Paris Encore

THE ZION COVENANT • BOOK 8

BODIE & BROCK THOENE

TYNDALE HOUSE PUBLISHERS, INC. • WHEATON, ILLINOIS

Visit Tyndale's exciting Web site at www.tyndale.com

TYNDALE is a registered trademark of Tyndale House Publishers, Inc.

Tyndale's quill logo is a trademark of Tyndale House Publishers, Inc.

The Zion Covenant series designed by Julie Chen

Designed by Dean H. Renninger

Edited by Ramona Cramer Tucker

Portions of *Paris Encore* were printed in *The Twilight of Courage*, © 1994 by Bodie and Brock Thoene, by Thomas Nelson, Inc., Publishers under ISBN 0-7852-8196-7.

First printing of *Paris Encore* by Tyndale House Publishers, Inc. in 2005.

Scripture quotations are taken from the *Holy Bible*, King James Version or the *Holy Bible*, New International Version® NIV® Copyright © 1973, 1978, 1984 by International Bible Society. Used by permission of Zondervan Publishing House. All rights reserved.

Library of Congress Cataloging-in-Publication Data

Thoene, Bodie, date.
   Paris encore / Bodie & Brock Thoene.
      p. cm. — (The Zion covenant ; bk. 8)
   ISBN-10: 1-4143-0544-3 (sc)
   ISBN-13: 978-1-4143-0544-8 (sc)
   1. World War, 1939-1945—France—Paris—Fiction. 2. Holocaust, Jewish (1939-1945)—Fiction.
   3. Jews—France—Paris—Fiction. 4. Paris (France)—Fiction. I. Thoene, Brock, date. II. Title.
   PS3570.H46P37 2005
   813'.54—dc22   2005002066

Printed in the United States of America

11 10 09 08 07 06 05
7   6   5   4   3   2   1

Dedicated to the memory of Rebekah Marie Swanson.

She loved books and people and Jesus and was loved by so many in return. She used to say of her mother, Rona Swanson, "I tell my mom everything. Why not? After all, we shared the same heart. . . ." They still share the same heart in a bond that stretches beyond this present world. Heaven is richer for Rebekah's presence, though earth is poorer without her. But the day will come when every tear will be wiped away by the gentle touch of Jesus. Until then we remember and honor the miracle of her life.

"There are only two ways to live your life. One is as though nothing is a miracle. The other is as though everything is a miracle."
—Albert Einstein

Paris Encore is a "Director's Cut,"
including portions of the Thoene Classic *The Twilight of Courage*
and thrilling, never-before-published scenes
with the characters you've come to know
and love through The Zion Covenant series.

The First Six Months of World War II

1939
September 1—Nazi Germany invades Poland
September 3—England and France declare war on Germany
September 17—Soviets invade Poland
September 27—Warsaw falls

October—"Phony War" begins

December 13—German battleship *Admiral Graf Spee* cornered in
South Atlantic

1940
February 16—*Altmark* incident

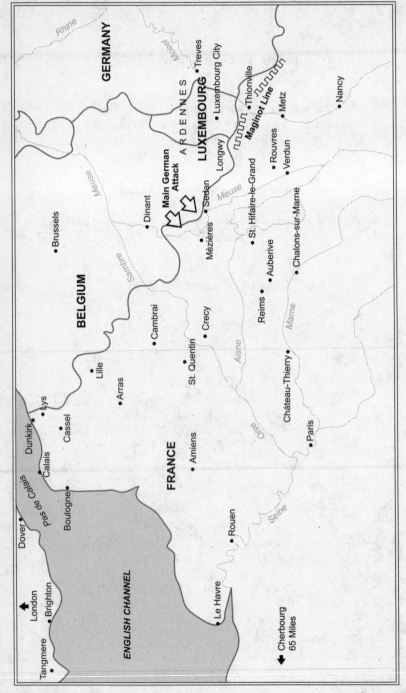

THE WESTERN FRONT

ENGLISH CHANNEL

GERMANY

LUXEMBOURG

BELGIUM

FRANCE

Rhine

Mosel

Meuse

Meuse

Sambre

Marne

Aisne

Oise

Seine

ARDENNES

Maginot Line

Main German Attack

Treves
Luxembourg City
Thionville
Metz
Nancy
Longwy
Rouvres
Verdun
Sedan
Mézières
St. Hilaire-le-Grand
Chalons-sur-Marne
Auberive
Reims
Château-Thierry
Paris
Crecy
Cambrai
St. Quentin
Dinant
Brussels
Lille
Arras
Lys
Cassel
Dunkirk
Calais
Boulogne
Amiens
Rouen
Le Havre
Dover
London
Brighton
Tangmere
Pas de Calais

↓ Cherbourg 65 Miles

← (London arrow)

THE BATTLE OF FRANCE BEGINS

ALLIES →

GERMANS →

North
Sea

• Amsterdam

• The Hague

• Rotterdam

NETHERLANDS

• Antwerp

• Dunkirk

Scheldt R.

Brussels •

BELGIUM

Cologne •

Lille •

Sambre R.

• Liège

• Arras

• Dinant

Meuse

• Amiens

FRANCE

A R D E N N E S

LUXEMBOURG

Siegfried Line

Aisne

• Sedan

Oise

Maginot Line

Marne

• Paris

PART I

A mighty fortress is our God,
A bulwark never failing;
Our helper He amid the flood
Of mortal ills prevailing.
For still our ancient foe
Doth seek to work us woe—
His craft and pow'r are great,
And, armed with cruel hate,
On earth is not his equal.

From "A Mighty Fortress Is Our God" by Martin Luther

1

Descent into War

FALL 1939

The appointment of Winston Churchill to the post of First Lord of the Admiralty in British prime minister Neville Chamberlain's War Cabinet on September 3 had been a political move. The position ensured that Churchill could no longer publicly voice criticism of the government.

Churchill knew this. The press was fully aware of the implications. The public war preparations had stumbled along at an agonizing pace as the country of Poland suffered and died day after day under the Nazi Blitzkrieg. Up to this point the governments of England and France had stopped their ears to the pleas of the dying Poles. But since England and France had declared war with Germany on September 3, frenetic activities of newly established petty bureaucracy had replaced prewar complacency. Blackout restrictions. Rationing plans. Evacuation billeting. All these issues became coupled with the term *British Patriotism* as England's allies perished alone and unaided.

It was with all this in mind that John Murphy, chief of Trump European News Service, met with Winston Churchill this afternoon in London. The reason for the meeting was a personal one, one friend to another, the note from Churchill declared. Murphy would not be granted a journalist's privilege of asking probing questions about the war.

Today Churchill was dressed in coat and tie, appearing much more official and governmental than Murphy had ever seen him. The ubiquitous cigar and water laced with a drop of whiskey were on the desk.

Churchill motioned for Murphy to be seated. "You have a bodyguard, as I suggested?"

"Yes, a good man. Very quiet. His name is Inspector Stone. He'll remain on the farm in Wales with Lori Kalner, Elisa, the kids, and a TENS employee, Eva Weitzman. And, of course, Elisa's mother and aunt."

"Yes, Elisa's aunt, Helen Ibsen. The widow of the German evangelical pastor Karl Ibsen, who was arrested by the Gestapo. I read the official Reich report given to the American Embassy, which claims Reverend Ibsen killed himself."

"None of us believe it." Murphy traced the brim of his hat with his finger. "Lori will remain in Wales with her mother. Mrs. Ibsen is a strong woman. She's taking it with courage. We are certain Pastor Ibsen didn't take his own life."

A single downward jerk of Churchill's head concurred. "Indeed, he did not." Sausage-shaped fingers stained by cigar tobacco pushed a tan folder marked *Confidential* toward Murphy. "It is just in from intelligence. I had a word about it with the prime minister. It is agreed that you have a right to know the truth about Pastor Ibsen."

Murphy hesitated before opening the report. The details concerning Karl Ibsen were sketchy, with long paragraphs blacked out. He scanned the document to the end. He felt the blood drain from his face as he absorbed the facts surrounding the death of Karl Ibsen.

"This is . . . correct?" Murphy breathed, barely able to speak.

Churchill responded quietly. "It has been confirmed. The Nazis have redefined martyrdom as a type of suicide. It is indeed suicide to speak out against attacks on Jews and euthanasia and abortion and sterilization in Nazi Germany. To protest and hold true to one's beliefs is suicide in a land where laws are reinterpreted and black is declared white by puppet courts. So, in a way, the pastor *did* commit suicide. He stood up for the right when everyone else accepted the new German laws as *law*. But though it may be suicide to protest against evil, Pastor Ibsen did not die by his own hand. I felt . . . perhaps the certainty of this fact is something Mrs. Ibsen and her daughter should know. Tell them if you like . . . or not."

"They're already certain Pastor Ibsen died heroically." Murphy replaced the document on Churchill's desk.

"Then perhaps the details—the horrible circumstances of the good man's death—are not for them to know. But the Nazi claim of suicide is yet another lie of the devil we must fight . . . and here is the proof."

"I . . . thank you." Murphy resisted the urge to ask when British military aid would be sent to Poland. Perhaps he knew the answer anyway. "What now, Winston?"

"We prepare. Years of slashing our military as Germany built her armies leaves England at a disadvantage. We have a lot of catching up to do. The entire energy of the nation must be focused on winning this war."

"How long?"

"As long as it takes. We will prevail. Whatever it takes. You can quote me on that."

Murphy left the Admiralty offices with the certainty that Poland had burned as a sacrifice to give the West time to rearm. There had been no one to quench the fires of that holocaust.

The British government led by Neville Chamberlain had met evil strength with moral weakness in the hope that weakness would bring peace. But the scent of Britain's fear had merely whetted the appetites of the dark gods of war.

Murphy ticked off the descent into the abyss of total war:

Years of official apathy when Hitler broke every treaty.

Disarmament of the British army and navy.

Appeasement.

Complacency of the Western nations in the face of Germany's policies of government-sanctioned murder against her own citizens and the unborn.

All this had, in the end, led to the moment when the death of one individual like Karl Ibsen no longer seemed significant. How many more would perish because of the misguided thought that peace could be won by bargaining with the devil?

Death had begun its march one soul at a time. Now it devoured thousands. In the end, Murphy thought, millions—men, women, children—would die. When the final tally came, the horrible sum of individual lives shattered would be unfathomable . . . incomprehensible to the human mind.

Murphy knew the mistakes of history would be repeated.

They cry, "Peace! Peace!" But there is no peace!

Murphy was certain of all this as he made his way toward home. He would write his story about war preparations in Britain. Wire his copy to the U.S., where it would appear in the morning papers. The newsreels shot by Mac McGrath would be played in theatres across the nation. But even now, who in America heeded the warnings?

Wilhelmstrasse was as slick as an ice-skating rink as the staff car of Gestapo Chief Himmler pulled away from the curb of the German Chancellery in Berlin.

Reinhard Heydrich, one of Himmler's chief lieutenants, sat beside him, gazing out at the colorless day. The only break in the monotony was the red banners draped from the cornices of the building, indicating that the Führer was in residence.

"He was in a mood," Himmler said without amusement.

Heydrich countered sullenly, "I thought you said he did not need to know about Richard Lewinski. That it was better left untold until we have taken care of the matter."

"Nothing remains a secret from the Führer for long. Not even internal matters of the Gestapo."

Heydrich nodded. He swiped his finger through the fog on the windowpane. "Sometimes I think he has eyes in the back of his head." He arched an eyebrow. "Like my mother when I was a boy. She knew everything I did. Everything I said."

"There is no dark magic to it, Heydrich. Have you not figured out that we are in rivalry with everyone else who has access to his ear? My guess is that fat Hermann Göring has an informer in my department who feeds him information. . . ."

"Göring's appetite is healthy, to be sure."

"And from Göring's mouth to the ear of the Führer."

Heydrich tugged at his collar. "It is irritating. Richard Lewinski is nothing. Nothing at all. I did not realize he was a Jew when he worked in the Enigma factory. I did not think of him at all. Just another engineer designing variations on the same theme. And when I found out, I sent him packing like every other Jew. Off to Poland. Dumped him on the Polish frontier with twelve thousand other vermin. How was I to know the rat would go underground?"

"You should have killed him."

"We were more careful in those days. World opinion mattered then. Lewinski is well connected in America. We still had some pretense of friendship with the Americans." Heydrich laughed. "Before the Führer started calling Roosevelt 'the Paralytic.'"

Himmler opened the snap of his leather portfolio and fished out a clean handkerchief. He cleaned his glasses and then blew his nose loudly. "I am catching cold," he complained. Then, "Lewinski is not in America. That much has been confirmed. Not in Rumania. Every acquaintance has been followed."

"You will not call off the American agents, will you? I still believe he will show up there."

"We have the best men on it. Our fellow in the U.S. State Department has access to files that would indicate a change of identity." Himmler sucked his teeth. "As I told the Führer, this is simply a matter for patience."

"It is a matter of cold weather. The army is stalled and he is bored, so we must amuse ourselves and him by tracking down some useless little Jew who may remotely be able to reconstruct our Enigma encoding machine." Heydrich slapped his knee. "Even though the code cannot be deciphered without the exact and perfect combination."

"We will find him. It will disappoint Göring if we do so. It will please the Führer. We will bring in 'the Russian.'" Himmler shrugged as though the matter would soon be settled. "A man like Lewinski cannot be hidden for long."

Heydrich nodded and wiped away the fog again as they drove along the Spree River. "He must be in the possession of one of the Allied governments. Or at least a neutral. Our enemies would not let a mind like that go free. They will feed him pastries and encourage him with praise as they keep up their hopes that he might be capable of doing us some mischief. But it is impossible. Enigma is invulnerable."

℘

The Russian, Nicholi Federov, had every reason to disavow his association with the Gestapo now that Hitler and Stalin had become so cozy. And the Gestapo could have handed Federov over to the Communist government of Stalin for a tidy sum, since Federov had been such an ardent and destructive force in the White Russian opposition to the Bolsheviks. But both Federov and Gestapo boss Heinrich Himmler knew that such a move would be counterproductive.

Possessing diplomatic papers known as a Nansen Passport, the Russian could move with relative ease throughout the neutral nations of Europe. He was a well-known wine merchant with connections in Switzerland and France and had first begun his work with the Nazi regime after being recruited in England by Hitler's foreign minister, Ribbentrop. Ribbentrop had also been a wine merchant before his rise in the ranks of Nazi power.

It seemed an innocent enough beginning for Federov. He was not particularly interested in the politics or the chaos of the German nation. He did not particularly like the strutting little Brownshirts of the Sturm Abteilung, also known as the SA or SS, except for the fact that they hated the Bolsheviks. The Nazis feared and despised Lenin and Trotsky and the rest of the Czar-killers who had renamed the Russian cities after themselves: Leningrad, Stalingrad. Disgusting.

And so, although Hitler did not drink wine, he shared similar tastes with the Russian wine merchant. In those days, Hitler had hated Stalin and all Communists with a passion that made him foam at the mouth like a rabid dog. This seemed an attractive quality when the Russian first observed the Nazi leader. Federov held to the old maxim "The enemy of my enemy is my friend." Hitler, upon coming to power, had proceeded to smash the German Communist cells with impunity. Thus, an alliance was made between Federov and the enemies of his great enemy.

Federov knew everyone who either drank wine or sold wine in Europe. Since this grouping omitted very few people, he provided the Gestapo with a large quantity of information gleaned from various talkative sources. Which high-placed German diplomats had anti-Hitler leanings. Who had ties to certain organizations that would like to see the Führer dead. It was Federov who had been key behind the scenes in the apprehension of the French singer Elaine Snow as she attempted to assist the would-be assassin and probable Bolshevik Georg Elser after his attempt to blow up Hitler in the Munich beer hall. The Führer had grown fond of the Russian. He was pleased to hear that Himmler and Heydrich had personally recruited him to handle the Lewinski matter.

Federov had been informed that the Jew, Lewinski, was a notorious Communist, certain to pull all of civilization down the drain after Russia if he was left to go free.

Since Stalin and Hitler were now allies, this should not have mattered to the Nazis on the face of it. Federov, however, understood the complex forces at work behind their extraordinary alliance.

With the unpleasant union between Hitler and Stalin, no one could imagine that Federov could have ties to the German Secret Police. But the wine business was slow, and Federov had grown accustomed to living well. In addition to the issue of money, he justified his perfidious existence with the certainty that the treaty between the Nazis and Stalin was just a marriage of convenience. Soon enough these strange bedfellows would wake up and notice that the other stank. By and by, Federov was certain, German troops would succeed in naming Leningrad for St. Peter once again. The Communists who had destroyed his homeland would be slaughtered like pigs, and Imperial Russia would be restored. After some agreement with the Germans, of course.

Even now, after the war had begun, the Russian was welcome in Brussels, Amsterdam, Geneva, London, and Paris. He was the perfect choice to sleuth out the whereabouts of a certain brilliant Jewish mathematician working for one of these governments. Someone who drank wine would know him. And after one drink too many at some embassy party, the Lewinski beans would be spilled. Then Federov would simply dial the local fifth-columnist thugs, and the issue of Richard Lewinski would be settled for good.

This game depended entirely on whom a man knew. Since Federov knew everyone, and was liked by most, he was very well suited to his occupation.

᧓

As the autumn weather cooled, the war against merchant vessels at sea heated up. Not a day passed that a German U-boat did not plow a torpedo or two into some unarmed ship carrying goods to France or England. When the Scottish freighter *Coulmore* was attacked by a U-boat two hundred miles directly east of Boston, it was a U.S. Coast Guard cutter that moved to its rescue.

Vessels carrying British children to Canada or the United States were sunk with loss of life so tragic that evacuation efforts were "regretfully" suspended by the British government.

In the United States Senate the debate on revising the Neutrality Act droned on. What kind of aid could be offered to the Western Allies? How should materials be paid for? Should the arms embargo be repealed? Colonel Charles A. Lindbergh, hero to millions, added his voice to the isolationist position: "I do not want to see American bombers dropping American bombs, which will kill and mutilate European children." In his view, not even Canadians, let alone Americans, should fight in a European war.

Despite the stature of the critic and the intensity of the debate, planes and supplies ordered before the war flowed north from the U.S. to Canada, where they were loaded onto ships bound for England.

At the same time, a handful of young American airmen also headed to Canada. There, at the loss of their American citizenship, they joined the Royal Air Force. Some joined up in the idealistic tradition of the American Lafayette Escadrille, which had flown for France in the Great War. Others came into the RAF with no other motive than the desire to fly the fastest planes in the world. Within days, each man found himself crossing the North Atlantic and in the middle of a real war.

Today foaming green waves burst over the bow of the SS *Duchess of Windsor* and poured around the lashings that secured the canvas-covered Hurricane fighter planes to the foredeck. As American flier David Meyer watched from his perch one deck above, the *Duchess* rode up the crest of another twenty-foot swell and dropped like an elevator into the trough beyond. Each breaker threatened to tear the aircraft loose from the transport ship and sink them in the North Atlantic long before they ever saw combat.

For all the freezing blasts of air, it was still more pleasant up on deck than below. A week out of Halifax, Nova Scotia, the convoy seemed no nearer to England. David knew that the course carried them far to the north to avoid the prowling U-boats, but there were times when it seemed that such a prolonged crossing actually exposed them to greater risk.

The night before, the seas around the *Duchess* had seemed empty of all other ships, so it was a surprising sight in the early morning to count two dozen laboring freighters. Ahead of and to either side of the convoy, two circling destroyers cast about like hunting dogs after a scent.

The first night aboard the *Duchess*, the Canadian and American fliers had been instructed to sleep in their clothing, wearing their life jackets because of the likelihood of U-boat attacks. They had all remained dressed, although none had been able to sleep. On the second day out, David had chanced to ask a sailor about the cargo the *Duchess* carried in addition to planes and men. When he was told that the holds of the freighter were filled with live ammo, David had grinned, shrugged, and thereafter undressed for bed and slept soundly.

Another enormous wave lifted the bow of the freighter and dropped it again. Forty feet of elevation were gained in three seconds and just as quickly lost. A sheen of ice from the freezing spray coated the railings and the safety lines, turning the decks into skating rinks. The fresh air was a nice change from his cramped quarters, but it was time to go below.

A bright flash south of the *Duchess* caught David's eye. A dark red flare rose into the sky from the black outline of a ship about a mile distant. A few seconds later the muffled *whoom* of a large explosion rolled across the seas. It was as if a giant hand lifted the unlucky freighter from beneath its steel belly while its bow and stern bent and drooped. To David's horrified view, the stricken ship broke in two. The forward section plunged almost straight down into the frigid water, while the aft piece floated dismally, half on its side, like a broken toy thrown down by a petulant child.

Ahead of their route, a blast of smoke erupted from one of the destroyers, and it heeled sharply into the wind as it circled around. On the *Duchess*, strident alarm bells began to ring. Under David's feet the freighter groaned and shuddered at the sudden demand for more speed. Sluggishly, unwillingly, the *Duchess* altered her course to the north and almost imperceptibly accelerated.

There was only a moment to note the tiny bobbing orange dots that were the life rafts from the torpedoed ship, and then the tragic scene aft was hidden by the intervening swells.

All around the *Duchess*, other ships of the convoy were steaming northward, their churning wakes evidence of their panicked flight. But like wolves, the rest of the U-boat pack waited across the line of the fleeing ships. The guns of the second destroyer boomed as the knifelike form of a submarine's bow appeared on the waves ahead. Another freighter exploded with a shattering blast that knocked David's grip loose from the rail and temporarily deafened him.

Two fleeing ships, both seeking to avoid the path of a torpedo, turned into each other's course and collided. The arrival of the torpedo tore the bow off of one and left a gaping hole in the side of the other.

Then it was time for the *Duchess* to receive the attention of the subs. The cries of three lookouts shrilled, "Torpedo in the water! Torpedo on the port quarter!"

David watched with fascinated horror as the *Duchess* began an agonizingly slow turn *toward* the torpedo's path.

"More to port!" a lookout screamed. "Come on, *Duchess*, move your bloomin' arse!"

The torpedo streaked into view, a lethal fish seeking to destroy the freighter and her cargo and crew. The *Duchess* swung sideways, the arc of its turn barely seeming to move.

David braced himself and ducked below the rail, anticipating the hammer blow of the torpedo's warhead on the far side of the freighter. When a few seconds passed like hours and no explosion ripped through the ship, David cautiously raised his head.

Racing away aft, the torpedo's trail of bubbles was inscribed on the waves and led back toward the unharmed *Duchess* like an exclamation point.

Three hours and eighteen course changes later, the freighter made its way back across the stretch of ocean where the original attack had occurred. At a cry from the lookout, the *Duchess* altered direction one more time to intercept a floating life raft.

Aboard the scrap of safety were four men. Two were freezing and comatose from exposure. The third had bled to death. And the remaining occupant had been blinded in the explosion.

It was that single moment, more than any other, that made David realize he could actually get himself killed in a war that was supposed to be none of his business.

2

The *Stinking Garlic*

Rusted iron rings were set in the algae-covered bridges of Paris and in the fortified stone of the Seine's riverbanks. A flotilla of boats and freight barges was moored to the ancient tethers and to one another. There, within the shadow of the Louvre, Notre Dame, and the opulent homes of wealthy Parisians, lived other citizens of the French Republic. Prostitutes, thieves, malcontents, and impoverished artists populated decrepit hulks that were berthed close to the motor yachts of the rich.

Beneath Pont Neuf, between a garbage scow and an ancient tug, was a narrow Dutch péniche that had hauled freight through the canals of Holland for fifty years. No one could remember how or when the barge had mysteriously appeared on the Seine. It seemed to most that she had always been there. Her masts and sails had long since been lowered and tied off to the eighty-foot-long deck. The giant rudder was secured to her starboard side. In those rare times she moved along the river, it was by the power of a gasping diesel engine.

The smoke from the exhaust had nearly covered over the once brightly painted name of some Dutch captain's favorite lady. Now only the letters *AIL* remained visible through the grime. In French, *AIL* meant "garlic." Thus she was known along the Left Bank as the *Stinking Garlic*. The English interpretation of the word *ail* also seemed appropriate to the appearance of the craft. The *AIL* had obviously fallen very sick indeed. The final degradation had come when, during a game of cards, she became home to an infamous Communist clochard by the name of Jardin and his two ragged children. Hardly a day passed without some kind of racket rising from the *Stinking Garlic*.

Today was no different.

"Jerome! Jerome, I say! Come here at once. You also, Marie. It is time for your lessons."

"Yes, Papa," came a small girl's treble from belowdecks. Six-year-old Marie appeared through the hatch near the helm station.

"Coming," agreed ten-year-old Jerome as he propped his fishing pole against the stern rail of the *AIL* and clambered over heaps of discarded rigging to sit on the stump of the mast.

Monsieur Jardin, in cast-off dungarees tied around with a length of rope and a threadbare sweater and black beret, did not look like a famous philosopher. However, neither that small matter nor his alcohol-fuddled brain kept him from thinking highly of his store of accumulated wisdom. Not in the least.

Jardin stretched upward with an elaborate contortion, broke wind loudly, and proclaimed himself ready to begin the day's lesson. At his feet was a bottle of vinegary red wine which he said had bravado, and which he could get for twenty-five centimes a gallon.

"Now," he said, waving an instructive finger so dirty that the nail could not be distinguished from the rest, "who remembers the name for the vilest and most flatuous of earthly villains?"

Jerome knew the answer, but he liked to give Marie a chance to go first. It pleased her when she got it right and did no harm to his standing with his father if he was called upon to help out.

"Cuttlefish," she said with a slight lisp.

Jardin laid his face sideways in the palm of one hand and stared reflectively into the gray Parisian sky. "Almost right," he allowed. "Jerome?"

"Capitalists," Jerome corrected.

"*Bon!* You both have the makings of scholars. But appearances are, as they say, discerning, so we must continue the lesson. Jerome, what is the greatest, most magnanimous fault man can possess?"

Jerome answered at once. "Greed, Papa."

"Even so. Greed is a source of much triplication in the world. It is a whip hand held over the brow of the poor and downtrodden, never forget."

After one of these profound statements, Jardin often helped himself to a swig from his bottle. Sometimes the length of the lesson depended on how much self-congratulation went on. Meanwhile the volume of the instruction got louder and louder.

Jardin took a drink and wiped his mouth on his arm through a hole in his sleeve. Then he turned again to Marie. "Here is a tough one for you, *ma chèrie.* What is another name for the wicked people who want to keep the poor always poor, in order to have them around to fight their wars?"

"Missionaries?"

"Well, that is a very fine answer, Marie. But I was looking for something else," explained Jardin grandly, taking another swallow of wine.

"Re-act . . . react-something," Jerome piped up.

Jardin snapped his fingers. "Bravo, Jerome. Reactionaries. Also known as warmongers. They are so busy looking backward that they cannot see the future when it hits them between the eyes."

Jerome was still trying to work out this metaphor while his father was already on to the next question. Such inattention was dangerous, to say the least, since a clout on the ear might result.

" . . . who ever lived?" Jardin was concluding.

Jerome breathed an inward sigh of relief. He not only knew what the question had been, he knew the answer as well. "Stalin," he said promptly.

Jardin removed his beret with respect at the pronunciation of the Soviet leader's name. "Leader of the most processive nation on earth," he proclaimed loudly.

"You mean *progressive*," shouted a passerby from the quai. "Or, more truthfully, *repressive*."

Jardin gestured angrily in the direction of the speaker and smiled proudly when Jerome and Marie both repeated the same arm movement.

"Papa," Jerome asked, raising his hand, "on the street they are saying that Monsieur Stalin has made a deal with Hitler. Did you not tell us that Hitler was the archfiend incarcerate?"

Jardin scratched his scraggly beard, then beamed as the proper response came to him. "Monsieur Stalin knows what is best. Perhaps he has converted this Hitler fellow to see the error of his ways." This last observation made Jardin reflective. There was a slice of sun streaming through the clouds. Just enough for Jardin to sit and warm himself. "Now, that is all the lesson for today, I think."

"What are we to do for food, Papa?" Marie asked. "We have nothing left in the cupboard."

"Jerome will go to the usual places . . . as usual . . . and catch something that might fall from the pocket of a capitalist. Or perhaps I will catch a cuttlefish." Jardin snapped his fingers in silent command for Jerome to fetch the fishing pole. "Now, Marie, go below and finish your chores. Jerome, I need to have a word with you."

Jerome wondered what sort of trouble he was in, or if the gendarmes had been around asking questions about too many handbags mysteriously disappearing on the boulevard. But this time it was his father who was in trouble.

"Jerome," Jardin said in a blast of vinegary breath, "I must tell you something in complete competence. The gendarmes are very angry that Hitler and Monsieur Stalin have made up their quarrel. It may be necessary for me to go away for a while, without saying good-bye. You are not to worry, but you must promise to take care of Marie."

"Of course, Papa."

Jardin held up his finger to emphasize the importance of his instruction. "Beware the gendarmes and the priests. If ever I am away, you must not let on that I am away and you are still here even though I am not." He paused for breath and squinted at the water of the Seine. "They would lock you in an orphanage. Think of the disgrace if your sister grew up to be a nun."

Jerome solemnly shook his head in horror at the image. "I will not let that happen, Papa."

"My son, I knew I could depend on you."

∽◐∾

American journalist Josephine Marlow was somewhat of a celebrity since her return to Paris. Men of the press corps who had known her before as Danny Marlow's widow looked at her with new respect since she'd been in Warsaw when it fell to the Nazis.

Then there were others who proclaimed that a woman had no place in the war.

"Stick to human-interest stories!" ordered Frank Blake at the Associated Press when Josie expressed a desire to interview the French prime minister, Daladier. It had been Daladier who, with British prime minister Chamberlain, had handed Czechoslovakia over to Hitler in exchange for the promise of "peace in our time." She simply wanted to ask the diminutive French politician what his thoughts were on the matter since the fall of Poland.

The Paris AP chief left little doubt that such questions were the domain of the male journalists. As some recognition of her ordeal, however, Josie had been given a raise of five dollars a week and sent out to interview dressmakers about the scarcity of French silk. She took the story an extra lap by tracing the sale of French-made silk to neutral Belgium, which in turn sold it to Nazi Germany to be made into parachutes.

Was it possible that the German Reich intended to return the silk to France one day? The question and the reply were cut from the story. The conclusion was that in the French textile industry, it was business as usual.

This morning Josie finished her work in the gloomy AP office. Most

of the masculine staff, resplendent in newly tailored military press uniforms, had headed for another guided tour of the Maginot Line. Alma
Dodge, who had traveled with Josie to work in Paris, manned the
switchboard and gathered up the tape streaming from the wire.

Josie was just wrapping up a story about the care and feeding of millions of soldiers. True to its national stereotype, the French army had
drafted civilian pastry chefs first. This army of bakers, equipped with
mobile stone bake ovens, filled the trenches daily with the aroma of
fresh-baked French bread. Nothing like it. Josie had toured the mobile
kitchens this morning and had come back with ravishing hunger. No
doubt this was some sort of new mental warfare against the German
troops. The Wehrmacht was, by now, faced with the threat of mass de-
fection unless the German bakers could learn to make French baguettes.

Since an army was only as good as its food supply, Josie presumed
that this was meant to be evidence of the superior quality of France's divisions. It was, as Frank Blake reminded her, clearly a human-interest
piece. Such a story would have no difficulty getting through the tribe of
French government censors who had taken over an entire floor at the
Hotel Continental on Rue de Castiglione.

"I'm taking this to the Continental," Josie called to Alma as she gathered her coat and handbag. "You want to meet someplace for lunch?"

Alma glanced at the clock. "Café Deux Magots? One?" Then her eyes
widened as the door to the AP office swung open and a tall, handsome
man entered.

It was the French colonel they had met on their journey to Paris.
Dressed as a civilian today in an expensive double-breasted brown suit,
he held a brown fedora in his hand as he leaned against the counter and
smiled at Josephine.

"Madame Marlow?" he began. "You probably do not remember me.
We met—briefly—on the train from Boulogne to Paris some time ago.
Colonel Andre Chardon. I need to speak with the AP station chief, Mon-
sieur Frank Blake. Is he in?"

Of course Josie remembered the colonel. The awkward conversation
in the dark compartment. The doll in his possession. The volume of *Paradise Lost* over his face as he slept.

"No, sorry, he's out. But of course I remember you," she replied. "I
have something of yours. A volume of Milton. I did not have your name
or I would have . . ."

He snapped his fingers. "I was hoping someone had picked it up. It
belonged to my mother."

"The notes are hers then."

"*Oui.*"

"She must be a very special lady."

"Yes. She was . . . Madame Marlow. A dear friend of hers gave me the volume as a gift. I have not yet had the opportunity to . . ."

"Lovely thoughts." Josie felt herself color. It was natural that she would have looked through the book, but somehow she felt as though she had been snooping. "She must have been a fan of Milton."

"Perhaps she was." Colonel Chardon glanced at his watch, obviously in a hurry. "You have the volume here, Madame Marlow? I am grateful."

"I've got to get my story through the censors at the Hotel Continental, and I'm afraid your book is at my lodgings. If you would like to drop by tomorrow . . ." It would be nice to see him again. To share thoughts on Milton's Paradise over a cup of coffee.

"You are staying at the Hotel Continental?"

Alma laughed.

Josie shrugged. "Nothing that upscale, I'm afraid. Foyer International."

"Foyer International. On St. Michel." Colonel Chardon made a note of the address with a slim gold pen. "May I send a courier by to pick it up this evening?"

So coffee and Paradise had not occurred to the handsome Frenchman. "I'll be out this evening."

"You can leave it with me, Josie," Alma chirped. Turning to the colonel, she said, "I'll make sure you get it. Just ask for Alma Dodge."

More scribbles and he snapped his notebook closed. "Done. My deepest thanks to you both." The colonel seemed pleased. He retrieved a fifty-franc note from his pocket and laid it on the counter. "The book is of great value to me. A small reward, Madame. Please. For your trouble."

"I wouldn't think of it!" Josie protested.

He left it there, backed up a step, and said cheerfully to Alma, "Take yourselves out for lunch on me." With that he bowed slightly and exited the AP office without a backward glance.

In silence the two women watched through a nearby window as he stepped into a sleek new Citroën and disappeared into traffic.

"I'd rather have lunch *with* him." Alma scooped up the fifty-franc note.

"How could you take that?"

"Of course, lunch on him might be nice, too." Alma tucked the bill into her pocket.

"He's not your type."

"Apparently we're not *his* type either. I thought these Frenchmen were interested in American women. Not even a glimmer."

"We've just met a man who loves his mother." Josie gathered up her papers.

"We'll have to settle for lunch. Deux Magots? One o'clock."

◯

It had been a wonderful meal. Jerome had stolen a lovely eel that was on display on a block of ice in the fish market. He had put the thing down his pant leg. His escape had been slimy and cold, but the thought of such a feast made it worthwhile. Papa had caught a catfish while fishing from the quai across from the Louvre. Old Uncle Jambonneau brought potatoes and onions from the kitchen at the Hotel des Invalides, where he lived with the other old wounded soldiers.

Tonight the *Stinking Garlic* reeked of grease and fish and garlic from the cooking. It was a lovely aroma to Jerome. Marie had eaten so much she had a bellyache and had gone to bed in her tiny bunk.

Alone on the deck, Jerome scrubbed the crusted skillet as Papa and Uncle Jambonneau discussed weighty matters belowdecks. Even in the blackout conditions due to the war, Paris was not entirely dark. Lights sneaked out the slits of blackout curtains here and there. The gendarmes did not seem to mind the violations. Jerome could plainly see the outlines of the buildings on l'Cité. A soft glow penetrated the cracks around the cargo hatch. The voices of Papa and Uncle Jambonneau were plainly audible.

Jerome wondered why Papa burned the lantern since Uncle was blind. His eyes had been burned by poison gas in the Great War. Now he was a grizzled old relic who tapped around the City of Lights with a cane and a canvas rucksack slung over his right shoulder. A very large white rat perched on his left shoulder and whispered things in Uncle's ear.

Jerome had been warned that Uncle Jambonneau did not know the rat was a rat. He believed it was a small dog with a long, hairless tail. When some foolish tourist or Right Bank stranger gasped and screamed and called the rat a rat, Uncle Jambonneau became instantly offended. He assumed they were talking about him, not the thing on his shoulder.

Uncle Jambonneau named his dog—which was not a dog—Petit Papillon, which means "Small Butterfly." All of this could be quite confusing to the uninitiated.

The boy peered down through the cracks at the top of the plank table as Papillon delicately held a bit of eel in his little hands and nibbled.

"There can be little doubt that my mother raised a fool," Uncle Jambonneau said to Papa. "Why did you have to become a Marxist?"

"I am content with what I am," Papa replied.

Jerome wondered, did Papa mean that he was content to be a fool or content to be a Marxist?

"Why not a Buddhist?" Uncle asked. "The French government is not arresting Buddhists. Only Communists."

"That is true. But I know nothing about such things."

Uncle Jambonneau snapped his fingers, and Papillon skittered up his arm to whisper something in his ear. "Well, little brother. You have one hope to stay out of prison, I think."

"What is that?"

"Perhaps you are not worth arresting. Not even the Communists of Paris will claim you. They say you are a fool."

"That may be true. But they are jealous," Papa said.

"Of what?"

Papa could not think of an answer to that. He leaned his head against his palm and gazed around the cluttered cabin of the boat. "They are jealous of my property."

"Yes. I can see that." Uncle Jambonneau nodded his white head and scratched Papillon under the chin. "By owning this boat, you have violated one of the principles of Communism."

"What right have they to constrain? I won the *Garlic* fairly at cards. She is mine."

"If Stalin invades France, you will have to give him the *Garlic*."

"If Stalin comes to Paris, by my honor, he may have her."

Uncle Jambonneau raised a gnarled finger in a gesture that reminded Jerome of an older version of Papa. "But will he want her?"

3

Small Miracles

No one would have imagined that the two old sisters had not always lived in Paris in the big house behind the gate at No. 5 Rue de la Huchette. They looked like any other grandmothers on the Left Bank: gray hair tied back in buns, aprons dusted with flour, run-down shoes, and navy blue dresses faded with many turns in the washtub.

They were spinsters, Rose and Betsy Smith of the Santa Barbara Smiths. That was Santa Barbara, California, USA. Rose was large, squarely built, strong, and fifty-five years old. Betsy, tiny and frail-looking, was nearing sixty.

They were the daughters of a fisherman who, as a young sailor, had nearly drowned in a gale in 1870 off Point Conception, California. He had cried out to God as green water broke over the decks of his schooner. The masts had snapped like twigs. The second mate was washed overboard, and the situation seemed hopeless. When the young sailor looked up, he saw silver angels moving in the sun-clipped clouds. A voice boomed in the thunder, and the sea became calm within moments!

Like the fishermen of ancient Galilee, he had heard the voice of the Lord, and he loved the mighty sound of it! Every day he sang God's words as he worked his nets off the Channel Islands.

As his daughters grew, he told them that except for the miracle in the storm, they would not have been born. In this way, the miracle came to belong to Rose and Betsy. Through the ears of their father they came to hear The Voice in the thunder. Through his eyes they saw the silver angels riding the clouds over Santa Cruz and the Anacapa Islands in the twilight hours.

They believed there was some reason their father had been spared, some reason they were born. They grew to womanhood certain that there was some larger purpose for their lives that they could not yet see.

And so they were not surprised when, at a tent meeting in Ventura in the summer of 1913, they heard The Voice calling them to leave Santa Barbara and serve needy children. But serve where? The dark continent of Africa was in fashion. The Voice was not specific.

Rose had bought a map of Africa and unrolled it on the kitchen table. She closed her eyes and plunged her finger onto the paper.

"Betsy," she called to her sister, who was sipping lemonade in the yard and praying as she watched the sunset, "God wants us to go to Algeria."

They had intended to do so. But the Great War of 1914 got in the way. Paris, the City of Lights, was far away from Africa. Their ship was sunk off the Canary Islands, and they were brought to Paris. They could not recollect just why that was, but that was the way it happened. It was a true story.

There were needy children in Paris, too, they discovered. So many little ones with papas killed in the trenches. The young fathers of France dissolved into the soil of Verdun and the Somme. So many mamas dead of the flu epidemic or simply dead in spirit.

The sisters had started caring for one baby, then three and then seven, until they had thirty—so many in need in those early days! The need had never ended.

One generation had grown up. There were always more to take the empty beds and toddle in at night to be rocked and sung to . . . one child at a time, with different faces, different names. Twenty-five years came and went without celebration, without recognition by anyone beyond the Left Bank of the Seine. Day by day needs were met by small miracles. Hour by hour love was dished out in generous helpings to little ones whose souls were in danger of starvation.

Two spinsters: Rose and Betsy Smith. They were an unlikely pair in the Latin Quarter. After twenty-five years, they spoke the language like native Parisians. Nearly everyone thought well of them.

The Jews who lived packed in little houses above the tailor shops off St. Germaine believed that Rose and Betsy were Righteous. Probably secret Jews.

The Catholics believed that they were perhaps doctrinally misguided but still worthy workers for the kingdom of God. Possibly secret Catholics.

There were very few Protestants in Paris. Those who were there either did not know that the sisters were Americans or were not aware of their existence. The pair served no church or ideology. They depended on God to provide for their needs.

They also took in washing.

Over the years Rose developed muscular washboard forearms like a carnival strongman. Little Betsy did the ironing. She remained petite, and unlike the broad-beamed Rose, she seemed to shrink as the years passed.

Their first children, all grown-up now, often came back to visit. Some, who had done very well for themselves, now brought their laundry and their offerings to the sisters.

Ernest Hemingway was a friend. He stopped in regularly to pick up or drop off his shirts. No one starched the way Rose did, he claimed. When his first novel sold and he traveled to Africa, he returned months later to tell the sisters about the wonders of the Dark Continent. After he left, Betsy confided that she was still willing to go to Africa if The Voice so instructed them. But in the meantime she was very glad that they had been shipwrecked like the apostle Paul and cast upon the shores of a city like Paris.

It was the children who kept them there in the hungry years of the twenties and into the thirties. And now, with a new war beginning, it looked as though the cycle was about to start all over again.

Those first few orphans raised by the sisters were now called to serve in the Grand Armees just like their fathers had done in 1914. Rose and Betsy prayed for each by name. They prayed for France. They even prayed for Germany—the new Dark Continent.

Mostly they prayed for the new generation of children who crowded into Paris from whatever country the Nazis crushed. It was always the little ones, the innocent ones, who suffered from the mistakes of politicians and nations, was it not?

Old ladies now, the sisters had come to believe that God had spared their father in the gale of 1870 so they could be here in Paris in 1939. It was a very long-playing miracle. It was not finished yet.

◌

For pilot David Meyer and the handful of other Americans who stepped off the transport ship in Southampton, the arrival at the Operational Training Unit at Aston Down made the Royal Air Force a reality. On that first cloudy evening after David's appearance at OTU, the RAF was also in for a shock at first meeting the Yank face-to-face.

While the rest of the new men lingered at the tables in the mess, David wandered out onto the grassy airfield to look over the object of his obsession. The Hawker Hurricane was larger than he had figured. It had a wingspan of forty feet and was thirty-two feet long. He reached up to touch the markings. Red, white, and blue concentric circles ominously resembled an archery target.

The Hurricane was not an all-metal aircraft. The front part of the fuselage and the wings were metal covered, while the back of the body and the tail were fabric. The Hurricane had a reputation for being light and highly maneuverable with no bad quirks. The thick wings accounted for a relatively slow top speed of 340 miles an hour even with the powerful Rolls-Royce "Merlin" V-12 engine that produced 1,280 horsepower.

In spite of that, the wing construction gave it an amazingly tight turning radius of something near eight hundred feet at three hundred miles an hour. This fact alone would make the plane a match for nearly any German craft in turns. Three summers performing aerobatics with a flying circus made David eager to try her out.

He climbed up to peer at the controls. Inside she was a single seater, with an austere, unlined cockpit. At his six-feet-one-inch height, it would be a tight fit for David. He was glad that he was slender. At the mess tonight he had spotted two pilots who, much broader than he, would have a tough time fitting into the plane. This could also mean serious problems if the time ever came when they had to bail out in a hurry.

David opened the canopy and, wanting to check the space for fit, slid in like a man trying to get the feel of a new car. He settled in easily, becoming part of the aircraft. He was instantly in love.

The Hurricane was controlled by a spade-grip stick that moved laterally about halfway up. The reduced play from that of a straight stick provided better aileron control than David had been used to in the old Jenny biplanes. He grasped the spade grip, which was a circular ring about eight inches around and an inch thick. On the grip was a large firing button and a ring with which the pilot could arm the guns. There were eight Browning machine guns with fourteen seconds of ammunition for each gun and a precise concentration of fire.

David planted his feet on the rudder pedals. He peered through the gunsight and moved the spade grip until an imaginary ME-109 was dead center. And then he pushed the brass button on the spade grip.

What happened next was *not* imaginary. The still evening of Aston Down was shattered as a burst of machine-gun fire tore into the rear fuselage of the Hurricane parked directly in front of the plane where David sat. Passing through the canvas structure, the .303 caliber bullets pierced a pattern in the wall of the mechanic's hangar one hundred yards farther across the field.

The two-second burst sent men tumbling out of the buildings in terror. Heads craned back in search of the airborne enemy who had disrupted their evening meal. They scrambled toward the slit trenches, and then a voice boomed in outrage, "It's the Yank! It's the new boy!"

A string of curses followed from Badger Cross, the largest and most gruesome assistant instructor at the OTU. "Look what the bloody fool's done to my Hurry! I'll kill 'im!"

୧୭

The French tricolor waved proudly over the great cobbled square in front of the main buildings of the Ecole de Cavalerie.

The sun beat hot on the black uniform and two-cornered hat of Cadre Noir instructor Captain Paul Chardon. A darkly handsome, compactly athletic man of twenty-seven, Chardon had begun his education here as a small child and had eventually graduated to the riding school at Saumur. There he had become a horseman of international reputation, winning gold medals in Olympic competition in 1932 and 1936.

Now he was *écuyer en chef*, chief riding instructor of the school on the River Lys. Because of his Olympic triumphs, he was secretly called Apollo by the students. He also possessed authority that could not be ignored. It was Captain Chardon who had the power to recommend promotion to the great cavalry school at Saumur, an honor enjoyed by only a handful of students each year. It was his dream to one day return to Saumur as chief instructor, but his youth and ability to work with youngsters kept him here for the time being. Today he inspected the long, straight lines of miniature soldiers for the last time.

Two thousand gray-uniformed boys, ages five to twelve, stood with their backs to the left wing of the massive four-story building that had once been a summer palace for Louis XV. Facing them on the right were 909 upperclassmen in the dark blue uniforms of the Cadre Bleu. These older cadets would remain at the Ecole de Cavalerie.

All of Northern France was on the move. Five hundred thousand civilians had been evacuated from military zones already. The train stations at Arras and Lille and Strasbourg were jammed with children being relocated. Some of these two thousand young cadets would be going back to their homes in the south of France or Switzerland or Monaco. The others would be resettled in a far less spacious school near Marseilles, where there were no horses or lessons in equitation. The majority of the staff were likewise being evacuated, leaving Paul with nine lieutenant instructors to govern nine hundred cadets. None seemed happy about breaking up the school.

Head held high, boots polished to a glossy sheen, spurs glinting in the sun, Paul Chardon walked among the little ones like a Gulliver among the Lilliputian army.

At the end of a column the chin of a small, pink-cheeked boy trembled with emotion. "Chin up, Jean-Claude." Paul patted him on the shoulder. "This will be over very soon. The Boche will be soundly beaten, and we will all be together here again."

Two rows back an eight-year-old named Pieter, who had grown attached to a bay broodmare named Germain, sniffled uncontrollably.

"Be brave, Pieter," Paul enjoined.

"It is Germain, sir. Poor Germain. I have heard what they did to horses in the last war. Will she be made to haul a wagon? Will they kill her for meat?"

"She is in foal, Pieter. When you return she will have a colt at her side. The broodmares of the Ecole de Cavalerie do not haul wagons. Ever."

At this the child brightened. And so it went on down the line. Colonel Michel Larousse, commandant of the school, made a stirring speech, calling on each cadet to wipe his tears and serve France with dignity by being good students and thus good soldiers.

But they were leaving the horses behind, and that was hard to take. Their first week in school they had memorized the words of Marshal Soult in his message to the school in 1840: "Horsemanship is not everything in the cavalry, but everything is nothing without it."

One hundred years later the Ecole de Cavalerie still operated on that principle. Therefore, without horses, everything seemed as nothing to the two thousand children with warriors' hearts who plodded onto waiting buses for the journey to the train depot in Arras. Suddenly they were mere foot soldiers.

In spite of the bright blue sky and the autumn colors in the trees, it was a gloomy day. The war was no longer exciting unless one was at least thirteen years old and dressed in the dark blue uniform of a Cadre Bleu cadet.

✑

The evacuation of two hundred thousand civilians from Northern France had taken place in the first forty-eight hours after the declaration of war. In Strasbourg, Alsace, on the German border, each person had been allowed only forty kilos of personal effects.

What to take? Old photographs or blankets? A precious heirloom or an extra pair of shoes? It was a terrible ordeal, and yet they knew from the last war that the possibility of occupation by the Germans was much more terrifying a prospect. Not everyone left, but nearest the border, entire villages now stood ghostly and deserted in the late-autumn haze.

The majority of the evacuees were placed in tiny farming villages like Perigueux. The Alsatian dialect was close to pure German. This problem was solved by double staffing in every store and public building. In the post office there were two clerks. One spoke Alsatian; the other spoke the local dialect. In the police headquarters there were now Alsatian policemen as well as the rural French gendarmes. So it was in the schools and even in the churches.

But double staffing did not prevent personal resentment against the Alsatian intruders. The farm communities had not been asked how many evacuees they could take in; they had simply been ordered to prepare for their arrival.

Ripples of refugees spread southwestward until the migration even affected the public and private charities in Paris. The nuns of St. Vincent de Paul were given a list of names of children arriving at Gare du Nord. They were ordered to make room in their orphanage to accommodate two hundred German-speaking Alsatian youngsters. Public institutions and private individuals were asked to open their doors to the overflow of Northern France.

Rose and Betsy Smith were visited personally by Monsieur Comperot, assistant minister of Civilian Relocation, who came to No. 5 Rue de la Huchette on a chilly afternoon.

He observed the ground floor of the three-story building that served as dining room, kitchen, schoolroom, and laundry. He smiled nervously at Madame Rose when she told him that the thirty children in their charge lived in dormitories on the upper two floors.

"Madame," he began, "it is very difficult. You are American, it is true, but what I must say is as one human to another. *Compre vous?*"

Rose was always delighted to speak as one human to another. Frequently, however, it meant that one human had a favor to ask of the other human.

"But of course, Monsieur. We consider ourselves citizens of Paris and of France. How can we help?"

"There are certain children among the evacuees . . . difficult cases, Madame. We simply cannot place them."

"Difficult?"

"They are seven children who have been residents of a sanitarium in Alsace."

Rose gestured out the window of her cluttered little office to the happy squeals of children playing soccer on the cobbles. "Our children are very healthy. . . ."

"These are not unhealthy, Madame. Not now." He swallowed hard. "They are crippled. Infantile paralysis. Polio, as you Americans call it. All of them affected in one way or another. Five in wheelchairs. Two manage on crutches. First they went to the community center in Perigueux. Farmers came in and picked children to take home. No farmer wants a child who cannot haul water or feed the milk cow. It is the same all over. We brought them by train to Paris. By then every place was full. There is some room at the insane asylum. But to put them into an institution would seem most cruel, Madame. They cannot climb stairs, which prevents them from being placed nearly anywhere. But as you can see, your facility is ideal. If you might make a place for them on the ground floor?"

Rose and Betsy shared a look of pleasant compliance. "But of course, Monsieur. We will make room for them. The other children will help us with them."

Monsieur Comperot mopped his brow with relief. "There are hundreds of others like them who are not so fortunate. They will be placed in hospitals for the duration." He drew a deep breath. "Of course the Boche will not pass the fortifications of the Maginot Line. Simply a precaution. But we all know what they did to unfortunate Polish children with physical limitations." He drew a finger across his throat. "Emptied the hospitals of useless mouths. Put them in a closed van and ran the exhaust fumes into it. They have no mercy, these Boche."

Betsy puffed up her tiny frame in indignation. "Rest assured, Monsieur Comperot. Even if they got past the Maginot, even if they came to Paris . . . if ever they came to No. 5 Rue de la Huchette, they would not pass!" She held up her fist, which seemed a fragile weapon to wave in the faces of imaginary Nazis.

Still, the gesture was sweet. Monsieur Comperot seemed comforted. "Ah. You Americans! You must write your president Roosevelt and encourage him to come along with France again. Together we will settle the matter once and for all. You are not truly neutral. Not at heart." He thanked them and finished his cup of coffee with a flourish.

"And how long do we have to prepare ourselves for the arrival of our new children, Monsieur?"

He glanced at his watch and stood abruptly. "Within the hour, Madames." He gave a Gallic shrug and placed his bowler on his head. "The nuns at St. Vincent de Paul assured me you would not refuse."

4

The Best Gunner

Badger Cross did not forgive David Meyer for shooting up his Hurricane. The RAF instructor dedicated himself to the task of making the three weeks at Aston Down Operational Training Unit pure hell for the young American. On every occasion, and to every newcomer, he introduced David as the best gunner in the RAF.

"Heartless, he is. Nerves of steel behind the gunsights. Or at least nerves of tin! The Nazis love this chap! He shoots up our own planes on the field!"

The combination of nerves of tin and heartlessness resulted in the moniker Tinman for David. Badger, who lived up to the ferocity promised by his name, meant this as an insult. By the end of the brief training period, however, David was putting out his hand and cheerfully presenting himself as the Tinman. He took the ribbing with unfailing good humor. This increased Badger's hatred. Like a fraternity pledge, David determined that the moment would come when he would turn the tables on his tormentor. Badger Cross, who outweighed the American by forty pounds, seemed to welcome the prospect of finishing off the Yank who had punctured his plane.

Three weeks of OTU were packed with formation practice, aerobatics, and night flying, all of which proved that Tinman was an excellent pilot. This fact disappointed Badger, who would have liked to see the "cocky Yank" flounder miserably. But the hostility of Badger only served to strengthen David's friendships with the other pilots, like Hewitt and Terry Simpson, who did not like the arrogant, acid-tongued Badger either.

However, on their first leave in London before being assigned to operational squadrons, David left the pub-hopping group of pilot officers. He struck out on his own after Badger chugged three pints of Guinness and declared, "I can whip any man here! Man of steel or—" he leveled his hot gaze on David—"man of tin!"

David did not fancy spending his first night in London behind bars. One more pint down Badger's throat would mean that an altercation followed by jail was a real possibility.

There were no affordable hotel rooms in the entire city, it seemed. When he inquired at the Savoy Hotel, the price of a single was too high after the wad he had just spent on a new RAF uniform at Moss Brothers. So David spent the night in the opulent lounge of the men's lavatory at the Savoy.

An RAF pilot snoozing in an overstuffed chair within earshot of the urinals did not perturb the elderly men's-room attendant who had himself fought in the last war in France. Running an officer out onto the cold, black streets of London would be positively unpatriotic, he declared. So David slept very comfortably until just before dawn, when the rattle of a custodian's buckets and mops woke him.

⌒∽

"Sir, wireless reports a contact with merchant ship *Collingwood*. It was attacked by a U-boat about two hours ago."

"Does it require assistance?" asked Lt. Commander Trevor Galway.

"Negative, sir. They were shelled but escaped. They can make it into port. Request that we alert other ships in the area."

"We'll do better than that. Mr. Fry, give us a course to the reported position of the sighting. Full ahead, if you please."

South of the Canary Islands, even the far-spent year had a pleasant, summery feel. Accounts like the one just rendered interrupted what was otherwise a quiet morning. Cruising along the coast of Africa, the destroyer HMS *Fortitude* patrolled the sea-lanes, protecting British shipping. There was a great need for such protection, despite the peaceful feel of the predawn air. Since the outbreak of the war, over one hundred merchant ships had been sunk by German submarines, raiders, or mines. Over half had been British.

An hour of steaming at top speed brought *Fortitude* to the area referred to by the freighter. From this point, the destroyer became a hunting dog, casting about over the surface of the Atlantic for any clues as to the whereabouts of the sub.

On the horizon was a fishing boat heading northwest. "Attempt to contact that craft," Galway ordered. "Ask if she has seen any other vessels in this area." While he waited for a reply, he studied the ship through his binoculars. The fishing vessel had two stubby masts and a jumble of nets heaped up on her stern.

"She does not acknowledge, sir," was the report.

"Well, she must have passed through long after the U-boat," Galway pondered aloud. "She's only making five knots."

"Should we warn her?" Fry asked.

"I can't imagine a U-boat skipper wasting a torpedo on a fishing smack," Galway said, still gazing through the field glasses. "She rides so low in the water and . . . Mr. Fry, sound action stations!"

Within seconds the stillness of the morning was shattered by the strident clanging of the warning gong. Sailors hastily turned out of their bunks and hurried into their battle gear.

Captain Pickering appeared at Galway's elbow. His uniform blouse was buttoned crooked, and a glop of shaving cream was behind one ear. "What's this, Mr. Galway? Attacking a fishing boat?" he asked incredulously.

"Take a look, sir," requested Trevor, passing the binoculars. "I noticed how long and low the profile was, but when I studied the cabin amidships it became clear."

"It's a U-boat!" Pickering exclaimed. "Mr. Galway, give the order to commence firing as soon as we have the range."

Fortitude carried four turrets of five-inch guns, two each forward and aft. Her gun crews needed no urging to rouse them to the attack; many had friends or relatives among the five hundred British lives lost at sea since the war began.

The two forward positions barked out their first rounds within a second of each other, vying for the honor of claiming the kill. The shots missed but bracketed the disguised submarine on both sides.

"What is the purpose of the deception?" Trevor asked. "To sneak up on victims?"

"Why would a vessel that can attack submerged need such a ruse?" Pickering said. "No, she must be damaged in some way and unable to submerge. She's hoping her trick will save her on the surface in daylight. Well done, Mr. Galway. Your sharp eyes have seen through the deception."

The next shot from number-one gun landed just astern of the supposed fishing vessel's cabin. The explosion blew one of the phony masts in half and exposed the gray metal of the conning tower. Movement was seen on the sub's deck. Sailors ran aft toward the pile of nets.

The heap of mesh was thrown aside, revealing the U-boat's own cannon. But before the German craft could fire a single time, another shot from *Fortitude* made a direct hit, splintering the gun and catapulting its crew into the water. The sound of cheering from the number-two gun turret was heard clear up on the bridge.

"She's settling lower, sir," Trevor reported. The U-boat sank beneath the waves, but whether because of the harm done by the shelling or to attempt to escape was not clear.

Another round from the number-one gun knocked the top off the submerging conning tower, and then the sea was empty of all but ripples.

"Cease firing," Pickering ordered. "Prepare to roll depth charges!"

The officer on the stern of *Fortitude* stood, stopwatch in hand, timing the rush of the destroyer to the exact spot where the U-boat had disappeared. When the clock's hand swept around the dial to the precise instant, he shouted, "Roll one! Roll two! Roll three!"

Moments after the warship rushed past, fountains of water erupted from the ocean, spraying three times higher than the radio masts. Four times she charged over the spot, making the figure-eight pattern of the hunting dog who has run his quarry to earth. After the tenth explosion, the face of the sea was littered with thousands of dead mackerel caught by the underwater concussions . . . and an oval-shaped oil slick that bubbled up from below.

"Cease depth charge," came the command. "That's finished it. Well done, lads; well done all. Helmsman, take us back to look for survivors of the German gun crew."

∾

It was the dog that Pilot Officer David Meyer first noticed that dawn as he walked alone in London's St. James Park.

An enormous Saint Bernard, with a curving white plume of a tail, a black-masked face, and drooping jowls, sniffed and lifted his leg against the white trunks of the plane trees, as if his aim in life was to mark every tree in the park. The animal was unaccompanied. Dragging his brown-leather leash, he chased a gray squirrel and then proceeded to relieve himself beside a heap of sandbags surrounding an antiaircraft gun emplacement. This drew verbal fire from the gun crew on duty.

"Get that bugger out of 'ere, mate! Why look! It's lef' a stinkin' pile big as one of the cav'ry 'orses!"

David was about to deny ownership when the thing turned, wagged, woofed, and ran to him. It jumped up on his new RAF pilot officer uniform. David pushed the beast down. Too late. A streak of muddy paw prints marred his trousers, and white strings of saliva clung to his tunic. Thwarting a second joyous assault, David grabbed the leash and, with a swift jerk, ordered the Saint Bernard to sit.

Miraculously the animal obeyed. With long dripping tongue lolling to the side, he gawked at David adoringly.

"Good dog." David patted the large square head firmly and scanned the wide expanse of the park for anyone who seemed to be missing a Saint Bernard.

And then he saw her. Red hair was pulled back in a single thick braid that glistened in the morning sun. She was petite and pretty, and her face appeared freshly scrubbed. In her early twenties, she was half jogging, walking, and holding her side as she hurried up the gravel path toward David. She was wearing a man's topcoat that hung almost to her ankles. The hem of a white cotton nightgown peeked out over the tops of large black galoshes.

"Duffy! You're lookin' for a trashin'!" she shouted angrily in a soft Irish brogue.

The dog's ears perked up. He glanced her way very briefly but remained contented and unconcerned at the side of the RAF pilot who held his leash.

David smiled and ordered his captive to heel. Duffy did so, and the two walked calmly toward the pained and angry pursuer.

"Looking for something?" David smiled and extended the leash to the young woman who was flushed and panting so hard she could hardly speak.

"The *Thing*!" she managed.

"He's a Saint."

"Saint, indeed!" She gave the inattentive Duffy a whack on his hindquarters. "A devil is what." Clutching the coat to her, she spotted the paw prints on David's uniform. Her eyes were brown and warm and full of remorse. She gasped and scooped up a handful of leaves with which she attempted to brush the saliva from his jacket. "Were you layin' down when he did that to you?"

"Standing up." David enjoyed the attention.

"Aw. You're such a brute, Duffy! Look what you've done now to the officer's uniform!" She tossed down the leaves and put a hand to her head. "I can't tell you how sorry . . ."

"My name's David Meyer."

They shook hands. Her hand was small and soft in his.

"Annie Galway. You've met Duffy, I'm afraid. So sorry, Officer Meyer."

"David."

"David. RAF is it? But you're a Yank, aren't you?"

He looked up at the leafless trees on St. James as if the answer were in the sky. "Guilty." He grinned down at her. She was beautiful. She had an oval face, wide eyes, and a pert nose. Her skin was fair and creamy smooth, and there was a hint of color in her cheeks. David thought how wonderful it would be to wake up to someone who could look this good with so little effort. "Has Duffy had breakfast?"

"No. I had just stepped out to bring in the milk when—"

"Bet he's hungry." Duffy wagged appreciatively as David patted his head. "Have you had breakfast, Miss Galway?"

"Not yet. This brute has kept me from it."

No wedding ring. Whose coat was she wearing? A large man, whoever he was.

"Neither have I. I know a little deli in the East End. All the cabdrivers eat there. The only place in London where a guy can get lox and bagels. My dad told me about it."

Still clucking over the paw prints, she seemed to be missing the point. "You must let me take care of your tunic. It'll need a good cleanin', I'm afraid."

"Live far from here?"

"The *Wairakei*. Victoria Embankment. Do you know of it?"

He did not, but he made an attempt at it. "Near the river?"

"Well done."

"I'll walk Duffy home for you if you'd like."

She surrendered the leash gratefully. "If you don't mind. He's Trevor's dog. Minds a man, but he has nothin' but contempt for me. I just stepped out for the milk . . . did I say that already?" They cut across the wide, leaf-covered lawn.

"And away he went."

"Exactly. I knew where to find him. Trevor always walked him here. St. James Park. Every mornin'. I just sort of flutter along behind on the end of his lead, and he tears about waterin' the king's shrubbery. I think he comes lookin' for Trevor."

"Trevor?"

"M' brother. He's in the Royal Navy."

Very good. The brother's dog. Annie must still live under the same roof with the family pet.

"Is that Trevor's coat?"

"My dad's. I just grabbed it off the hook and out I went. And I'd best be gettin' it back to him." She smiled as an idea penetrated her brain. "Did I hear you say you'd not eaten breakfast?"

"Not yet. But I know this deli where we could go."

"The *Wairakei*. That's the ticket. We've got milk and we've saved some eggs. Would you like to eat with me and Da, then? It's the least I can do. And I do mean the least. I'm a terrible cook, but Da is a regular miracle worker when it comes to stretchin' eggs. Learned every trick in the navy. You can put on Trevor's things, and we'll get your uniform set right. Unless you have somethin' to do? What do y' say?"

"It's dinnertime back home. This is the best offer I've had since I left the States." David let her think it was all her idea. He glanced down at the lumbering dog. "Thank you, Duffy."

Duffy led the way out of the park along Birdcage Walk, through Parliament Square, beyond Westminster Abbey and the Houses of Parliament, before turning left along the riverbank at Westminster Bridge. The course of the River Thames was marked by barrage balloons that hovered over the river like a school of great silverfish, preventing the German Luftwaffe from mining the waterway.

By the time they reached Victoria Embankment, Annie knew all about the Newfoundland retriever David had owned as a child and that he had spent his tenth summer as a cabin boy on a rumrunner named *Jazz Baby* off the coast of New York. Then he told her about the convoy crossing the North Atlantic and the U-boat attack and how there was more war going on at sea than in all of England, France, and Germany put together.

In that same time, David learned that Annie had been born in Ulster, Northern Ireland, and had lived there until her father moved to Scotland to go into the shipbuilding business with his brother-in-law. The *Wairakei* was not an apartment block or a hotel, but a boat moored in the shadow of the Egyptian obelisque known as Cleopatra's Needle. Duffy had made his mark even on that distinguished relic, Annie told him.

A handsome, forty-two-foot, ketch-rigged motor sailor of the Brown Owl class, the *Wairakei* had been built by Annie's father and an uncle at Rosneath, on the River Clyde in Scotland.

"As a lad, Da sailed round the globe. Said he never saw a place as fine as Waikiki and when he built his own ship, he'd name 'er *Waikiki*. Well, the painter, who was a drunken Irishman, got it all wrong."

Annie paused, leaned against the stone railing of the embankment, and pointed down to the double masts of the well-kept ketch that was moored behind a row of deserted water taxis. The tide was up and the wind was up. The metal fittings on the rigging clanked a melody against the masts.

"Why didn't your dad have the painter put the proper name on her?"

"Oooooh! That's bad luck, doncha know that, Yank?" Those words were exclaimed in thick Irish brogue, as though they needed extra attention. "You never can change the name of a ship and have a thimble of good luck ever after. Would be like changin' . . . like changin' your own name! Someone would call you by the new thing, and you'd not be able t' answer!"

He looked at her there in the soft morning light and thought that if he had a ship he'd name it *Annie*. He'd paint it on the stern in flaming red letters trimmed in gold.

And then the words blurted out. "If I had a ship, I'd name her *Annie*."

She cocked an eye at him in amused disbelief. "Are all you Yanks so bold? Or is it all pilot officers?" She shrugged.

He was blushing.

She seemed not to notice. "Dad, Trevor, Duffy, and me sailed 'er down from Scotland through the Forth and Clyde Canal, down the East coast to Chelsea, on the Thames. Dad's just got a contract refitting motor launches for the Admiralty. Patrol duty. Small, wood-hulled ladies are less likely to blow up in a brush with those magnetic mines the Nazis have been seeding in the estuary. We'll be moving down to Dover when I finish school."

She turned and glanced back toward Parliament. "I'll miss this. London, I mean. She's a grand city even with the blackout and the air-raid wardens and such. At night I lie in my bunk and feel the tide coming in and going out. The lady rocks a bit as the riggin' rings like little bells. Through the porthole I can just make out Big Ben there. And I think what it must've been like in the old days. Before electric lamps. Charles Dickens and the like. It's quite nice, I think, unless you get run over by a taxi in the dark."

David recovered enough to tame his brain into thinking of suitable questions. "What do you do while your father is refitting patrol boats?"

"I'm studying to join the CNR—Civil Nursing Reserve. Last year I was at University of Edinburgh. Trevor was to have been Da's assistant, but he joined the Royal Navy. Just what I would have done if I were a man. Lucky Trevor. He's on HMS *Fortitude*. I love the sea. It's in the blood I suppose." She smiled at Duffy. "I wanted to see the world. At least I've seen London. And what about you, David Meyer. Yank. What are you doin' in a war that's none of your business? Come to see the world, did you?"

He wanted to tell her that he would have traveled the world just to meet someone like her, but the impression of impetuous American had already been received with amusement on her part.

"I was barnstorming between terms at UCLA."

"Speak English, if you please," she warned him as an enormous man with a bald head stepped out on the deck of the *Wairakei*. She gave him a playful wave, which he returned. He did not seem surprised that his daughter was having a conversation with a soldier.

She called to her father, "We'll be havin' a guest for breakfast, Da!" The big man nodded and grinned up at her. She leaned closer to David.

"Da doesn't think much of Yanks. Says they speak gibberish and drink too much."

"Winston Churchill is half American."

"Exactly. Da cannot understand why they've made him First Lord of the Admiralty. He says a man who talks so much ought to be prime minister."

David tried again. "I was a student at the University of California in Los Angeles. Summer term I performed in a flying circus. The war started. I heard they'd be flying Spitfires and Hurricanes, so I went north to visit family in Montreal and I joined up. The RAF seemed pleased to have me."

Annie stared at him in astonishment. "You mean you've come all this way . . . put your life in danger . . . just so you could fly a particular aeroplane?"

He shrugged. "That was my original motivation, yes."

"And now?"

"Now it doesn't look real promising. So far, the only reason the RAF is flying over Germany is to drop pamphlets. BUMF, we call it. Bum fodder, toilet paper. Warning the Germans to be good little Nazis and stop this nasty quarrel. I think the war may be over before I get to France."

"What would you do then?"

"I don't know. What about you?"

"I suppose I'll go back to Edinburgh to university."

"Nice place, Edinburgh?"

"I suppose so. If you like old castles, bagpipes, and the history of John Knox."

"I'd like to see it. Maybe have a look at your school."

Annie shook her head. "All of this because my dog ran over the top of you?"

By the time breakfast was over David was convinced that if he never saw action in a Hurricane, he had come to England for one reason. And she was sitting directly across from him in the teak-paneled salon of the *Wairakei*. Annie Galway was burned into his mind in bright red letters trimmed in gold.

5

Visitors' Day

Today was visitors' day. Jerome and Marie waited patiently for Uncle Jambonneau beside the arched stone gateway that led to the inner courtyard of Hotel des Invalides.

The Invalides was an enormous building that housed the old soldiers of the French Republic. Napoleon himself had walked upon these very cobblestones to review his troops, Uncle Jambonneau had explained. It was a very proud and historical place.

The golden dome of Napoleon's mausoleum shone above the rooftops of the buildings. Last month Jerome and Marie had gone with their uncle to visit the emperor's burial place. It was a wondrous monument of green and black marble towering up two stories from a huge, round, polished-stone pit. Jerome thought that Napoleon Bonaparte must have been a very large man to need such a big tomb.

The building had been quiet and solemn. Jerome had been suitably impressed. Uncle Jambonneau had spoken about the great Napoleon and how the present honor of France was threatened by Hitler and his Boche, and Jerome had almost wept.

It had been a very good day until Papillon leaped from Uncle Jambonneau's shoulder onto the hat of an Englishwoman. Who could blame a rat for wanting to taste grapes and strawberries? Even Jerome could see that the chapeau looked like a basket of fruit.

Unfortunately the woman was one of those who did not know that the rat was Uncle Jambonneau's pet dog. Her ill-mannered English husband had tried to kill poor Papillon with an umbrella. It was a very noisy and unpleasant scene. After the woman was carried off, Uncle

Jambonneau, Marie, Jerome, and Papillon were escorted out and asked never to return. It did not matter. They had seen everything there was to see and a good deal more.

The incident gave Uncle Jambonneau many hours of pleasure as he angrily talked with the other soldiers in his ward about the stupid and arrogant race known as "The English." It was the English, said the old soldiers, who got France into this present war with the Boche.

"Now here we are. We have already made the great sacrifice, but we French must fight and die for England once again. They have no self-respect!"

Jerome could not think how Papillon jumping on the English-woman's hat had brought about such prolonged discussion about war with the Nazis, but Uncle Jambonneau seemed extremely lively when it came time for Marie and Jerome to go home. Uncle Jambonneau had not been by to visit them at the *Garlic* since then, perhaps because of the colder autumn weather. Jerome had missed him and Papillon, too.

These once-a-month visits were perhaps the most wonderful thing about des Invalides. On this day the pensioners were allowed to have two guests for the noon meal. Some of the soldiers had no guest to invite, so Uncle Jambonneau shared Jerome and Marie with them. Some had no legs or were missing a hand or an arm. All of them had smiles, however, when Jerome and Marie came to visit. This was perhaps the only place in Paris where they were welcomed without suspicion.

In the enormous dining room, they sat at long tables and ate delicious hot food and all the bread they wanted. Jerome usually stuffed his pockets full of rolls so they had enough to last for several days after.

They were also given free admission to the museums and even the Eiffel Tower. Of course, Uncle Jambonneau could not actually see anything, but he still had a good deal to say about everything. Papa called the monthly occasion with Uncle "an educational outing." Papa also thought that it was very good that it did not cost anything. This was an event Jerome and Marie never missed.

Last night they had bathed in the big copper washtub belowdecks on the *Garlic*. Papa had boiled their clothes clean and hung them to dry near the kerosene stove. The thin cotton of Marie's dress dried quickly. The waist of Jerome's trousers was still damp, but he wore them without complaint. He had not wanted to miss even a minute of the day.

But it was Uncle Jambonneau who was late today. Most of the other guests had already been admitted into the courtyard and led beneath the columned porticos to the reception halls. It was cold out here. Marie was already shivering, and soon it would be time for the meal to begin. Where was Uncle Jambonneau?

The uniformed poilu in the small guardhouse peered through his window at Jerome and Marie. He was a new fellow, young, with a pointed face and a thin mustache. He leaned partially out the door because it was too cold to come out entirely. "What are you urchins waiting for?"

He was an unpleasant man, Jerome decided. "My uncle Jambonneau is coming. He is a resident here. My sister and I are invited to lunch."

At the mention of lunch the poilu ran his tongue over his teeth and ducked back inside. He opened a tin lunch box and pulled out three kinds of cheese, a thick sandwich piled with ham and chicken, two oranges, and a bottle of milk.

"I wish Uncle would come soon," Marie said through chattering teeth.

Jerome watched the poilu grasp the sandwich with both hands and maneuver his mouth around the bread and meat. Jerome's stomach was growling. If Uncle Jambonneau did not come soon, they might miss lunch altogether.

The poilu finished off the sandwich and licked mustard from his fingers. He guzzled down the milk. He ate the cheeses and then peeled his oranges one at a time.

Beyond the gate the courtyard was quiet and deserted. No visitors were walking about looking at old cannons or discussing Napoleon or the old wars.

Where was Uncle Jambonneau?

The guard finished his lunch and wiped his hands on a napkin.

Jerome approached the guardhouse and tapped on the window.

The poilu considered him with some irritation, then shouted through the glass. "What is it? Can't you see I am busy?"

Jerome called back, "My uncle is a resident here. My sister and I—"

The poilu held up his hand in impatience. He opened the door a crack. Jerome could feel the warmth of the little guardroom as heat escaped.

"Now, what do you want?"

"My uncle Jambonneau is a pensioner here. We were invited to come for the luncheon."

"Well, you have missed that, to be sure. They have eaten everything and picked the bones clean by now, little beggar."

"I am no beggar," Jerome flared. "My uncle lives here. My sister and I have been waiting, and he has not come for us."

"What am I supposed to do about it?"

"He is a patriot blinded by poison gas in the Great War. Perhaps he has fallen or become lost." Jerome doubted this, because little Papillon forever whispered to Uncle Jambonneau which way to go and where he should walk.

"Well." The poilu was humbled a bit by the fact that Uncle was an old soldier and blind. "I will telephone the reception. His name and yours, if you please."

"Corporal Jambonneau Jardin. And I am his nephew, Jerome, and my sister, who is shivering there as you see, is Marie."

The poilu nodded and closed the door. With Jerome's wary eye upon him, he telephoned reception and in a muffled voice repeated the names of all parties and the situation. He studied his nails as he waited for the reply.

"*Oui*. I shall tell them." Down went the receiver. The door slid open a crack. "No free lunch today. Your Uncle Jambonneau Jardin is gravely ill. Pneumonia." This he announced as if he were telling Jerome when the next bus would come. "He is in quarantine. Since you are enfants, you will not be allowed to see him. Run along home now and tell whoever might be concerned that the old man may die very soon."

"How do I look, Jerome?" Papa adjusted his blue beret in the dim mirror that hung beneath the hatch of the *Stinking Garlic*.

"Well." Jerome scratched his chin in wonder.

"Very well!" Marie piped. She had not witnessed the transformation and so did not know who the stranger was who examined himself in their mirror. "Now, who are you, Monsieur?"

"Papa," replied the fellow. He had the voice of Papa but looked entirely like someone else. It was an amazing thing to see. Papa was clean. Not only had he washed his hands and face, but he had washed himself all over in the copper washtub. Also he had shaved his scruffy beard until only a pointed black goatee spiked his chin. He had Jerome trim his hair in the back. He smelled like soap and mothballs. The frayed white cuffs of his shirt hung out from the too-short sleeves of his old blue suit, and there was a gap between the hem of his trousers and the tops of his shoes.

All the same, it had been a long time since Jerome and Marie had seen Papa looking so good. Perhaps it had even been since the funeral of Mama. A very long time indeed.

"Now they will let you in to visit Uncle Jambonneau," Jerome said positively. "They will not even suspect you could be the same fellow."

Marie, perched on a stack of coiled rope, concurred. "You can tell the poilu at the gate that you are the other brother of Uncle Jambonneau."

"Jambonneau has no other brother than myself," Papa said sternly.

"But you do not look the same as that brother." Marie studied the face of her father. She could hardly see any resemblance to Papa. "Monsieur, you look entirely different from our other papa, who is Uncle

Jambonneau's other brother. I suppose it will not make any difference to Uncle Jambonneau who you do not look like, since he is blind."

"But Marie! Uncle Jambonneau has only one brother! We have only one papa," Jerome declared in exasperation.

"*Oui*, Jerome!" she replied in a haughty tone. "I have eyes to see that. There he is . . . the Monsieur . . . only one person. But all the same, I shall miss the other papa now that he is gone. He was very good, even though he smelled badly and beat us sometimes."

Jerome and Papa frowned down at her. Papa put his hand to his cheek and sighed. "She is too young to remember me, Jerome. It has been a long time since she has seen me as I was, I suppose." He knelt beside Marie and smiled into her face. "I will tell you a story that will help you understand that I am he." He looked upward as though the story were written on the cargo hatch. "When your papa was a boy on the farm he had a pig. He was a very dirty pig, covered in mud from head to foot. Before we took him to market, Papa's father washed the creature. The skin of the pig was white underneath all the mud, and suddenly your papa did not recognize him because he was clean. But, *voilà*! It was the same pig! Soooooo." Papa dipped his head slowly. He held up his hands in a gesture that indicated the story was finished.

"*Oui*." Marie thought it over. "So?"

"So, *ma chèrie*! Think of it! I, myself, even I . . . am that pig!"

Marie pivoted slowly on the rope coil and eyed Papa with grave suspicion. "If you say so, Monsieur."

Papa smiled with satisfaction, clapped his hands once, and rose to his feet. "There. Take a lesson, Jerome. Speak plainly, and you will not fail in your meaning."

☙

Monsieur Pierre Mazur was not a religious Jew. He had been an active political campaigner back in the days when the French Socialists like Leon Blum were in power.

How quickly the flower fades!

In France, various popular political dogmas went in and out of fashion about as frequently as the Ritz arcade changed the dresses on their dummies in the shopwindows.

Mazur was definitely out of fashion. He turned his attentions to other matters.

He was a Zionist. He seemed about as Jewish in looks, belief, and habit as bacon on a bagel. The rabbis did not approve of him, and yet when the Jewish Quarter was close to bursting at the seams from newly arrived refugees, they grudgingly agreed to work with him.

The Jewish orphanages, both religious and nonreligious, were dangerously overcrowded. Soup kitchens were feeding many more thousands than could be properly cared for. Occasionally the French became irritated and threatened to burn down a synagogue or shoot a Jew for old times' sake. In those moments a man like Monsieur Mazur became an important intermediary between the religious Jews and the nonreligious Jews, between all the Jews and the hostile French population.

Today, in the Beth-el Children's Soup Kitchen, there was great upheaval. The conflict was between the religious children and the nonreligious group of five Viennese Goldblatt brothers who had just arrived via Warsaw and Bucharest.

It was obvious to all the religious males that the children from Vienna were more Austrian than Jewish, no matter what their surnames might be. They looked Austrian. They spoke with rolling German tongues and had arrived in Paris dressed in lederhosen and knee socks.

In the middle of lunch, which was strictly kosher, one seven-year-old Goldblatt expressed too loudly that what he really missed and wanted more than anything was his mother's bratwurst, sauerkraut, bread and butter, and a tall glass of milk. Did they ever serve such things in this soup kitchen? he wanted to know.

One thing led to another from the religious side of the table. Phrases like "ham-eating goy" grew violently to insults like "pig-kissing Nazi."

A food fight ensued. The kosher soup kitchen was devastated. The nonreligious culprits, who should never have been brought there in the first place, were deposited in the Zionist Office of Welfare.

Thus they came to the attention of Monsieur Mazur. They stood, covered in dried lentil stew, waiting for some more suitable place to be found for them, someplace where eating bratwurst and drinking milk at the same meal was not a transgression against the Eternal and an affront to fellow Jews.

Monsieur Mazur spent a long time on the telephone. Who in the Jewish neighborhood had even one square inch of space left for five little boys?

No one. No room at the inn, it seemed. The door of hospitality for these wild Deutsch-cluckers was unequivocally closed once word got around that they had done battle against fellow Jews with all the fierceness of miniature Wehrmacht troops. Spoons and tin plates had banged little Jewish heads. Not even the rabbinical students in attendance had been spared the indignity of black coats splattered with food.

"What am I going to do with you?" Mazur glared at them.

The five brothers were without remorse. They glared back. Mazur thought what very good pioneers they would be in Palestine. What wonderful soldiers they would make against the Nazis if only they were older.

Their papers were stamped with the large *J* for Jew. They were among those who had left Austria just in time. They had been sent to temporary safety in Warsaw and then had managed to escape there as well. From Poland they had journeyed to Rumania. Why had they been sent to Paris? Mazur asked the question.

They shrugged. "Where are we supposed to be?" replied the eldest, who was eleven and already bitter.

Mazur leaned his cheek upon his hand. He stared at the documents that allowed temporary residence in Paris for these stateless persons. His brain ached. He could not send them to the Catholics. Boys like this would turn the Catholics upside down or die trying. Such a move would be bad politics—sending Jewish delinquents to the priests.

Who was strong enough to handle such a force? And yet soft-hearted enough to see the deep wounds in the soul of each boy?

A light came on in Mazur's mind. He held up his finger in mental exclamation. "The American sisters! Madame Rose and Madame Betsy!" He grinned as five sets of eyes narrowed in doubt.

Mazur picked up the telephone and dialed. He spoke to the defiant ones as the telephone of Rose and Betsy Smith buzzed.

"Madame Rose is an interesting woman. She has arms like a Titan. Once I saw her capture a thief who was attempting to steal the *Mona Lisa* at the Louvre. She tossed him to the ground and sat on him until he turned blue. I believe he died. In the 1924 Olympics, she threw the shot put. After that she boxed a Russian bear in the circus for a living. She does not like boys, but perhaps she will accept you so you will not starve."

6

You Will Be Well Cared For

Uncle Jambonneau was very ill indeed. He was so ill that Papa brought Papillon, the white rat, home in a box and gave him to Jerome to care for.

"It is Uncle Jambonneau's last request that you take care of his dog. Of course, if Uncle Jambonneau does not die, he says you will have to give Papillon back to him."

Jerome accepted the solemn responsibility. Now Papillon perched on his left shoulder and tickled Jerome's ear with his whiskers. Jerome could not understand one word that Papillon spoke to him, however. But all the same, the dog that was a rat made very pleasant company for a small boy.

Marie got used to the new papa, even though she often spoke wistfully about the old one. This papa was very solemn, and he was not often drunk and jolly. He combed his hair and stared into the mirror for long periods of time as though regarding someone he did not know. He reminded Marie of the self-portrait of the artist named Rembrandt who Uncle Jambonneau said had cut off his ear and given it to a lady. When Marie pointed this out to Jerome, Jerome said that Papa did not look anything like Rembrandt. Rembrandt had red hair, and his skin was yellow and green. Papa had black hair, white skin, and two ears. Marie replied that Jerome just did not know what part of Papa she was thinking of.

After each visit to the hospital ward of Uncle Jambonneau, Papa came home and talked about things he had never mentioned before. "Do you know that your uncle, my brother, has very good care at des Invalides? And it is free."

Jerome and Marie had known this for a long time. They missed their free lunch visits.

And Papa would continue. "Did you know that when a French soldier is killed in battle, his wife and orphans also receive a pension?"

Jerome and Marie did not know that.

"So," Papa said, as Uncle Jambonneau grew stronger, "a French poilu receives fifty centimes a day. And there they sit. Warm clothes, new boots, socks, hot food, and grog every day. And what do they do for it, I ask you?"

Jerome thought about Uncle Jambonneau and his burned eyes and all the old soldiers without arms or legs or other body parts. "A poilu is a soldier, Papa. Soldiers go to war and get hurt and killed."

Papa wagged his finger in disagreement. "That is only when the war is real, Jerome. I have two ears, you know."

Jerome nodded and gave Marie a look to remind her how foolish she had been to compare Papa with the crazy painter Rembrandt. "Yes, Papa. Marie and I have noticed your ears."

"These ears have heard some very interesting things about the Funny War, Jerome. They say at des Invalides that there will not be a war. No one is killing anyone at the front. A very boring affair as wars go. Perhaps very soon everyone who is mobilized will be called down, and then it will be over." He checked his image in the mirror. "It will be over, and everyone else will get pensions. Everyone else will come back wearing new boots and warm coats. When they are old and sick like Uncle Jambonneau, they will live in luxury at des Invalides and get free cigarettes and wine and food every day while I am here on the *Stinking Garlic*, trying to catch a bottom-sucking fish for my dinner."

Papa appeared very sad at that thought. Jerome had never heard Papa speak so rudely about the fish he caught for dinner in the Seine.

Jerome tried to console him. "Marie and I will be here, Papa."

"No, you will be grown and gone. It is the way of life. A man must think of his old age. I will be fifty."

"When?"

"In twenty years, if I live so long."

"But you are only thirty now."

"Opportunity passes me by." Papa sighed. "Not even the gendarmes think I am a good enough Communist to arrest. Every worthy Communist is in prison for seduction against the government or has fled. I have no employment. My children are ragged and hungry. If I perish now, where would you be?"

Papillon sensed the seriousness of the discussion. He ran up Jerome's arm and tickled his ear. "The same place we are now," Jerome said.

"This is what I mean." Papa scratched his head. "I could enlist and send you my pay. And then when they disband the armies in a few months, I come home with the same rights as my brother. You see how it works, Jerome?"

"But what about Stalin?" Marie was very worried now at this crazy talk.

"He would only take our boat from us," Papa said with conviction. "It is a very difficult world we live in, Marie. There are times a man must join an army and fight for important things. Security."

"Like Uncle Jambonneau," Jerome said. "And the old men at des Invalides."

Papa took one last glance at himself in the mirror. "They will not refuse my enlistment." He licked his palm and smoothed his hair. "I will look fine in the uniform of a poilu."

Marie's face puckered in consternation. "But who will take care of us if you enlist in the armees?"

"Who indeed!" Papa scoffed. "I have given the matter some thought. Madame Hilaire has just been evicted from her establishment."

"Madame Hilaire!" Jerome and Marie blurted in unison.

"Well, what is wrong with her?" Papa frowned, although he knew the truth.

There were a million things wrong with Madame Hilaire. A former circus performer, she had been shot from cannons from her youth and was stone deaf by the age of thirty. Being deaf herself, she believed that the whole world was hard of hearing, so she shouted every word she uttered until one's head ached. Her hair, singed by constant exposure to black powder, stood out from her head in a permanent frizz. At the age of thirty-six, she grew too large to fit into the cannon. She tried working in the concessions, but her shouting made small children cry, which was bad for business. After leaving the circus, she took up the oldest profession in the world. Unfortunately age, strong drink, and her ear-piercing voice made her unattractive to all but a blind man. Uncle Jambonneau was thus her only friend and customer.

Jerome and Marie sat in grim contemplation of living with Madame Hilaire in the small confines of the *Garlic*.

"It will not be so bad," Papa said. "I will send money home from the armee, and you will all eat well. Uncle Jambonneau says she is an excellent cook, and she is the only woman I know who is fond of Papillon. It will not be for long, my little chickens. You must remember that this is not really a war at all. We will all be better off for it."

◀▶

The terrible news had come the night before.

The wire from the Ministry of War arrived at the tiny studio flat above the bookshop at No. 26 Rue St. Severin just after 9 PM.

Michelle Fain had put young Claude and Jean to bed. She sat down to write the weekly letter to her husband, Jean-Paul, who served France at the Maginot.

There was a sharp, official rapping at the door. She called out to ask who was there.

The reply was chilling. "War ministry telegram for Madame Michelle Fain."

It was all so cut-and-dried:

> MADAME FAIN,
>
> WE DEEPLY REGRET TO INFORM YOU THAT PRIVATE JEAN-PAUL
> FAIN PERISHED IN AN ARTILLERY ATTACK. . . .

And so ended the life of her dearest Jean-Paul and all Michelle's hopes for happiness. Only last autumn she had married Jean-Paul, a young widower with two small sons. They were good boys, but they were not her own. What could she do now?

This afternoon she packed a small wicker basket with the clothes of the children. It was the same hamper they had packed with lunch and carried to picnic beside the Seine last summer.

Were they going on a picnic, little Claude wanted to know?

Michelle did not reply at first. What could she say to Claude, who was five, and little Jean, who at three was already so much like his papa?

"I am going to be with your papa," she replied at last. "You will be well cared for."

Claude fought back tears. He was too old to cry, was he not? And little Jean did not understand, so he played with his blocks on the floor and paid no attention to anything.

After sunset Michelle led the boys by the medieval church of St. Severin, past the ancient well of the pilgrims and the gnarled tree in the courtyard. It was very dark, but they were not far from Rue de la Huchette. They walked up one narrow lane and down the next, until they came at last to the heavy arched gate of No. 5.

"Why have we come here, Mama?" Claude asked, peering up at the black wood of the gate. He always called her Mama because his papa said he should.

"There are lots of children here," she replied in a detached voice, as though she were already somewhere else. "You will be happy here."

She put her hand on Claude's shoulder and her other arm around Jean.

"When will you come back for us, Mama?" Claude asked.

She touched his cheek. "I am going to be with your papa." She placed the basket on the ground. "Stand on the basket, Claude." She helped him onto the lid of the hamper. "Can you touch the rope?"

He reached up and grasped the frayed end of the bellpull. "*Oui,* Mama."

She kissed him and embraced Jean. "Take care of little Jean. They will help you here." She tucked the hand of little Jean into the larger hand of Claude. "Count to one hundred and then ring the bell. Keep ringing until they open the gate. It will be good for you here. Better for you than with someone who has no money, no job. *Adieu, cheri.*"

Claude began to count. "*Un, deux, trois, quatre . . .*"

Michelle left them there and retreated along the dark street to a narrow space between two buildings. She hid and watched unseen as Claude counted slowly. She should have told him to count to fifty. It would have been quicker.

"*Quatre-vingt-dix . . . cent!*"

"Good boy!" she whispered with relief when he skipped impatiently from ninety to one hundred.

The bell began to clang, loud and insistent. True to her instructions, he did not stop ringing until the latch of the massive gate clanked back and a sliver of light escaped, illuminating the two young boys on the street.

"What is this? Lord in heaven!"

A large woman stepped out from the courtyard and peered up and down the pitch-black lane in hopes of seeing some movement. Then she bent down very close to Claude. "Are you lost, little man?"

"No, Madame. We are brought to you."

"Where is your papa?"

"At the war."

"Where is your mama?"

"Our first mama is gone to heaven. The other one goes to join Papa. She cannot keep us, Madame. She has no money."

Good boy! From her hiding place Michelle cheered him. The large woman clucked her tongue in sympathy, asked their names and if they were hungry now. And then, with one more look out into the blackness, she turned and led them in behind the safety of the gate.

"You will be well cared for, Claude. And you as well, little Jean." It was a kind voice, raised just enough so Michelle could hear her clearly.

The gate slammed shut. The iron bolt slid back in place. Michelle retreated alone back along the Huchette the way she had come.

⚬

Trevor Galway and his ship, HMS *Fortitude*, were still off the coast of South Africa. Having successfully escorted a convoy of ships past the Cape of Good Hope and into the Indian Ocean, the destroyer was headed northward again. She kept company with a freighter called *Doric Star*. For months there had been reports of a German raiding vessel operating in the South Atlantic, but the pocket battleship had not been located.

Captain Pickering was in a relaxed mood. A coastal steamer had just notified the destroyer of seeing the British battle cruiser *Renown* a hundred miles up the coast. *Renown* was more than a match for any German ship afloat.

The British presence in the South Atlantic was increasing, and as a result, the losses to merchant shipping were declining. No matter that the land war was a hopeless stalemate; at sea the Allies were succeeding. A battle group including the cruiser *Essex* was operating off of South America, and soon the ocean from Brazil to the Ivory Coast would be as safe as a pond back home.

When the outline of another ship appeared on the horizon, Lt. Commander Galway studied her intently, as did the captain. "It's *Renown*," Pickering announced. "Have wireless contact her."

"Sir," the helmsman reported, "there has been an explosion of some kind."

Pickering and Galway jammed their glasses back to their eyes.

A bright flash appeared on the other vessel. A billow of gray fumes drifted upward, from which the prow of the ship speedily emerged like the snout of a dragon coming out of its lair. Another flare of light and then another. "Where is that wireless contact?" Pickering demanded. "Mr. Galway, go below and attend to it personally."

Trevor had just exited the bridge into the alleyway that led sternward when a shell ripped into *Fortitude*. It struck the destroyer between the two forward gun turrets, shredding number one and leaving only the revolving ring to show where the second emplacement had been. Trevor was knocked off his feet by the impact and thrown against a bulkhead. From behind him he could hear Pickering shouting to break out the signal flags. To let *Renown* know about this terrible mistake.

The freighter sailing behind *Fortitude* was also being shelled. Trevor caught a glimpse of the *Doric Star* just after a blast amidships blew a gaping hole in its side. The steamer went dead in the water, and a column of thick black smoke rose upward.

Trevor had only regained his feet when another crash rocked the *Fortitude*. This one penetrated the armor of the hull opposite the base of the first stack. Like twisting a dagger in someone's ribs, the piercing shell penetrated into the vitals of the destroyer and exploded with devastating force.

The deck under Trevor's feet leaned away from him as the *Fortitude* sagged in the middle. The stern of the warship rose out of the water, as if a giant hand were pressing down between her funnels and bending her into a U shape.

Clanging gongs and shrieking sirens mingled with the screams of men. Explosion followed explosion as the destroyer folded in on herself. Aft, the canisters of the depth charges fell from their racks, crushing the men caught on deck. The aft gun turrets pointed uselessly up at the sky, and their crews struggled to escape the confines of the steel cages.

The ship was doomed. Trevor lost his footing again and rolled down the passageway, jolting against the partition that was now more a hatch than a doorway beneath him. The loudspeaker was blaring, "Abandon ship! Abandon ship!" *Fortitude* was settling, sinking. In a minute more she would go to the bottom, carrying most of her crew trapped inside the hull. Trevor got up quickly and tried to pull the hatch cover upward while standing awkwardly on the frame around it, when it suddenly dropped open and fell the other direction.

Wavering above a fall to where the ship's midsection had been, Trevor saw swirling blue water rushing over the hull. As he hesitated, still another blast ripped into the ship, propelling him through the opening and into the sea.

When the bridge and the bow of the ship poised like a giant shark leaping down to devour him, he struck out swimming in frantic terror. More men were around him in the water, some paddling and others floating lifelessly. A sailor in a small raft beckoned to him. "Come on, sir, you can make it!" The young seaman pulled Trevor over the side of the inflated island of safety. Less than three minutes had passed since he had left the bridge.

Together the two paddled away from the dying destroyer. For all the violence of the attack, the end was a silent one. *Fortitude*'s bow and stern saluted each other, almost touching, and then the warship sank beneath the waves.

Thirty minutes later, Trevor and the sailor, whose name Trevor never learned, were plucked from the water by a boat from the attacking ship.

Trevor could see that one of its smokestacks was a sham, and part of its superstructure was camouflaged to make it resemble *Renown*.

"What is that ship?" Trevor asked in Deutsch of the obviously German officer who retrieved him.

Thickly accented English answered him in a tone full of pride. "*Graf Spee*," the Kriegsmarine lieutenant replied. "Greatest commerce raider in the world."

⟨∞⟩

Stormy weather grounded the fighter patrol on the Kentish coast. If British aircraft were unable to fly, it was reasoned, neither would the German Luftwaffe venture out in gale-force winds.

David Meyer had taken advantage of every occasion to visit London . . . and Annie Galway. Today he opened his umbrella as he stepped onto the West Canterbury train platform. The wind instantly tore the black fabric and twisted the frame into something that resembled a feather duster. Pulling up the collar of his topcoat, he caught sight of Annie and Duffy laughing at him from the warm comfort of the depot. He tucked his head and dashed into the building. The door slapped open in the wind, refusing to close again until David leaned his full weight against it.

"Lovely weather we're havin'," Annie teased as his breath exploded with relief in the warmth of the station. Duffy rushed past her and jumped up to put his enormous front paws on David's shoulders in an eye-to-eye greeting.

"Lovely enough." David pushed the dog down and slapped the rain from his coat. "I'm not flying today, and here you are. Very nice weather, if you ask me. Thanks for coming."

She kissed him lightly and let her hand linger on his cheek. "Yesterday they had all of us student nurses cleaning out the basement of University College Hospital as a maternity ward. Air-raid precautions order. They say women will be having babies even in air raids, and we should be prepared. Truth is, we all think the war will be over by Christmas. The hospital will be left with a very lovely basement."

"I'm glad you got it all done yesterday."

"I caught the first train to Canterbury the minute your wire came. I've missed you, Davey," she whispered quietly. They were not alone in the depot. Two elderly women observed the meeting with interest as they warmed themselves beside the coal fire at the far end of the small room.

The sight of Annie was enough to make him forget the bone-deep chill of the howling storm outside and the scrutiny of the old women inside. "You're famous. I've named my Hurricane after you. *Annie*. Painted in bright red letters. Trimmed in gold."

Suddenly shy, Annie inclined her head toward their audience. "Let's get out of here. What do you say?"

The torrential rain let up just long enough for the couple to make their way up St. Dunstan Street to the tiny Falstaff Inn in the shadow of the ancient West Gate of Canterbury. The sign above the heavy wood door of the inn rocked crazily in the wind, threatening to pull loose from the iron standard that held it.

The head of the proprietor snapped up with surprise at the entrance of David, Annie, and Duffy. The beams above the bar were set low, requiring the tall barkeep to duck beneath each timber as he stroked the zinc-topped bar affectionately with a cloth. He was permanently stooped after years of duty at his station. With every step his head bobbed forward on a long, thin neck, giving him the appearance of a turkey strutting in a coop. The dark oak-paneled room of the pub was nearly empty except for an English cleric who read the *Times* and languidly sipped his tea at a snug little table in the corner. What fool would venture out in such weather?

"A day trip," Annie explained as they took a table before the fire, and Duffy curled up in contentment at their feet.

"Lousy weather for it." The proprietor grinned. "Pilgrims come t' see the cathedral, or just t' sun yourselves?"

"Picnic," Annie replied.

"Well, here's the place for it. Me missus makes the best kidney pie in England. Isn't that so, gov'?" He addressed the cleric, who seemed either not to hear him or to choose not to reply. "The old padre is deaf as a post. You can say what you like an' he'll not hear a word. Can I get you a bite to eat? It's a slow day, and I've got a bit of work to do in the cellar."

They ordered hot tea and a ploughman's lunch—heavy bread, stilton cheese, and tart chutney. This was served and then the barkeep disappeared down the narrow steps, leaving David and Annie alone in front of the fireplace. Soft dance music was playing through the static on the enormous radio. The walls of the room were decorated with etchings of Falstaff and scenes from Shakespeare's play *Henry IV*.

David leaned close to examine the fat, drunken character of Falstaff. "Did you ever notice how much this Falstaff guy resembles Hermann Göring?" he quipped. "Comforting to think that somebody who looks like that is head of the German air force. A couple of Spitfires shot down a German bomber off the coast yesterday. Laying mines most likely."

Annie's expression was sad and serious as she listened to him talk. "You're not in danger . . . I mean, not a lot of danger, are you?"

"Does this mean you lie awake at night and worry about me?"

"Of course. I can't help it. You're the only pilot I know."

"Are there other fellas who keep you awake thinking about them, too?'

"Yes. Sailors mostly." At his obvious disappointment she added, "My brother Trevor and the crew of the *Fortitude*."

"In that case, I'll let you in on a secret so you only have to worry about one of us . . . I haven't even seen a Jerry. The closest I've gotten is sitting here looking at Falstaff and wishing I could get a target that big in my sights."

She reached out and took his hand across the table. "I'm glad. I hope you never meet a German plane. I hope you stay here in England and that things go on like this forever."

"Me too."

The hour passed quickly. David tossed a load of coal on the fire as Duffy snoozed. The cleric in the corner sat as unobtrusive as a wooden Indian. Then the music on the radio was interrupted by the sound of the BBC Westminster chimes. The pub owner reappeared at the top of the cellar steps.

The reality of war suddenly intruded on the timeless peace of the rainy Canterbury afternoon:

> "Information has been received that the HMS Fortitude has been attacked by a German raider and sunk with all hands. The urgent communiqué was received from the ship yesterday at . . ."

Annie was ashen. "I've got to ring Da. Got to get in touch with the Admiralty. They'll know about Trevor." She scanned the room for a telephone.

"What is it, miss?" the pub man asked, catching her alarm at once.

David answered for her. "Her brother is on the *Fortitude*."

The barkeep led them upstairs to his apartment and pointed at the telephone as the news droned in the background.

> "The HMS Fortitude was the second British ship to be sunk within a week and the seventeenth ship to go down in the Atlantic since Saturday."

Winding the crank of the old-fashioned telephone, Annie raised the operator and asked to be connected to the offices of the Admiralty.

> "It is reported that she has been sunk in the South Atlantic. The presumption, therefore, is that she was attacked by the German pocket battleship Admiral Graf Spee, which is reported to have been in that area."

The wait for the call to reach London seemed interminable. Annie wiped away tears with the back of her hand and stubbornly refused to sit when the wife of the pub's owner brought her a chair.

David stood beside her as the Admiralty secretary transferred her call.

"My name is Annie Galway. My brother, Trevor Galway, was lieutenant commander aboard HMS *Fortitude*. Yes. Yes. I'll wait." She closed her eyes, and her lips moved in a silent prayer of hope. A moment later her eyes snapped open with alarm, and her ashen complexion grew more gray. "I see." Her voice was barely audible. "Yes. Thank you. My father . . . you say the wire has been sent. Yes. Thank you. . . ." She clicked the receiver and sank into the chair. There was no need for anyone in the room to question the outcome. She covered her face with her hands. "Ah, Trev." She sighed.

"I'll fix some tea," offered the owner's wife.

"A spot of brandy would be better," argued the barkeep.

Annie looked up pleadingly at David. "Da'll be needin' me in London. Can you come?"

David nodded. "For a couple days."

"You've just got time to catch the train, lad," said the barkeep. He solemnly shook Annie's hand as though he were standing in the reception line at a funeral of an old friend. The missus was crying, wiping her tears with her apron. They did not even know Annie's name. "Our fine, brave lads. I'm awfully sorry, miss. Do come back on a better day, will you?"

7

In the Interest of Foreign Relations

The duties of patrol and intensified combat training did not give David any additional time to spend with Annie. David had seen her only once since she'd heard the news about her brother—on the day of the remembrance service held at St. Paul's for the sailors of twenty ships that had fallen victim to German raiders. She clung to the hope that Trevor had somehow survived, that possibly he had been rescued. There was no word of hope, yet Annie was resolute in her belief.

But now she was all alone. Her father was burying his own worry under a mound of twenty-four-hour workdays in Dover. Annie stayed aboard the *Wairakei*, still moored on the Thames, and labored toward the completion of her nursing studies. More than anything else, she seemed to miss David. Her letters, like the one he kept inside his flight-jacket pocket, were full of brave sentiments, but David could sense that she was terribly lonely.

Coming out of his turn, David looked down from ten thousand feet on the length of the railway line between Ashford and Tonbridge. He was on a refresher flight in cross-country navigation, and the next marker he needed to spot was the second branch line to the right. Locating it would anchor the Hurricane onto the last leg of the Iron Dog route that led directly to the Croydon aerodrome—the goal of this exercise. Miss the turn, and he could end up over the coastal defenses, where some eager antiaircraft crew might put embarrassing holes in the Hurricane. They might even scratch the gold-trimmed red letters on the engine cowling that said *Annie*.

There it was, just where it was supposed to be. David guided the

Hurricane into another turn, adjusting the throttle and correcting a little swing with a touch of right rudder. This flight had gone so well that David had a lot of time to think about Annie, and he realized that he missed her terribly, too.

He also knew that there was nothing to be done about it. Now the young pilots were given almost no spare moments. If it wasn't flying patrols over the Channel, it was the endlessly repeated drilling: formations, attacks, evasive maneuvers, gunnery drills. It just went on and on, and David got more and more withdrawn as he fretted about Annie. He was so on edge that he had quarreled with his mates, Simpson and Hewitt, and that was no good for a combat team. David had hoped that the long cross-country hop would give him a chance to think things through. But with the end in sight, he felt no closer to sorting it all out.

David roused himself to go through the mental checklist for landing: flaps, trim, propellor pitch, throttle. All as it should be. David took his left hand off the throttle knob to release the undercarriage lever. His eyes flicked over to the indicator lights, then looked again. Instead of a pair of green lights, one of the two continued to wink red.

David's first reaction was to grab for more altitude. Back up to twelve thousand feet he soared, to give himself time to think things over. There was no other problem with the aircraft, and ample fuel, but this one snag was bad enough. After several futile attempts raising and lowering the control mechanism, David radioed for assistance.

"Croydon," he called on the radio, "I have a little problem here."

"Reach behind the gear-release lever," he was told. "There you'll find a T-shaped handle. Pump it vigorously, and see if the increased hydraulic pressure won't release the gear."

"Negative. I tried that already, Croydon."

"Try it again. It may take several minutes, but it should fix the problem."

It did. Less than five minutes later, David was rolling to a stop beside the Croydon hangar. As he got out, he noticed a number of airmen stare at him curiously, but no one spoke as he went into the headquarters office and reported in. He had to file an incident report and got a lecture on being more familiar with the equipment, so it was two hours before he could get back outside. David was even more glum than he had been before.

Since the second half of the mission was night navigation back to his base, David left the airfield and headed for the nearby Kings Arms pub for a bite to eat. When he got there, some of the bystanders who had watched his landing were already present, and it was clear from the volume of their voices that they had been drinking for two hours.

And Badger Cross was one of them. The burly man approached David.

"So, assassin . . . Tinman," he said with a little slur to his words. "Heard you had a spot of trouble today."

"No, nothing to speak of," David replied.

"Not surprised you couldn't manage it properly. Didn't you learn anything? Why don't you go back home where you belong? We can get along without your help. Isn't that right?" Badger called over his shoulder to his fellows at the bar.

"Ah, pipe down, Badger," one of them responded. "Pay him no mind, Yank. He's tight."

"The gear was stuck," David said hotly. "It could happen to anyone. Now let me by, please. I want to get something to eat." David slipped off his flight jacket, and as he did so, Annie's letter fluttered to the floor.

Badger beat David to it, snatching it up and holding it out of reach. "Ooh-la-la," he said, leering and waving the letter for all to see. "Lilac and lavender for the Yank. Where's she from, Yank? London postmark," he reported to his audience, tucking the letter in his pocket. "You Yanks come over here and wave a wad of dough about, so all the women drop their knickers for you. Some poor sod off in the service will be pining away, while his girl is doing the dirty with the likes of you."

"Give me back my letter," David demanded. He could feel the prickle on the back of his neck that he had always noticed right before a fight, ever since he was a kid.

"Say, 'pretty please,'" Badger taunted, mugging for his friends.

"Pretty please," David replied and threw his jacket in Badger's face. While Badger was clawing at the coat, trying to clear his vision, David hit him in the mouth as hard as he could.

Badger spun half around, stumbling over a bar stool, then tried to respond with an overhand right that would have felled an ox if it had landed.

But David ducked under the blow, landed two punches in the other pilot's ribs, and danced out of the way.

"Get him, Badger," called one of the bystanders. "Don't let him do that to you!"

Badger nodded and came toward David, a thin trickle of blood running from his nose and over his lip. David tried a couple more punches that bounced harmlessly off the heavier man's forearms.

"Caught me when I wasn't looking," Badger said in a panting voice. "Try it again, why don't you, Yank?"

David circled to his left, keeping the other man off balance. Tiring of the game, Badger gave up boxing in favor of grappling and forged straight in, trying to grab David around the middle.

David got in two blows that hammered Badger's eyes before being borne back against the edge of the bar. The force of the rush threw David down hard, and his head cracked sharply on the walnut counter. Badger raised both fists together over his head, preparing to smash them down on David's face.

Without an instant to spare, David thrust his right into Badger's throat, who gave a gurgling sound and rolled off. Outside there was a shrill whistle as the local constabulary came to investigate the uproar.

"'Ere now, what's all this?" demanded the policeman, thumping his nightstick against his palm with evident relish. "Drunk and disorderly, are we? Brawling?"

"No sir, Constable," spoke up one of the fliers. "The Yank there was just showing Badger some new boxing moves, imported from the States."

"Uh-huh," said the policeman, eyeing the blood dripping from Badger's nose and the lump on the back of David's head. "And I suppose they both slipped and fell into each other's arms?"

"That's it exactly, Constable," Badger pledged. "A friendly little tussle in the interest of better foreign relations."

"Uh-huh. Well, see that your diplomatic efforts don't go any further, or I'll call the watch and you can take your tussle to the guardhouse."

When the policeman had gone, David yanked his crumpled letter from Badger's pocket.

Badger moved as if he would renew the battle, but the stern look on the pubkeeper's face must have convinced him that this was not the time.

"I won't forget you, Yank," Badger said. "I've got you down in my book."

⚭

The richly appointed corridors and rooms of the French censors at the Hotel Continental were crowded with the junior staff of press agencies filing stories wired in from their frontline correspondents in Nancy. Former guest rooms decorated with delicate floral-print wallpaper and lace curtains were the backdrop for conflict between the censors and the members of the press.

Josephine Marlow was at the back of the queue. A lively argument ensued from a suite just up the hall. Josie recognized the voice of Mac McGrath as one of the combatants.

"What do you mean . . . won't do?"

"It simply will not do, Monsieur. For the sake of morale—"

"Morale! These guys died up there fighting for France! Well . . . they died anyway. Don't they deserve . . . ?"

"It is the decision of the committee, Monsieur McGrath. The footage has been confiscated."

"I've driven all this way from the front lines at Nancy to bring this. . . ."

"You were in a forward area without an official press officer, in a place where you had no business to be."

"So that's it then?"

"Oui! As you say it. That is it."

Josie searched for a place to hide. The linen closet was locked. She tried to squeeze into the nearest room but was warned off by angry glares from a crowd of male journalists who had been waiting for hours.

Too late. Mac left his oppressor with a string of uncensored American expletives and exploded, red-faced and grubby, into the corridor just a few feet from where Josie waited.

For an instant she thought he would storm past without seeing her. No such luck. He stood for a long moment, unshaven and rumpled. He had come straight from the front to the censors' offices at the hotel without stopping to clean up.

He glanced her way, did a double take, and then ran his hand through his hair. He looked like a kid caught with his hand in the cookie jar.

"Hello, Mac."

"Hullo, Jo." His expression clearly displayed that he would rather not be seeing her right now either.

"Quite a ruckus in there."

He shrugged and changed the subject. "So you made it back to Paris."

"You were right. Things have changed since the war began."

"Lousy censors. Herr Joseph Goebbels in Naziland is easier to deal with than these French poets and literary critics turned officials. Give 'em a little power and—"

"When I said things have changed, I was thinking more of other things."

"Yeah. I haven't slept in a couple days."

"I meant the restaurants. They're only serving half a cup of coffee, and there's no more butter on the tables."

"War is hell. I'm glad that's all the trouble you've had." He gave a bitter laugh. "Where you staying? I heard they requisitioned your block of flats for the French armees."

"Foyer International."

"Yeah?" He grinned. "With Mama Watson? Like being an inmate in a girls' school, isn't it?" His breath exploded in a sigh as his tension dissipated. "Well, nothing I can do around here." He laughed and wiped his hands on his muddy coat. "Except take a bath and sleep for a week. And I'm hungry. You had lunch?"

"I am meeting—"

"Never mind," he interrupted sharply. "I look like something the cat dragged in; I know."

"You could use a bath. But I was about to say I'm meeting Alma Dodge for lunch if you'd like to come. If you want to go upstairs and bathe, we'll meet you there."

Josie blurted the invitation without thinking. What could be more awkward than sitting across from Mac and pretending that there was nothing between them? His nearness only sharpened her loneliness, making her nights longer. No more journalists! Why had she opened her big mouth?

He stared at the toes of his boots for a moment, then stepped closer to her. "Tonight?"

"Tonight . . . there's that Polish thing at the Ritz," she said too cheerfully.

"Right. The Polish thing." Mac took her arm and put his face next to hers. He lowered his voice as though he were in pain. "Look. I can't do this, you know? Pass you in a crowded hallway and end up sitting across from you with a teacup in my hand. I hate tea. I don't know why I mentioned lunch just now. You confuse me, Jo. Last time we were together at the Langham I told myself I wouldn't ask again. Better for me, I think. Sorry." He ran his hand across his cheek. "Guess I need a shave. See you around."

◦◦◦

Darkness descended on Paris like a black curtain.

The interior of the Ritz Hotel on Place Vendome was as bright as ever. The lobby was a blaze of holiday lights that reflected endlessly in the massive gilt mirrors. A string quartet played Mozart as eminent men in dinner jackets and dress uniforms accompanied women in satin and jewels. The guests moved familiarly through the corridors and sitting rooms furnished with Louis XIV chairs and tables. A long arcade lined with shops lured browsers with diamonds and designer fashions. It seemed as if there was no war at the Ritz, and yet it was the war that drew such a distinguished crowd tonight.

The Society of the Friends of Poland had spared no expense in their reception for the former American ambassador to Poland, Anthony Biddle. The tables were laden with a buffet personally supervised by the head chef of the Ritz. An ice sculpture of the Eiffel Tower rose from the center of the buffet table; hors d'oeuvres were assembled to create a replica of Warsaw's Cathedral of St. John. Polish flags draped the walls, and a banner stretched across the room proclaimed in French *Forget not Poland!*

In spite of the sentiment, the general attitude among the non-Polish guests in the crowd was that they would very much like to forget Poland. Invitations had been sent to every ambassador on Embassy Row. Of all the top diplomatic officers, only William Bullit, the American ambassador to France, was in attendance. The majority of the ambassadors from neutral nations had felt it was more proper to send their assistants. How would it look to Berlin, after all, if the top representative of a neutral nation nibbled caviar and drank champagne beneath a sign imploring them not to forget Poland, which had just been incorporated into the Reich?

Even the newsmen in attendance viewed the occasion as a very fancy wake for a very cold corpse. But the food was excellent, and here was opportunity to eat well and drink freely.

"Remember the Alamo," Mac McGrath said as he raised his champagne glass, gulped the contents down in one go, and then took another from the serving tray of a passing waiter.

"A first-rate spread for a third-rate cause," said Frank Blake, the squat, balding tyrant of Paris AP.

John Murphy eyed Blake disapprovingly. "Cynic. I should have stayed at the Maginot. At least there they think there are some things worth fighting for."

"Right, Murphy. Ol' bleeding heart Murphy!" commented Blake as he took another hors d'oeuvre off the steeple of the cathedral, giving it an ominous, bombed-out look. "I'll tell you what they fight for. The English fight for tea, crumpets, and mother. The French fight for sex, a good table in a restaurant, and the right to a pension. Sensible people, the French. Trust me. I've been here long enough to know. First Kraut the Frogs see bobbing across the Meuse and they'll cut and run."

Mac could tell Murphy had already had enough of Frank Blake. It did not take much. Angry, Murphy grinned, thumped Mac on the back in farewell, turned, and wandered off into the babble of the crowd, leaving Mac alone to argue the point with Blake. Blake was already half drunk, and the evening had only begun.

"I saw Josephine Marlow at Hotel Continental today." Mac tried to turn the topic to something he cared about. He had not stopped thinking about her. "How is she getting along?"

"That is one lady I do not talk politics with! I keep her covering the Paris bread lines. It's safer, if you know what I mean." Blake snorted and consumed another glass of champagne. "An idealist, that one. Raving lunatic when it comes to Poland and the Nazis. She was a lamb before she left Paris last August. Lovely little political cretin, she was. Now she's Winston Churchill and Joan of Arc in one pretty package. Bonkers. Too bad. The whole thing spoiled a very nice, docile-type, feminine dame, if you ask me. Good writer though. Gets the job done. Good as ol' Danny was that way."

"Is she here?" Mac had been looking for her since his arrival thirty minutes earlier. He wanted another chance before he returned to Nancy. He needed to talk to her again.

"Josephine Marlow? You think she'd miss this? Bleeding heart Polacks." Blake jerked his thumb at the shrinking edible edifice of the cathedral, then at a table across the room. "What say we go over there? They've built the Belvedere Palace out of smoked salmon."

"Go on. I'll catch up." Mac watched Blake weave through the mash of Polish uniforms and tuxedoed bankers and oil magnates to the replica of the Belvedere Palace. Oblivious to the platter of smoked salmon and melba toast surrounding the sculpture, Blake thrust his fork into the dome and removed the roof—toast and salmon slices—onto his plate. *A little Hitler, that one,* Mac mused. He did not know how Josie could get along with him in the same office.

Knowing Josie, this would be a perfect topic of conversation. He mentally framed the hook for his lead paragraph. *"Hi, Josie. Frank Blake is a real putz, isn't he? He just ate half the caviar off the Cathedral of St. John, and now he's attacking the Belvedere Palace. How can you stand working for this guy? What do you say we get out of here? Talk it out over coffee some-where—"*

Then Mac's mental ridicule of Blake stopped short. What kind of heel was Mac acting like himself? One encounter with Josie Marlow and . . .

Mac patted the letter from Eva Weitzman he carried tucked in his coat pocket and felt more confused than ever.

8

A Rare Piece of Art

The reception at the Ritz was a logical place for Nicholi Federov, the White Russian, to continue his search for Richard Lewinski. Nearly everyone who had anything to do with his escape from Poland was in attendance.

Federov was certain of this fact because, as a member of the Friends of Poland Committee, he had helped make out the guest list. His firm had supplied the champagne. The bill, along with the rest of his expenses, would be submitted to the Gestapo.

His niece accompanied him on the social rounds and then wandered off somewhere while the Movietone film of the dramatic footage of Biddle's escape from Warsaw was shown.

Federov made certain that he stood beside Mac McGrath during the showing. McGrath seemed distracted, disinterested in the whole affair.

"Magnificent footage, Mr. McGrath." Federov spoke to him in English so there could be no misunderstanding. "An exciting trip, was it?"

"The last decent film in the war."

The clip moved toward its climax, and the figure of Lewinski in his gas mask appeared close up. He pulled the mask up and mopped the perspiration from his brow.

"An odd-looking fellow," Federov probed, taking care that McGrath could hear the amusement in his voice. "Who is he?"

"Some character taking up room in our car." McGrath looked over his shoulder toward the door, as if searching for someone.

"He has to be something more than just a character if he escaped with the ambassador."

"I suppose. Just another pretty face to me. Ask Biddle." The American excused himself and walked to the entrance of the dining room. He scanned to the right and the left and then disappeared as applause from the appreciative crowd swelled.

Federov decided that Mac McGrath knew more than he was saying. There was, of course, no way to ask Ambassador Biddle about Lewinski. Biddle certainly knew everything or he would not have spirited the Jew out of Poland. Therefore Biddle would have nothing to say about his identity and less to say about the man's current whereabouts.

As for the cameraman, Federov would put his Gestapo contacts to work on him. There were ways to find out what McGrath really knew about Lewinski.

"Americans." Federov sighed as the lights came up. He pondered his problem. It seemed obvious that the neutral Americans were holding all the cards in this matter. Probably they were also holding Lewinski. Or had they allowed this film past the censors to throw the Gestapo off the trail? Who else rode in the automobile with Lewinski from Warsaw to Rumania? McGrath would answer that after a little sensibly applied pressure.

There was only one way to confirm what Federov suspected. An active branch of the Friends of Poland was lobbying in Washington even now. Friends of Lewinski would doubtless also be active in the organization.

୧୨

It was the color of the dress that first caught Andre's eye. Cobalt blue satin, cut low in the back, it was worn by a tall woman with a graceful neck and thick, upswept, plaited chestnut hair. If the hair color had been blond, Andre might have mistaken her for Elaine from behind. He could not help himself. He stared at her, wishing she would turn around.

Attractive from the back, she apparently was worth looking at straight on as well. A semicircle of four male guests stood in front of her like smitten adolescents. Andre recognized Johnson, who had served as assistant to the American ambassador to Poland; at her right were the Polish Count Radziwill, grim and intense, and Clive Blackwell, the London journalist who had championed Chamberlain's pacifist policies before the war. Finally, crowding in at her left hand, was Federov, the White Russian wine merchant, whose main interest in life was not commerce but social functions and beautiful women.

And then the blue dress turned enough so Andre could see the face in profile.

Madame Josephine Marlow. This was his first glimpse of her out of that khaki press uniform. Impressive. Unlike the other women in the crowd, she wore no jewels, no furs; she did not carry a beaded handbag.

She was just there in the blue satin dress. Her face was fresh as a farm girl's. Nose straight. Forehead high. Classic. And she was beautiful.

Andre had noticed that much about Daniel Marlow's widow before, but he had not given her much thought. Perhaps it was the sight of the Russian, Federov, lusting after her like a third-rate museum curator lusts after the *Mona Lisa*. There was something about this woman, like a rare piece of art, that was out of reach.

Andre excused himself from the mindless buzz of conversation and moved toward her.

"Marlow," said Blackwell. "Marlow? Any relation to Daniel Marlow?"

"We were married."

"I was in Paris with him for a year in 1934 before I left for Ottawa, and I never knew Marlow was married. How long were you married?"

"Six years."

Blackwell counted on his fingers. "You mean he was married . . . ?" There was an accusation of the late Daniel Marlow in the comment. Everyone knew the reputation of the American journalist. He never behaved like a married man. But why bring that up now? Blackwell was a soul entirely without tact.

Andre sauntered up and patted the journalist on the back. "Well, Blackwell, good to see you back in Paris. Did you just arrive?"

"Yes."

"Did the fresh Canadian air do you some good?"

"It's the best air in the world, Colonel Chardon."

"Your tuberculosis is better these days, I take it. Very good."

Blackwell gaped at Andre. What was he to say? "But I didn't have tuberculosis."

"Whatever it was . . . terrible thing. We all thought you would die. All the same, my congratulations that you are out of the sanitarium, Monsieur." Andre crowded in beside the speechless Blackwell and kissed the hand of Josephine. "Madame Marlow, we meet again. A pleasure."

The others in the group cast concerned glances at Blackwell, bid Madame Marlow adieu, and sauntered off to less contagious parts of the room.

Andre took her arm and led her away from the stunned Blackwell.

"That was a slick piece of work." She smiled as they halted beneath a Polish flag. "No wonder you are a colonel."

"He is ridiculous, this British journalist. Ungallant."

"It's all right, Colonel. Blackwell doesn't shock me. I was aware of my husband's reputation."

"It is difficult to imagine that Monsieur Marlow would have had a reputation when one sees you."

"We were apart for a long time."

"That is also difficult to imagine. To be apart from you by choice?" His eyes flitted to her throat, her hair, her mouth. "Very difficult."

"When I came here two years ago, I intended to divorce him."

"And when he saw you again he would not let you go? That I believe. At times it takes a second look, and a man knows he was first blinded by the sun."

The wall was at her back. "Why is it that I feel like I've just jumped from the frying pan to the fire?"

"The frying pan?'

"An old American saying. It means that you are . . . skilled at conversation, Colonel." She eyed him with doubtful amusement.

"Just Andre, Madame."

"Well then, just Andre." She pointed to herself. "I will be just Josephine."

"No. Josephine the Just, I think . . . or Josephine the Gracious. Or the Beautiful."

She laughed—great uproarious laughter, the way American students on the Left Bank laugh when they have consumed too much wine. It embarrassed him.

"What is it?" he asked.

The laughter subsided, and she patted him gently on the cheek, the way a sister pats a little brother. "You're just so good at it; that's all! And I thought you were such a gloomy person the first time. Then that day in the office. I might as well have had a bag over my head. Now this!"

◦⁂◦

Wasn't that just the picture? Mac watched them from a distance: Josie in the blue dress with her back pressed against the wall . . . the French colonel in his dress uniform and tall boots . . . one hand in his pocket, the other hand touching her hand. The colonel stood close in front of her, like a fraternity man making time with a freshman coed.

She laughed at something he said. The kind of laugh that made a guy feel as clever as William Powell with Myrna Loy.

Mac wanted to break the Frenchman's handsome face. He wanted to thump his chest like Tarzan and hit the clown over the head with a Louis XIV gilt chair.

"What's with you?" John Murphy pounded Mac on the back.

"What do you mean?" Mac snarled and looked away from the too-cozy scene.

Murphy spotted Josephine and the colonel, then studied Mac. "Oh, I get it."

"No, you don't get it!" Mac controlled his urge to pop Murphy in the kisser for being too nosy and for knowing too much before Mac even said anything about it. "You don't know nothing! Look, Murphy, just what kind of a louse am I, anyway?" Mac's hand dove inside his coat pocket and produced a crumpled sheaf of Eva's letters. "What do I care what Josie Marlow does? Do I think just because Eva's in England and I'm across the Channel, I can just ditch her and go to trying to corral someone else?"

"Whoa, easy there, partner," Murphy kidded. "You're a rescuer, is what. For ladies in distress you're the knight—in tweed armor—riding to the rescue!" Then Murphy's tone grew more serious. "But which one can you see yourself spending the rest of your life with? growing old with?"

Mac caught sight of his own reflection in a mirror. His tweed suit was wrinkled. His red tie, which he'd owned since college days, was tied like a red rag around the neck of a bulldog. He needed a haircut.

Sheepishly he replied, "Now that you mention it, Josie always makes me feel like the biggest hick just in from the country. With Eva, well, I can be myself and no worries. . . ."

"Well, there you go, then. Besides, it's no crime to admit that Josie Marlow's ripe as a peach in June for plucking. That French colonel's got it figured, all right. But Mac . . . she's a big girl. She can take care of herself."

"Ah, it's just the fancy braid," Mac countered.

"Yep. They all go for it. Good thing I married Elisa before all the journalists were out getting fitted for uniforms. 'Course, if it was now, I'd visit Mussolini's very own tailor if I thought it'd make Elisa look at me. Now . . . who do you feel that way about? Josie or Eva?"

Mac's crooked smile emerged from the corners of his mouth to meet in the middle of a wide grin. "Say, Father Murphy, you're quite a counselor, you are. Confession does a body a heap of good." He tucked Eva's letters safely away and patted his coat just to make sure.

"Good, my son," Murphy replied solemnly. "Now go and sin no more."

9

For Such a Time As This

Andre Chardon brought Josie to the Casino de Paris and, with a bribe of fifty francs to the headwaiter, procured a table on the first balcony. He then ordered champagne at a cost that exceeded an entire week of her income. It was obvious to her that he was living on something more than the pay of an army colonel.

Back home in America, Josephine had been content to crowd into the movie theatre like everyone else for a black-and-white glimpse of Maurice Chevalier. Now here he was in the flesh.

It had taken the war to bring Chevalier home from Hollywood. Cheeks rosy and lips red in the footlights, his white-straw boater was pulled down over one eye as he sang the most popular song in France. Called "In the Maginot," it was set to the tune of "La Marseillaise." It provided a complete picture of the democratic army of France.

> "The colonel was in finance,
> The major was in industry,
> The captain was an insurance man,
> The lieutenant had a grocery.
> The adjutant was an usher at the Bank of France.
> The sergeant was a pastry cook,
> The corporal was a dunce,
> And all the privates had private incomes."

Josie smiled at Andre across the small round table as he sipped his champagne. "Everyone in the army was something before the war," she said. "What did you do?"

"I kept myself busy with horses and wine." He raised his glass to her. "And beautiful women."

"Back home we would call that a recipe for poverty."

He laughed. "It is not as bad as all that, Madame Marlow . . . Josephine. . . . As a young man I trained as a cavalry officer at Saumur. Thus the horses. My brother, Paul, carries on the tradition."

"And the wine?"

"My family owned vineyards in Bordeaux, which Paul and I inherited."

She smiled and thought, *Thus the money.*

His gaze moved to her throat, her ear, her cheek, and then lingered on her mouth. "As for beautiful women? I suppose they are also family tradition . . . one which, with your assistance, I may carry on in spite of the war."

What could she say to that? *"Very smooth, Colonel Chardon? Top of the class, Colonel Chardon?"*

Chevalier belted out his melody as sequined showgirls strutted their stuff around him.

> *"D'excellents Français!*
> *D'excellents soldats . . .*
> And all this makes fine Frenchmen,
> Fine soldiers. . . ."

Josie did not look at Andre. "I suppose you are highly skilled at what you do."

"I manage. I am out of practice in some things." His look warmed her. "Equestrian pursuits, for instance. And I find that my palate is not as sharp as it used to be. As for other matters?" He gestured toward the entertainer, as though the words to the song provided some answer to his final pursuit.

> *"Qui marchent au pas;*
> Marching in step;
> *Ils n'en avaient plus l'habitude;*
> They'd got out of the habit, but
> *Mais tout comm' la bicyclett' . . .*
> Like bicycle riding you don't forget!"

It occurred to Josie that in the mind of the colonel, she was the bicycle. It was an interesting idea, but it also frightened her. Soldiers were as bad as war correspondents. Shiny medals and brass buttons attracted bullets. She had had enough of that for a lifetime.

"I am not sure I want to get to know you, Colonel Chardon."

"Call me Andre, please." He seemed undeterred by her frankness. "And then tell me why you feel that way when we know each other so well."

"Not so well."

"We slept side by side on the train. You know I do not snore. Usually women do not discover such things until it is too late. Even when a husband snores, it is difficult to divorce him in France. There are laws. So, I do not snore, I am rich, and I ride well. What more can you ask?"

She laughed. "You must have some flaws."

The amusement in his eyes faded. There was the look she had seen on the train. The look of a lonely man.

He nodded curtly. "Many." He turned to stare at the act. The song ended to thunderous applause. The game was over. What had she said to kill his pursuit so entirely?

"I should take you home." He crooked a finger at the waiter and asked for the check.

The image of the doll jumped to Josie's mind. She blurted, "Did she like the doll?"

He looked at her as though she had read some small line in his thoughts. "How do you know . . . ?"

"I saw it on the train. I assumed you were taking it to someone."

He drew a deep breath. "I have a daughter."

"And did she like it? A beautiful thing."

"She has not seen it. Nor has she ever met me." He shrugged as though the words had escaped unbidden. "My greatest fault." An embarrassed smile. He counted out the bills to pay the check and had to count again.

Josie felt suddenly tender toward him. "I like you much better when you are not trying so hard."

"I suppose I am out of practice with beautiful women as well. It has been a long time since I could look at anyone else. . . ." His words trailed off.

"Anyone else?"

"The child's mother. She is dead now. It was hopeless long before she died. And yet I hoped. I noticed you tonight. Beautiful. Aloof. Intelligent. But . . . I have forgotten how the game is played."

"Not really. It is just that I prefer honesty to the game. I have had too much of the first and not enough of the other."

Andre bit his lip and leaned closer, like a man wanting to share some secret plan. "She is only five, my little girl. Living with her grandfather in Luxembourg."

"A beautiful little place."

"A dreary life. He is a grim and bitter man."

"Well? Have you thought about bringing her to Paris?"

"I know nothing at all about little girls. Children."

What was that in his expression? A plea for help? Josie sensed she was coming near to a dangerous situation. Here was a man who wanted to bring his child into his home, but how could he manage? Was he looking at Josie as some sort of potential nursemaid? Sweet, but no cigar.

"They are something like puppies. Feed them, love them, teach them manners, and they usually grow up to be quite decent."

"I have no experience with puppies either."

"You are deprived."

The spark returned in the colonel's eyes. "Do you know about such mysteries?"

"Puppies. Kittens. Colts. Six brothers and sisters. You name it."

"Would you share your advice with me? If perhaps I went to meet the child?"

She considered his request for a long moment. "Is that why you asked me out?"

He tucked his chin. "Honestly?"

"I told you how I feel about honesty."

"Well then . . . no. Honestly, you have a beautiful face. I noticed your eyes even when you were wearing your press uniform. But this color blue suits you better. Now I find there was much beneath the khaki that I had not seen before." He took her hand and lifted her fingers to his lips. "Beneath your tunic I see there is a fountain of maternal instincts waiting to be uncovered."

His appreciative gaze made her want to reach for her coat and button up. On the other hand, it had been a long time since any man had looked at her this way. She was enjoying it, but she did not give him the satisfaction of knowing how much.

"All instincts aside, Andre . . . common sense is what is required here."

He sat back and drummed his fingers on the table. "You are right, of course. What do you suggest?"

"If I were you, I would wrap that beautiful doll for Christmas and make a trip to Luxembourg."

"I was considering it." He frowned down at his hands in thought and then raised his eyes to meet her gaze. "Thank you for saying it. Would you go with me? I may need a friend to hold my hand."

☙

Mac felt the presence of danger even before he could see the vague shadows of the two men following him.

It was a short walk through the darkness from the Ritz Hotel to Hotel Continental, but the list of pedestrian fatalities since the blackout far exceeded the casualties at the front. Paris was entirely without the benefit of streetlamps. Muggings were as common in the City of Lights as they had been during the dark times of Charles Dickens. Every alleyway and narrow space between the close-packed houses and arcades could be a hiding place for a thug. Not even the blue-uniformed gendarmes were immune from being robbed; they traveled in pairs these days.

So who was on Mac's trail? He listened for voices but heard only the heavy footfalls of two men. They slowed when he slowed and sped up when he began to walk faster.

Other shadowy forms slipped past him in the dark. The drunken laughter of a group of revelers echoed across the square and reverberated beneath the portico.

The footsteps did not stop when Mac turned on Rue de Castiglione and quickened his pace toward his own hotel three blocks away. A cold wind blew up from the Tuileries, carrying on it the dank scent of the Seine and the sewers that emptied into the river in the night.

He pulled the collar of his topcoat up around his ears and clutched his keys so they protruded from his fist like spikes. He carried only ten francs in his wallet—hardly worth dying for. But his hard-won clearance papers were worth a fortune on the black market these days. To anyone interested in buying and selling false identities, the papers of an American were certainly worth killing for. There were a number of unidentified bodies fished out of the river every week. They were laid out in the morgue until someone recognized them. They were never found accompanied by their documents.

Mac wished he had a revolver. A number of men in the press corps carried sidearms just for such occasions. Benny Morris could get anybody any kind of weapon he wanted. It had been foolish for Mac to refuse. He had told Benny that the DeVry camera was enough to shoot. Now Mac would have been glad just to have the DeVry to hit one of these guys over the head. Too late for that now.

A car roared past on the street, driving too fast in the darkness. Blue light glimmered feebly from the slits in the headlamps. Mac attempted to glimpse the features of the men he was certain would assail him. Bulky silhouettes stood out in momentary relief against the white stone of the building, but he could not make out their faces.

The Rue de Castiglione was deserted. The voices of the drunks died away behind him. He was still a full block from the corner of Rue de Rivoli but remembered that somewhere along the block was the side entrance of the Continental. But where? He groped for the door like a blind man in unfamiliar surroundings.

The footsteps quickened, closing the gap. Mac stopped and plastered his back against the hard stone wall. At least he would face them when they jumped. Nobody would club him from behind and dump him, unconscious, to drown in the river!

"Hey!" he shouted. "I'm ready for you!"

The footsteps halted abruptly. Silence. Right. It was two men the size of prizefighters.

Mac challenged them again. "I've got ten francs, pals. If you think it's worth a try, come ahead."

"You don't say?" The accent was American. "Is that you, Mac?"

It was John Murphy and Ambassador Biddle. The three men entered the hotel together.

Mac wished the interior of Hotel Continental was not so bright. Biddle and Murphy said his face was as red as the lantern on a caboose. He glowed even in the dark. There was no escaping their ribbing.

The elevators were not working, so he plodded wearily up to his room. Inserting the key, he turned the lock and entered.

He swayed in the darkness for a minute, making certain that the blackout curtains were drawn. They were not. The notion that something was wrong rushed back. Or maybe he really had gone paranoid, as Murphy had suggested.

The window onto the fire escape was open. Cold air billowed in. Mac crossed the room in the dark, while something crunched underfoot.

Drawing the curtains, he turned on the light and stared at what he saw. The mattress and pillows had been slit. Every bit of his clothing was dumped onto the floor. Toothpaste was squeezed out of the tube . . . soap smashed . . . safety razor taken apart, the blades scattered like leaves on the bureau top.

He could live with all of that. Only one thing mattered. The rucksack containing his film was gone. And his DeVry camera was smashed. It lay in pieces on the floor.

◌◐◌

Trevor Galway had been imprisoned in the dank cargo hold of the *Admiral Graf Spee* for days before he was transferred onto the prison ship *Altmark*, whose only purpose was to collect the human flotsam of British shipwrecks and transfer captives back to the Fatherland.

As senior British officer, Trevor had at first been questioned courteously about the mission and destination of HMS *Fortitude*. When he refused to answer, he had been lowered into a cargo hold with forty-five other men, and the hatch had been battened down.

It was still an hour before dawn, yet the tropical heat had already begun to turn the prison hold into a steam bath. Trevor figured that the *Graf Spee* and the *Altmark* were somewhere near the equator, possibly off the coast of South America. He had not given up hope that the British navy was tracking the German commerce raider with the diligence of a good pack of hounds after a fox.

Beside him on the bare wooden pallet that served as a bunk for eight men, Frankie Thomas, a Liverpool boy of seventeen who had been captured from the British ship *Trevanian*, moaned and raised his hand toward the hatch. Even before his imprisonment Frankie had been thin and frail from his first voyage on a merchant ship. Captives' rations on the *Altmark* consisted of three thin slices of black bread twice a day and a pint of tinned potatoes. Now every bone was visible through Frankie's pale, stretched skin. He was like a baby bird, Trevor thought—all eyes and wide, hungry mouth. Unlike the other prisoners, Frankie had no beard.

The boy gasped and coughed at the stench of urine and human excrement overflowing from the waste bucket into the bilge. "I gotta breathe fresh air today or I ain't gonna make it, Commander Galway."

"Steady, boy." Trevor tried to soothe Frankie, although he also felt the pressure of filth, heat, and humidity bearing down on his chest. "You can't talk like that."

"Sure he can," barked the bitter voice of John Dykes from the dark pallet opposite. "And he can die if he wants. He probably will. You'd think the young'uns would be the strongest, but they're not." The Australian Dykes had been on the *Altmark* longer than any other prisoner in the hold. His freighter had been blown out of the water off the Cape of Good Hope at the end of September when the war was barely three weeks old.

"Shut up, Dykes," threatened Nob Jenkins, who was over sixty and had sailed in the merchant marine since he was the age of young Frankie. "Leave him be."

Dykes snorted in defense. "Just sayin' what I know. The young'uns always die."

"Somebody open a window," moaned Frankie. "I gotta breathe."

"Window!" Dykes scoffed. "He's off his head. Thinks he's at his mum's house in Liverpool! I've seen it. He's a goner all right!"

"Not yet, he's not," Trevor spat. He put his hand on Frankie's forehead. The boy was burning with fever.

"Why d'ya suppose it's always the young'uns?" asked the Australian. "Mum used t' say only the good die young. Y' suppose it's because they ain't had time to live bad enough t' fear dyin'?"

"Shut up!" Trevor snapped. "That's an order."

It was still at least two hours before the hatch would be opened and fresh water and rations lowered. Frankie Thomas needed to be lifted out of the hold and placed in a doctor's care immediately, or Dykes' prediction would be a certainty.

Trevor crawled out from the cramped space and groped in the blackness for the oil drum that held the discarded tin cans from the potato rations. Finding the drum he grasped an empty tin. Next he woke George Daly.

George was a merchant marine who spoke fair German, along with a half-dozen languages he had learned in ports around the world.

"We've got to get Frankie topside," Trevor said. " I need you to translate for me."

George moaned. "I was dreaming, Commander. A good dream, too."

"Stow it."

"You know the Huns can't hear us down here." At that George let loose with a string of insults in German at the top of his voice. "See there? If that wouldn't bring them down on us, nothing will." This was followed by a chorus of curses from the other men. "You see? Nothing."

"Pick the worst of the lot and repeat it, George. Slowly and distinctly, please. Think of der Führer and spell out every word in German."

Trevor did not ask the meaning of George Daly's communiqué. He stood on the pallet and began to clang the can loudly against the hatch, reciting each letter in Morse code. Once, twice, three times the message was tapped.

Within two minutes the hatch was peeled back, allowing a blast of fresh air to penetrate the suffocating gloom.

Nob Jenkins touched the sick boy on his head. "Look, Frankie. The sky."

Frankie opened his eyes and blinked up at the square of star-flecked heavens. "Thanks," he breathed.

A cluster of German faces peered down angrily into the hold. Pistols were drawn.

"What'd you say to 'em, George?" hissed Dykes. "You was only supposed to make 'em a little mad."

George seemed pleased. "Just repeated a rumor that Hitler's mother's name was Schicklgruber. A Jewess. Sure to get us shot."

Dykes, a wild man with a long beard and matted hair, peered at

George with eyes like two burned holes in his filthy face. "The name of Hitler's mother?"

George had just opened his mouth to explain when the glaring face of Captain Thun appeared in the opening. A blaze of light stabbed the darkness, causing the men below to shield their eyes.

"Who has done this!"

Trevor held up the tin can as admission of guilt. "We have a seriously ill man here."

"What has that to do with this matter? Such slander against the purity of our Führer's Aryan blood is punishable by death in the Reich. Strictly *verboten*. Since you are ignorant of the ways of National Socialism, however, we shall spare your life."

"We could think of no other way to get your attention. If this boy does not get help soon . . ."

But it was already too late. Frankie reached both spindly arms skyward, as if to grasp the stars and pull himself up by beams of light. "Oh, look!" He smiled. "Look at them!"

Nob clasped the boy's shoulder as if to hold him down. "Stay with us, Frankie. We're goin' home to England soon!"

"Home," Frankie murmured, and his arms fell in a limp tangle across his chest. The light left his eyes, sailing past the German captain to freedom.

"Dead," said Dykes. "Always the young'uns."

"So, Lt. Commander Galway, you have the attention of the Reich." Then the German captain shouted the order to have Trevor dragged out of the hold for public flogging to precede the burial at sea of young Frankie Thomas.

PART II

Did we in our strength confide,
Our striving would be losing,
Were not the right man on our side,
The man of God's own choosing.
Dost ask who that may be?
Christ Jesus, it is He—
Lord Sabaoth His name,
From age to age the same,
    And He must win the battle.

10

The Interruptions of War

On a quiet afternoon in the neutral nation of Belgium, the peaceful life of farmer Leopold Dumas was about to be interrupted by the war.

The Belgian farmer scooped grain out of a gunnysack and into the canvas feedbag. An enormous draft horse put his great shaggy head over the stall and neighed with anticipation. Then the horse's ears pricked upward, and he turned his head toward the open door of the barn that framed a square of gray light.

A moment later the farmer noticed it also: an intermittent buzzing as if a mosquito were turning its shrill hum on and off. Leopold straightened up and listened, twirling one end of his bushy silver mustache in thought. "What can that be, eh?" he asked the horse. "What is an aeroplane doing around here, and in this weather also?"

The horse's curiosity about the unfamiliar noise ended, and he nickered again for his supper. Leopold shrugged and finished filling the feedbag as the humming receded.

The farmer was slipping the leather strap over the animal's ears when the buzzing returned with a rush. It seemed to come from a great height, faint at first, and then increasing until the sputtering hum was directly above the barn roof.

There was a *swoosh* of air through the open doorway that scattered the chickens and swirled the dust. An instant later came a sharp crack, as if a frozen tree limb had broken off, followed by more snapping noises and the rattle of breaking glass.

Leopold hurriedly retrieved his heavy coat from a wooden peg near the door and slipped the cap with the long earflaps over his head. At first he could see nothing amiss as he scanned the fields covered by early snow. Then a man staggered into view at the far end of the pasture, climbing out of the culvert.

Leopold started toward him. A little closer and Leopold could make out the crumpled outline of a small plane. It lay half across the drainage ditch with its nose on one side and its tail on the other, but it had buckled in the middle as if the bug Leopold had thought of earlier had been squashed. A Nazi bug, judging by its markings.

A second man in uniform staggered out of the ditch and joined his fellow. They appeared to be having a hurried conference involving a leather portfolio that the first officer waved excitedly. Both men patted their uniform pockets, looking for something.

They turned at Leopold's approach, and the man with the pouch spoke. "*Sprechen Sie Deutsch?*"

"I speak German," Leopold acknowledged. "So, your flying machine is broken, yes? Are you hurt?"

"No, no, we are very fortunately uninjured. I am Major Kurt Hulse, and this is Major Reinberger. And your name is?"

Introductions over, Hulse made an odd request. "Have you any matches, Herr Leopold?"

So the search of the pockets was explained. "Yes," Leopold agreed. "Why?"

"We need . . . that is . . . it is so cold. We need to build a fire, Herr Leopold."

"Come into my house," urged the farmer. "It is just beyond the barn there."

"Ah, no, we . . . we cannot leave the plane, you see . . . we must guard it."

"From what?" Leopold asked, eyeing the empty fields. A car turned the far corner of the hedge-bordered pasture.

"Please," Hulse begged. "Our orders, you see. Could we build a fire here to keep warm?"

Leopold hesitantly produced two matches from his jacket and handed them to Hulse. Reinberger upended the portfolio, spilling a pile of papers onto the frozen earth.

A light snow was beginning to fall, and the first match sputtered and died without catching in the heap of typewritten pages. The auto pulled up across the hedge nearest the plane and slid to a halt on the icy road. A gendarme jumped out.

"*Schneller,*" muttered Hulse.

The second match flared, and Reinberger cupped it against the wind and touched it to the corner of a page. The damp paper seemed to refuse the fire for a second; then a bright yellow flame jumped up as the gendarme vaulted the ditch, pistol in hand.

Hulse turned to face the policeman, blocking his view of the scene as Reinberger, in a sudden change of mind, stomped on the tiny blaze and hurriedly stuffed the papers back into the case.

"Leopold," called the local gendarme, a man named Albert. "This plane . . . it is German."

"I know that," remarked Leopold with irritation. "It has chosen my field in which to crash."

Albert waved his pistol at the two Nazi officers. "You will move away from the plane," he directed. "Leopold, we will please go to your home to await my superiors. We saw this plane circle the village, obviously in difficulty. Others will be following me shortly."

Reinberger and Hulse exchanged a look, then complied with the policeman and started across the snow toward the farmhouse. Reinberger cradled the pouch under his arm as they went.

☙❧

Information about the German plane crash in Belgium and the attempted destruction of top-secret Nazi papers reached French Military Intelligence two days after the event. By then the Belgians and the Dutch and the officials of tiny Luxembourg had already taken their turns interrogating the two German airmen. The suspect papers had been examined a dozen times and were the subject of grave concern in the governments of the neutrals. The trembling caused by the revelation of what was in the papers about the Germans' plan had somehow filtered down into the villages on the border, causing unconcealed suspicion of every stranger who passed through.

Andre Chardon, as French Military Intelligence liaison officer, was the obvious choice to travel to Belgium to check out the papers and talk to the German airmen. In spite of the frigid weather, he elected to motor the route from Paris to Brussels and pass through the Ardennes along the way. The roundabout route was intentional. He wanted to review a growing suspicion about German objectives. Richard Lewinski, working in Andre's basement to unravel Enigma, grudgingly accepted Gustave Bertrand as a temporary guardian.

After a long, uneventful drive and a night in Luxembourg City, Andre left for Brussels early the next morning. A fine rain mixed with wisps of fog. The trip up through the rough terrain of the Ardennes was long and wet with plenty of time to consider the improbable possibility of German invasion by this route.

He passed through the frontier checks into Belgium without a problem, but upon entering the town of Arlon, he found that the hint of a Wehrmacht assault had sent a wave of panic through the Belgian populace.

The streets of Arlon were without markers. Barricades of logs lay across each of the main thoroughfares. These obstructions, Andre noted, were pathetic attempts by the citizens to block an expected German invasion of their town. The heaviest obstacle could have been simply pushed aside or crushed beneath the treads of a German tank. The only result of the ramparts that Andre could see was crazy bottlenecks in intersections that were nearly impassable at the best of times. Driving from one side of Arlon to the other was something like trying to find his way out of a maze in the gardens of Versailles. If and when the Germans did decide to overrun Arlon, the town's pitiful fortifications would only impede the advance of friendly troops and artillery sent out to face the Nazi menace.

Finally reaching the center of town, Andre found further evidence of panic. All the men who might have manned the outer blockades were in the square listening to an inspiring speech by the major. Even here the word was "The Boche shall not pass!"

It seemed that the townsfolk did not want *anyone* to pass, not even a French military officer with official business in Brussels. Andre was pulled to the side of the street. Military police came at the bidding of the metropolitan police, who responded to the summons of the traffic police. Each group examined Andre's documents down to his French driver's license. Was he a spy dressed in French military uniform? Was he a fifth columnist out to take pictures of the little town of Arlon and pass information to saboteurs? Andre was held and questioned for two hours.

Finally cleared, Andre proceeded by a back road north toward Dinant and the bridge that crossed the Meuse River. There he was stopped by a cheerful captain of the Belgian military police, who instantly read the irritation on Andre's face.

"What is it, Colonel?"

"I might have been burned for a witch in Arlon. They have gone mad."

"It is the rumor, Colonel. No one knows where it began, but there is hearsay that the Germans will soon attack through Belgium and Holland."

Andre knew the source of the rumor would be the documents on the German plane. He did not know, however, how the information had escaped the confines of Belgian Military Intelligence to affect the intelligence of the ordinary citizens in Arlon.

"If there is a spy in Arlon, no doubt he has his papers in order and is carrying the briefcase of the town magistrate."

The captain laughed and passed Andre's documents back through the window. "Yes, and if there was a German spy in Arlon, no doubt he would have been the first to run and examine your papers, Colonel."

"Their hysteria is a bad sign. Frenzy and self-assurance do not go together."

"That is true. Poor little Arlon. Always the first to be invaded. Yet there is not much hysteria in Belgium. I, for one, do not believe the Nazis will attack us today. But who is to say?" He gestured toward the opposite bank of the river. "If they do, we will cut them to shreds without the help of either the French or English army. You see this bridge? There will never be a German tank passing over it unless all of us are dead. We Belgians shall do it ourselves."

Andre did not argue with the Belgian captain, but he thought about the roadblocks on the main highways from France to Belgium. He shuddered at the difficulty they would cause for advancing French and English troops, should Belgium and Holland call for their assistance.

The Ardennes. Andre pondered the rolling forest country as he continued toward Brussels. The French High Command had simply looked at the hills of the Ardennes through the dim eyes of generals who had fought in the last great war. The conclusions reached were logical according to the tactics of 1914–1918 trench warfare. It was not that the Ardennes was impassable to troops, but its twisting roads could not accommodate heavy siege guns. It was unthinkable to the old French generals that German infantry might be brought forward to fight without first having the advantage of artillery bombardment. Therefore, the German offensive against France would not come through the Ardennes. It never had. It never would. That territory was in itself a kind of Maginot. The French and the English were secure in that.

Who was Colonel Andre Chardon to question generals like Gamelin and Georges, or the British general Lord Gort? Yet he found himself glancing up through his mud-spattered windscreen at the gray skies and thinking of Stuka dive-bombers. A new kind of artillery. The narrow roads of the Ardennes meant nothing to the Luftwaffe. That thought made him uneasy.

Andre found no comfort in the visible preparations of the Belgian defenses. There were, he knew, seven hundred thousand men billeted in the beautiful hills of little Belgium. On the fire lanes leading off the main highway red signs announced that the area was prohibited to all civilian traffic. Steel gates and armed guards blocked the bridge approaches. A massive red steel fence ran up hills and down valleys for the entire length of the country in hopes of catching stray German tanks. Just in case . . .

A few miles beyond Dinant, the drizzle turned into a serious downpour. Twilight and then darkness descended like a curtain. Andre drove slowly along the back roads. Belgian troops were coming forward one brigade at a time. The troop lorries tracked red clay onto the pavement until it was as slick as ice. Andre peered cautiously through the windshield and cursed the vigilantes of Arlon who had kept him from his journey too long for safety.

There were explosive traps set every kilometer along the highway from Arlon to Brussels, land mines recently set in place, meant to destroy the road and halt any enemy advance. Andre noticed trenches cut from the center of the road to the shoulder and filled again as though someone were laying a pipeline halfway across the highway. Beside every trench stood a rain-drenched soldier with a rifle, warning Andre to reduce his already slow speed.

He came to an intersection where the soil in the trench had been churned to thick, gooey mud. There was a problem. Military vehicles had come to a stop on the crossroad. An angry officer was standing in the downpour, trying to figure the best angle with which to turn tractors, supply trucks, and an enormous 155 mm gun around the land mine.

"Who put this so close to our turn? Stupidity!" the officer railed at the sky. "Dig the thing up!"

The sentry eyed the booby trap with respect. What did he fear more: the little trench or the officer? "I cannot dig it up, sir. I do not know where the thing is. I am afraid to touch the string."

The string was a feeble piece of twine set between two sticks. Under slight tension, it held back the trigger of the land mine—a very dangerous thing for vehicles on the road.

The officer handled the inconvenience. He ran a tractor back and forth over the brush beside the road, cutting an alternate path for all his machines. Within minutes the bottleneck was broken.

Now, Andre thought grimly, if the Belgians could so easily bypass their own traps, could not the German Panzerkorps think of the same solution?

Andre drove on after the military equipment, rolling through mud that was nearly axle deep. He tried not to look at the little string. He made himself think about things other than the simplicity with which the trap had been bypassed.

Following military trucks all the way, he finally reached Brussels close to midnight . . . and spent a restless night in his hotel.

ॐ

Andre Chardon's brother, Paul, watched with amusement from the top landing outside the Ecole de Cavalerie entrance hall as the army lorry squealed to a stop on the slick cobblestones in front of the steps.

Paul's three senior cadet captains also observed the arrival from across the square. Their poses—arms folded across their immaculate uniforms and their weight leaned back on their polished boots—spoke of distrust and disdain. It was obvious the idea of turning the cavalry school into a hospital—and an English hospital at that—was repugnant to them.

The driver's door opened, and a tall, very British doctor emerged. "You are Captain Chardon," he said in very bad French. "I am Surgeon Officer Roberts."

Paul acknowledged the introduction. Roberts and his staff were to take over the now-vacant wing of the junior school, turning it into a Casualty Clearing Station for the British Expeditionary Force.

"And this is Chief Nurse Abigail Mitchell," Roberts said as a passenger slid across the seat of the truck and stood gazing up at the imposing brick facade of the school.

Nurse Mitchell was tall—almost Paul's height, in fact—and had dark brown hair and eyes. Her complexion was ruddy, outdoorsy, and she had the lean, muscular look of a horsewoman. *Striking* was the adjective that came to Paul's mind. So striking, in fact, that he repeated it to himself, creating an awkward pause when he failed to respond promptly to Miss Mitchell's greeting.

"You are very welcome," he said. "I mean, I am also pleased to meet you."

Paul shot a glance at the three students who were studying him intently. Was his bumbling shyness around women that easy to read, even from fifty yards away? He gave a peremptory gesture to Gaston, Sepp, and Raymond to come forward and present themselves.

"I want you to meet the ranking student officers," he added, silently wishing that they would walk faster. By eye contact, he told each boy in unmistakable language to be on his best behavior.

When the three were introduced, each stepped forward, bowed stiffly, then stepped back to form an unbroken rank of disapproval.

"Right. I will leave it to you then, Captain Chardon," Roberts said. "Miss Mitchell will do the inspection, and you two can discuss the necessary modifications."

As Paul left to escort Nurse Mitchell through the school, he saw the three boys exchange another look of disgust. Modify the school to accommodate a British nurse? Unthinkable!

It was clear from the start that nurse Abigail Mitchell preferred the title Sister Mitchell. With great pride she wore the coveted scarlet cape of Queen Alexandra's Imperial Military Nursing Service—QAIMNS for short.

Paul Chardon soon discovered that she was a formidable woman.

On the day the war had been declared, she was only twenty-eight. But she had previously served in Calcutta, India, and then in Cairo. She had only returned to England two weeks before the Nazis invaded Poland and was among the first nurses to cross the Channel with the BEF.

Had she been a man, a Frenchman, she would have been a general, Paul thought as she strode through the corridors of the junior school, issuing immediate orders.

All mattresses in the dormitories were to be cleaned, aired, and sterilized. Every inch of window, wall, and floor was to be disinfected. Little schoolboys carried germs, she said, and what a pity it would be if some brave British soldier was saved from his battle wounds only to die of some lurking measles bug. And so it went.

The kitchen of the junior school, thanks to its tile counters and stainless-steel sinks, would be converted into an operating theatre. Shadowless lights would be rigged and a generator installed as a source of backup power.

Probably because of her years in the warm climates of the British Empire, Sister Mitchell seemed to have a morbid loathing of cold weather. At her command, tons of coal were laid in, enough to heat the entire Maginot for a year or more, Paul thought.

The Casualty Clearing Station, or CCS, at Lys was set up to be the short-term holding component, receiving casualties from Field Dressing Stations and Advanced Surgical Units. Only urgent surgery would be dealt with in the field. All other cases were to be brought here, tended to, and then nursed until they were able to be transferred to the hospital ships a few miles away in Channel ports like Dunkirk or Calais.

Hardly a shot had been fired, but Sister Mitchell seemed to work under the assumption that the Ecole would soon be overrun with wounded men. With impunity, she recruited the school cadets to slave for her.

There were complaints.

Big, muscular Gaston, his face smudged with soot, his mouth turned down in indignation, and his uniform and tall riding boots filthy, reported to Paul: "Captain Chardon, I must protest the arrogant behavior of this arrogant Englishwoman! No wonder our countries have been so many times at war! The Englishwomen are much worse than the men, I think. Probably because they had a queen for so many years. Today Sepp and I were walking past from the stables to study for the calculus examination when she called down from the window that used to belong to the seven-year-old boys. You know the little boys sometimes wet their beds! *Mon dieu*, Captain! What a job! She put Sepp and me to work hauling down the mattresses and burning them in the field. Look at my boots! My uniform! I am a cadet officer, not a janitor!"

Paul considered the muscular young man with a disapproving eye. "I have told Sister Mitchell that every young officer in the Ecole is a gentleman and that we are all willing to help in whatever task she sets us to."

This was not the truth, but Gaston was ashamed that he had complained. He apologized and went off to study calculus without further words on the matter. But from that day on, he walked to the stables the long way round the junior school.

Paul resolved to speak with Sister Mitchell about keeping cadets from classes and duties. But when he faced her, she beguiled him, thanking him for sending his "little chaps" round to help out with such an enormous task.

Well, what could he say? "Thank you, Mam'zelle . . . pardon. I meant to say . . . that is . . . *merci*, Sister Mitchell."

Andre would have handled it better, Paul thought. Under the guise of having pressing business to attend to, Paul took refuge in the stables. There he explored matters he knew something about. Bowed tendons and the difficult temperaments of mares in heat were discussed with the school veterinarian, Lieutenant Rappollo. Rappollo, Paul discovered, had also been nabbed by Sister Mitchell to paint the ceiling of the receiving room. Three cadets had likewise missed a chemistry test and had received demerits when the stalls of their horses had not been mucked out.

All military order had been disrupted by this woman. Everyone was angry, and there were only three patients in the CCS. One fellow had broken his leg in a motorcycle accident. Another had a very bad appendix. The third had the measles, contracted elsewhere, and was in quarantine.

Paul had sent in his request for transfer to active duty, he confessed to Rappollo. The request had nothing to do with Sister Mitchell. He had, in fact, made it before she arrived. But now that he had experienced the fearsome Englishwoman firsthand, he hoped to face the German army very soon.

11

I'll Be True to You

Standing upright in his half-track, German Wehrmacht major Horst von Bockman surveyed the encampment of his new command. To be the officer in charge of a reconnaissance battalion in the Seventh Panzer Division meant that Horst was responsible for over a hundred vehicles and the troops who manned them.

An armored car bristling with radio aerials pulled up alongside Horst's location. General Erwin Rommel, the commander of the Seventh, got out and crossed to where Horst stood rigidly at attention. "At ease, Major," he ordered. "This is not a formal inspection. Not yet, at any rate. I want you to drill your men hard in rapid deployment through wooded countryside. Troops employed in assessing an enemy's strength on the field of battle must be able to get in, gather information, and return alive."

"*Jawohl*, Herr General," Horst agreed. "We'll start immediately."

"He talks like a textbook," observed Sergeant Fiske after Rommel had driven away. "Where was he when we were fighting our way across the Vistula in Poland?"

"That is enough, Fiske," Horst ordered. "No criticism of our commanding officer, if you please."

Nevertheless, even in Horst's mind, Rommel was something of an unknown quantity. He had been the commander of Adolf Hitler's personal guard during the invasion of Poland but did not have a background in tank warfare. But Rommel had been convinced by what he saw in Poland that the onslaught of armored units would deliver the Allies into German hands, and he wanted to be where the most glory was to be won.

Horst believed he knew what was coming. The Seventh was biv-
ouacked near the town of Kalenborn, close to the river Ahr. The Belgian
frontier was only a scant eighty kilometers away. Studying topographical
maps of the area, Belgium's Ardennes Forest jumped to mind. Horst now
knew that his aviator brother-in-law, Kurt Hulse, had been right. There
would be no frontal assault on the Maginot defenses. The attack, when it
came, would be through Belgium and Luxembourg, neutral or not.

The area of timbered terrain called the Ardennes was not fortified because it had long been believed to be impenetrable to the movement of
large numbers of men and equipment. That might have been true in the
days of horse-drawn artillery and the painfully slow deployment of foot
soldiers, but not in the mechanized days of 1939.

"Sergeant Fiske, contact the company commanders," Horst ordered.
"Give them my compliments and tell them I wish to see them in one
hour."

The boredom so prevalent among the poilus on the French side of the
line was nowhere to be found in the ranks of the Wehrmacht. The Germans thought of themselves as the best soldiers in the world, and they
were anxious to prove it, even if it meant continuous practice and drill.

Horst organized his command into recon patrols. Each unit had
three armored cars and a screen of motorcycle officers. "Today's drill will
be to cover the area from here to Staffel," he told his captains. "Each
team will be assigned a route and an objective that are roughly equiva-
lent in difficulty. The units will have to effect a crossing of the river—no
using the highway, gentlemen! Sergeant Fiske will be in Staffel with the
packets that represent the information you are to obtain and return to
me here. Are there any questions?"

Captain Grühn raised his hand. "And what will the winning team
receive?"

Horst grinned. "Did I not explain that? The unit that returns the fastest without any demerits will receive five-day passes for Christmas!"

The day following, Horst was in his half-track, roaming the dirt roads
of the practice area. He seemed to be everywhere at once, correcting mistakes and preventing cheating.

"No, Lieutenant Gelb," he scolded. "Go back and start over. You did
not dispatch your motorcycles down that country lane about a quarter
mile back. What if an enemy tank squadron had been waiting there to
hit our main force in the flank? You are the eyes of the entire division;
you cannot afford to have one eye closed!"

Horst managed to keep the tone of his reprimands light, even
though the subject they were studying was deadly serious. In the back of
his mind was the hope that all this practice warfare would never become

real. Perhaps just the spirit and ability that they were demonstrating would convince the Allies that their only hope lay in embracing the bargaining table and avoiding the battlefield.

"No, Shultz! You cannot leave your artillery observer behind as a guard. Look—up in those trees—don't you see that enemy machine gun? It has pinned down the entire advance. Think, Shultz, think! You need that observer to call in supporting fire, and you need him right now!"

In the end, it was the unit of eager Captain Grühn that carried off the honors. Arriving back at a tributary of the Ahr a bit behind schedule, they found that the narrow bridge was blocked by a broken-down transport truck. Rather than give up, Grühn reconnoitered upstream and found a bank of dirt that projected over the stream. The captain delighted his commandant by jumping his 500cc BMW motorcycle thirty-six feet to the other bank.

"Bravo, Grühn." Horst applauded. "You and your men have carried the day. You win the holiday passes."

"Thank you, Major," Grühn said. "What about yourself? Will you be going home for Christmas?"

Horst's mind flashed to Katrina and their home. He shook his head to clear the images before answering. "No . . . that is . . . yes, I will be away for a few days. Taking care of some business." Then, trying to recover some of the previous pleasant mood, he added, "By the way, you may tell your team that they especially deserve this victory."

"Why is that, Major?"

"Because, to make things more interesting, I am the one who arranged for the truck to 'break down' on the bridge."

☙

The cold had settled over London tonight, but the nearness of Annie warmed David. In the moonlight, the Thames gleamed like a ribbon of tinfoil as it snaked past the wharves and under Tower Bridge. David had not intended to stroll so far when they left the *Wairakei* to walk Duffy along the Embankment, but he was glad for the distance. Although David had not told Annie, he knew that this was their last night together for perhaps a very long time.

By tomorrow morning he would be nearly to Tangmere, the airfield twenty-five miles west of Brighton, between the South Downs and the Channel. But he would not be there for long. *Posted to France*, his orders read. At Tangmere he was slated to join a formation of replacement pilots ferrying Hurricanes to the BEF. Once there, he would belong to 73 Squadron body and soul.

That was why David was taking his time tonight. He realized that when they turned back toward the *Wairakei,* it would mean their final good-bye was near.

Duffy tugged David along to the next unlit lamppost and then to an ornate bench with camels decorating the ironwork. The pilot made no effort to slow the dog or turn him back. The farther Duffy pulled them away from home, the longer the walk home would last.

Wordlessly Annie took his hand, intertwining her fingers with his. It felt natural, as though their hands were meant to fit together. This gesture, which had become so familiar to him in their days together, made him ache inside. How he longed to tell her he was leaving and that he loved her. His desire was bigger than words. It dwarfed his thoughts until they were mere shadows of his feelings.

"You've been quiet all evenin', Davey." She stopped and leaned against his arm. "What's wrong?"

He could hardly breathe. He could not answer her question about why he was quiet. She was the reason. There was the river and the moonlight and Annie. She tugged his wrist and pulled him down to sit on a bench.

"Like a silver ribbon," David murmured, commenting on the shining river as if he was not thinking of her lying in his arms, yielding to his touch. He was certain that he loved her. He wanted her as he had never wanted any woman. But if he loved her, how could he take her tonight and leave before dawn, maybe forever? She knew all the stories of the lines soldiers pulled on their "last night before going off to war." What could David say that would not sound like that?

Helpless in the face of reality, he remarked on the water, the shadows cast on the Thames by London Bridge, and the shining dome of St. Paul's Cathedral. When he had finally run out of travelogue and was trying to think what else to say about the moonlight without repeating himself, he chanced to look down at Annie, curled up beside him on the bench. She was grinning at him.

He caught on at once. "Rambling like an idiot, huh?"

"Blitherin'," she agreed, but with a dazzling smile that took the bite out of her comment. "Why don't you just say it?"

"Annie, I . . . ," David began and then paused. "I'd like to ask you to . . . marry me. I never would have believed that I could fall so much in love so fast. You hit me like a ton of bricks."

She smiled again. "That's good, is it? The ton of bricks, I mean?"

"More pain than I've felt in a long time . . . but as I say, I want to ask you, but I can't, not now. To ask you to wait for me, not knowing when or even . . ."

Her smile faded. She knew. "You're leavin' then. You've been posted to France?"

"Annie, do you know how much I . . ." He did not finish.

Annie's father was in Dover. They could be alone on the little ketch tonight. The rising and falling of the tide. The rigging playing a melody against the masts. Her softness beneath him. He had imagined it all. He dared not speak it. Would she say yes?

"I love you, Annie. I won't ask for a commitment from you that I may not be able to keep. If anything should happen . . ."

"Shhh!" she insisted hurriedly, putting her hand across his lips. "Don't even be thinkin' that, Davey Meyer, not for one instant!"

They sat together in silence, both reflecting on what the unspoken words had been. The RAF casualty list for the first three months of the war had recently appeared in the London *Times*: 380 fliers had been killed since September, and everyone agreed that the fighting had not even started to heat up.

"It's just better for you to not get tangled up with me now," David said.

"David Meyer," Annie said with spirit, "don't you be tellin' me about what's better for me, without even askin' my thoughts!"

Duffy got in the middle of the argument, laying his great sorrowful head on Annie's lap.

"This is tough on me, you know. Right now I wish I could change places with Duffy."

"I've been thinkin' the same thing." She laughed and he laughed, dissipating some of his anguish. "I'd be a liar if I didn't tell you I get a hunger when I think of you. I feel it now. I've never . . . been with a man, Davey."

He wanted to kiss her, but she turned her face away.

"It's a good thing we've walked so far from the *Wairakei*," he ventured. "Or I'd . . ."

"I know. Me too." Annie lapsed into silence.

David and Annie stared across the luminous river, watching the way it flowed past Tower Bridge, as if they could see all the way to the Channel, all the way to France.

"Do you see this river, Davey?" she asked. "Men and women have been sayin' good-bye on this spot for maybe a thousand years. It has always been a fearful thing to be waitin' for one you care about to come home. But sayin' that it's hard doesn't mean you can stop carin', even if you wanted to. Are your feelin's like a spigot that you turn off when you've a mind to? Or are they like this river, rollin' so strong that you cannot hold them back? I can wait. And you can leave me knowin' that I'll be true to you, because I'm true to myself. The river will be here when you come back."

David studied her eyes, her nose, her lips, memorizing her features in the moonlight. He took her face in his hands and, pulling her close, kissed her. She slipped her arms beneath his coat and buried her face in the rough fabric of his uniform jacket. David stroked the feathery texture of her hair. He buried his face in the nape of her neck and inhaled her sweet fragrance. He felt his pulse race as she pressed against him. He wanted to commit every sense of her to a forever part of his mind.

"I love you," he whispered to her. "Will you wait for me? Will you marry me when I get back?"

She nodded in reply.

She said she dared not let him walk her back to the mooring. And so they said good-bye beside the river, like ten thousand others had done for a thousand years.

Like clockwork, three francs a week arrived for Jerome and Marie from Papa. Madame Hilaire was always on board the *Garlic* to accept the letter from the postman. She would open it, cackle like a chicken that had just laid an egg, and hold up the three francs in glee.

"A good man, your papa!" she would shout so every head along the Quai d'Conti would pivot to stare. "We will eat well tonight!"

Each payday the old hag would indeed cook a wholesome meal: fresh baguettes, mounds of fried potatoes, a piece of cod. She would raise her wineglass and drink a toast after she screamed this sentiment: "To the health of your dear Uncle Jambonneau, wherever it has gotten off to."

Then she would drink another toast. "To your brave papa, who serves the glorious armees of France! May they raise his pay and increase his ration of grog!"

There were numerous other toasts. Some were drunk to the rat, who Madame Hilaire said was the cousin of the president of the French Republic. As the contents of the jug decreased, she would begin to weep copiously and raise her glass to various old circus performers Jerome did not know. At last Madame Hilaire would drink the last drops of her gallon and lay her head on the table to sleep in peace among the dishes.

But when the morning after came, Jerome and Marie would awaken to the quiet lapping of the Seine against the boat, and Madame Hilaire would be gone. The pattern was always the same. Jerome did not mind that the woman disappeared for six days and reappeared to collect the money and cook one meal a week. On the day that Papa had enlisted, Jerome had decided that he would rather live with a booming cannon than the shrieking voice of their guardian, Madame Hilaire. Good riddance. If she had not departed, Jerome might have done so himself.

This left Jerome to fend for Marie six days of the week, however.

Some days the task was more difficult than others. This morning would not be difficult.

Jerome rose before dawn, stuffed little Papillon into his shirt, and made his way to Rue de Buci. There was a break in the rain and the cold weather, which meant that the merchants would be setting up their stalls on the street. In the predawn light without streetlamps, the place was easy pickings for a skilled thief like Jerome. He raised his hands in joy and blessed the blackout.

The air of Buci Market smelled like fresh-baked bread and flowers. The flowers had been shipped from greenhouses in the warm south of France as if there were no war on at all.

Jerome passed the stall of the citrus seller. He nabbed an orange and slipped it into a canvas bag. What could be more simple? Would the merchant notice one missing orange? It could easily have fallen off the table and into the gutter, where Jerome might have found it!

The loudmouthed wife of the baker was barking orders at her unfortunate little husband. He should move faster! The sun would soon be up, and the housewives would come! He should cover the barrel of baguettes in case it rained!

When the baker argued that the sky was clear and that there was not a cloud, she roared and pointed upward. "How can you know what the day will bring? It has rained all week! Cover the baguettes!"

The baker bent beneath the table to fish among the boxes for something to cover the long loaves of bread that were packed upright like pencils in a pencil cup. At the same instant the broad backside of the baker's wife turned toward Jerome. Here was his opportunity! He reached out and grasped a loaf, pulling it out and breaking it in two. He dunked the two halves into his bag and hurried on.

Breakfast was taken care of. Now, what to do about dinner?

He gazed longingly at the hooks in the butcher shop. Salamis by the dozen hung on the right of the open window. The hooks on the left held skinned rabbits and thin chickens. There was seldom any beef since the armees of France got all the best meat these days. Jerome's eyes narrowed with intensity as he considered some way to snag a salami. A salami would be the prize of all prizes. He would not have to cook it, and it would last for days. But they hung too far out of his reach. A pity.

A large American woman, the keeper of an orphanage, tugged her little wagon to the window of the butcher. She was out early. Jerome often saw her in Buci Market, pulling her wagonload of groceries from stall to stall and arguing over prices like a common Parisian. Perhaps if she would distract the butcher long enough . . .

"*Bonjour*, Monsieur Turenne," she called in a loud voice that hardly displayed any of the flat American accent.

The large butcher greeted her cheerfully. She was a regular customer and a good one, Jerome knew. "Ah, Madame Rose!" the butcher cried. "How lovely you look today, Madame!"

"It is too dark for you to know how I look, Monsieur Turenne." She laughed. "That is why I come early. I like your compliments."

"You are the light of Buci Market."

"If you look upon the soul, then I hope that is true, Monsieur."

"Ah, Madame." The butcher, whom everyone knew was a lonely widower, lowered his voice. "To think that such a plum as you remains unpicked."

"Plum?" She laughed again. "Coconut is more like it. Hard and tough."

"But sweet inside."

He was definitely distracted, although Jerome thought he would have to be as blind as Uncle Jambonneau to mean what he was saying. Madame Rose could have passed for a fair-sized side of beef in the dark. But maybe such a figure was what butchers were attracted to.

"Enough, Monsieur!"

Jerome inched forward toward the salami.

"How can I help you this morning, Madame Rose?"

Jerome was at her elbow, moving his hand up toward the hook.

"I need chickens for my children today."

"Chickens, Madame! Fowl is very expensive these days. Rabbit would be better for the cost."

"No, chickens. We have thirteen children down with bronchitis. Sister Betsy is not well either. Chicken broth, that is the thing. Four chickens, if you please. That should do very well for thirty-two little ones and two old ladies."

"Old! Madame! You are in your prime!"

Jerome wondered who the butcher could be talking to. Madame Rose was gray-haired beneath her scarf.

"Always you flatter me, and after we argue about the price of the chicken, you hate me. But I always come back."

Jerome touched the rounded end of the lowest salami. His fingers just grasped it at the bottom, but he could not get a firm enough grip to pull! He jumped, grabbed, and jerked the salami off the hook.

The butcher shouted. Madame Rose whirled around much faster than Jerome would have imagined such a large woman could move. She grasped his hair, jerking him back mid-stride and holding him firmly.

Thinking to terrify her, Jerome reached into his shirt and held up

Papillon. The rat blinked at her with pink eyes and twitched his whiskers curiously.

Madame Rose was unimpressed. "You have a rat. Put him away or Monsieur the butcher is likely to carve him up and grind him in his sausage."

Jerome obeyed her warning instantly. She still did not let go of his hair.

The great lumbering hulk of the butcher hurried out the door of his shop. "Well, well, well! So, so, so! Madame Rose!" he cried. "You have caught the little beggar Jardin!" He yanked the salami free from Jerome's hand and held it aloft triumphantly. "I owe you a debt of gratitude."

"Gratitude is nice, but I would rather have ten centimes off the price of each chicken."

The butcher grimaced. "Thievery, Madame. But . . . done. Now I shall call the gendarmes to haul this rat away."

The big woman leaned down and studied Jerome with one eye. She poked at his ribs. She pinched his cheeks. "He hardly weighs more than that salami, Monsieur. If he was a fish, I would throw him back in the Seine. Not enough to fry."

"He is a thief."

"I have seen him here in Buci. Perhaps he meant to ask you if he might borrow the salami for a time?"

Jerome's hair hurt. He peered up at the large woman defiantly. "Borrow?" The boy snorted. "I meant to eat it all. Monsieur the butcher has enough to go around. He is fat as a pig! And . . . he has two large dogs at home to whom he feeds scraps. My sister and I would eat such scraps very happily. Are we not better than dogs?"

The butcher began making incoherent angry noises after the reference to the pig. He held the salami like a sword, as if to stab Jerome with it.

Madame Rose swung herself between butcher and boy in a series of moves that kept the butcher jabbing the salami around her.

Jerome yelped as he swung from side to side by his hair. Would not a thump on the head with a salami be less painful than Madame Rose's fingers in his hair?

"Monsieur Turenne, you must stop this at once!" she cried. "I . . . I wish to purchase that salami as well!"

"You may do so, Madame!" he huffed. "After I beat this boy with it!"

"No!" she shouted, putting her free hand up and shoving Monsieur the butcher back. "I protest. Children do not beg unless they are hungry."

Jerome shot back defiantly. "I do not beg from the capitalist pig, Madame!"

"He steals!" the butcher bellowed.

"Not if I buy the salami for him."

The butcher stepped back and lowered his weapon. "If you do not allow me to call the gendarmes, Madame, then I shall have to charge you full price for your chickens and for the salami!"

Jerome peered out from behind the skirt of the American woman. The butcher had her there.

"As you wish, Monsieur Turenne, but it is not gallant of you."

He shrugged and went back inside to wrap the chickens.

Madame Rose released her grip, letting Jerome free. She bent low and put her nose to his. Her face was very fierce, and her mouth was straight and wide like a bullfrog's. "Do not move," she warned, then turned her attention to paying the bill.

Jerome did not stir. He stood at her back and petted Papillon through the gap in his shirt caused by missing buttons. The sun was coming up. The bunches of flowers in the barrels of the florist's stall were bright and pretty. It would be too light to steal now, but at least he was not going to prison.

Now Madame Rose turned on him. "What is your name?" She took him by the arm and hauled him after her with the same determination as she hauled the wagon.

"Jerome Jardin."

"Now what am I supposed to do? I have paid full price for the chickens, and I have a salami I do not want."

"I am sorry, Madame." Jerome felt bad. The large American was a kind woman, after all. Everyone said so, except for Papa who said that Madame Rose and her sister, Betsy, were only kind because they got something for it in return. Jerome could not think what Madame had gotten out of this act of kindness. The deal seemed quite a bad one to him.

"You do not have to steal, you know." She pulled the wagon out of the way of a gaggle of housewives and bent until her eyes were level with Jerome's. "You could have asked if you were hungry."

"I am not a beggar."

"I do not know what I will do with this salami." She extended it to him.

The salami was wrapped in white wax paper, but he could smell it through the wrapping. His stomach growled. He looked away. "I am sorry," he said again.

"Would you like it, Jerome?"

"You are a religious person," he said in a lofty way as Papa had taught him. "Dangerous."

She laughed. Then she laughed louder, as though what he said was the funniest thing she had heard in a long time. "Well, I suppose that is a matter of opinion."

"You are a spider of the church. Papa says never take charity from church. Charity is the web that catches the . . ."

This time her mouth twitched like she might laugh, but she did not. "So, you are a man of honor, I see," she said seriously. But her eyes were laughing. "I would not entice you with a gift." She placed the salami back on top of a heap of cabbages in the wagon. "But I suppose that if I turned my back and looked away, there might come someone who took the salami right off my cart." As she spoke, she turned slowly away from him and stared off at the vegetable stalls across the street. "If someone stole my salami, I would never know it."

Jerome gaped up at her. She was a giant silhouette against the sun. She was not looking. There was the salami. He picked it up. Then he picked up a cabbage and shoved it into his bag.

"Leave the chickens, Jerome," she warned. "If you and your sister are hungry, you may come eat with us. Our church does not look like a church, boy. It is inside our hearts. Get going."

Madame Rose was a confusing person. Their church was a church but did not look like a church? Well, he could not think of that now. Sun would stream through the portholes of the *Garlic*. Marie would be waking up. She always called Jerome her hero when there was breakfast waiting when she woke up. Dodging through the trudging shoppers, Jerome happily took off toward the river. This salami would be enough to eat every night until Madame Hilaire showed up again at the end of the week!

12

The Great Problem

The garret room at the top of seven long flights of stairs was ideal for Josephine Marlow. She alone occupied the floor that had been an attic storage space. Tucked beneath the eaves of the Foyer International, two tall dormer windows overlooked slate and green copper roofs and the leafless trees of Luxembourg Gardens. To the left, the golden dome of des Invalides marked the burial place of Napoleon. Above the tangle of chimney pots, the large square towers of Notre Dame marked the center of l'Cité. To the right, the distant hill above Montmartre was crowned with Sacre Coeur.

In their time together in Paris, Josie and Daniel had climbed the north tower of Notre Dame a dozen times to view the city. They had picnicked on fresh warm bread with creamy Brie and washed it down with red wine as they waited for the bells to toll. No doubt they had glanced toward the windows of this very room and yet had never imagined that Josie would be standing here alone one day, waiting for the same bells to ring.

It was best, she thought, to hear them at a distance now. To turn her face to the north tower and imagine Danny there still, looking her way.

The room was small. A single iron-frame bed rested against the wall beneath the sloping ceiling. Madame Watson provided a desk and chair where Josie could write. A tall chest of drawers was maneuvered up the stairs with great difficulty by two sweating deliverymen who were past their prime. The wood-planked floor was covered by a blue floral rug Josie had purchased at the flea market a week after her arrival.

Alma was quartered two floors below and down the hall from two of their friends, Irene and Helene. No doubt Josie's isolation had been planned by Madame Watson to protect the other residents from the clacking of an Olivetti typewriter at all hours.

Whatever the reason, it was worth seven flights to be spared the constant borrowing and unending chatter of the lower floors that reminded Josie of a college dorm. If someone needed a word with her or a telephone call came in, the message was relayed by banging on the radiator pipes that twisted up to heat her living space. No one, after panting up four or five stories, wanted to climb the rest of the way just to visit Josephine Marlow. Josie was grateful for the privacy and the view.

As a foreigner, she was required to register and be fingerprinted at the police station just around the corner in the Latin Quarter. But she did not feel like a foreigner. Her favorite café, Deux Magots, was a short walk. In spite of the cold, the bouquinists, the booksellers, still displayed their wares in sidewalk bins. There were fewer students poking through the crates these days, but still the old Left Bank neighborhood had the look and feel of Paris before the war. It was good to be home.

Even so, as Josie listened to the conversation of taxi drivers and waiters and shopgirls, she felt uneasy. She lunched with French government officials and visited neutrals and fellow journalists at the Crillon and the Ritz but left each meeting with a heavy lump of foreboding in her throat. It was not the bitter cold of winter that made her tremble in her attic room; it was something else. France did not want to hear that what had happened in Warsaw was possible in France.

She had promised the little priest of the Cathedral of St. John that she would tell the world what had transpired there, but no one wanted to be reminded of war. They wanted only to talk of politics.

As she walked toward Deux Magots to join her friends for lunch, Josie knew she would have to talk of politics again. And she was right.

Delfina and Helene, Alma, Irene and Josie now sat beneath the grinning wooden effigies of two Chinese Mandarin lords and sipped their coffee. They argued with an old waiter who had been pulled from retirement after the young waiters had all been sent to the front.

The old man winked at the young women and proceeded to enlighten them about "The Great Problem Facing France."

"Russia has a Man. Italy has a Man. Germany has a Man. If only France had a Man, we could beat them all." He shrugged. "But we have Prime Minister Daladier, who gave Czechoslovakia to Germany's Man. England has Chamberlain, who did the same."

Delfina, Russian by birth and anti-Bolshevik by religion, flared. "If France and England were run by dictators, then what would make them different from Russia, Germany, or Italy, Monsieur?"

"If we had a dictator," said the waiter somewhat sadly, "at least he would be our Man . . . a French Man."

The waiter may have been a secret Fascist, a Socialist, a Communist, or simply a confused Democrat, but he expressed the longing of nearly every Parisian for a strong national government that would inspire national pride. Beyond that, government should leave the common man to live.

This desire—to be left alone to live according to one's convictions—was common to all French political positions. A strong leader was the one concept that united all parties. It was just that no one in France could agree upon whose point of view the Strong Man of France should represent. Each political faction believed that all the other camps should be brought into line with their own. All that resulted was confusion.

Helene, who worked as a seamstress at Redfern, simply shrugged. "*Mais que voulez-vous?* We French like our own politics, but we deplore those of everyone around who does not agree. It is not always convenient, but we manage. . . ."

"*Oui*," concluded Irene. "When the occasion demands it, we will put aside our differences, to be resumed at a more convenient moment. In the meantime, we all unite to defend our beloved France."

Josie remained silent through all of this. Her companions did not know, could not conceive, what it was they were defending their beloved France against.

If all that was required for an acceptable existence was to remain alive and relatively untroubled, then what difference would it make to the French if their government was Fascist, Communist, Socialist, or confused Democrat? One was just as good as another, was it not? Laissez-faire; as long as an individual was left alone to live day by day, one set of principles was as good as another. Provided that the Man at the helm of French government was French, perhaps even Fascism could be tolerated.

Josephine had been too quiet. All heads pivoted toward her.

"Well, Josephine?" Helene probed.

Alma added with a laugh, "In England she could not stop talking politics. What's this? Run out of opinions?"

Josie sat back and drew a deep breath. "You sure you want my views?"

"This is France," Delfina remarked sharply. "Everyone has an opinion."

"And every one is different," Josie interrupted. "All right, then. Unlike France, there is only one opinion in all of Nazi Germany, and here it is: Warfare is as sacred to men as motherhood is to women."

There was silence around the table for a second and then a nervous giggle.

"Is that all, Josephine?" Helene laughed.

Josie shrugged. "They all agree on that. Or if they don't agree, they can't argue with it. Germans no longer talk politics on the Ku'damm in Berlin. They talk about war."

"Well, is that not what we have been doing?" Irene twittered.

"No!" Delfina shot back hotly. "Politics and war are not the same. It is war that ultimately decides politics, religion, and what your life will be like day to day! Not the other way around. Right and wrong survive every battle. But only the victor has the privilege to choose between the two. The Nazis have known that from the beginning. Hitler . . . Stalin . . . they are all the same. They enslave their own people by giving them something that politics and religion can no longer provide. They give them meaning to their existence that is beyond narrow self-interest. Give them a sacred war to fight! A reason to sacrifice! Some unity in a bloody cause! The real degradation begins when people realize they are in league with the devil. But they feel the devil is preferable to the emptiness of life that lacks larger significance. The Cause becomes their god. Right or wrong? What is that? The Cause is everything."

Josie considered her friend with sympathy. Delfina's family had fled from Russia to France during the Bolshevik revolution. Her *cartes d'identite* was still the Nansen Passport—the passport issued to displaced persons after the last war. She had suffered enough to know what she was talking about.

The others sat speechless at Delfina's outburst. There was an uncomfortable pall over them as she continued. "France is waiting for its French Hitler. The churches are empty. Lives are empty. What is your purpose for existence? Only to exist. To keep breathing and eating and . . . it all frightens me very much."

"War as sacred as motherhood?" Alma laughed. "Ask any French poilu at the Maginot how he feels about that! He will tell you he much prefers making some woman into a sacred mother to making war. There's the difference between Germany and France!"

Helene shook her head in horror. "Dreary little Nazis! To imagine men who value fighting over making love!" She put a finger to her temple, indicating the madness of it. "*Vive la France!* It is them or us this time, girls."

❦

Three days' leave in Paris! The only way the prospect could have been more exciting was if it had been London, or if Annie had somehow managed to be in Paris, too. Hewitt had teased David when he said this. "The last place you want your regular girl to be is in Paris, Tinman!"

The train pulled out of Rouvres at noon; the trip would take only a few hours. David had never been to Paris before. He made a mental vow to store up sights and sounds to share with Annie. She had never been to the City of Lights either. He would take her there someday and be her tour guide to the most romantic place in the world.

The countryside of eastern France rolled by. Hewitt and Simpson were asleep as the train pulled away from the platform at Chalons-sur-Marne. David leaned on the window ledge along the corridor outside the compartment, looking at the Marne River. He compared the twin towers of the church of Notre Dame de Vaux to its description in a guidebook. "Romanesque nave," he read. "Gothic choir and vaults."

"What's this?" a gravelly voice belched. "Trying to improve your mind, assassin?"

A reedy, high-pitched tone agreed. "Sure he is, Badger. That's it exactly."

It was Badger Cross and his toady friend, Dinky Mertz. From the slur in both their voices it was clear they had been drinking. David wanted to ignore them, hoping they would go away. The last thing he needed was to get into an altercation with Cross and maybe get put off the train.

Badger snatched the volume out of David's hands. "Too high-and-mighty for the likes of us, eh, Tincup? Can't be bothered to speak to an old acquaintance?"

"Give it here, Cross," David said as Badger passed the guidebook to Dinky. "I don't want any trouble with you."

"He doesn't want any trouble with me. Isn't that sad, Dinky? Is that any way to speak to a comrade in arms?"

"No, not at all polite." Mertz hiccupped.

David tried to reach past Badger and grab the book, but Cross swatted his arm aside and wheezed his beery breath in David's face. "Didn't know I lost me cushy instructor job on accounta you, did you, Teacup? Someone ratted on me for the little tussle we had in the pub . . . was that you, Tincan, Buttercup—whatever your name is—was that you?"

"It wasn't me. Now get lost, Badger. I don't want to fight you again."

"Well, shall we let bygones be bygones then?"

David regarded Badger's meaty, outstretched hand with suspicion. "Sure," he said at last. "Just as soon as you give me my book back."

"How thoughtless of me. Dinky, the book." Badger reached his right hand back over his shoulder as if to take the guide from Mertz. But when his fist reached shoulder height, he threw it straight forward, toward David's nose.

David had expected something of the kind, and that instinctive warning, combined with Badger's drunken reflexes, was enough to get

David's nose out of the way. The punch did land on his ear, though, flinging him sideways into the window and knocking out the glass.

He lashed out with his leg as he fell and hooked Badger behind the knee. The big man also tumbled against the window, catching Dinky with a flailing forearm and whacking him to the floor as well.

Quickly on his feet, David said, "Okay, so we still have something to settle. But not here, you idiot! Do you want to get thrown off the train?"

"Ha! Did you hear that, Dinky? The Yank has got no stomach, besides no heart. He's yellow."

"Sure he is, Badger." Mertz wiped his bloody lip with his sleeve. "But c'mon, he's right. We don't want to get put off."

"You little traitor. Just have to get the job done quickly then."

Badger put his head down and charged, more bull-like in his actions than his namesake. David caught him around the neck with one arm and brought an uppercut into the center of Badger's mouth. The force of the rush carried the pair down the corridor till they impacted the wall at the end, breaking out another glass panel.

Having Badger's twenty-stone weight behind the shoulder in the center of David's chest took the American's breath away. Badger threw his head back and brought his hands together up under David's chin. "I'll throttle you good, Tinfoil," he said, squeezing David's throat. Cross braced himself against the motion of the train with a wide stance.

A mademoiselle came into the corridor from the far end. When she saw the struggle, she screamed and ran back out the door. "Hurry, Badger," urged Mertz, "'fore the gendarmes get here!"

Though David's head was swimming, his early dirty fighting skills had not deserted him. He brought his right knee up into Badger's crotch.

Badger grunted once and dropped his hands. David wound up his right and fired, smacking Badger in the eye and flinging him backward into the just-arrived train conductor.

That worthy was knocked down, breaking his glasses and a gold watch. But the French damsel's screams had brought assistance: Two stewards from the dining car and an off-duty policeman had come along as well.

Dinky Mertz disappeared.

When David and Badger were hauled before the magistrate in the town of Epernay, the judge was an understanding man. He was willing to let the two brawlers go, he said, provided they pay for the damage to the train, the glasses, the watch, and Monsieur the conductor's nose. Five hundred francs should cover it.

It was more than both had, put together.

"*Trois jours*," he said. "Three days in jail."

☙

Luxembourg City was an anachronism—a hodgepodge of architecture and ages that somehow managed to live together in harmony. It was the city where Elaine Snow had lived. It was the place where Andre and Elaine's child now resided with her grandfather, steel magnate Abraham Snow, in a tall, Gothic house overlooking the Petrusse River.

Andre's official trip to Belgium was reason enough to make a detour back into Luxembourg City on his return to Paris from Arlon. This time he spent the night at the Brasseur Hotel in the same room where he had often met with Elaine.

The staff recognized him at once. Henri, the proprietor, and his wife, Agnes, greeted him solemnly. Did they sense that he had returned to their establishment on a sort of pilgrimage dedicated to Nazi-executed Elaine? They did not mention her name. Henri simply handed Andre the key to their room.

Agnes, who sat knitting in the shadows beside the lift, turned her eyes upward in pity for an instant as he passed. The needles clicked like those of Madame Defarge watching the condemned climb the scaffold of the guillotine. Her eyes seemed to ask, *"Are you putting yourself through this ordeal willingly? Poor fool."*

He took his meal, *roti de veau* and *asperges*, alone in his room. He was hardly able to swallow. What little he ate was washed down with an entire bottle of Chateauneuf-du-Pap. It was a mediocre vintage, but he drank it all. The wine did not help him sleep as he had hoped. He lay on the bed and closed his eyes and saw Elaine.

Blue satin negligee. The thin strap slipped down, revealing her shoulder. Her lips parted in a smile of expectation. He reached out for her, but she was gone. . . .

He hardly slept, and when he did, his dreams were full of her. When she was alive, he had still held some hope that one day they would be together again. Now there was nothing but the ache of longing.

At last his thoughts turned to the child, to Juliette. She was no more than a ten-minute walk from the hotel. Ten minutes away, yet Andre had never laid eyes on her. And so, in the morning, he got up determined to see the child that he and Elaine had created.

It was raining. At eight o'clock Andre ate a croissant and gulped a cup of coffee in the small dining room of the hotel. He left his car in the garage and borrowed an umbrella from Henri for the short walk to Boulevard de la Petrusse.

Andre crossed the street and walked along the quai. With the river at his back, he stared up at the tarnished stone of the great house. Six smoking chimney pots topped the steep slate roof. The window shades were drawn as if the structure had closed its eyes in grief. The black crepe of mourning was hung above the massive door. Would Juliette come out and walk to school? Or should Andre go boldly up the steps, knock on the door, and ask to see the child? Should he risk being refused by Abraham Snow, who had good reason to hate him? That could mean a scene in front of Juliette. Hadn't she been through enough?

Andre could not make himself move toward the house.

Rain drummed hard on the umbrella, like impatient fingers drumming on a tabletop. It splashed up from the stones until the cuffs of his trousers were damp. How long had he been waiting? A lone man beneath a black umbrella on the riverbank. He must be a curious sight. He thought he saw the edge of a curtain of an upper-story window stir and then fall back. Was someone watching him even as he watched the house? Perhaps it was little Juliette behind the glass.

He wished someone would raise the shades, that he could have even one glimpse of Elaine's child—his child. But no one appeared at the windows. No one left the house.

It was almost eleven when Andre returned to the Brasseur Hotel. The proprietor and his wife each glanced up furtively as Andre placed the umbrella on the marble top of the reception desk.

"Was your meeting a pleasant one, Monsieur Chardon?" Henri asked.

"It is very wet." Andre did not tell him that he had been standing several hours in the rain.

"Your trousers are damp, Monsieur Chardon," offered Agnes, setting down her knitting. "Perhaps you would like to have them dried and pressed?"

He shook his head and did not look her in the eye. "I have a long way to go today. It will have to wait."

He left Luxembourg City feeling foolish. What had he accomplished except that he was more miserable than he had ever been? He felt the loneliness of his life more acutely than he had ever felt any emotion, and in the end what difference did it make?

13

Defense Strategies

Andre's mission to Belgium had left him with a sense of foreboding about the defensive strategies of his own generals. Staying with Lewinski had left Gustave Bertrand grim and confused. Andre sat silently beside Bertrand all the way to the prime minister's office at the Palais Bourbon in Paris.

They entered the building and went directly to Premier Daladier's suite. The group that was already present and awaiting their arrival included Daladier, Supreme Military Commander Gamelin, and Gamelin's aide, Colonel Pucelle.

The diminuitive figure of Daladier straightened his already squarely set shoulders and invited Andre to begin. "Everyone here is already aware of your mission, Colonel, and everyone knows its importance. Please proceed."

Andre opened his briefcase and extracted a crumpled sheaf of papers. These he fanned out across the table, carefully laying aside two pages that were partially charred. "You understand, gentlemen, that these are not all the contents of the German major's portfolio," he explained. "My Belgian counterpart has the rest, but we were provided with these originals so as to better judge their significance and authenticity."

"Can you give us a summary of what they are?" suggested Daladier.

"These papers purport to be the air-fleet operation orders for the Luftwaffe division based at Cologne."

This much of the papers' secret was already known to the men at the table, but not what came next.

"And what are the orders?"

Andre drew a deep breath. "They direct the targeting of air attacks in connection with a German invasion of Holland and Belgium."

"Exactly!" said General Gamelin. "This is confirmation of what we have always said. The Germans would be fools to try a frontal assault on the Maginot Line. Therefore the attack, when it comes, must be through the Low Countries."

Andre frowned but said nothing.

Daladier prompted, "You said 'purport to be.' Is there some doubt about their authenticity?"

Colonel Pucelle, in a tone that spoke of how anxious he was to curry favor with his commander, answered before Andre could speak. "Pardon me, Prime Minister, but what doubt can there be? The German officer carrying these orders attempted to destroy them, as we can see from the burned pages. In fact, we understand that he tried twice."

"Is this correct, Colonel Chardon?"

Andre acknowledged the accuracy of Pucelle's statement. "The gendarme who apprehended the two Germans did not see the first attempt to ignite the papers. Later, when they were awaiting the arrival of the chief inspector, Major Reinberger made a second effort at their destruction—this time in the parlor stove in the farmhouse."

"But quick action on the part of the gendarme stopped him from succeeding," announced Pucelle with a triumphant tone. "Surely this proves that the papers are genuine. If the German scheme was to send us false information, why try so hard to eliminate what they wanted us to have?"

There was a murmur of agreement from General Gamelin and Minister Daladier at this reasoning, but Andre still sat silently frowning.

"Colonel Chardon, you are still unconvinced," said Daladier reasonably. "Tell us what you see that we have missed."

Andre cleared his throat before replying. "It is directly contrary to the policy of the German High Command to ever transport top-secret documents by air, in exact anticipation of what has occurred here. Secondly, the German majors stated that they crash-landed because they became lost and ran out of fuel, yet when the ME-108 was examined, it still had enough fuel to have continued flying."

"A malfunctioning gauge, or ice in the fuel line," interrupted Pucelle.

"Please continue, Colonel Chardon," Daladier urged.

Andre nodded and spoke again. "Thirdly, the two attempts to burn the documents are suspicious, to me anyway." He looked directly at Pucelle as he continued. "These are Luftwaffe officers . . . not fools . . . carrying highly sensitive papers directly against orders. How many tries does it take to burn something so incriminating?"

"Bah," snorted Pucelle. "Colonel Chardon is striving to unravel a mystery where one does not exist. General Gamelin stated as long ago as 1937 that any future Nazi threat to our border would have to come through Holland and Belgium and would precisely follow the German Schleiffen Plan. The same strategy they followed in the Great War . . . unsuccessfully, I might add."

There was a general air of agreement around the table, which only Andre and Bertrand did not share. To be fair, Daladier gave Andre one more chance to speak. "If this is an elaborate trick, Colonel, what could possibly be the intent?"

Andre cleared his throat nervously. "I do not believe this is a trick. However, I do believe that the German officers Hulse and Reinberger allowed these documents to come into the hands of the neutrals intentionally."

There was an undertone of surprise around the table. Daladier leaned close to drum his fingers on the documents. "Then you feel these Germans wished that we possess the complete details of Luftwaffe plans? They are traitors, in other words."

"They were reticent to speak with me, Prime Minister, because I am a Frenchman and the enemy of their Reich. But through a two-way mirror I observed a conversation between the German Kurt Hulse and a Belgian plainclothes officer who has befriended him."

"This Hulse will speak to the neutrals then."

"I believe his plan was to warn them. But there is more." Andre drew his breath in slowly. What he was about to say flew in the face of all current military thinking. "At my urging, the Belgian asked this Hulse if he knew of any plans concerning the Ardennes. . . ."

Pucelle snorted. "There could be none. Impassable to artillery . . ."

Andre continued in spite of the prevailing attitude of scorn. "Hulse said that it was just as easy for a Stuka dive-bomber to fly over the Ardennes as it was for it to fly over flat terrain."

"A dive-bomber could not carry enough explosives to make a dent in—," Pucelle began.

Bertrand leaped into the argument. "You are forgetting Warsaw, Colonel! You are forgetting Barcelona!"

"Cities!" Pucelle retorted. "Vulnerable to air bombardment. But the entire French front could not be dented!"

"I tell you," Andre said quietly, "Hulse and Reinberger were warning the neutrals. But we Frenchmen should also be warned about the Ardennes."

Gamelin shook his head and stuck his lower lip out in disdain at the very idea. "A guess is not good enough, Colonel Chardon. I will not move whole divisions to sit idle before an impenetrable line because of an unsubstantiated guess." He slapped his hand down on the German documents. "This is what we go on. If these documents are authentic, and you believe they are . . ."

"But incomplete," Andre insisted.

"What other information do we have? Show me proof, and I may look at the Ardennes. But for now you waste our time with speculation!" The general stood, and the meeting was at an end. Andre was dismissed like an errant schoolboy. He would not mention the Ardennes again until he had proof that his theory was correct.

On the way out to the waiting Citroën, Bertrand drew Andre aside. "I know you are disappointed that you could not convince them. But remember that they know nothing as yet about the project going on in your basement. Perhaps our friend Lewinski has come up with something definite."

Andre gave Bertrand a bleak look. "The truth, Gustave? I do not even know what he is up to."

Early December in the South Atlantic was hotter than any summer Trevor had ever experienced back home. Once a day the prisoners were allowed a ten-minute turn on *Altmark*'s deck. It was an amazing relief, if only to have the temperature drop to a hundred degrees from the sweltering hundred and thirty of the hold.

Trevor realized that nothing in the Nazis' hearts had softened to allow this brief exercise. As Captain Thun had so grandly informed the prisoners, they were to be taken back to Germany and displayed. Britain's vaunted sea power was being humbled, and the parade of British sailors was the proof. As such, hostages to German propaganda had to be transported alive, if only barely.

The incident of the death of Frankie Thomas had resulted in a curious postscript. As additional proof that the Germans were still far more concerned with discipline than with the welfare of the prisoners, an official proclamation had been posted inside the hold:

> *Notice to Prisoners:*
> *On account of today's behavior of the prisoners, they will get bread and water only tomorrow. Further, I have given orders that the doctor will not make his regular rounds after this. Cases of severe sickness must be reported at the time of handing down the food.*

But if the iron enforcement of German authority had not changed, something in Trevor's relationship with the rest of the prisoners had. After Frankie's body had been unceremoniously dumped over the side, every Brit had taken the time to squeeze Trevor's hand in approval of his attempt to intercede. When Dykes had complained about the loss of their rations, Nob had taken him aside. In a low, unmistakably menacing tone, Dykes had been informed that if he didn't shut up, his would be the next body going over the rail.

As the calendar slowly crept toward Christmas, the day finally came when *Altmark* was once again rafted up next to the *Graf Spee* to receive more prisoners. When the newly transferred captives were added to the crowd in the hold, each was quizzed for news of the outside world and the prospects of rescue. Trevor latched on to a tall machinist's mate named Dooley who had been on the freighter *Huntsman*.

"They've got the wind up about somethin'," Dooley reported. "Heard two Heinie swabbies gabbin' about a big battle comin'. There may be nothin' to it, but they made a course change, sudden-like."

Before Dooley had even finished speaking, orders were shouted and the lines securing the battleship to her smaller accomplice were cast off. Sirens blared on the battleship, and the steam whistle of the prison ship shrilled a farewell. In the confusion of the abrupt departure, no one had been commanded to shut the lid over the hold. To come out of the cell unordered would mean being shot, but Trevor risked standing on the ladder and poking his head up just far enough to get a narrow view of the sea across the deck.

At first he could not make out anything but the giant steel wall that was the hull of the *Graf Spee*. But gradually the raider drew apart from the *Altmark*, and then Trevor could make out what had caused the sudden departure: Two columns of smoke on the horizon were moving at high speed toward the German ships. As Trevor watched, a third smudge of dark fumes appeared a short distance behind the first pair.

The guns of the *Spee* roared. She carried three sets of enormous eleven-inch cannons, capable of throwing huge projectiles across miles of ocean. The crash of the guns reverberated within the confines of the hold, as if *Altmark* herself were under attack.

"What is it? What's happening?" came the urgent shouts from below.

Trevor had forgotten that he was supposed to be a reporter and not just an observer. "Can't make out the hulls yet," Trevor yelled back. "From the way they are coming straight ahead, they must be at least battle cruisers. Maybe the *Exeter*."

"Get on with it, man," Dooley urged. "Tell it all!"

"*Spee* has the range," Trevor said. "The cruisers are firing, but the shells are falling way too short. Every time one of those eleven-inchers hits, it throws water two hundred feet in the air. Now I can see . . ." Trevor stopped awkwardly.

"What, man, what?" Dooley pleaded. "I mean, sir. Don't stop!"

"One of the cruisers has taken a hit," Trevor reported. "There was a bright flash, and it's falling back now."

A groan went up from all the prisoners. "What about the other two?" Nob asked.

"They are zigging—making a smoke screen," Trevor recounted.

"To cover their retreat, the no-good cowards," Dykes muttered.

Altmark bore away northeast, leaving the battle scene behind as the *Spee* headed southwest. It was clear that there would be no rescue today. All the attention of the British warships was focused on the German raider.

The accidentally uncovered hatch was discovered, and Trevor was curtly ordered to drop down or face more punishment. Just before he complied, he hauled himself up on his hands and peered across the intervening water at the battle. He got a clout on his ear for his audacity and was knocked backward into the hold.

"What'd you do that for?" Dykes muttered. "Tryin' to get us on bread and water again?"

Trevor came up holding the side of his head, but he was smiling. "Think what you want, Dykes. But it was worth it. The cruisers aren't running away. They are dashing in and out of that smoke like dogs after a lion. One of them closed to point-blank range before plunging back into cover."

"And? Go on, man, finish!" Dooley urged.

"I saw the *Graf Spee* take a hit on her bridge."

A cheer resounded in the cramped space of the hull that could not have been any greater if liberation had come. This behavior did, in fact, earn the prisoners another day on reduced rations, but not one, not even Dykes, complained.

ℴ

Mac and Murphy boarded the 7 AM train to Nancy from Paris.

The compartment was occupied by a man who snoozed soundly. A copy of the *New York Times* covered his face. He snored softly beneath bold headlines, declaring the defeat of the German pocket battleship *Graf Spee* by the British navy at Montevideo Harbor in South America on December thirteenth.

Mac and Murphy leaned forward in unison to read the fluttering newspaper. It had been weeks since they had seen an American publication. The capture of *Graf Spee* had all of England waving the Union Jack as if the war had been won.

Photographs showed the proud German ship before its defeat and

then the smashed hull as it sank slowly into the waters at the mouth of
the River Plate. Proclaimed as a glorious victory for the British fleet, the
sinking of the warship was an Allied public-relations victory as well. The
naval battle, fought an ocean away from France, had been the most exciting news event in the conflict for several months.

The *New York Times* rose and fell with the even dance of the man's
breathing.

A reprinted German communiqué beneath the photograph of the
captain of the battleship announced:

> *The commander of the* Graf Spee, *Captain Hans Langsdorf, did not
> want to survive the sinking of his ship. True to the old traditions and
> in the spirit of the Officers' Corps, of which he was a member for
> thirty years, he made this decision. Having brought his crew to safety
> he considered his duty fulfilled, and he followed his ship. The navy
> understands and praises this step. Captain Langsdorf has in this way
> fulfilled like a fighter and a hero the expectations of his Führer, the
> German people, and the navy.*

Mac read the bit and let out a low whistle. "Really something. The
guy went down with his ship."

From beneath the newsprint a familiar French voice bellowed,
"Nonsense, Monsieur! Langsdorf was ordered by Hitler to shoot himself. Which he did in a hotel room in Buenos Aires." The figure sat up
and extended the paper to Mac. It was Leon Noel, the former French
ambassador to Poland. He had just returned to France after a trip to
Washington, during which he had personally informed Roosevelt of
the events in Poland. He had taken along a reel of Mac's film as proof.

"*Bonjour*, McGrath. We meet again. This time no one is shooting at
us, eh?" Noel ran his hand through his thinning hair. "Your newsreel
has been a great success back in the States. It had the president and
Madame Eleanor on the edge of their seats. I suppose you have not had
such exciting film since we escaped the Messerschmitts in Poland?"

For the next several hours Noel proved to be a prime source of real
news. Having just arrived from the States, he was a fountain of information to the two journalists who had been living with the filtered, one-
sided versions allowed by the censors. They sat like starved puppies
waiting for the next morsel.

"And furthermore, the Royal Navy may have caught the *Graf Spee*,
but not before she off-loaded several hundred British prisoners of war
onto a German freighter called the *Altmark*. The British Admiralty is not
printing everything." Noel yawned. "Oh, by the way, did you hear that

the Russians attacked Finland with Hitler's blessings? It is my opinion that Hitler wishes to let his friend Stalin wear out his army in the blizzards of Scandinavia this winter. Then Hitler will fight Stalin."

Poor Finland seemed very far away. Would England and Britain send troops to assist? Or would they simply be content to bluster and bellow and let the Finns fight their own war? Noel, who did not like the English or his own government, believed that the fate of Finland would be the same as Poland. Enough said.

After that the conversation turned to news from home. Clark Gable had done a smashing job as Rhett Butler in *Gone With the Wind*. The German, French, and British ambassadors had all shown up at the theatre for the Washington premiere. It made for added excitement during the burning of Atlanta. Noel rather enjoyed it.

The New York World's Fair was still packing in the crowds in spite of the cold weather. The German, British, and French exhibitions attracted all sorts of sinister characters who all ate at the same hot-dog stand. Noel himself had enjoyed a beer from Munich under the watchful eye of two Gestapo men. They had even been bold enough to strike up a conversation with him about his escape from Poland. He had told them their pilots were very good shots. Noel was quite certain he had been followed everywhere he went, as if he knew anything of vital importance that the Nazis did not already know. He had not minded, he said. He found the whole thing amusing.

In conclusion, most people in America, including the resident Germans, French, and British, treated the war as if it were nothing more than a staring match across a concrete fence, with a few muttered threats thrown in for interest.

Noel made a prediction. "How much longer can it last? A German captain ordered to shoot himself for the sake of tacking on a dignified ending? War without nobility soon becomes tiresome. We shall hope that by spring some disenchanted German will shoot Hitler, and everything will get back to normal."

❧

"You are looking at me strangely," Richard Lewinski said as he tapped the top of his soft-boiled egg with a spoon.

Andre glared at him across the breakfast table. "You are tapping Morse code on your egg, Richard. You said, *Donnez-moi du sel.*"

"That is correct. So? Pass the salt."

Andre did so with some irritation, then returned his attention to the newspaper.

The tapping continued, this time against the egg cup: *Thank you and good morning.*

Andre lowered the paper and narrowed his eyes as Richard continued. *Why are you cross?*

"I will tell you why, Richard. Because it has been a long and difficult week. My superiors at Vignolle think you are a lunatic up to no good. Therefore they think I am a lunatic for continuing my support of you. You tell me virtually nothing about what you are doing in my basement all day. Therefore I have nothing to tell them."

Lewinski smiled and raised his spoon like a conductor's baton. "Tell them . . . I am building an organ. I intend to put a Nazi monkey on a chain and become an organ grinder in Geneva."

"You are mad."

"Yes—" Lewinski nodded—"but there is method in it." He leaned his elbow against the table and gazed intently at Andre. "Tell them . . ." He smiled. "Tell them this is all a child's game."

"Deciphering enemy codes is no game for children, Richard."

"But it is." He blotted his mouth and smoothed his napkin out on the table. "Remember when we were children? Remember the code?"

"No."

"Yes, Andre! You must. We made up a list. Every letter in the alphabet was substituted for another letter." He began to write on the napkin:

H=T, E=Q, L=Y, P=N. HELP=TQYN

"Yes. A child's game. I will give you that. We have an entire team working to decipher the German substitution codes."

"Too simple. *E* is the most common letter. One progresses from there. We learned that from Sherlock Holmes. Remember, Andre? *The Adventure of the Dancing Men.*"

Andre had lost his appetite. There was nothing in this that he did not know. "Richard, the problem is that we are deciphering German codes too late. It takes months. They change their ciphers every day."

"Exactly. Enter Enigma. The original commercially marketed machine has three wheels, each of which contains connections for twenty-six letters of the alphabet."

Andre nodded, hoping there was some point to Lewinski's lecture. "This we know was sold on the open market as a business encoding device just after the last war."

"The machine is no secret. When the operator types the letter *A*, the setting of the first wheel might change it to the letter *R*. The second changes the *R* to a *Y*, and the third changes the *Y* to an *H*. Which is the first letter of the word *HELP*."

"Richard, Intelligence is aware of the problem. What is the solution?"

"Someone who knows how to set the wheels could read the message running the *H* back through the machine to the letter *A*, to decipher it."

Andre stared glumly at the word *HELP* on the napkin. "Changing one of the wheels changes the outcome by possible millions of combinations. And the Nazis alter the setting each day."

Lewinski added cheerfully, "It is much worse than that, Andre. Since the Nazis have added two additional interchangeable wheels to their Enigma machines, there are now *billions* of possible combinations."

Andre nodded. That meant the code was virtually impossible to break by any human.

"You see why the Nazis are not afraid to send thousands of these machines up to the front lines of battle?" Lewinski continued. "Why, they are on every ship and every command car. They are supremely confident that all your work is too little, too late. And it is. Your cipher experts are ants in combat with a bull elephant."

Andre's brow furrowed as the implications became clear. Accurately coding and decoding messages depended on three things: using the right three wheels, putting them in the Enigma machine in the correct order, and setting all three wheels to the correct starting position.

"Is this what I am to report to Bertrand at Vignolle? That Lewinski says it is hopeless?"

"Indeed not, Andre. What is needed is another machine that can duplicate and electronically interpret the impulses of the Enigma transmissions."

"And where is this miracle?"

"In your basement." Lewinski picked at the shell of his egg as though they had merely been chatting about the weather.

"Richard . . . is it possible?"

"A child's game. Multiplied a million times. But still, a child's game."

"When will it be ready?"

"When it is finished." Lewinski salted his breakfast, and the conversation ended.

Affairs of the Heart

Cold weather hit Northern France with a fierceness that sent all brave soldiers on both sides of the Maginot Line burrowing into their bunkers. Apart from the daily ritual of artillery rounds, the war was very slow indeed.

There were no wounded soldiers in the Casualty Clearing Station at the Ecole de Cavalerie. There were, however, about a hundred patients with either bronchitis or pneumonia. The entire wing reeked of linseed and antiphlogistine poultices and camphor steam inhalations that clung to the clothes and skin of the nurses.

Including Sister Abigail Mitchell.

As was his custom, Paul strolled through the stables after dinner, not so much to check the horses as because he found comfort in the warm, earthy scents of horseflesh and the quiet of the place during the study hour.

This evening he was troubled by what had passed between him and Andre in Paris. Paul felt he was right about Andre's treatment of Elaine Snow. Andre had let their grandfather keep him from marrying the woman he loved—the mother of his child. And now it was too late—Elaine was dead. Andre had, indeed, sold a piece of his soul, Paul had told his brother. But perhaps he had spoken too frankly. It was a fault of his—speaking too frankly. The same fault had put him into disfavor with General Gamelin when he had argued on behalf of de Gaulle's military strategy.

So here he was—acting headmaster of a cavalry school and likely to stay until the war was over one way or the other. He stroked the soft nose of a broodmare and felt sorry for himself.

Suddenly the aroma of camphor assaulted his nose. He turned too late to escape the smiling greeting of Sister Mitchell. She was quite pretty, even though she was an Amazon personality type, Paul thought.

"*Bonjour*, Captain Chardon!"

This meant "good day," and it was evening. Her French, as always, was very bad. Paul decided to speak English, a language he managed masterfully.

"Good evening, Sister."

"You speak English very well."

"My mother was English," he explained.

An expression of surprise crossed her face and then unusual warmth, as if he was forgiven for whatever it was he had done. "I thought there was something different about you." She pulled her coat tighter around herself and leaned against the stall door.

"Different?"

"Polite. Like an Englishman. A gentleman. Not like the rest of the . . ." She faltered. "Oh, I didn't mean that. . . ."

"What did you mean?"

"The very thing I came to discuss with you. It seems that one of your officers has been seeing one of my younger nurses."

"Yes?" Paul cast through his mind for the right match. Probably Jules Sully, the chemistry instructor, and that cute little thing from Jersey. The Channel Island women were beauties and spoke decent French as well.

"It is that chemistry teacher and Miss Bremmer from Jersey."

He nodded. "A very pretty couple."

"No! I forbid it! He actually wishes to marry her, and it simply cannot . . . we must put a stop to it."

Paul had heard quite enough. "Mam'zelle, I am only half English. I do not admit it often, and in matters of the heart I am entirely French, I assure you. As was my mother, who, even though she was raised in England, was French to the core. A woman of great passion and understanding in such matters as affairs of the heart. Therefore, do not assume, though you yourself have no understanding of love, that I will allow you to direct heaven in the matter of a man and a woman who wish to be married. I am not so cold as that."

Her jaw dropped. She blinked at him in amazement. "But you cannot mean it."

"Mam'zelle . . . Sister . . . whatever. You may direct your CCS. You may scrub your little life away and tend to your camphor poultices, but there is more to life than that. I will grant my permission when the request is made. I would suggest you do the same, lest you reap the disdain of every citizen in Lys and every feeling heart at the Ecole de Cavalerie."

"Well!"

"Very well, indeed." He bowed slightly. "It is no wonder you require so much coal to warm yourself. Now if you will excuse me. The smell of camphor has opened my head in ways I had not imagined. I bid you good evening, Mam'zelle Sister Abigail Mitchell."

☙

When his brother, Paul, arrived in Paris to spend the Christmas holiday, Andre was even more on edge than usual.

The hair of Richard Lewinski gleamed like molten copper beneath the lamp that hung from the ceiling of his basement workshop. Laboring over a mass of wires and gears, he barely looked up as Andre and Paul descended the steep steps.

"*Bonjour*, Richard," Andre called. "Paul is back in Paris, my friend."

"Merry Christmas, Richard," Paul said cheerfully.

Lewinski replied with a grunt as he continued his work. Sometime later, Andre suspected, his absentminded guest would ask where Paul had been and for how long. Of course, Andre had to admit the possibility that Richard Lewinski had not even noticed Paul's absence.

"He is no trouble, really," remarked Andre with a shrug. "Although he is more vacant than in the old days, I think. Not one word of conversation. We played a game of chess two nights ago, and he was winning, too. Suddenly he got up and ran down to the cellar. Odd. I rarely see him eat, but Cook takes him his food, and when she returns later it is gone." He laughed.

"What is he up to, anyway?" inquired Paul.

Andre avoided the question. "The mad scientist. You know Richard has never been happy unless he is tinkering with something."

"Something from a Jules Verne novel, I expect. A time machine. Perhaps he will vanish and return with Napoleon at his side."

"An excellent guess." Andre clapped his brother on the back as they entered the study. "France could use another Napoleon these days."

Paul laughed. "Some of our generals are so old that I would swear they knew him personally."

A porcelain doll dressed in white lace was perched on a bookcase bearing red-leather first editions autographed by the author Jules Verne, and another set signed by Victor Hugo, both of whom had visited the house in former days.

Paul warmed his hands by the fire. "Will you try to see your daughter on this trip to Luxembourg with your pretty American friend?"

"I thought I might take Mother's doll to give to her. A Christmas gift."

"Have you thought of bringing her to Paris?"

"I have thought of it." Paul's straightforward questioning made Andre uneasy.

"You should keep Lewinski away from the child. He's apt to frighten her. The way he peers through that gas mask and prowls around at all hours."

Andre sighed and shook his head. "This is crazy. I doubt that her grandfather will even let me see her. And if he did? How could I manage with the war on?"

"As a gentleman, do you have a choice, Brother? There is really nothing else to be done under the circumstances."

Andre did not acknowledge the opinion of Paul about his personal affairs. The comment irritated him. What could Paul know about it? Andre fell silent, pretending to busy himself with unopened mail.

At last Paul broke the stillness. "So how is the political side of the war?"

"The British are ecstatic about the destruction of the *Graf Spee*, the German battleship. Full of self-congratulations, as if the British navy had won the war. Winston Churchill, as First Lord of the Admiralty, is quite the celebrity. We would all be better served if he headed the government of England, I think. Hitler hates him. That's a good sign."

"It will not be like the last war," Paul countered grimly.

Andre nodded in agreement. "I saw Charles de Gaulle last night at a party. Swaggering giant. He is arrogant and outspoken as always, but he's right. Tanks, he says. Tanks and planes. Mobility. But our generals are from another century, Paul." He half turned to gaze at his brother, who still wore the uniform of a cavalry officer. "We still have the finest horses in the world."

Paul bowed slightly. "Horses and French courage will defeat the Boche. My cadets are convinced of it. If only every poilu had the courage of my boys. They are certain the Boche will melt in the face of our bravery."

"It must have been the opinion of the leaders of our Republic as well. Or why would they have gone to Munich with the English to give Hitler Czechoslovakia and the Skoda Arms Works?" Andre gave a bitter laugh. "I hear the Panzer divisions are now driving Czech-made tanks of French design."

"But we have our eighty-year-old generals to inspire, do we not? General Petain, the hero of Verdun. He glares down at me from the dining hall of the Ecole de Cavalerie, accusing me of being too modern for a cavalry officer. Petain, good horses, and courage. The Nazis cannot over-come such a combination."

The brothers fell silent. The fire crackled. Andre looked at the doll on the bookshelf. "The English have evacuated their children from London. I have considered speaking to Juliette's grandfather about sending her to England. Perhaps it would be best if she came here to Paris."

"So. She is the reason behind all this talk of war." Paul laughed. "It is easier for you to consider mass destruction than fatherhood."

"That's not it."

"There are a few months until the offensive will begin. Trust a horse soldier in that. Hitler will wait until the roads dry out. Try to bring her here to be with you until then. She needs someone."

Andre nodded. "I was thinking that it might be better if she does not become . . . attached." Running his hand across his face, he muttered, "Should I give her the doll at once? Should I go alone to the house to meet her? Or will it be better to bring a woman with me? Josephine seems fond of children."

"How do you know such details about women after so short a time? They are inscrutable to me after months of conversation. You amaze me, Brother." Paul shook his head in amusement and turned toward the fire.

Just then through the window Andre glimpsed a sleek black limou-sine as it turned left on Quai d'Anjou, slowed, and pulled to a stop in front of No. 19. "Josephine Marlow is here," he announced quietly.

"Shall we go?" Paul rocked up on the toes of his boots and added in a tone thick with sarcasm, *"Papa?"* He tugged at the tunic of his cavalry uniform in a nervous gesture and squinted out the window as Josephine Marlow emerged from the vehicle. "Very nice. I am disappointed in only one thing."

Andre's brow furrowed. "Yes? What is that?"

"I should have met her first."

Old Brezinski perched on the top rail of the stall as the spindly legged colt stooped to probe his mother's underside in search of supper.

"He is a beauty," Katrina von Bockman said softly, taking a seat be-side the Polish Jew.

"He will be black as a crow's wing by the time he is a yearling," Brezinski observed with pleasure. "His father was the same at this age, and look what came of him: Othello, black as night and the most mag-nificent stallion in Poland."

"Shot out from under Count Gratz in the battle of Krakow." Katrina brushed her hair back impatiently. What was the use of talking about what had gone before? It all had vanished now.

"The stallion was bred for battle, Katrina. Perhaps it is not wrong that he should have ended his life in such a way."

"A waste."

"So it always seems, except that courage in battle—of men and horses—is the stuff legends are made from."

"Legends," she scoffed. "We would be better off to have Othello standing at stud right now, passing on some of his legendary qualities to his offspring."

The colt found the faucet and latched on with an enthusiasm that made the mare stamp her rear hoof three times.

"Starbright has taken to motherhood," said the old man. "She was such a flighty thing. It always settles them." He did not look at Katrina as he spoke. "It will be good for Horst to see her and the colt. It will cheer him."

"He is not coming home for Christmas." She raised her chin regally, as if expecting an argument.

"That is a shame. I would have liked for him to see this one."

"You are too kind, considering."

"Considering?"

"What he is part of."

Brezinski pushed his cap back on his head. "Horst is like Othello, Katrina. Have you not noticed?"

"I have noticed all right. I have asked him to leave me, to gallop off and fight his war, even though he does not know what he is fighting for."

Brezinski appeared to contemplate her bitterness before he replied, "He is fighting because he must fight."

"For the Nazis?"

"For us, perhaps."

"You are a Jew. How can you say such a thing?"

He gestured broadly and turned his eyes upward at the sound of children's footsteps. "Your husband is a Wehrmacht hero, Katrina. His loyalty is unquestioned. Though the Nazis do not have his heart, they have his oath as a soldier. And as long as he continues to fight well for the Fatherland? Well then, we might remain relatively safe. If there is any safety for a Jew in Germany, it is only that he might be useful in the service of a German hero."

She blinked at him in astonishment. "But, Brezinski . . ."

He turned his gaze on her. "Your brother-in-law? Kurt Hulse? His plane down in Belgium? *Lucky* fellow. Your sister and parents are in Switzerland. You think the Gestapo is not watching you now?"

"How do you know this?"

"Everyone from the kitchen to the stable knows it. The little girls whisper about it. The nuns pray. Are you leaving the Reich as well?"

She frowned at the back of the colt. "I had no plans to leave."

"Why?"

"This place . . . all of you."

"You are fighting in your own way then, instead of running. If you leave us, you know they will come for us."

"Yes."

"And if Horst is disloyal to his oath?"

Her eyes narrowed. "He is not fighting for us. He is fighting because he loves it."

"Not every man in the Wehrmacht is evil, Katrina. You know the Nazi law. If one family member commits a crime, all are punished." He took her hand. It was ice-cold. "So now the only honest men left in Germany are in concentration camps. Holy places, those prisons. Full of saints and martyrs. Everyone else? Hostages, true fanatics, or terrified liars . . . or fools who rage at a wind that will blow them away."

"It has become so complicated. I can't sort it out anymore."

"It is simple for me because I am a Jew. Hitler made the decision for me. But what about you? And Horst?"

She sat sullenly, considering the old man's words. "We should have left before the war."

"And what would have become of us? My family . . . the others you hide here?"

"I cannot guarantee your safety even now."

"Nor can you guarantee your own. But at least we are still breathing." He smiled.

"Why didn't you leave Europe?"

"I wanted to go to America. I was there for a short time with the Kellogg Arabians. But I could not get visas for my family, so I returned, even knowing that this was a possibility. You see? For the sake of my family."

"That is different."

"Is it? Horst loves you, Katrina. Love sometimes calls for a peculiar kind of duty." He shifted his weight on the narrow rail and rubbed his chin. "I used to think of it when I was young. When my wife, Tanya, was alive and the pogroms were so fierce against the Jews in Poland, here was the question I put to myself: A man comes up to me on the street and puts a gun to the head of my wife. He tells me he will blow her brains out if I do not break into the house of my neighbor and steal his gold. What will I do?"

He shrugged. The choice seemed obvious. "For the sake of her life, I will become a thief." He looked away as some terrible image crowded into his mind. "In Poland now the Nazis have made Jews to be policemen to arrest their fellow Jews. Good men are made to be traitors to their own friends. Their wives and children are hostages. The Gestapo learned that trick first in Germany, did they not?"

"What can I do?"

"You are doing all you can. You have put yourself at risk for all of us. So be smart. But you must have mercy also on your husband. They hold a gun to your head, and he loves you. Believe that he will do what he can, but also what he must."

A Margin of Safety

It was a chance meeting with a major in a Wehrmacht artillery regiment that turned Horst von Bockman's interest back to Poland.

"Holiday leave?" The major swirled his glass of whiskey and soda like an Englishman. "I'm taking my pay back to Poland. Why should the SS swine get all the profit, while those of us who fought and won the war end up buying Polish goods in Germany for double the price? I tell you, von Bockman, there's a profit to be made in Poland in everything from lace doilies to horseflesh. The best for practically nothing!"

The wealth of Poland was finding its way into Germany. Coal and grain flowed west with antique furnishings, tapestries, and art. Jewels, furs, china, silver, and gold that had been smuggled out of Russia during the Bolshevik Revolution were now in the coffers of the Reich or for sale at bargain prices for Christmas.

The trains ran unhindered across former Polish territory into Danzig and East Prussia and the now-humbled, broken Polish cities of Lublin, Krakow, and Warsaw. Enterprising merchants with the permission of the Reich general government traveled east to examine the possibilities of establishing manufacturing centers manned by slave labor.

Major Horst von Bockman presented his request to enter the occupied territory to a minor clerk in the Offices of Commerce in Berlin.

"Yes, Major von Bockman. You say you wish to examine and purchase livestock from the general government of Poland?"

"That is correct."

"What is your purpose?"

"In private life my wife and I own a stud farm. Arabian horses. I understand there are still many more to be had in Poland. The Poles are slaughtering horses and selling the meat on the black market. It is a waste beyond contemplation."

It had occurred to Horst that somewhere in the horror of the stock pens of Poland were the finest Arabian horses waiting to be butchered and hung on hooks in a meat shop. If he could purchase a dozen of the best and return them to the farm for Christmas, Katrina would have to speak to him again.

"How much cash do you intend to take into the general government?"

"Five thousand Reichsmarks."

"A considerable sum."

"We purchased a number of Polish horses from Reichsmarschall Göring. The amount seems modest for the quality of animal I have in mind to bring back to the Reich."

At the mention of Göring's weighty name, the eyebrows of the clerk raised in respect. The rubber stamp bearing the eagle and the swastika thumped down on Horst's travel permit.

⚭

Andre Chardon had clumsily wrapped the doll in red tissue paper and tied it with string. His efforts at packaging his daughter's gift embarrassed him, as did the fact of his paternity. Driving Josephine north from Paris along the Chemin des Dames, the highway named for the daughters of Louis XV, he felt awkward.

To the wonder of Josephine, who had not been able to secure passes into the Zones des Armees, his documents gave them unhindered admittance through the concrete chicanes that blocked the roads leading toward the border of Luxembourg. Sentries saluted him, bade him good day, and sent him on his way.

He spoke little, although there was much he wanted to share with the beautiful woman beside him. She must have sensed his uneasiness, for she filled the silence with conversation, answering his questions about her life in America.

Born in Fort Smith, Arkansas, Josie had moved to California with her family when the drought and the Depression withered their world in 1930. She confided, "We lived in a tent beside a river until my father found work in the oil fields. I was sixteen, gangly, and self-conscious. The girls made fun of me because of my Southern accent. Like the teasing done to the evacuated children from Alsace who are billeted in Paris—just the same. In California, the more of us who came west, the uglier things got. Compassion wore a little thin."

Andre wished he could have known her then. He glanced at her. Thick chestnut hair was plaited and pinned up. A strand curled at the curve of her cheek. Her gaze held the knowledge of sorrow too great for her years. Had such depth come with the privations of her childhood? Or was it more recent grief that had burned its image onto her soul? There was something in her expression that made him want to gather her into his arms, stroke her face, and hold her. "But you were beautiful. The young men? They were all in love with you, no doubt." He slowed the car behind a troop transport till the road was clear, then accelerated around it.

She laughed at him in genuine amusement as she had laughed at the Ritz. "Plain brown hair . . . ordinary . . . too tall. I'm glad of it now, but back then? I hid in the library and read until my eyes crossed. I excelled in French class. When I spoke French no one noticed my Southern accent, you see? I spoke as well as—better than—the other girls in French class. In the summer I worked as a laborer in the vineyards outside a little shantytown called Arvin. See how much we have in common, Andre? You own vineyards in Bordeaux, and I once harvested grapes in Kern County, California." She laughed again. "But I was good in school. I got a scholarship to UCLA."

"And your husband?"

"We met in a literature class. Danny was the first man I ever loved. The only man up until then. I thought when two people were in love they got married, had children, worked, and went to church on Sunday. Danny surprised me. He married me, got a job with AP, and left for Europe."

"And you followed him."

"Not for five years. I taught in a little one-room school in the mountains above Bakersfield, California. When I came to Paris, I thought we were finished. But I fell in love with my husband all over again . . . then I lost him."

Rows of leafless poplar trees slid past like a picket fence bordering snow-laden fields.

There was so much Andre wanted to know about her. She was different than any woman he had ever met. From a childhood of poverty she had a nobility of spirit and a strength untainted by bitterness. She was far from ordinary, yet she accepted his compliments only with amusement, as if she had never really looked at herself in a mirror, as if his attentions were simply empty attempts at flattery.

"You have loved other men?"

"One." Rubbing the fog from the window, she gazed at the countryside.

Her silence made Andre wonder if she still loved the Other One. "Where is he now?"

She smiled. "Probably out here somewhere chasing a story about the war, wishing he could befriend some French colonel who would get him through the roadblocks as easily as you! He is a newsman, a cameraman. I promised myself after I lost Danny that I would not get involved with another journalist. So common sense prevails over love, and he's gone."

"But you are a journalist."

"Danny didn't believe in life insurance. I have to eat. I love Paris. No one in Paris minds the fact that I was born in Arkansas. No one in France even knows where Arkansas is. America is just one big dreamland to the people over here. Writing for AP beats harvesting grapes in the vineyard of Colonel Andre Chardon."

He looked at her with surprise. It had never occurred to him that she was actually working because she had to. She was smiling, but her words seemed like a rebuke. Driving into the courtyard of a small inn, he shut off the motor and set the brake. Andre turned to face her as sleet began to fall. Taking her hands, he raised them to his face. For the first time he noticed the remnants of callouses on her palms.

She eased her hands from his grip and closed her fists, suddenly self-conscious. "Everyone in France did something else before the war, Andre. How does the song go? 'The colonel owned a vineyard. The correspondent tended vines. . . .' Something like that. 'Like riding a bicycle, you never forget.'"

He pulled her against him and touched her cheek. "I would make you forget, if you will let me." Then he kissed her as the sleet drummed on the roof of the car.

◌

It was bitterly cold in Warsaw. With some relief Horst von Bockman noted that the snow covered some of the scars of battle. Trams had been righted and the rails repaired from the Umschlagplatz to the hotel. On the streets, open-backed lorries transported prisoners to shovel snow or to work on repairing the roads. Horst did not look at their gloomy faces as they passed.

In the late afternoon, Horst retraced his steps to the Vistula River. There was no sign of what had transpired here some months before. Sections of the river were frozen, yet black water lapped around the pilings of the bridge that joined the right and left banks of the city.

He imagined the body of the woman, Sophia, still beneath the water. Or, in death, had she escaped Poland and drifted down to the sea? It seemed so long ago now. Why could he not forget her face? Why did he hear her repeat the name of her child each night as he lay down to sleep? *"Jules! Oh, poor Jules."*

He thought about the child of the dead woman. Once again he replayed the incident in his mind, wondering if he could have done anything different. Would the SS have arrested him if he had not stepped aside? Would they have shot her regardless? And if Katrina had been there with him, would her courage have brought about a different ending to the tragedy?

Katrina had a way of changing the world by her will. Perhaps that is why she believed that her will would change him now. How he ached for her approval and her love, yet her self-righteousness angered him. Why had she chosen to reject him now when he needed her more than ever?

"Herr Major!" A ragged boy of about eleven approached from behind a heap of rubble. His coat was thin. Dark circles were beneath his eyes. He had the look of malnutrition. His German was barely passable.

"It is almost curfew, boy. You should get home."

"You look lonely, Herr Major. I have a pretty sister for you to spend time with." The boy took a cautious step closer.

"Little beggar," Horst scoffed, even as he wondered how evident his loneliness was in his expression. "Any sister of yours would not be something I want to spend time with."

"Oh no, Herr Major!" the boy blurted eagerly. "She is not like me. A beauty, I assure you!"

"I am not interested in Polish women or Jews, boy."

"We are not Jews," the child spat. "She is very Aryan. Blond. Blue eyes. Young. Pretty. Better than the whores in Berlin." He moved his hands in the shape of an hourglass. "And she does not cost much to make a major very satisfied indeed! Come see! It cannot hurt to look. There is a gramophone for music. Vodka to drink. A pleasant way to pass a lonely evening. If you do not like her, you can leave. But you will be well pleased; I promise!"

To forget. That seemed the primary concern of Horst this evening. He was in need of diversion, he told himself. And what harm was there in just taking a look at the merchandise the boy was selling?

The sky was steel gray as a thick fog descended over the city. Horst followed the beggar, keeping in mind that German soldiers had been led to ambush by partisans with the promise that a pretty woman waited at the end of a short walk.

"I will be discreet, Herr Major. You must not seem to be following me."

The boy was cheerful, walking a few paces ahead of Horst like a native guide. On deserted streets, he pointed at the windows of shops and flats whose shattered glass was pieced together with lead and putty. Those spaces too large to be repaired were simply boarded up, the boy explained. It would not matter until summer when the weather turned hot. Maybe by then everything would be back to normal. Maybe by then there would be no more war, and the Germans would see that the Poles were really their friends. There would be whole panes of glass in the windows of Warsaw again.

They crossed a bomb-pocked street and passed a knot of sullen Poles who separated at the sight of Horst, retreating into shadowed alcoves as if they did not know one another.

At twilight Horst and the boy entered a building that had been moderately damaged in the bombardment. The stonework of the five-story building was scarred by shrapnel. The cornice work was broken, and the windows here were more boarded up than patched.

The door into the lobby had once been glass. Now it was completely covered by bits of scrap wood. The interior of the entryway seemed entirely without light. Holding the door wide, the boy peered past Horst into the fog. "Come on, Herr Major. No one will see you."

Horst unsnapped the leather flap of his holster and rested his hand on the butt of his Luger. After a second's hesitation, he stepped in after the boy. The door swung shut as the child leaped onto the narrow stairway. A glimmer of light from a single lightbulb identified the spiral staircase and each vacant landing. Other than that, there was an oppressive gloom. Horst listened for the sound of any footsteps besides their own. He glanced at each door as they passed, half expecting an ambush.

"It was a very nice flat before the war, Herr Major," the boy chirped as they passed the landing on the second floor. "Maybe next year . . ."

Horst was sweating by the time they reached the third floor. The climb had been uneventful, but he still felt the presence of danger as the boy knocked softly and called, "Smyka?"

There was a long pause; then the sound of a Schubert waltz penetrated the wood of the door.

"She will just be a moment." The boy turned apologetically. "You know . . . these females."

Horst kept his hand on the Luger. How stupid it would be to have survived battle and be murdered on a gloomy backstreet in Warsaw. "Of course."

The doorknob clicked, the hinges groaned slightly, and the door opened. A stream of light spilled out on Horst and the beggar.

Silhouetted in the light was a girl with blond, shoulder-length hair. Dyed, Horst reckoned, to make herself more appealing to the German clientele who were fixated on all things Aryan. Her eyes were wide and blue in an oval face and reflected her nervousness. Or was it fear? She was not much more than eighteen, if that. Wearing a flimsy, light blue cotton robe, she was small and thin, but not as starved-looking as her brother. Nevertheless, the spectre of hunger was in her eyes.

"I have brought someone, Smyka," said the boy in an urgent tone, as if he was warning her to keep a bargain.

She did not smile or raise her eyes as she stepped aside. *"Guten Abend,"* she said timidly.

Horst brushed past her into a small, musty smelling room. The windows here were boarded. Fresh air would have been a relief. There was a neatly made bed in the corner and a tiny kerosene stove on the opposite wall. A curtain provided a partition for what might have been a second room, but there was nothing else.

"He is a major, Smyka," said the boy. "I have told him you are very nice. That you have music and vodka, too."

The girl's eyes darted up. "I am out of vodka, Herr Major. But if you like, my brother can get some."

Horst nodded and gestured toward the curtain.

"Oh that," the boy said brightly. "It is nothing. Just clothes and things." He put out his hand. "If you want vodka, you will have to pay in advance, Herr Major."

Horst dug in his pocket and retrieved a handful of change. "Yes, I would like a drink."

The brother and sister exchanged a look. The girl leaned in close and murmured some instruction in Polish. Then the urchin was out the door, clattering down the stairway. Schubert played on, skipping and scratching through one waltz and popping onto another.

"You will want to remove your gun and your tunic, Herr Major."

The girl glanced at the bed and began to take off the robe.

"Wait until your brother comes back. I want to drink first."

She managed a weak, self-conscious smile and tied the belt again. Was she relieved? "As you wish, Herr Major. Would you like to dance then?"

The curtain stirred. Someone was behind it. Horst felt the hair on the back of his neck prickle. He stepped away from her as she put her arms around him.

"Who is there?" he demanded hotly.

"It is nothing, Herr Major. Nothing!"

He pushed her away roughly and drew his Luger, as if to shoot through the cloth.

The girl shrieked and stumbled, throwing herself between the muzzle of the pistol and the curtain. "No! It is nothing, Herr Major! Do not shoot! Please! I beg you!"

Horst flung her aside and tore away the fabric, revealing not an

enemy waiting in ambush but a crib with a child of about twelve
months standing, clutching the bars.

The girl wept and clung to Horst's boots. "Please! I told you! You
see? Only a baby, Herr Major! You cannot hurt him!"

A wave of dread enveloped Horst. Suppose he had fired?

The baby began to cry.

"Why did you hide him away?" Horst shouted at her. "I might have
killed him!"

"I thought . . . you would not . . . want me. I need the money, Herr
Major. Please! Do not leave me! I will do anything you want!"

Horst's breath exploded from his lungs. "Is the child yours, girl?"

"My baby brother."

"How old are you?" He grabbed her arm and pulled her roughly to
her feet. "Do not lie to me. How old?"

"Sixteen," she cried. "Please . . . it is only me to care for them. For my
brothers. Don't leave yet! There is no other way! You can see. No kerosene. Nothing left to eat. Please stay! I will make it up to you, Herr Major!" She sank to her knees and covered her face with her hands. "God,
help me! God help us!"

The record bumped to an end. The ticking of the needle against the
label marked time with her sobs. Horst shoved the Luger back into the
holster. He reached into his pocket and pulled out a one-hundred
Reichsmark note and handed it to the baby.

Then he strode out of the room and out of the building into the foggy
streets of Warsaw.

⟨෴⟩

The road into Luxembourg City climbed out of a canyon and across a
narrow ridge known as the Bock. Since Roman times this had been the
main approach to the heights of ancient Luxembourg.

Like a broken tooth against the sky, the ruins of a tower marked the
remnants of the city's original ramparts. Legends about the founder of
Luxembourg claimed that Count Sigefroi sold his soul to the devil, who
built the fortress for him in a single night.

As the evening mists swirled up from the Alzette and Petrusse rivers
to drift among the sloping medieval streets, it was not hard for Josie to
imagine that the legend might be true. Here in this tiny neutral nation,
other pacts were being made with the devil. The city was full of Gestapo
agents, she had been told. Deals were struck and military information
bought and sold as commonly as vegetables on market day.

Andre had changed into civilian clothes at the border. Any military
uniforms made the citizens of Luxembourg nervous. They preferred the

"see no evil" approach to the war. Trusting in their policy of strict neutrality, they crossed their fingers and closed their eyes to the fact that they were snug against the borders of France and Germany.

As for the state of their own army, Luxembourg kept a troop of three hundred fifty men. Who would want to overrun the Grand Duchy, they reasoned, when it was such a useful meeting place for spies of both sides?

Andre knew the city well. This fact surprised Josie, since while his little girl lived here he had never been to visit her. With the certainty of a homing pigeon, he made his way past the Gothic cathedral of Our Lady of Luxembourg and the Grand Palace and the National Museum, finally stopping at the Brasseur Hotel.

The place exuded the faded grandeur of the last century. The lounge was draped in deep red. A portrait of the Grand Duchess Charlotte hung over the mantel of a large open fireplace in which the logs blazed cheerfully. In the stone of the mantel beneath Charlotte was carved the national motto of Luxembourg:

> "*Ir woelle bleiwe was mir sin—*
> We want to remain who we are."

Was the motto merely wishful thinking?

There was a large Christmas tree in the corner behind a grand piano. A thin-faced man in an old-fashioned cutaway coat played Mozart. The lounge was populated almost entirely by middle-aged men with grim eyes that darted from the pages of their newspapers to examine other grim men. With the piano providing the mood, the setting reminded Josie of an old silent movie she had seen about Mata Hari.

It was clear Andre knew the proprieter of the Brasseur. The man peered up at Josie with interest as Andre signed the register for two rooms.

"Adjoining, Monsieur Chardon?" His inquiry was discreet, but heads turned all the same. Had Andre been here with other women? Perhaps with the mother of his child?

Against her will the color rose to Josie's face.

"No. *Merci*, Henri," Andre replied. "My regular room for me. A suite for Madame Marlow."

There was no need for a bellman. Josie had brought only a small carpetbag with one change of clothes and the blue dress. Andre carried the red-wrapped doll and an expensive leather valise.

Her suite was on the second floor near the stairs. His was on the third floor at the end of the corridor.

"Is an hour enough time?" he asked. "Dinner at eight-thirty. The dining room. I'll come by, and we can go down together."

"I'll meet you," she said, not wanting to take the chance of asking him in. He stooped to kiss her mouth. She turned her face away, and his lips brushed her cheek. "Please don't," she whispered. "Not now. Not . . . tonight. I am . . . vulnerable."

He backed up a step and inclined his head in a slight bow, like a junior officer coolly accepting a command.

She closed the door of her room and turned the lock without thinking. Was she locking him out, or locking herself in? The last thing she needed was to get romantically involved with a French colonel. At this moment she wished they were each staying at different hotels. In fact, the way she was feeling, separate cities might be the only real margin of safety.

Caught on the Playing Board

Hot water. Josie lay back in the tub in her room at the Brasseur Hotel and let it wash over her in delicious waves. She almost regretted her promise to be ready in an hour. How wonderful it would be to simply throw on her nightgown, climb between cool sheets, and sleep for a while!

The telephone rang. She wrapped in a towel and answered it on the fifth ring. The tone of Andre was too cheerful. "*Chèrie!* I've met some old friends who are staying here. I hope you don't mind. We are invited to join them at their table. I could not refuse without compromising you to gossip."

She suppressed her vague sense of disappointment with the knowledge that there was safety in numbers. The way she was feeling, dinner by candlelight with Andre could be fatal. "Of course, Andre!" Did her too-cheerful tone match his?

Dressed in the cobalt blue evening dress, Josie entered the lobby of the hotel on time. Andre had already seen her in the gown—her only one. She felt like a caterpillar among the butterflies he must see all around Paris.

"Fantastic," Andre uttered, as if seeing her for the first time.

Escorting her to the dining room, he explained that a number of foreign nationals would be at the table tonight, including an American oilman and a Polish colonel in exile.

"All men, I fear. Most English speaking." He leaned close to her as they entered the dining room. She felt his breath on her shoulder. "You said you were vulnerable tonight. I have taken you at your word. I have provided you with, I hope, an entertaining diversion, but I cannot always say that I will be such a gentleman."

His frank gaze made her blush again. Suddenly wide-awake, she could feel the color climb from her throat to her cheeks. He smiled at it, and she imagined that he said such things on purpose. There was a kind of power in a man who could warm a woman with a look. Was it an acquired skill, she wondered, or just some inherited talent peculiar to the French? She forced herself to remember the wizened old face of the railroad ticket clerk in Boulogne. What was it he had said about the French bulls?

"May I speak frankly?" she asked.

"But of course."

"On our first meeting on the train to Paris, I am relieved that your eyes were closed and your mouth open most of the way from Boulogne. Otherwise I might have thought you were a dangerous man."

"Oh, but I am! You'll see when you know me better." He laughed, but Josie had the distinct feeling that he was no longer joking.

The large round dining table was set before a fireplace at the far end of the salon. Four men rose in unison as they approached.

Andre introduced Josie. "This group will be all politics and war. The food is the best in Luxembourg, and this was the personal table of the German kaiser in the last war." He pulled out her chair. "This was the kaiser's chair."

Introductions passed clockwise around the table: the American oilman, Hardy, thickset and sunburned, with a Southern accent; the Polish colonel, Wolinska, fine-boned, grim, and steely eyed, as though thinking about Christmas misery in Warsaw; a Canadian journalist, Tibbets, who had arrived on the Continent too late to make Christmas on the Western Front with his colleagues; and Medard, the elderly French assistant minister of commerce, who looked like a librarian.

The Canadian squinted curiously at Josie. "Marlow. Marlow? I knew a Marlow. Quite a ladies' man. Put us all to shame. Danny Marlow. Any relation?"

So here it was again. Right out. "My husband."

The Canadian swallowed hard. He scratched his chin and took a sip of wine. "I never knew Danny was married."

Andre glanced at her with that inscrutable smile. Was he enjoying the fact that she was blushing again? Thankfully the conversation rushed past the subject of Daniel's forgetting to tell anyone he had a wife back in the States. The Canadian murmured words of sympathy, and then the topic leaped to offensives, defense, the Germans, the English, politics, and war.

"Neutrality," spat the Polish colonel. "Americans call themselves neutral, safe on the far side of the Atlantic. I say Americans are another yellow race."

The face of the oilman grew redder with the affront. "I'm in Europe to put French tankers under the protection of our flag. France will be in need of American neutrality in shipping if this goes on a long time."

"The last war was a long one," said the French commerce minister, "and we won it. Therefore this will likely be a long war and we will win."

"History repeats itself," agreed the Canadian journalist. "Time won for the Allies. In 1914 the Allies were disorganized and unprepared. But time, working for us, assured our victory."

Andre Chardon remained silent, complacent, as if the topic bored him.

The French minister went on. It was apparent he was a well-read man. He quoted every government newspaper and magazine and arrived at his version of the truth about the inevitable outcome of this war. "An impregnable defense cannot be taken. The Maginot Line constitutes an impregnable defense. The Belgians also have their own Maginot between them and Germany. Belgium is on our border and is impregnable. And Luxembourg! A maze of mountains and valleys. Impassable to artillery. Therefore France cannot be taken. We wait it out. And if France cannot be taken, Germany is beaten."

"That may be true," commented the American oilman, "but suppose Hitler has some secret weapon? I sent my family home at the thought of it."

The French minister scoffed. "He has nothing but the tanks and dive-bombers he used against Poland, a very weak and unprepared nation."

The Polish colonel bristled. "You are wrong! It was not the tanks or dive-bombers we were unprepared for. It was the way the Germans used them. It was not history repeating itself, but something new and terrible. A war of movement!"

The French minister wagged his head at the naïveté of the Polish colonel. "Of course they moved across the Polish plains. But through the Maginot? Never. Through tank traps and barbed wire? Through the Ardennes and Dutch floods and the Belgian defenses? In the face of our air force? C'est ridicule, Monsieur! France is impregnable. If we cannot be beaten, then Hitler is beaten."

For a moment it looked like the table might come to blows. Josie shifted her gaze from one debater to the next as though she were watching a tennis match. Andre Chardon continued to say nothing at all. Josie found his calm demeanor disquieting. Did Andre have any opinion? Was he unmoved by the terrible fate of Poland? For the first time she saw him as cold and detached. She smoldered inside as she listened to empty prattle that could not alter what she had lived through in Warsaw.

The Polish colonel, a cavalry officer, was the only man among them who had tasted battle. He now found himself in what he considered a group of ignorant café generals. He became increasingly sullen as the minutes ticked past.

Dinner was ordered. Colonel Wolinska recited tales of horror to the unimpressed French minister, who babbled about the need to maintain the French economy. The oilman agreed that commerce must be protected.

"While France delays converting commercial factories into armament facilities for fear of harming a peacetime industry, the German nation puts all its energies into preparation for war," said the Polish colonel. He narrowed his eyes in disgust. "You are talking politics. There is a difference between politics and war. The Nazis know that. The Allies do not. France talks and talks while the Germans march and kill. That is the weakness of France—why France remains unprepared."

The Canadian replied in a patronizing tone, "Unprepared? The French fortifications are unlike any the world has seen before, my dear colonel."

"The only defense for France is to attack first. But even now it may be too late for that. Poland is destroyed. The Germans are moving their armies again. This time they gather at your precious, invincible Maginot."

The first course was served.

The colonel was calm again for a moment. He had angered the complacent allies at the table and so had won a small battle in his own bitter eyes.

"Defeatist!" spat the French minister.

It was evident that Josie had been meant to somehow restrain the potential volatility of the dinner guests. At least the Polish colonel and the French minister had not yet thrown the goose-liver paté at one another. But Josie was falling down on the job. The conversation moved on to poison gas, which might humanely murder all of Paris in its sleep or possibly peel the population alive like so many ripe bananas.

Then the inevitable question arose: What was this all about, anyway? It was no longer about Poland. Poland was gone. So why the naval blockade against Germany? Why the blustering on both sides?

"And what do you think, Colonel Chardon?" asked the American. "Is this a righteous war?"

Andre turned his gaze first on the Canadian journalist and then on Josie. "Some poet said it. That boys and girls and women who would groan to see a child pull off an insect's leg all like to read of war. It is the best amusement of our morning meal. Until we face death ourselves, until it touches someone we love, the death of strangers is an amuse-

ment we savor in the papers. Other people's sons. Other people's brothers, husbands, and fathers. Hitler says war is about honor, dying with
courage. I think it is more about breaking the tedium of ordinary life . . .
a terrible game of chess between Hitler and every other government in
Europe, and we are all caught on the playing board."

Outraged, the Polish colonel tossed his napkin onto the table. "Not
for me, Monsieur Chardon! It is about my homeland! The national
honor of Poland! There is cause enough to die for!"

Andre touched his fingers to his brow in salute. "And yet, when Hitler invaded Czechoslovakia, Poland darted across the border like a hungry little mongrel dog to grab the Czech province of Teschen! Hitler let
you have it, too, Colonel, because he knew all along he would take it
back. Check and checkmate. Where were all our high ideals when Austria went under and Czechoslovakia was overrun? Do ideals only apply
when what *we* value is stolen? I, for one, am still hoping, as General
Gamelin says, that France will not be bled white again. Not for any cause
or nation beyond our own borders."

"You would negotiate with Hitler after what has been done?"

"I would negotiate with the devil if I thought there was a chance that
this could all be stopped."

"But Poland!" The colonel sputtered with indignation.

"No matter who wins, I fear your nation will be lost. Spoils to be divided among the victors. A point on the negotiating table. The war is no
longer about Poland."

Red-faced, the Polish colonel leaped to his feet, wavering as if he
would like to strangle Andre. Then he stormed from the dining room.

Josie, her expression matching that of the Pole, simply stared hotly at
Andre as if she could not believe what she had heard. He smiled at her,
but she averted her eyes. While the others recovered easily from the rage
of the Polish colonel, Josie finished her meal in stony silence. Whatever
warmth she had felt toward Andre had completely vanished by the time
coffee was served.

ᏀᏉ

Horst stayed on the snowy bank of the Vistula until almost dawn.
Leaving the river, he walked through the deserted streets until he came
to the Cathedral of St. John. The broken spire was profiled in the predawn light. He entered through a side door that hung from one hinge.

It seemed a dead place. Holes still gaped in the ceiling. Morning stars
shone through the vaulted stone. Rubble had been cleared from the
floor in front of the altar, where a colony of red votive candles burned
beneath a crucifix in the otherwise dimly lit interior.

He removed his cap and crossed himself, more out of habit than conviction. Some years before he had visited the magnificent Warsaw structure with his red Baedeker's guidebook in hand. Now there was little left that he recognized.

As he turned to go, a man called from the shadows in German, "We are inconvenienced, but still in business, for the moment." There was a sharpness in his voice. "It was five centuries old, this cathedral."

"Yes," Horst replied. "My wife and I were here before . . . very old. I remember."

"This *building* you have destroyed, but you have not—cannot—destroy the truth."

"You Poles have one truth. We Germans another. So? What is truth?"

The voice was nearer. "Curfew is not lifted, Herr Officer. I knew you had to be a German officer. Your friends are shooting Poles and Jews for being out past curfew—those who are only looking for wood to warm their families—shooting them as children shoot sparrows in an orchard, and leaving them in the snow." As he spoke, the popping of a rifle sounded distinctly. The priest crossed himself. "As I was saying."

Horst could not reply to that. He closed his eyes briefly and saw the young mother being hurled into the oblivion of the Vistula. He was suddenly ashamed that he had come here.

"I did not mean to intrude, Father. Forgive me." Horst inclined his head as the priest struck a match and lit another candle a few feet from him. He was a tiny, dark-eyed man.

"Forgive you?" The priest held up the light as if to study the uniform of Horst. "Well, you are not SS." He sounded relieved. "I thought . . . I have been expecting the SS."

"No, Father. I am Major Horst von Bockman. Seventh Panzer Division."

"And I am Father Kopecky," the priest said, nodding slightly. "You are Wehrmacht. I thought most of you had been withdrawn. To leave us to the vultures."

"I came back . . . on business."

"You are a Catholic?"

"I was. But I only meant to . . . I have brought something." Horst retrieved an envelope from the pocket of his overcoat. Giving it to the priest, he shifted his weight nervously. "I have heard . . . you feed people here."

Father Kopecky opened the folded paper and examined the crisp new Reichsmarks. His expression displayed neither surprise nor curiosity as to why so much money would be given to feed the hungry. "You must carry a heavy burden of guilt, Major."

"Yes." Horst did not argue but briefly recounted what he had seen of crucified men, murdered women, and starving children.

"God is not some sort of court magistrate who accepts a fine in payment for the crimes of men."

"I did not know where else to turn."

"The condition of your soul is between you and the Almighty. No one else. Not the church. Not a priest. The only hope for any of us is that God alone is good and merciful. It gives Him joy to forgive us freely. Even the angels rejoice at the turning of one sinner's heart toward heaven. So says the Scripture. But then we must be willing to live as if we are forgiven. Showing mercy to others."

"Where do you see mercy or goodness in Warsaw?"

Father Kopecky held up the envelope as though it was some small proof. "The Almighty is also a pragmatist, I think. There is more at stake here at St. John's than your peace of mind, Major. The sun and the moon do not orbit around your guilty conscience. There are other more helpless lambs in the flock who also need mercy. So many Reichsmarks will feed many hungry children. We were down to the last of our provisions."

❧

Andre awoke before dawn and lay in bed, impatiently waiting for the hours to pass before he could telephone the home of Abraham Snow.

He showered and ate breakfast early without ringing Josie to join him. Then he retreated back to his room and placed the call to the father of Elaine. There was a long silence on the other end of the telephone when Andre announced his name.

Then the gruff voice of Abraham Snow replied, "Colonel Chardon, why do you bother me? My daughter is . . . Elaine is gone. There is no changing it. Leave us to our grief."

"I wish to see Juliette."

"Why are you suddenly interested? She is getting along as well as any child might who has lost her mother in such a way. Your sudden appearance in her life would simply disturb her mind. She has never known a father."

Andre glanced at himself reproachfully in the mirror. His eyes flitted to the red-wrapped package on the bureau.

"You are right in what you say, Monsieur Snow. I mean nothing to her, of course. But I have brought her a gift. Something for the holidays."

"A gift? It will only be a gift from a stranger. Meaningless. Why not send it with a messenger, Colonel? What purpose can it serve to meet her? If she knows you are her father, it can only hurt her. I must refuse."

"Please, don't hang up. I wish only to see her. I would not hurt her for anything, Monsieur Snow. I will not tell her. I have something that belonged to my mother . . . a doll. I wish only to give it to her."

A bitter laugh emanated from the telephone. "Yes, I know these kinds of presents. You do not bring it for Juliette but for yourself. To ease your guilt? To satisfy your curiosity, perhaps? Or do you hope to see what Elaine must have looked like when she was five? To see the child is to see the mother. Well then?"

He was right, of course. Andre had brought the gift thinking somehow that to behold the child would be to recognize some tangible part of what he had lost when he lost Elaine. His motives were selfish, yet . . .

"Five minutes is all I ask. You will be there. I will be discreet. I will tell her I am an old friend of her mother's who has just dropped by. I implore you."

There was silence as Abraham Snow considered the request. "Bring your gift then."

The phone clicked hard in Andre's ear as the old man slammed the receiver down.

Clutching Juliette's package, Andre hurried to Josie's room. But she was not there. The door was open, and the hotel maid was already hard at work, stripping the linens from the bed.

He did not wait for the groaning lift but ran down the stairs to the lobby. Josie was taking coffee with the Polish colonel in front of the fire. The two were speaking in low, sympathetic tones. The Pole glanced up, caught sight of Andre approaching, and stiffened. He muttered something at which Josie turned. Her expression was less than friendly.

Andre was unintimidated by their dour expressions. The morning was too full of hope to be ruined. "*Bonjour.* I am glad you have found pleasant company to breakfast with, Josephine. I had a telephone call to make."

"A success, I take it," she replied.

He held up the package as indication that he was going to be occupied for a while.

"We finished breakfast some time ago," Josie said. It was apparent from her icy tone that she had not forgiven Andre for insulting the Polish colonel with the truth last night. Now here she was in the lounge, conversing with the very man Andre had insulted. Andre was certain he was meant to feel this as a kind of unspoken chastisement.

At the moment Andre did not care if she approved or disapproved. He did not mind that she was sipping coffee with a vain peacock of a man like the Polish colonel. Water off a duck's back, as the English would say. Andre was about to have five minutes with his daughter! To meet his child face-to-face for the first time! It was not much, but it was something. Perhaps a beginning.

"Take as long as you like, Andre." Josie seemed pleased that he was on his way. The reserve in her eyes was unmistakable. "Colonel Wolinska and I are going to the cathedral to have a look around. Regular tourists. Do you mind?"

Andre glanced at his watch. It was 9 AM. "I thought we would leave for Paris by eleven this morning."

It was clear that his timetable was not hers. She had come all this way for one very unpleasant dinner at the kaiser's table and not even a full morning in Luxembourg City.

Her smile was forced. "You are the man with the travel pass."

A few minutes later, Andre arrived at the great house on Boulevard de la Petrusse. This morning the blinds were open, and the sunlight shone through the tall windows. Glancing up at the facade, Andre caught a glimpse of a small figure dressed in red, peering down from an upper-story window.

"*Juliette!*" He said her name, and in that instant the face vanished. The broad steps of the house were guarded by two stone lions, blackened by time and the all-pervasive coal smoke of the city.

Andre hung back; a twinge of apprehension knotted his stomach. He could not touch the door or cross the threshold without the awareness that this had been the house where Elaine had lived. How vast and empty the rooms must seem now without her.

He swallowed hard and prayed that he would say the right thing, that he could remain calm, even though he wanted nothing so much as to wrap his arms around Juliette and tell her everything!

He rang the bell and waited. Behind him a cloud passed in front of the sun. The door was opened by an elderly butler in formal dress. Chin high, expression aloof, the man did not step aside to admit Andre.

"Monsieur Snow told me to expect a messenger." The servant studied Andre with surprise.

"No. I am . . . Colonel Chardon. I am expected by Monsieur Snow. I have come to pay a call on Monsieur Snow and his granddaughter, Juliette."

The man still did not budge. He considered Andre with a look of pity. Perhaps he was fully aware of the identity of Andre. Perhaps he knew as much as anyone about Elaine Snow and her child.

"I regret, Colonel, that Monsieur Snow and his grandchild have only just left for a long trip to Belgium." He raised his hand regally to indicate the back bumper of a large, black American Buick fast disappearing around the long curve of the boulevard.

"But I only just spoke to Monsieur Snow! Twenty minutes ago from my hotel. He told me to come."

"Be that as it may, they have gone."

Andre pointed up at the windows. "I just saw a little girl in the window upstairs."

"You are mistaken, Monsieur. That is the daughter of our cook." The man wagged his head in dignified refusal to accept Andre's protest.

So that was it. Even if they were in the house, Andre was not to be admitted. He could not charge past the servant. Nor could he make demands. Abraham Snow had simply decided that he and Juliette would not be at home when Andre came. There was nothing to be done about it.

The shadows around him deepened. He glanced down at the gift in the rumpled red paper.

"I am sorry, Colonel," the butler blurted in a voice thick with sympathy. "Shall I take that for you? Give it to Mam'zelle Juliette?"

Beaten, Andre nodded. "I was in hopes of giving it to her personally. I have not written a note. Will you see that she knows the gift is from me?"

"Of course, Monsieur Colonel." He looked past Andre, as if the sight of him there on the doorstep was painful. Like a lost puppy in the rain.

Andre fumbled in his pocket for a pen and a small notebook. What to write?

> *Merry Christmas, dearest Juliette.*
>
> *I give you a beautiful little girl in search of a loving home. Take care of her.*
>
> *Best regards,*
>
> *Colonel Andre Chardon.*

He tore the paper out and placed it in the outstretched hand of the butler. As Andre looked at the dignified face of this man, it occurred to him that this servant knew Juliette very well. So he dared to ask, "What is she like?"

The brown eyes softened still more. "She is very sweet, Monsieur Colonel. Beautiful as her mother was at that age. Except—" he almost smiled—"she has brown eyes. Much like the color of your own. And she sings like a lark. You would be proud."

So he knew.

Andre handed over the gift. "This belonged to my mother. If she ever asks, tell her I was . . . a dear friend of her mère."

"Yes. My solemn oath, Colonel."

17

Now They Are Dust

B flight of the 73rd RAF Fighter Squadron completed its early morning patrol and winged in toward the base at Rouvres. All six planes touched down safely, none showing any sign of having been damaged or of having even been in battle.

Terry Simpson examined each returning plane's unscarred outline and sighed heavily. "Right-o, chaps," he said. "Our turn to 'ride boldly, ride'. . . . Death to the Huns." He flicked the butt of the Players cigarette onto the ground and crushed it beneath his heel.

"More likely we'll footle around with nothing to show for it," growled his wingman, Hewitt. A sly look crossed Hewitt's face, and he tossed the next remark casually into the circle of men that made up A flight like a nonchalantly dropped hand grenade. "Unless we jump some Messers, like Tinman here."

David Meyer colored up to his hairline until his freckles glowed.

"Put a sock in it, Hewitt," ordered Simpson.

"Aw, he knows I'm just havin' him on a bit. Right, Tinman?"

David gave a negligent wave of his hand to indicate that he had taken no offense, but as he walked toward his waiting Hurricane, his ears were still burning.

Three days earlier, in an excess of zeal borne of frustration, David had spotted and attacked a formation of what he took to be German aircraft. He pulled up abruptly when he discovered that they were French Morane fighters, but not before the French section scattered in all directions, and a startled French pilot had loosed a string of machine-gun fire. The incident had brought a vociferous complaint from the French squadron's officers and a severe dressing-down from his own squadron leader. David had held his breath during the reprimand, fearing that his section—he, Hewitt, and Simpson—would lose their furlough, but the captain had let him off with a caution.

David settled into the cockpit of his Hurricane with a sigh and adjusted the parachute harness. After the engine roared to life and David checked the gauges on the run-up, he throttled back and looked over toward Simpson's plane, getting a nod and a wave. He gave the thumbs-up to his ground crewman to pull the chocks, and a minute later the Hurricanes were speeding toward the end of the runway and leaping up into the clear blue French sky.

A flight orbited at twenty-five thousand feet and, as Hewitt had forecast, "footled about" searching for nonexistent targets. "Right," came Simpson's muffled voice through David's earphones. "Let's have a looksee southwest."

The new course carried the flight across Verdun. David looked down over the snowy hills and thought again how five miles of altitude could hide a lot of tragic history. Verdun had been the setting for the ten bloodiest months of the Great War. Close to a million men—French and German—had been killed or wounded there. And after close to a year of attacks and counterattacks, the line of battle had ended almost where it began.

David peered over his right wing at the wintry calm below and was brought up sharply when Simpson's voice crackled in his ear. "Meyer, what's that black spot at your nine o'clock low?" David's head snapped around, and he grimaced at his inattention. Too much of that would get a man killed.

Red section—Simpson, Hewitt, and ·Meyer—broke off from the other three planes of the flight and dove southeast to investigate. A few seconds passed; then Hewitt gave a yelp of exultation. The long, pencil-slim silhouette and twin tails identified the craft as a Luftwaffe Dornier Do 17. It was probably heading back to Germany after a reconnaissance mission, although the twin-engine planes were also used as bombers.

"Right!" Simpson's voice was crisp. "Form line astern. . . . Attack from dead aft. . . . I'll lead, and we'll break left, right, left. Here we go!"

The orders called for the three Hurricanes to change from their V formation to a line with Simpson in the lead, Hewitt next behind, and David following last. They would attack the Dornier from directly behind it, since that area of the bomber was not protected by machine guns.

The crew of the German craft spotted them at the same moment the Hurricanes formed their line, and the top turret machine gun opened up. A streak of tracers reached across the void toward Simpson's plane, and his guns responded as if the two aircraft were trying to tie each other together with lines of deadly fire.

Simpson dove below the cone of defensive bullets, stitching the fuselage of the Dornier before flashing past. He broke abruptly left before his plane came within sights of the bottom turret gun.

As David watched, Hewitt repeated the maneuver, scoring hits on the left engine of the German plane. Then it was David's turn.

Matching his craft's position to that of the bomber, David also matched the German pilot move for move. The Dornier jostled from one side to the other, like an animal trying to shake off a predator that has landed on its back. At two hundred fifty yards, David watched as his sights slid along the body of the twisting Dornier, raking its length.

When the Hurricanes reformed, the Dornier's left engine and midsection were in flames, and one of the rudders flapped raggedly. As the three RAF pilots closed again from astern, the Dornier made a lazy half roll and began a vertical spiral toward the ground.

"Shall we give 'im another go?" Hewitt inquired.

"No," came Simpson's rebuke. "He's done for. Give them a chance to get out . . . poor sods."

As red section circled overhead, one German appeared at the hatch of the doomed plane and launched himself out. In quick succession the white blossom of a parachute appeared and then, only an instant later, the German aircraft slammed into the countryside—a black, flaming meteor against the white hills.

⚭

Andre and Josie's return journey from Luxembourg on Christmas Eve day followed the course of the Meuse River. Once again his military pass and rank gave them easy access through the barricades and checkpoints along the road. He spoke little, but his expression reminded Josie of her first impression of him on the night train to Paris. A sort of tragic figure, she had told Alma. What had happened when he went to see his child? He had not spoken about it, and she did not ask, but she was certain it had not gone well.

She had been angry with him last night and earlier this morning, but her anger had cooled when she had seen the pain in his eyes upon his return from delivering the doll. Now there was something else. It was as if he had a secret he wanted to share with her.

They passed through the tiny, empty village of Bras and then turned away from the river onto a road that was little more than a cart path. The trees were young, with slim trunks and unscarred bark. The contours of the hills and ridgelines were ragged and uneven, as though some giant spade had dipped down, turned the earth in great chunks, and dumped it in useless heaps. Josie could see beneath the undergrowth that there were lines of trenches and broken barbed wire mired in the mud.

"Where are you taking me?" she asked, even though she knew this was a battlefield.

The line of Andre's mouth hardened at her question. He did not reply but turned off on a winding, rutted side road that climbed a hill crowned by slim beech trees. At the crest of the ridgeline, he stopped the car and sat staring through the windshield for a long moment. He gestured with his hand at the sign beside the road: *Louvemont, village detruit.*

"There was a village here when I was a very young child," he said in an almost inaudible voice, as though he had entered a cathedral in the middle of Mass.

There was nothing beyond the sign—no houses or shops, no parish church or cobbled square—only the heaps of earth and scattered stones that might once have been a wall or a foundation.

"My mother was born here." Andre cleared his throat. "My grandparents lived here." He pointed toward the next ridge. "It was a beautiful place. They were good people. They left when the war began in 1914. My mother came back to see my father here near the front in Louvemont and so now, together, they are the dust of Louvemont."

"You do not owe me an explanation."

"You think I am a coward."

"I do not! No, Andre! I just think . . ."

"You think!" he said fiercely. "But you cannot know what France was before. You ridicule Gamelin for saying that we will not be bled white again. But you cannot know whose blood watered this place! How can you know? There are too many to count. But I can see the faces of some just as clearly as I remember that the village of Louvemont was here. My mother and father died in one day at this place." He shook his head.

"I am sorry, Andre. I had no intention of prying into your life."

"It is not only my life, Josephine. There is more for you to see, if you will understand what this war must mean to France."

He started the car again and drove on slowly through the emptiness, as though there was something to witness. On each side of the road signs were posted in short intervals: *TERRAIN INTERDIT*, "forbidden ground."

"The woods and fields are still littered with unexploded shells and canisters of poison gas. A million acres and more, the land cannot be farmed or grazed. No couples can picnic or make love. These are fields of death for any who walk here even now."

He glanced at her. She knew she must appear pale and unhappy as a result of his macabre revelations. "For eight months it was quiet here. The sons of France waited in their muddy trenches, praying that the Germans would wear down through the long winter. And all the time they were building up. Time was not on our side. The Germans were waiting for spring. As they wait now."

There was no stopping him. It was as though he had to tell her, had to make her see the peace of these fields and know what ghosts still lingered here. "My father was a colonel. Mother came here to Louvemont often to be with him during that time. It was his birthday. They had a friend in the High Command who secured her a pass." He swallowed hard. "She would not let Paul and me go with her. Maybe she sensed what was going to happen . . . just as I am certain that hell is coming again to France, Josephine."

His knuckles were white as he gripped the steering wheel. "Look at it. On the day before the German offensive began in 1916, there was snow on the forests . . . on the fields and rooftops of the village. I have seen such days as a child . . . beautiful . . . peaceful. My parents must have awakened in an embrace and smiled at the sound of a lark outside the window. Who could imagine what would come? Just past dawn it began. The artillery shells fell like so many drops of rain. The church exploded. The houses exploded. Pits erupted across the fields like the craters of the moon. Trees and animals and barns and men . . . gone. The heat melted the snow everywhere. By noon, peaceful Louvemont had vanished."

"And your mother? your father?"

"Gone. They were never found. There was not enough left to bury. A million people died here in this place. One man in love . . . like me. One woman, beautiful and passionate . . . like you. Here! Look around you, Josephine, and know what war is . . . what it means to France. My mother and father? They are only two who died on the first day. A million lives were swallowed up right here. Only 160,000 bodies of that million were ever identified."

He fell silent again as the road wound up the slope of a long hill crowned with two granite monuments that stood at the empty crossroads and overlooked the killing fields. For a moment he stopped the car and waited, as if thinking whether to take her all the way to the center of his knowledge.

"Come," he said, getting out and opening the car door for her.

The wind was biting as they stepped out and stood in the center of the road between the two facing monuments. One was a granite structure of blocks topped with the bronze helmet of a knight. On it was carved, *AUX MORTS DES CHARS d'ASSAUT 1916.*

The other was a simple stone crucifix inscribed with the words:

> *Ossements qu'animait un fier souffle naguere,*
> *Membres epars, debris sans non, humain chaos,*
> *Pêle-mêle sacré d'un reliquaire,*
> *Dieu vous reconnaîtra, poussiere de heros!*

"Say it in English, Josephine, and then you will remember."

She stood shivering before it. Around her the fields seemed to awaken with the ghosts of a million young men who had barely lived before they died. Who had disappeared into the maw of war without leaving even a trace of themselves to bury.

She began to read. Her voice was carried away on the wind and sounded to her ears as though it was some other voice.

> "Heaps of bones once moved by the proud breath of life,
> Scattered limbs, nameless debris, chaos of humanity,
> Sacred jumble of a vast reliquary,
> Dust of heroes, God will know you!"

Silence. The wind. The distant memory of a day like Armageddon. The thunder of artillery mingled in her mind with the screams of dying men.

She turned to Andre, who searched her eyes and then held out his hand to her.

"Time levels all men. Good and evil alike. A century will pass in the blink of an eye, and who will sort the particles of dust? 'God will know you!' I look in the mirror each morning and say to myself, 'Andre, one day everything you think you believe about yourself will be put to the test! Then there will be no more empty talk over the dinner table. Honor? Love? Faith? Courage? They will become suddenly tangible truths that stand before you and require you to make a choice. You will live out your Truth even to the death, or Truth will die inside you even if you survive.' Do you see what I am saying?"

"Forgive me." Josie did not look at him. Leafless branches reached up to touch the gray sky. She felt suddenly ashamed of her empty talk about principles and courage. In the face of reality, such talk was hypocrisy. She had seen the reality in Warsaw. Could she forget so soon? "I have made this into a philosophical debate, haven't I?"

"Perhaps debate is the beginning of courage. There are no righteous wars. There is only, regrettably, sometimes the necessity to fight. I would negotiate with the devil to stop what I know will come. But there are no words left to stop him. So I will stand with France and fight the devil for the sake of my own soul. Now we wait. When the waiting ends this spring, I know what real war will mean. When it comes to this place . . . to France, to us . . . you and me."

He pulled her against him. "I have already made so many wrong choices. Hurt so many. Thrown away so much. Everything important, wasted on my own selfishness. Now I may lose my life, when living is precious to me at last. But for the first time in a long time, I think I have found something—*someone*—to live for."

～ᗕᗝ～

David navigated the borrowed 1928 Citroën to the village nearest the snow-covered field where the Dornier had crashed. From there, an icy track led into the countryside. They stopped the car when they caught sight of a lone soldier standing guard beside an opening in a hedgerow. The trio of fliers piled out gratefully from the battered car's single seat and stretched.

As the three approached the short-statured French poilu, he came away from the hedge, shook his fist, and waved the bayonet on the end of his rifle in their faces. "Easy, mate," instructed Hewitt, pointing to the RAF badge on his cap. "We're the ones who shot down the German."

David looked past the guard, through the gap in the fence, toward the skeletal wreckage of the German bomber. What he saw chilled him worse than the wintry air. "Shut up, Hewitt," he urged. "Look!"

Though the rolling hills were barren for miles around, the fallen Dornier had crashed on top of a farmhouse. The nose had struck the roof dead center and punched a hole into the structure. Then both plane and farmhouse had burned together. Only two stone walls remained upright around the gutted interior.

The French soldier's head pivoted in the direction of the debris, and when he turned around, he was crying. *"La famille entier,"* he said. *"Tous ensemble."*

"What'd he say?" whispered Hewitt.

"He said, 'the whole family,'" Simpson muttered.

Outside the charred hulk of the house lay a row of bodies. They were all wrapped in tarps. Three of the bundles were very small indeed, only half the size of the others.

Hewitt was violently ill and had to be helped back to the road by David, who felt far from well himself. The three pilots packed into the Citroën again and drove away without speaking.

18

The Great Spiderweb

Jerome Jardin was desperate. He thought of the two American sisters, Madame Rose and Madame Betsy. He remembered the salami and the cabbage and imagined chicken boiling in a very large stewpot today.

Something would have to be done.

"I should throw you into the Seine and let the fish of Paris eat you!" Jerome gave Marie a threatening shake as he pulled her up the stone steps beneath the bridge that spanned the river. The rat balanced precariously on his shoulder. Compared to life with Jerome, surely Papillon's life with Uncle Jambonneau had been dull.

"No! Jerome! Please do not kill me," Marie wailed. She had been wailing all morning about her empty stomach, and Jerome was sick of it. She was picking up noisy habits from Madame Hilaire.

"I will use you for fish bait if you do not shut up! I will catch myself a big fish with your toes. And then I will only have myself to feed."

"I die anyway with the hunger!"

"Ingrate!" He shook her again and came very near to carrying out his threat to throw her off the steps of Quai d'Conti. A man riding his bicycle across Pont Neuf frowned down from the bridge with disapproval, and Jerome controlled his anger.

Jerome had done the best he could with breakfast. It had been raining early this morning when he left the barge for the market. The vendors had not wheeled their pushcarts onto the sidewalk of Rue de Mazarine lest their baguettes grow soggy, their cabbages mold. The capitalists had remained inside their warm shops where bells tinkled a warning above doors whenever anyone entered or left. It was difficult to steal a croissant when all the bread was inside the pâtisserie and under guard.

This morning at the pâtisserie the little bell had dinged and the overstuffed wife of the baker had looked down her long nose to see that it was Jerome who entered the shop. She announced his arrival very loudly to a dozen customers. They had all turned at once to stare at him as if he were a cockroach swimming in a bowl of soup, even though Jerome had left the rat at the boat.

"Look here, Papa. Is this a stray cat dripping on the clean floor? What sad brown eyes! Soaked clear to the skin! I will bet it is hungry, too."

"Look again, Madame. It is no cat but a scruffy river rat and the son of a rat. Madames and Monsieurs, hold tightly to your purses, if you please. Meet Jerome Jardin, unfortunate offspring of that drunken Communist clochard, who would rather sit on his filthy barge moored beneath Pont Neuf and read the works of Karl Marx than work an honest day. But of course! Little Jerome is here to rob us rotten capitalists again. You want to eat something, little rat? Go to the soup kitchens. We serve only honest citizens here. Out of my shop, if you please!"

On days when the street market was open Monsieur le Baker had no opportunity to humiliate Jerome. The boy was too quick for the fat man. It was easy enough to hide outside behind the baskets of the florist and wait until madame and monsieur were each busy with a customer and then . . . he would dash in, steal a baguette, and be gone. But it had been a long time since the days had been warm enough for that.

Now Madame Hilaire was gone again . . . somewhere. It was three days until Papa's letter would arrive and Madame Hilaire would make The Dinner. Jerome was not worried about this . . . not much. But it had been three days since Marie had eaten anything but the stale crusts Jerome had gathered from the garbage bins behind the Ritz. She was getting on his nerves. She did not appreciate that he had to scramble even to get bread from the garbage. They were not the only hungry Parisians these days. Refugees had crowded into the city, making it more difficult to scrounge.

"Where are you taking me?" Marie shrilled as he led her toward Pont Neuf and Quai Augustins, which followed the Left Bank of the Seine.

"We are going to eat," he said firmly, fixing his eyes on the great statue of Henri IV that towered above the center of the bridge. The old king had been melted once during the Revolution and had become cannons for Napoleon. Later someone had melted down a statue of Napoleon and made a new King Henri. Now he was back on the bridge overlooking Ile de la Cité.

Last summer the old king had attracted tourists who posed for pho-

tographs on the parapets and were often careless with wallets and handbags. Jerome had been a better provider in those days. The head and
shoulders of King Henri also served as a roost for pigeons. Pigeons were
easier than fish for Jerome to catch. Being fed by tourists, pigeons had no
concept that they could themselves be eaten. But today not even pigeons
cooed on the head of Henri.

A crisp wind assailed the two children as they trudged beside the
river. Marie's spindly legs turned pale blue beneath her ragged coat, and
her wail diminished to a whimper.

Jerome took Papillon from his shoulder and handed him to Marie.
"Put him in your shirt. He is cold." He said this not because the rat was
bothered by the cold but because Papillon's extra warmth against Marie's belly might help her.

"He will be warm there." She cradled the creature. "Thank you,
Jerome. Where will we eat?"

"The soup kitchen," he replied with the stern authority of a young
man of ten. Just then, across the river, the towers of Notre Dame came
into view beyond the buildings of the Prefecture of Police.

Marie balked. "No! Not the church, Jerome! Papa says they poison
people there!"

"Poison in the head, Marie." He tapped his finger against her temple
and softened a bit at her terror. Papa had been arrested many times and
taken to the fortress of buildings that flanked the cathedral. Sometimes
Jerome thought that Marie did not know the difference between Notre
Dame Cathedral and the police headquarters. Papa hated both places
with equal fervor. He was always talking against the charity of the soup
kitchens. Always he spoke about the priests as spiders waiting to pull the
unsuspecting person into a web of religion by feeding empty bellies.

"I do not want my head poisoned!" she insisted.

"If you do not eat, you will die of hunger before Madame Hilaire
comes back with potatoes. Or I may kill you to shut you up. You will eat
where I say or I will leave you somewhere terrible and not come back."

"Papa says the church is . . . the . . . something . . . of the people!"

"Opiate." Jerome glanced at his little sister with respect. Not bad for a
six-year-old. Marie had been learning her Marxist catechism well. Papa
had taught them both to read and cipher. He told them that the schools
of France were corrupt. It was better to stay home and learn the truth
than to attend public school and be filled with lies.

"What is op-i-ate?"

Jerome ran a hand over his face in frustration. Papa had taught the
words but not entirely the meaning. It was something terrible, he knew.
Something worse than death, according to Papa.

"It is . . . something . . . I don't know."

"They will lock us in cells because we are Marxists. Then Papa will beat us because of the charity soup kitchen." Marie sighed and shuddered. She was confused again. "I am scared." Papillon clambered up and poked his head out of her collar to have a look around.

"Are you more hungry than scared? Or more scared than hungry?" Jerome stopped in resignation at Pont St. Michel, the bridge that would take them to Notre Dame. He leaned against the parapet and stared off toward the twin towers of the cathedral, the great spiderweb of France.

How Papa hated the towers and the bells that rang out morning and evening! How he cursed the priests when the bells sounded! *"The people will not be free until every priest is strung up and Notre Dame is a gymnasium."* He often spit on the sidewalk after a priest walked by. He taught Jerome to spit as well. He seemed very pleased when Jerome spit first.

Marie was right. When Papa came back, he would beat them if he found out where they had gone. And surely someone would tell him. Maybe even Madame Hilaire, who often ate there when times were bad. Ile de la Cité was a small place. No doubt someone would see Marie and Jerome go into the soup kitchen. Someone would see Jerome there talking to a priest or a nun about the soup and bread. How could he spit on the floor of the people who fed him? Everyone knew how his father felt about the church.

Jerome could not see the line of people waiting to go into the Cloisters Soup Kitchen, but he knew it was there on the far side of the cathedral. Once a day at this time a line formed along the Rue du Cloitre, waiting to go into the cloisters, where the long tables were set and the nuns ladled out bowls of hot soup.

The wind cut through Jerome's thin cotton coat. Marie rested heavily against the stone wall and laid her head in her arms, careful not to crush Papillon.

"All right," she said miserably. "All right."

Jerome put his hand on her shoulder in a wave of pity. For Marie to agree to go to this place meant that she was very hungry indeed. "Maybe there is somewhere else. Another kitchen where no one will know we are the children of the clochard. If no one knows us, he will not hear about it. We can eat and . . ."

"But where, Jerome?" She raised her head slightly but did not try to stand without the help of the wall.

"Can you walk, *ma chèrie?*" he asked in a voice so kind that he surprised himself. He had not done well by Marie. He had eaten the best stuff himself. He had not cared for her as he should have.

"Very far?"

"Quai d'Orsay."

"So far?"

It was a long way for small legs carrying a hungry belly to go. "Only four kilometers back along the river. There is a place . . . they feed refugees and ragged people bread there. Beside a université. American . . ."

"But Papa hates the American."

"Those people do not even know how to speak French. How could they tell him we were there?"

Hope shone in her eyes. "Yes? And so?"

"There is a building that looks like a church. But it is not. We will go into the building that is not a church, even though it looks like one outside. So you will not have to be afraid. And there we will eat."

Marie nodded as he took her hand, more gently now. She had never been in any church. She would not know the difference if he did not tell. Her face was set. Small mouth turned down slightly as her dark eyes fixed on the farthest bridge she could see across the Seine. It was a long way.

"*Je marche!*" she said solemnly as they set out.

☙

This afternoon Lewinski carried his gas mask in a canvas shopping bag. He was less likely to be noticed without the thing on his face, he decided.

It was Christmas Eve. Lewinski had not bought gifts for either Andre or Paul, so now he strolled beside the open bookstalls on Quai des Grands Augustins, searching for some last-minute prize. The scent of roasting chestnuts filled the air. Lewinski bought a bag and munched them as he browsed through rare volumes in hopes of finding something not already on the shelves of the Chardon library.

American titles would be most appropriate. Herman Melville and *Moby Dick*? Washington Irving and *The Legend of Sleepy Hollow*? During his years of study in America, Lewinski had read every volume of the works of Mark Twain. *Roughing It* and *Huckleberry Finn* were not among Andre's classics. A pitiful oversight, Lewinski thought.

Andre needed help. Now that he was spending time with an American woman, he would certainly desire at least a rudimentary knowledge of American literature. He could not talk to the lady all day about wine and horses, could he? Well, yes, perhaps it was possible with Andre. But Lewinski had never found it possible to speak to a woman about anything unless he had prepared well ahead of time. Literature and art were always safe topics. If he spoke of physics or mathematics, nearly everyone but Albert looked at him as if he had dropped off the moon.

Albert. How Lewinski wished that Albert Einstein were here to discuss the enigma of Enigma with him. Together their two minds were flint and steel. The sparks would fly, and the riddle would be solved in no time!

Lewinski longed to send his old mentor a cablegram, but Andre had forbidden it. So instead he wrote it in his head as he walked:

HAPPY HOLIDAYS, DEAR ALBERT! I AM NOT DEAD!
I AM RICHARD LEWINSKI!

He laughed loudly at his own joke. Heads turned to see what was so amusing. But they did not hear it, so they did not know.

He jingled his change. Enough for *Roughing It* but not for a cablegram, too. Too bad. Such a message would cheer poor Albert up. No doubt Albert was also depressed over there in America. So many minds like his and Lewinski's had been extinguished here in Europe.

Lewinski found Andre a copy of Twain's masterpiece. He dipped into his pocket and fumbled with his change again. French money. So confusing.

"May I help you, Monsieur?" asked a young lady. She was a student from the look of her drab clothes and run-down shoes. But she had a pretty round face, brown eyes, and thick black hair beneath a blue beret.

He smiled at her. "Are you fond of the American author Mark Twain, Mam'zelle?"

She gazed up at him as if she had not understood the question.

Did he ask the question aloud or only think he said it? "I said . . . ," he began again.

"You are—" she unsheathed thick glasses and put them on—"Doctor Lewinski!" She said this very loudly.

Richard reached for his gas mask as heads turned. Two tough-looking fellows with determined expressions pivoted in unison to glare at Lewinski.

"You are mistaken. I am not."

"Pardon! But you *are* Doctor Lewinski! I heard you lecture at University of Berlin. Four years ago. A moment! My boyfriend is just there! He teaches mathematics now at the Sorbonne. He attended your lectures each week . . . oh, Jan! Look here! It is Doctor Lewinski!"

"No, it is not." Lewinski backed away as panic welled up in him.

She turned aside for an instant. "But I remember . . ."

Lewinski slapped down his payment for the book and hurried off. The young woman called after him. The two toughs put their hands into the pockets of their overcoats as if they had guns.

The woman smiled and waved as she shouted down the quai, "Merry Christmas, Doctor Lewinski! I am so glad that you are not . . ."

". . . dead." Richard finished her sentence as he rushed across Pont Neuf and forgot to turn toward home.

ॐ

The organ of the Cathedral of St. John was miraculously intact. The steps leading to the organ loft were blown away, so Horst watched as an old man in the robes of a musician climbed a ladder to reach his instrument. He was followed by two boys who would tread the bellows. There were a few moments of wheezing as the bellows awoke; then the building rang with the joyous strains of Bach's chorale *Nun Danket Alle Gott*—"Now Thank We All Our God." The music resounded through the shattered windows to the outside, drawing in still more worshippers from the streets until the place was packed. Still there was room enough on each side of Horst for several more to crowd in.

The melody of Bach formed a sharp contrast to the somber congregation. In the vast sea of people, Horst could see no spot of holiday color in their attire. Black dresses, shawls, and scarves adorned old and young women and girls alike. Old men and young boys wore black coats and sweaters. Their complexions all reflected varying degrees of the same shade of gray.

Horst's gray green uniform made him stand out from everyone. The presence of a German officer at the mass seemed as inappropriate to the prevailing mood as the music of Bach. He caught the fearful glances of the Poles who worshipped here. *"Why does he not go with his own kind?"* their eyes seemed to ask. Was it not a fact that the German military had their own army of priests and pastors who preached the doctrines of the Reich and spread their poison even on this holy day? Why then was this German major disturbing what small comfort the faithful found in this sacred place?

How could they know that he was not the one they should fear? Horst knew he was not the only German attending this afternoon's Christmas Eve Mass at the cathedral. He easily spotted the plainclothes Gestapo agents among the congregation. While men and women knelt in prayer, the Gestapo looked on with disdain and scribbled notes and phrases from the Father Kopecky's sermon in black notebooks. From the diligence of these agents, Horst was certain that the days of the diminuitive priest were numbered.

And what was the priest's crime? Today he preached the old sermon—the same story Horst had heard every Christmas Eve as a child growing up in Germany. Yet now, in the context of Poland, the story of the birth of a Jewish baby in a manger took on a new and irritating significance to the servants of Hitler. Horst knew their questions:

Was there some political reason the priest dwelt on the jealousy of King Herod and the murder of every baby boy in Bethlehem in an attempt to destroy the foretold Messiah?

What did the priest really mean when he spoke about the desperate flight of Joseph and Mary from the slaughter? He used the word *refugee*. Was he drawing parallels, perhaps?

Why mention the death of the tyrant of that age and compare it to the victory of the one life that began in the degradation of a stable? Was he intimating the treasonous hope that the Führer would perish?

And why did he mention that the child was a Jew descended from Abraham? Surely he knew the edicts of the Führer on the unfortunate matter of the Jewish heritage of Christ.

Why did he read aloud those promises of Old Testament prophets whose writings were now banned in all churches of the Reich?

Horst saw suspicion and judgment in the faces of the Gestapo as the crowd filed out. Father Kopecky had condemned himself—not because he had uttered one word different from the Christmas story told in all previous years but because the story itself was the ultimate reproof of all tyranny. The ancient tale could be taking place at that moment in Warsaw, could it not? Simply substitute Nazis as the antagonists determined to slaughter every Jewish child in Poland.

Horst considered that perhaps he had never really understood the story before now. Like the minions of Hitler who had mingled today with the faithful of Warsaw, he had also listened with new interest.

Thinking that he would warn the priest about the hostile members of the congregation, Horst lagged behind. The booming organ fell silent. The organist descended from his perch. Nearing the high arch of the foyer, Horst noticed three of the Nazi officials conferring beside a massive pillar pocked by shrapnel. Horst averted his eyes before he drew attention to himself. Leaving the building, he determined that he would come back later and inform the priest of the danger.

19

A Strange Entourage

As Jerome and his sister, Marie, walked toward the American church, the Paris shops began to close early because of the holiday. Traffic thinned out as men and women hurried to get ready for family gatherings and midnight Mass. It seemed that all of France had become religious again since the war.

Jerome had not remembered that everything in the city closed up tight on Christmas Eve. From the great Louvre to the lowliest butcher shop, the signs were hung and the doors were locked. This fact worried Jerome. It seemed that he and Marie were the only two in Paris who were headed away from home.

"How much longer? I am tired, Jerome."

Marie looked like a half-drowned cat. Brown hair hung in limp strands around her face, her ears protruding like the open doors of a taxi. Her clothes were soaked through, which had to be unpleasant for her and poor Papillon as well. Shoes that were already too large got bigger with every puddle. Her feet shuffled on the sidewalk, and she lagged farther and farther behind her brother.

Jerome stopped in front of a closed bakery. He put his hands on his hips and tried to look stern, but she was so pathetic that he could not. "You need to walk more quickly, Marie."

"Why are the shops closed?" She bit her lip and stared at the display of pastries in the unlit window. "Where is everyone?"

"You can see that all of Paris is closing and going home for roast goose. It is the night before Christmas. The food at the soup kitchen will be better than every other day. We should hurry." He looked at the threatening sky. Soon it would begin to snow. Night would surely come before they got back to the *Garlic*.

Marie leaned against the stone facade of the shop. "Can I wait for you? You can run ahead and bring back roast goose for me and Papillon."

"No," he snapped. Taking her by the arm, he pulled her along. "I never said that we would have roast goose. Other people have it on Christmas. We will have . . . something else. I do not know what. But you will be glad we walked so far. It will be warm there, and the food will be good. You'll see."

He was talking now just to keep her on her feet and moving. She did not reply. Her eyes were dull. It was too cold for her to be out without a much heavier coat. Her sweater underneath was drenched as well.

Jerome spotted the ornate spire of the American church rising above the buildings. "There it is, Marie! It only looks like a church, but it is not," he lied.

Marie lifted her face and blinked against the raindrops. Jerome thought that maybe now it no longer mattered to Marie what the place was. As long as she could eat and be warm.

"Good," she said, and at last her legs began to move a bit faster.

The last two blocks were not as difficult. Marie did not ask to stop and rest even one time.

There was no line of hungry people winding down the street like at the cloisters of Notre Dame. "Everyone is already inside eating," he told her.

There were no sandbags heaped outside. Jerome explained that this was because the Americans were not at war with Hitler, so their building would not be bombed.

Jerome helped Marie up the broad stone steps. For a moment they stood before the bronze doors, deciding where to go in. Jerome pushed hard on the biggest door. It swung back easily, and the two tumbled onto the hard stone floor of the lobby. Beyond them, the church was dimly illuminated by the soft colors of stained-glass windows on each side.

Jerome had sneaked into a church before, and he knew that this was how a church was supposed to look. Very old. High, arched ceiling. Stone columns. Candles in golden stands at the front—and a large cross behind a big table that was covered with a red-velvet cloth. A bright red banner with golden words in English hung down from the ceiling. And there were rows and rows of benches with red cushions on the seats. In an alcove behind the pulpit was a large oil painting of a kind-looking man. It was very serene and beautiful. This was all part of what made it so dangerous, Papa said.

Today this church was also very empty.

"Keep Papillon out of sight," he warned as the head of the rat protruded from between two buttons of Marie's dress front. "Soup kitchens are very strange about pets like Papillon. They will think he is a rat."

Marie shuddered. "Where are the people? The food?" Her voice echoed hollowly.

"Maybe in the cellar." Jerome bit his lip. He hoped he had not made a mistake. Where was the cellar? He pointed at the steps at the far end of the foyer. "There." He held her hand and guided her down the stairs.

"It is nice here," Marie said hoarsely.

"Warm," he agreed, hoping they had not arrived too late for the food.

At the bottom of the steps was a long corridor with dark wooden doors on either side. Jerome tried all the latches, but all the doors were locked. At the far end of the corridor was another set of stairs leading up. The two ascended, only to find themselves in the very front of the large auditorium. There was no soup kitchen, no roast goose. Only this big, peaceful, empty building.

Marie sank down onto the front pew and began to cry very softly. "I was too slow," she moaned. Her tears mingled with the water dripping from her hair. She was shivering through her wet clothes in spite of the fact that the interior of the building was much warmer than outside. "They ate without us."

Jerome sat beside her and stared numbly at the red banner and the golden English words written on it and the red velvet cloth on the long table. He sighed. "It is my fault. I brought you all this way for nothing."

He glared at the picture of the kind man in the alcove. The figure had a beard and wore a long white robe like a nightshirt. One hand held a lantern, and the other knocked on a door that looked very much like all the locked doors downstairs.

"This is why Papa hates you"—he lifted his voice to the vaulted ceiling—"and now I will hate you forever also. We come all this way, my sister and me and Uncle Jambonneau's dog, and you are not really here. We will go away cold and with empty bellies from this place that looks like a church but is not a church."

"It is . . . a church. . . ." Marie trembled harder now. Her teeth chattered. She could not get warm even with Papillon snuggled against her. She had nothing in her stomach to help her get warm. She needed a blanket.

For the first time it occurred to Jerome that she might die if she was not warmed and fed very soon. He felt afraid. "I am sorry I brought you here, Marie," he said bitterly. "Yes, it is a church. I thought you would not come if you knew. It doesn't matter. Now you see Papa is right."

"What is your papa right about?" asked a muffled voice behind them.

Jerome whirled around to face a creature as horrible as the gargoyles that gaped down from the facade of Notre Dame. Marie gave a little cry and covered her face with her hands. The thing looked something like the head of a locust attached to the body of a man. The tails of a heavy red-checked flannel shirt stuck out from baggy corduroy trousers held up by suspenders.

Jerome leaped up and doubled his fists in defense against the monster who cackled wildly. Then Jerome realized that the thing was not a thing but a man in a gas mask.

Unruly red hair protruded like wire from the rubber thongs of the mask. With an odd sucking sound, like water going down a slow drain, the man pulled the mask back on top of his head. "What are you doing here?" he asked Jerome.

"We just came to eat something." Jerome was defiant.

"Yes." The man stared around the place as if he was looking for something, too. "Where is supper?"

"But there is nothing to eat in your church."

"Not my church. I'm Lewinski." He cackled again as if his name explained everything. "No one is here. I was hoping to use the telephone, but there is no telephone that I can find." He walked slowly up to Marie, who peered up at him in terror through her fingers. "What is wrong with her?" Lewinski asked, glancing at the alarm clock that was tied around his waist by a length of twine.

"She is hungry and wet," Jerome said. "Leave her alone."

"Why do you not feed her and get her a blanket?" Lewinski glanced over his shoulder as he said the words, giving the odd impression that he was addressing someone behind him. Then he bounded up the low steps to the altar at the front. He looked upward and touched the gas mask on his head as if in salute. "You can plainly see the little girl is cold and wet."

Like a magician in a performance at the Tuileries gardens, he pulled the red-velvet cloth from the altar.

Marie gasped from behind him. "Jerome, look! Look what is here for us!"

It was like magic. Marie applauded. On the marble table, three braided loaves of bread were heaped on a large brass plate. Beautiful loaves they were, with golden crusts, baked to perfection. Had there ever been such beautiful loaves of bread?

"How did you do that?" Jerome cried. He had always been impressed with magicians.

"Well, I do not know." Lewinski seemed surprised by his trick. "But dinner is served." He scratched his head and tossed the red cloth to

Marie. "You will look very nice in that color, Mam'zelle. And warm. Well, well! Put it on!"

Jerome gaped at the feast and then, with a whoop, he joined Lewinski, who tossed a loaf into Jerome's arms. The boy ran to Marie. "Get up! We have to get out of here quick before he changes his mind!"

Marie had an odd smile on her face, as if she knew some wonderful secret. She stood up on unsteady legs. She raised her face ever so slightly toward Lewinski. "Thank you, Monsieur," she whispered. Then, "Are you . . . a priest?"

The hall reverberated with Lewinski's laughter.

"Well then . . . an angel?"

Lewinski howled and fell to the ground at the humor of such a question. Tears streamed from his eyes. Then suddenly he stopped laughing and stood up. "I am lost," he announced in a very serious tone. "I went out shopping and realized that I was somewhere else."

"Somewhere else besides where?" Jerome sniffed and eyed Lewinski suspiciously. He was almost certain that this fellow must be an inmate escaped from the lunatic asylum. If so, he was quite far from his place of residence.

"Andre will be looking for me," Lewinski said. "Last time they called the police. Or the police called Andre. It is very dangerous for me to be out alone, they tell me. But you two look harmless enough." He bowed to Marie. "And you look very pretty in your red blanket, Mam'zelle. Also you have a rat climbing out of your collar."

She giggled as Papillon emerged and leaped from her shoulder to the arm of Jerome. Jerome nudged her in the ribs for silence.

Yes. So it was the asylum, after all. Jerome took Marie firmly by the arm and stepped back. "We have to be going now."

Lewinski frowned. "Do you know the way to No. 19 Quai d'Anjou?"

"*Oui!* On l'Ile!" Marie clapped her hands, obviously carried away by the clownlike appearance of the lunatic Lewinski. "We will take you home."

"No, Marie," Jerome hissed.

"Yes, we will!" Marie tore free from Jerome and ran to the side of Lewinski, who cackled with relief, checked his alarm clock, and replaced the mask.

"Marie! You heard him! Police!"

"*Oui!* He is magic. He got me a blanket and made the bread appear." She took Lewinski's hand. Lewinski tore off half a loaf of bread from his hoard and presented it to his guide. She broke off a piece for Lewinski, who could not eat it because of his rubber mask. Together they marched up the center aisle and out onto the street, with Jerome trailing at a safe distance behind them.

⟨◎⟩

David and Simpson had decided between them that they would drive to Nancy instead of returning directly to Rouvres. "If we go back to the base too soon, everyone will want to know what we made of the crash," David suggested.

"Too right," Simpson agreed. "Besides, it's Christmas Eve, and we've need of some good cheer."

Hewitt shivered but offered neither argument nor support for the plan; he only sat with a stunned look and stared out at the French countryside.

David pushed the protesting Citroën to its maximum speed, wanting to reach Nancy before the darkness and the blackout restrictions made travel more difficult. The icy roads were deserted except for one farmer and a wagon drawn by an ancient draft horse. The car swung through the wrought-iron-encircled Place Stanislaus and into the crooked medieval lane named the Grand Rue just as the sun was setting.

"Here we are then," Simpson pronounced grandly, trying to lighten the mood. "The Excelsior Brasserie—finest food and drink in at least . . . five kilometers."

Hewitt shook his head as if waking up from a long and especially unpleasant nightmare. He pointed at the number of impressively uniformed men going in and out of the Excelsior and finally spoke. "I don't know," he said doubtfully. "There's a lot of blokes about. Can't we find someplace a bit quieter?"

"Nonsense," Simpson reassured him. "None of these are our chaps, Hewitt. Most of them aren't even soldiers. By their uniforms they're either North American correspondents or South American dictators. Either way, they're no concern of ours. Come on."

Three bottles of the local red wine improved the spirits of the trio, and their returning appetites led to the consumption of enough potato-and-rabbit pie to have served twice their number.

David was relieved when Hewitt leaned back in his chair and looked much more his usual self when he patted his stomach and belched. An extravagant stretch backward brought one of his large hands into abrupt contact with the back of an American correspondent's head.

At Hewitt's apology, the correspondent scooted his chair around to the table with the pilots. "RAF," he noted. "I thought so. Two English and one American? Fighter pilots."

"Right," David agreed.

"What gave us away?" Simpson inquired. "Our keen eyes and deadly serious expressions?"

The correspondent laughed. Hewitt's eyes were anything but keen, and his goofy grin was not at all serious. "Yeah, that's it exactly. Anyway, you three are in a lot better shape than the other fliers I bumped into tonight."

"Is that so? What was wrong with them?" David asked.

"Couple German prisoners out of a plane shot down by some of your boys. One's busted up pretty bad and the other's burned. They got brought here for treatment; then they'll be sent on to Paris."

David and Simpson snapped to attention as Hewitt struggled to follow along.

"Did you catch what sort of craft?" David asked. "That is, where did this happen?"

"A Dornier. Shot down between here and Verdun."

"Quick, man! Where did you meet these two?" Simpson demanded.

"They're under guard upstairs, not that they could . . ."

David tossed a few franc notes onto the table and was halfway to the stairs as the newsman called after them, "Hey, what's the rush?"

Hewitt staggered to his feet, but even so was only a few steps behind David and Simpson. "Because," he remarked over his shoulder in a rush of slurred words, "we're the lot who put 'paid' to that beggar."

David had no difficulty talking his way past the guard outside the door at the top of the stairs. Apparently this poilu—like the keeper of a small menagerie of dangerous beasts—had been making a profit by charging admission to any who wanted to view the Nazi aviators.

But the first sight of the two prisoners gave David no impression of menace. He eyed them with an unexpected and unwelcome sense of guilt. As if he had accidentally injured an opponent in a football game and needed to find a way to apologize. What could he say to these two young men, his enemies?

The first German had a thick shock of dark hair. His thin face was boyish and worried. He was still wearing a ragged flight suit from the waist up, but his legs were in plaster casts from ankles to thighs.

The other man was wearing a bathrobe. His head was so swathed in layers of bandages that only a pair of glaring, bloodshot eyes could be seen. His hands were similarly rolled in white gauze. It occurred to David that if it were not for the bare feet that showed below the robe, the German would have seemed to be a very thoroughly wrapped mummy.

David, who had a rudimentary grasp of the German language, became the spokesman for the group. "I don't know if you understand English or not," he began; then he introduced himself and the others in clumsy German. "We are the Hurricane pilots who shot down your Dornier. We are glad that you made it out all right."

"I speak English," replied the man with the broken legs. "I am Unteroffizer Hammel. Klinger is here." He gestured toward his companion. "We—" he searched for the words—"parachute . . . three others in our crew did not."

"We . . . we know. . . ." The vision of the wrecked Dornier and the lingering odor rose fresh in David's imagination, causing his stomach to churn. "How did two of you survive? We only saw one chute."

"Ja," answered Hammel with a shrug. "I carry Klinger. His hands so burn . . . jump we together. The weight is too great and my legs . . . who can think snow will be so hard?" Tears welled up in his eyes. "But we will not have lived if you . . . continue shooting. We are told you English fire on parachutes."

"We would not do that!" Simpson remarked with horror.

"We would!" snapped a voice from beneath layers of gauze.

David had supposed that the burned man spoke no English, but now it was apparent that he spoke it well and that he had plenty to say.

"We do not believe in letting an enemy escape!" Klinger added with venom. "If we had been in a Messerschmitt, the outcome would have been far different!"

"You feel this way, too?" David asked Hammel.

"I . . . it is hard to . . ." Hammel caught a ferocious glare from Klinger and subsided in misery. "War is a terrible thing," he concluded lamely.

"Come on, Tinman," said Simpson, moving toward the door and pushing Hewitt ahead of him. "We've done what we came for." Halfway down the stairs he remarked, "Officer Hammel probably has family back in Germany."

ℚ⧉

It was a strange entourage that paraded through the streets of Paris at sunset. Jerome followed ten paces behind Lewinski and Marie. She was wrapped in yards of bright red cloth stolen from the church. Wiry red tufts of the madman's hair protruded through the straps of the dark green rubber gas mask as if Lewinski's head were a flowering weed.

Jerome thought about calling out for help. After all, their route to Quai d'Anjou led right past the Palais de Justice. Normally all the gendarmes in the world stood around under the awnings on the Ile de la Cité smoking their Gauloises and chatting. But today, what with the showers, the cold wind sweeping down the river, and it's being Christmas Eve, there were no blue-jacketed figures in view.

Sighing heavily, Jerome thought that perhaps it was just as well. He and the law were not on the best of terms anyway. How could he explain about the altar cloth? Jerome's father had taught him that the police were the arm of the oppressive power of the privileged classes—whatever that meant. Something to stay away from, no doubt.

But how to get Marie free from what was obviously a lunatic. There she was, clinging to Lewinski's hand and chattering away like a magpie. Jerome could have strangled her.

The lunatic Lewinski led the little procession across the rain-slick pavement of Pont St. Louis. The red-haired figure pushed the gas mask up on his forehead and divided another chunk of the magic bread with Marie. They seemed to have forgotten that Jerome was still behind them, fretting and worrying.

At last the Quai de Bourbon became the Quai d'Anjou, and Lewinski pointed to the curve up ahead as if he recognized a landmark. Now what?

Lewinski and Marie were walking very carefully, staring down at the paving stones. Jerome could see they were being very cautious about not stepping on any of the cracks in the sidewalk. It made Jerome watch where he was stepping, too, until they had passed the bend in the road. Then Jerome abruptly looked up.

There, not half a block away, was a police car. It sat in front of the house to which Lewinski was leading Marie. It was a trap!

"Run, Marie!" Jerome yelled, sprinting up behind his sister and yanking her hand loose from Lewinski's grip. "Run, I say! He is trying to turn us in to the police!"

Jerome dragged a stumbling Marie away from Lewinski and back down the block. When they came to an alleyway, he ducked in, pulling Marie in after him.

Marie was blubbering. "I did not get to tell him thank you for the bread."

20

The Promise Is Fulfilled

At the evening appearance of Horst von Bockman in the foyer of the Cathedral of St. John, the old custodian leaned against his broom and stared fearfully at the heap of dust on the floor. He crossed himself as if he was in the presence of great evil.

"I am looking for Father Kopecky," Horst said, stamping the snow from his boots before proceeding across the newly swept flagstones.

The old man cleared his throat nervously and probed at his ear with a bony finger. He did not acknowledge Horst.

"It is important that I see your priest, old man." Horst had no time for guessing games. "For the sake of his safety."

The *swish* of the broom against the stone was the only reply. The custodian nudged the heap of debris toward the entrance as though he were the only one there.

Horst tried again. "You must believe me. I am a friend of his. Will you take him a message? Tell him Major Horst von Bockman has come to say good-bye. I leave for Berlin tonight. Tell him it is urgent that I speak with him."

The thin face looked up slowly. Beneath bushy eyebrows, dark eyes glinted with unconcealed hatred and mistrust. The old man leaned his broom against a stone column and, without a backward glance, padded down the long aisle and vanished in the shadows of the auditorium. Horst heard the creak of heavy hinges and then a strange metallic rattle, like sabers clashing, before the unseen door slammed shut again, blocking out the sound.

There was no heat in the building, and Horst's breath rose in a steaming vapor. He blew on his hands and stamped his feet against the cold. Pacing the length of the foyer and back again, he considered how meaningless this visit was. What difference would it make if he told the priest that he had been watched? that his words had been recorded in little black books?

"Merry Christmas, Major von Bockman."

Horst turned at the priest's voice.

Father Kopecky was alone. "We will have no midnight Mass tonight. The curfew, you know."

"I did not come for that, Father. I wish it were that simple."

The cleric was coatless yet smiling as though he did not notice the cold breeze blowing through his church.

"I was at the afternoon Mass."

"I saw you. I could not help but notice. You were the only one not dressed in mourning." The priest shrugged. "I was glad you came."

"There were three Gestapo officers there as well."

"Only three?" Father Kopecky was not surprised, nor was he alarmed.

"Probably more. But I saw three myself. There is no mistaking their kind, although they attempt to blend in."

"The presence of the secret police is to be expected these days, is it not? It is cold here since we lost the windows. Would you like to go where it is warmer?" Taking Horst by the arm, Father Kopecky led him through the cathedral to the maze of vaulted corridors in the cloisters. Before a heavy wooden door he stopped and looked up at Horst. The odd clacking sound penetrated the wood. "I knew you would come tonight."

"How could you know that?"

"I knew." He pulled down the latch to open the door. The corridor was filled with light and warmth and happy voices that bubbled up from a steep stairway. The priest made no move to enter but stepped aside so Horst might peer down into a deep storage cellar that now served as a dining room. Long tables set among the pillars were packed with several hundred children who laughed and talked over tin plates laden with thick stew. It was the banging of spoons against the plates that had reminded Horst of clashing swords. Horst spotted four nuns carrying pots and ladles. The sisters glided behind the benches to cheer the diners and refill empty bowls. The din was deafening.

"Three hundred and twenty-six children. Each has lost mother and father. Some were brought to us, but many made their way on their own. Some from Warsaw. Others from a great distance. Look at them, Horst. Look at their faces."

Horst gazed at a table packed with young boys who wagged their spoons in conversation and laughed at some joke that was lost to Horst beneath the racket.

"I am glad to see happy children on Christmas Eve. I am cheered by it . . . by your good work for them."

"Yes." The priest's voice was not so joyful. "I want you to remember them. Think of it. Any one of them might be the child of one of the men you saw crucified or the woman who sank into the Vistula."

Horst's pleasure vanished. "Why do you say such a thing to me?" He stepped back from the doorway as though he had been kicked.

The priest closed the door on the scene and shrugged as if the reason for his cruel statement was obvious. "Each of them has a story much like the one you told me. They are only children, yet all have come here along the path of grief and brutality. They are not here by their own choice. Others made this choice for them. German soldiers."

"I did not come to hear this," Horst snapped. "What can I do to change that now? It is not my responsibility." He caught himself and began again. "At some risk to myself, I came to warn you. The Gestapo . . . the SS."

"Thank you. I am warned."

Horst stared bleakly at the black door. "You do not care if you are arrested . . . but what about the children? What will become of them?"

"You know the answer."

The vision of the future exploded in Horst's mind as though it were already the past:

The priest was tortured by the Gestapo and hanged. The sisters imprisoned. They died of hunger, dysentery, and typhus. Those little boys who laughed and talked over their tin bowls this Christmas were herded into a room and stripped naked. They were sorted like animals being prepared for market—Jew from Gentile. This was easiest with male children because of the practice of circumcision among the Jews. Those confirmed or suspected of being Jewish were liquidated. The Polish children were placed in Nazi detention centers, where they were abused and starved and taught to read a few necessary German commands and trained in the proper attitude toward the Reich, the Führer, and their Aryan masters. Most of them perished, too, before it was over. . . .

Horst covered his face with his hands to shut out the images. "What do you want from me? I cannot undo what is past!"

"It is in your power to change tomorrow. I knew you would be here." Father Kopecky put his hand on Horst's shoulder. "Come with me now."

Horst followed him down the shadowed corridor, although he wanted to turn and run the other way. The children were singing in the cloister now. Christmas carols. Happy voices pursued the priest and the major until they turned a corner and entered a warm and quiet room with ten cribs and a dozen sleeping infants. Christ, crucified, looked down from the wall above them.

An elderly nun sat in a rocking chair near the coal fire. She held a baby boy a little over a year old in her arms. She curled his dark hair around her gnarled finger. He sucked milk from a bottle and kicked one foot free of the blanket as if in time to the old woman's lullaby. She touched the tiny toes and tucked the blanket over his foot again. The slurping sound stopped a moment as the boy gazed at the old woman with trusting blue eyes and gurgled in happy response to her humming.

Father Kopecky glanced up sharply at Horst. Was the future clear in the priest's mind as to the fate of these little ones as well? Horst wondered.

"Enough," Horst whispered, staggering back to lean against the wall. His stricken face reflected in the glass of a picture of Christ surrounded by children.

"You are here tonight as one of God's footsteps," the priest replied quietly. "You came tonight because tomorrow may be too late."

"There is nothing I can do to help these—" Horst waved his hand over the room as if it were already empty.

"You can save one."

"Save?"

"It is in your hands now to change the future of one."

"How can I . . . ?"

"I have a plan."

"You're talking nonsense, Father."

"You must do exactly as I instruct you. It came to me clearly as I prayed."

"How can anyone choose which of all these? It is impossible to save one while the others . . ."

The priest gestured toward the painting of Christ encircled by children. "Jesus said, *'Whoever welcomes a little child like this in My name welcomes Me.'* Don't you see, Horst? How God loves them! Their angels are constantly before His throne. To have compassion on a child . . . there is no act so holy. It is as if you carry the Christ child in your arms!"

Horst raised his eyes as the baby leaned his head against the old woman's shoulder. Heavy eyelids began to droop in contentment. A drop of milk dripped from the corner of his mouth and clung to the black fabric of her habit.

Father Kopecky took the child from her and laid him in Horst's arms. "It is Christmas, little one. The sword of the tyrant is poised above all the children of Israel again. You must go." And then to Horst, who cradled the little boy with awkward gentleness, the priest said gently, "To save one small life, Horst. Perhaps one day the world might be saved by that life. His name is Yacov Lubetkin."

ᏀᎠ

The mess hall of the Maginot Fortress echoed with the sounds of shouts, laughter, and loudly sung, off-key Christmas carols. Mac had to lean close to Murphy's ear and yell to make himself heard. "Do you s'pose these guys would even know if they were under attack?"

"Not unless they took a direct hit," Murphy shouted back. "They're making more noise than an artillery barrage now."

The Christmas Eve scene inside the underground French fortification was one of raucous merriment. As Mac and Murphy watched, one corner of the room erupted with men pelting each other with pieces of bread. Across the huge, concrete-walled chamber, another set of four soldiers climbed up on the table and began an impromptu cancan, accompanied by whistles and lewd suggestions.

"How long will this go on?" Mac bellowed, giving the cancan dancers ten seconds of film time.

"Till dawn," Murphy replied, "except for a short interruption at midnight for Mass."

Mac took a step back to change the way the scene was framed in the viewfinder of his new camera and stumbled over an empty wine bottle underfoot.

Murphy caught Mac by the elbow to keep him from falling. "And they better pray for a hangover cure at that Mass. If the Germans attack tomorrow, these guys will surrender at the sight of an aspirin bottle."

Mac turned at a tap on his shoulder. A French artillery captain started to say something to the two journalists, then shrugged because of the noise and gestured for them to follow him. When the three had gotten into the corridor and closed a steel door on the merrymaking, the officer tried again. "The colonel would like you to join him for a late Christmas Eve supper."

Up two flights of concrete steps and down two long corridors that rang with the passage of their boots, they arrived at the officers' dining room. Once there, Mac and Murphy were introduced to Colonel Benet, the commandant.

To Mac, Benet looked like a marshal of France from the time of Napoleon. He was an elderly man but tall and straight, and he carried himself with ramrod correctness. The shock of white hair combed back from his high forehead was matched by the gleaming sweep of an elegant mustache. Among the medals and ribbons on his uniform was the Croix de Guerre.

"Please be seated, gentlemen," the colonel urged. "We have just enough time for an aperitif before the meal."

A junior officer rapped on a connecting door, and a nervous soldier dressed in a white apron entered, pushing a serving trolley.

"I must apologize for the poor quality of our hospitality," the colonel said, "but there is a war on, you know." The soldier-waiter offered each officer a choice of whiskey, sherry, port, Madeira, Armagnac, or any of a dozen other liqueurs.

"I am a banker in civilian life," Colonel Benet explained over the first course of the supper—bowls of vichyssoise. "But old soldiers never die, as they say, so I dusted off my uniform from the Great War and returned to duty."

"And are you expecting to have to fight the Great War over again?" Murphy asked.

"The Germans are without imagination," the colonel maintained, carefully brushing the ends of his mustache with a linen napkin. "Right now they are holding back because they realize what an error they have made to come to blows with us at all. Sooner or later Herr Hitler will have to launch an attack—to save face, of course—and when it is repulsed, the politicians will settle things."

Mac accepted a plate of roast pork with cauliflower in cheese sauce from the waiter and allowed the colonel to swallow a sip of wine before raising another question. "And your men are ready to face a German attack?"

Spreading his broad hands, the commandant gave an expressive shrug. "But of course! You have seen for yourself what good spirits they are in. Here we are, on our own soil, behind the greatest fortifications in the history of the world. How could we be more ready?"

The colonel studied his platter of food and then in an abrupt change of subject said, "Our cook is just like the Boche . . . completely without imagination!"

When supper concluded, Mac asked, "Has there been any activity by the Germans in your sector? Could we go to one of your lookout posts and get a peek across the line?"

Colonel Benet cleared his throat with disapproval. "I was going to suggest that we adjourn to the auditorium. The enlisted men are putting on an amateur musical performance. It should be very droll."

"With respect, Colonel," Murphy added, "just a quick look at what the other side is up to."

"Very well," Benet grumbled, "but you will not see anything. Nothing going on tonight, I can promise you."

The observation platform of the fort was four stories above the mess hall and directly above the outpost's armament of 75 mm cannons. The sentry on lone guard duty stamped his feet against the wintry air that swirled in through the open small-arms ports. He snapped to attention as his commandant arrived, and Mac wondered what crime the man was being punished for to draw this duty tonight.

"Anything to report?" asked the colonel.

"Nothing, sir," answered the guard, "except that it has been snowing again."

"What about that light over there?" Mac asked, pointing to a faint yellow glow that dimly outlined a knobby hill about a half mile off.

"Ah, that," snorted Benet. "That is Spichern Hill. Until recently it belonged to us, but a patrol of Boche crept round behind it and captured it." His tone sounded as if he thought the Germans had done something unfair. As if they had not played by the rules or cheated somehow. "We will retake it, never fear."

"There seems to be some movement going on there now," Murphy observed. "In fact, the light is brighter now than it was when we first looked, and it seems to be moving toward the top of the hill."

"Shall I ring the battery and give the order to fire?" asked the sentry, stepping toward a telephone on the wall.

"Absolutely not!" corrected the colonel, his mustache quivering with indignation. "How can you think of such uncivilized behavior? They are enjoying a quiet Christmas celebration the same as we. Why should we do something so antagonistic? Come now, we've seen enough. Let us adjourn to the auditorium. I am sure the singing is already in progress."

⊙෨

A soundless snowfall dropped onto the outlines of Spichern Heights. Sturmann Geiger hunched his shoulders against the cold of the Western Front. It was a mistake. The movement caused a tiny avalanche to cascade off the back rim of his steel helmet and into the collar of his greatcoat. A thin stream of icy water trickled down his back, adding to his misery.

Sentry duty in the Saarbrücken sector was not enjoyable in December of 1939, and especially not on this cold and sodden Christmas Eve. The tree trunks below the ridge commanded by the pillbox were black skeletal forms against the snow. Geiger had seen dead men that looked like that: Polish soldiers killed by machine-gun fire and abandoned by their comrades, left hanging over fences to rot.

The quiet Western Front was different, to be sure, but in the lonely darkness, it was easy to conjure up all the spectres that haunted Geiger's dreams. Even the pride that the German soldier had felt at taking part in the capture of this tiny piece of French soil had frozen into a corner of his mind. He could take it out and examine it, but it refused to give warmth or comfort.

Instead he tried to shake off the oppressive dread by thinking about his home in Munich: the family gathered for a festive meal in a house filled with light, food, and warmth. But try as he might, he kept seeing phantoms lurking in the darkness and the reproachful stares on the remembered faces of the dead. He frowned and shook his head, reminding himself that just to the west, no more than a half mile or so away, a live French sentry was also standing guard, along with ten thousand of his fellows.

Wondering if the French would send out a patrol on this darkest night of the year made Geiger peer through the swirling flakes toward the French lines. Counting off ten paces to the end of his duty area, a slow pivot faced him back toward the concrete pillbox that guarded the unremarkable chunk of French territory called Spichern Heights.

Geiger snorted with the contempt shared by his entire regiment at the French defenses. This machine-gun emplacement was impressive enough in its solidity, but there was one major flaw: Like the entire strategy of the Maginot Line, its designers were so convinced of its invulnerability that its guns faced only toward Germany. There had been no allowance of either men or equipment that had prepared the French for the encircling German infantry patrol that had looped through the woods to attack Spichern Heights from the rear.

But that triumph had been some time before, and it was back to business as usual on the Western Front. Another hour to go before his relief showed up. It was difficult to judge the passage of time on the lonely walk, and it dragged all the more because Geiger stopped to listen to the night. The squishing of his boots made thin echoes that sounded as if someone else were marching when he marched and stopping when he stopped.

He made five circuits of his post before drowsiness began to replace his earlier terror. It was a cold, miserably wet night after all—nothing more. Geiger stopped again to listen, but it was more out of habit than expectation.

That was when he heard the footfalls . . . real ones that continued on though he stood rooted in place, his heart racing as apprehension flooded over him again. He tried to call out a challenge, but his voice was only a harsh croak of meaningless noise. His fingers fumbled with the safety catch of the rifle but were so numb that he could not tell if he had moved it or not.

Geiger forced himself to look down at his weapon, to visually determine what his sense of touch could not confirm. Yes, the catch was off. He raised the gun to his shoulder and sighted along its barrel . . . into a hazy yellow glow that had not been in front of him a moment before.

"Halt!" he cried, finding words as last. "Who goes there?"

An advancing mass, black against the frosty background, resolved itself into separate dark shapes approaching his position. "Halt!" he ordered again, "or I will—"

"*Achtung*, Sturmann Geiger!" the voice of the company commander demanded. "We are coming to inspect the post!"

The captain and four other figures moved with the glow of a shielded lantern to join the sentry on the ridge. Whether because of his earlier fear or because of the stiffness induced by his hours on guard, Geiger was slow in lowering his weapon. When he allowed its muzzle to drop, it slid across the form of a short man clad in a black leather coat.

A low chuckle came to the young man's ears. "Would you shoot your Führer?" a familiar rasping accent asked.

The Führer! Sturmann Geiger snapped to attention—or did his best—but the leader of the Third Reich paid him no further heed. Instead, Hitler addressed the men in his entourage. There was a tone of smug satisfaction in his voice. "In 1918 I vowed to never again stand on French soil until I could give it to the Fatherland! Tonight that promise is fulfilled! You and your men, Captain, have made it possible."

The captain made a modest rejoinder that the emplacement was a very small attainment in the scope of the war, but Hitler interrupted him.

"*I* am Germany," the Führer said, "and the ground where I stand is symbolic of *all* of France." His voice rose in pitch and trembled with excitement. "Of the whole world! I stretch out my hand toward the west so . . . and it is as if it were already taken!"

The Führer swung a Nazi salute over the hilltop at Spichern Heights . . . and over the whole of the darkened earth.

PART III

And though this world, with devils filled,
Should threaten to undo us,
We will not fear, for God hath willed
His truth to triumph through us.
The prince of darkness grim,
We tremble not for him—
His rage we can endure,
For lo! his doom is sure:
   One little word shall fell him.

21

On the Edge of the Abyss

Horst von Bockman carried Yacov Lubetkin in a wicker laundry basket packed with diapers, one baby bottle, and two cans of milk. The aged sister at the Cathedral of St. John had warned Horst that the fourteen-month-old baby was getting another tooth and that if he should fuss, the best thing for it was straight rye whiskey smeared on the gums.

But baby Yacov did not fuss. Wide-awake now, he smiled up at Horst. In the Warsaw train station he squealed happily as an SS colonel leaned over the basket and tickled his chin. It was, Horst thought grimly, something like a lamb being licked by a tiger. Then the child took the colonel's finger and pulled it to his mouth. This pleased the SS colonel. He roared with laughter.

"He is teething." Horst looked away uncomfortably.

"Yes. I feel two teeth coming through on the bottom." The SS colonel displayed his patience and affection with Aryan children. "Your child, Herr Major?"

"A strong child, I am pleased to say," Horst said cheerfully. He controlled the revulsion he felt at the hand of a murderer so near the baby's face. How many Jewish children had that hand slaughtered?

"I can see the resemblance. The eyes. Beautiful blue eyes, Herr Major. Where is his mother?"

"I am taking him home."

"A son?"

"I do my duty for the Fatherland. This son is the only gift an honorable soldier can offer the future of the world in such a dark time."

"Indeed! So says our Führer. If a soldier might lose his life for the

Reich, he has left behind a legacy in a child. And this boy will be the best to come from Germany; it is plain to see. Very bright. I can spot a future general. This grip! A child who will sink his teeth into life!" He laughed at his joke and held up his wet finger. "What is he called?"

"Can you guess?" Horst gulped as the name escaped him. "Named for a great leader, Herr Colonel."

"Adolf! Well done! A well-mannered infant. A handsome German son. I myself have four sons in the Hitler Youth. There is nothing like sons. You have done well for the Fatherland."

"Thank you, Colonel. And now we are off to Berlin."

The SS colonel offered advice for dealing with the ordeal of teething . . . whiskey on the gums. With a pleasant pat on Horst's back, the tiger strolled away without suspecting the truth. Reeling, Horst hurried off to hide with Yacov in his first-class sleeping compartment.

On this night the train from Warsaw to Berlin was nearly empty. Except for a handful of drunk soldiers heading home for leave, everyone was already wherever they were going. Horst was grateful for this. There would be no grandmotherly types to croon over the baby.

But they were an hour out in the dark Polish countryside before his hands quit shaking and he could turn his thoughts from the SS colonel to the child who slept beside him in the basket. The priest's plan for his escape seemed fantastic, and yet it might work.

"It is good that you are too young to know what all this is about, little one. You sleep on the edge of a flaming abyss, yet you are not troubled. What voice whispers peace to you?" Horst looked out at the star-flecked sky. "The priest says your angels ascend constantly before the throne of God and back to you again. . . . If there are angels who follow you, boy, they descend into the center of hell tonight."

Horst tucked the blanket around the child's chin. His gaze lingered on the pink cheeks and the long lashes. Here was contentment: Yacov's tiny fist was clenched and his thumb placed in his mouth. Touching the velvet-soft hair, Horst considered the story the priest had told him about Etta and Aaron Lubetkin. Where were they and their other children now? What kind of world was this that made mothers and fathers thrust their infants into the arms of strangers, then turn away forever?

"I can make you no promises," Horst whispered as though the parents of his ward could somehow hear him. "I cannot even promise that he will survive. But on my own honor as a soldier and my very life, I vow I will do everything I can to see your child safely home." He closed his eyes. "I am so sorry . . . God? Hear me."

He took the hand of Yacov, so small and soft and perfect, into his big fingers. The child stirred and breathed a ragged sigh.

What man could think of stopping such sweet breath? What kind of national government could call for the crucifixion of such innocence— to drive spikes through hands like these? What sort of people could allow it?

Had Horst known all along what was being done? The truth of Nazi racial doctrines had lingered like a dark shadow in the back of his thoughts like everyone else in Germany. But tonight he was certain of what Hitler meant when he threatened the annihilation of the Jews of Europe if there was war. The threat was not merely rhetorical!

The vision of the future loomed before Horst tonight in the image of a million nameless children. His eyes stung with tears of rage and shame. *So many! How many are there?* Too many to count! And it was only just beginning! This is what Katrina had tried to tell him. This is why Kurt had chosen to warn Belgium that their hope of neutrality was in vain. The shadow must not reach any farther beyond the borders of the Reich!

"I must do this," Horst whispered. "But I cannot think of the others. Too many . . . too much . . ."

So it came down to the life of only one child in the mind of Horst von Bockman. For this one life he could risk everything! Exhaustion swept over him. With his fingers closed gently around the hand of the baby, he leaned his head back, and for the first time in months, he slept.

∽〇〇

Had Katrina received his message?

Horst spotted her as the train chugged beneath the dome of the Friedrichstrasse Bahnhof in Berlin. Wearing a loden green wool skirt, sweater, and beret, she leaned against an iron pillar draped with red swastika banners.

The baby was wide-awake. Fed, washed, and changed, he perched on Horst's arm and watched the world slide by with interest. Horst stepped from the compartment onto the nearly deserted platform with the last huff and shudder of the train. He left the wicker basket behind, carrying only his valise and the baby.

Enormous posters of the Führer glared down at them from every wall. Katrina glanced, unseeing, toward Horst and then away. Her expression changed with the startling realization that the man walking toward her was indeed Horst, and he was not alone. She looked back again, held her astonishment in check, and pretended that the strange child in Horst's arms was fully expected.

"You made it! Welcome, my darlings!" She hurried toward them.

Well done, Katrina! How beautifully she improvised in a world where the expression of surprise could be cause for official investigation.

Horst spotted the ubiquitous Gestapo agents lounging around the lobby of the uncrowded depot in search of any traveler who displayed even a glint of apprehension. Two plainclothes officers near the stairway. Another was beside the news kiosk, while a fourth pretended to read the paper.

"There is Mama!" Horst said loudly, pointing toward Katrina. It seemed a very ordinary reunion. The Gestapo barely glanced up as Katrina kissed Horst and took the child from his arms with delight.

There was other quarry to be sniffed out. A small, dark man with a haunted face walked too quickly toward the exit and glanced over his shoulder as if he was being pursued. Two of the Gestapo exchanged knowing looks and strolled after him.

The charade of Horst and Katrina played out. "Look at you! How I have missed you!" She kissed the baby and held him up over her head. Yacov frowned down at her and, for an instant, seemed as if he might break into tears. "No, my angel! What is it? Are you hungry? Horst, where is her bottle?"

"Teething," Horst replied.

The light banter went on with Katrina calling Yacov *she* and *her* until at last they passed through the portals of the gleaming marble edifice of the Friedrichstrasse Bahnhof and settled into the car with Horst behind the wheel and Katrina holding Yacov. Two policemen on the sidewalk, arms crossed, seemed not to see them.

Horst started the engine and ground the gears, his only sign of nervousness.

Katrina eyed him coolly. "So, hello, Horst. I am a mother, am I?"

"He is a boy."

Katrina shot him a look. "Polish?"

"From Poland. Jewish."

"A Jewish boy?" Katrina kissed Yacov on the cheek and brushed his hair with her fingers. She studied him for a moment, and he smiled curiously at her and batted her nose. "Very pretty. But Horst, a boy? He is circumcised?"

"Yes." Horst pulled from the curb and drove down the deserted street.

"Well, well, little one," she said. "We must not let a Nazi change your diapers."

"With any luck he will not be in Germany long enough to need a change of diapers."

"It is already too late for that. Do you have any clean things?"

"The valise."

She fumbled with the latch and retrieved a diaper. Changing the baby on her lap as they drove toward the suburbs, Katrina said with a touch of wonder in her voice, "You might have told me about this."

"There was no safe means."

"The Gestapo could have seen how surprised I was and then . . ."

"You are a good enough actress, Katrina. I was counting on it."

She was silent as they passed the new Chancellery building. The enormous Nazi flags were on display, indicating that Hitler was in residence. Katrina shuddered and instinctively held the baby nearer. "Where are we going, Horst?"

"Home."

"That is not what I meant. I mean . . . us. Where are you and I headed? What has happened to you since you left me? Why have you done this? brought this baby to me? Is it because you thought it would change my mind about us? pacify me somehow?"

Horst thumped his hand angrily against the wheel and swore.

The baby began to cry.

"An arrogant thing to say, Katrina!"

"Look what you've done. You have frightened him!" She caressed Yacov and tried to quiet him, then fumbled in the bag for a bottle.

Horst pressed his foot down hard on the accelerator and sped across the bridge over the Spree River. "I have done this because . . . because I must! That is all! It has nothing to do with us . . . with where I stand with you. Or whether I remain a soldier or abandon my men in a fight because I do not agree with the politics of my country." He ran his fingers through his hair. "What is the use? The child will be out of Germany soon enough. Safe. I need your help with him for a day or so. No more than that. It has nothing to do with whether or not you still care about me. It is his life and my soul! For once it has nothing to do with you. Can you understand that?"

Katrina stared straight ahead. Her jaw was set. "Good. That is all I wanted to know. Because . . . I wanted to tell you . . . you need not do anything to prove yourself to me . . . but this . . . well." She turned toward him and put her hand on his shoulder and slid her fingers down his arm to touch his hand. "I have missed you, darling."

❧

This time Madame Hilaire came back on board the *Garlic* with a man in tow. He was dark-eyed, unshaven, and ominous in the way he wandered around the cabin, picking up everything as though he were shopping in a flea market. He looked at Papillon, who was perched on Jerome's head, as if he might crush him.

"Who are you?" Jerome demanded of the man. After all, this was Jerome's home, and what right did Madame Hilaire have to bring a stranger onto the *Garlic* without asking? And what right did this ragged character have to examine everything so closely?

"Who am I?" The man acted like he might strike Jerome for asking. Then he shouted to Madame Hilaire, "He wants to know who I am."

She snorted at the impudence of such a question. When Jerome tried to get an answer from her, she did not look at him. She reeked of sour wine. Her hair was even more unruly than usual. She stood with her hands on her hips and stared with proprietary satisfaction past the children at the bed, the table, the dish cupboards, and the pans stacked in the dry sink.

The man lifted the hatch and peered into the engine compartment.

"What are they doing, Jerome?" Marie asked. She was troubled, even frightened, by the intrusion.

Jerome took his sister up the ladder and onto the deck. He instructed her to sit on the rope coil and hold Papillon. The sun was bright and beautiful. The stone faces on Pont Neuf gaped at the two children. Jerome took a seat beside the open cargo hatch and leaned down to listen to the conversation. With the shouting of Madame Hilaire it was not hard to understand the intent.

"Well, Captain, what do you think of it?" she screamed.

He shouted back, enunciating each word. "She is a reeking *Garlic* all right, Madame!"

"But what will you pay for her?"

Marie jumped to her feet. "Pay? Does she mean buy? Buy the *Garlic*?"

"Stay here!" Jerome ordered. Then he bounded down the hatch. "Monsieur." He was panting as he stood at the elbow of the man, who ignored him. "I do not care what Madame Hilaire tells you. Our ship is not for sale. It is not hers to sell. She is our guardian only."

The man turned and laughed, throwing his head back and opening his mouth wide to reveal blackened teeth. "She is your guardian, boy?"

Jerome put his hands behind his back so the man would not see how he was shaking. Something terrible was happening, and Jerome did not know how to stop it.

"She is meant only to watch over my sister and me, Monsieur. The *Garlic* is ours. It belongs to our father, who is a poilu at the front."

Again the laugh.

Madame Hilaire looked at Jerome as she would regard a fly to be swatted or brushed away. She shrugged.

Jerome knew that his words were of no consequence. The scheming hag was up to something.

"Look, boy." The man shoved him back. "Let me tell you something. Madame Hilaire has this paper, see? It is from your papa. He gives her the power to tend to his affairs while he is gone. Do you understand, boy?"

"But Papa did not mean—"

"She has the paper. He has signed it. Madame Hilaire is authorized to sell this tub. Of course the money will be used to care for you and your sister."

The hag nodded broadly and grinned in agreement with whatever she thought she heard.

Jerome rushed at her ferociously. He grabbed her arms and pushed her back against the wall. "Thief! You cannot do this to us. I will tell my Uncle Jambonneau. I will write Papa, and he will have you thrown into jail!"

"Get the rubbish off me!" she wailed.

The man picked up Jerome by the back of his shirt and held him aloft. Jerome swung his fists, but the man was out of reach.

"Look, boy, your father was in debt. This is the only way his debts can be paid. What can he do? Settle his accounts on fifty centimes a day?"

Madame Hilaire brushed herself off in indignation. She tugged up her sleeves and waddled to where Jerome dangled. She spit on the floor of the cabin and then slapped Jerome hard across the cheek. Much worse than the slap was the way she lowered her voice and spoke to him in a sinister whisper for the first time.

"Little beggar! There are plenty of charity wards for scum like you and your sister. You think I can support myself and you on what Jardin is paying me? Now get out of here! I am selling the *Garlic*, and there is nothing you can do about it! When the war begins, your father will die anyway. They always put the stupid sheep in front of the cannons. A charity ward is all you have to hope for."

Jerome heard the sobs of Marie from on deck. The eyes of the stranger turned up. He guffawed. "A pitiful thing, this is, Madame Hilaire. Tragic. That a man does not even care for his own children properly. Ah, well. This way they will begin life with a clean slate . . . with nothing at all to encumber them."

22

· Surprising Solutions

Jerome Jardin was worried. It was as if something had turned on a water tap in the eyes of Marie, and Jerome could not turn it off again. She was not blubbering or making even a sound, but every time Jerome looked at her face, there was an unending stream of new tears trickling down her cheeks. Very quiet and troubling. The noiseless suffering of his sister made him feel even more miserable inside. He felt bad enough already.

Madame Hilaire had tied up some clothes in a bundle and thrown them from the *Garlic* onto the quai. She told Jerome and Marie that if they came back she would call the gendarmes and have them sent to a charity orphanage. Jerome would be conveyed to a home for boys. Marie would be dispatched to a home for girls, and they would never see one another again.

"Do not feel bad, Marie," Jerome had said. "We will go to the hospital. We will send word to Uncle Jambonneau. He will know what we should do."

Marie had nodded and sniffed. Yet her nose was still dripping even now. Marie was like a sponge, Jerome thought, oversaturated with liquid. It was as though Madame Hilaire had stepped on poor Marie, and all the juice was squishing out of her at once. Could there be so much dampness in one so little? It was a pathetic sight.

Even Papillon was worried. Sweet little rat Papillon—he had the kind heart of a dog, even if he was a rat. Sitting on Marie's shoulder, he patted her salty tears. Putting his paw to his mouth he tasted her grief and twitched his whiskers in concern. When Marie finished this weeping, would she be all shriveled and dry like a raisin?

The entrance to Hospital de la Charité, where Uncle Jambonneau had been moved, was in the Rue Jacob among a warren of little shops and old buildings. The hospital was itself a dreary place. Its stone facade was black with years of exposure to coal smoke.

Marie now stood on the steps and craned her head back to peer up at the sooty windows.

"Stay here," Jerome instructed her firmly. He tried to sound like he was not really worried at all about her. "There are nuns and nurses inside. They will think Papillon is just a common rat. They will not like him in their establishment, *ma chèrie*. So you will have to stay out here with him."

She nodded wordlessly. Jerome, in an impulse of compassion that surprised even him, leaned down and kissed her quickly on the head. Papillon leaped up and clung to his shirtfront.

"No, Papillon, dear little dog. You must stay here with Marie. She is afraid of the nuns, you see." He pulled Papillon loose and replaced him in Marie's pocket.

Marie would watch over Papillon. Papillon would watch over Marie.

The inside of the hospital smelled like antiseptic and mold. The plaster of the ceiling was flaking. The green linoleum squares of the floor were chipped. Two long benches in the foyer held grim-faced men and old women cradling cranky children. Above their heads was a crucifix. On the opposite wall was a large framed photograph of the pope. In an alcove was a statue of Mary and the Christ child.

This was familiar to Jerome because his mother had died in this place. He remembered sitting on the long bench and wondering when it would be time for lunch. Even now he could recall the red, swollen face of his papa. From that day on, Papa had blamed the sisters and the priests and the doctors—and especially God—that Mama was gone. Jerome wished very much that Uncle Jambonneau was in a different hospital than this one.

There was a nun behind a very tidy desk. She was talking on the telephone when Jerome approached her. She smiled at him as she spoke to someone else. She winked at him and held up a finger to ask him to be patient. And then . . .

"Yes, young man? How may I help you?" She looked at his cap to indicate that he should take it off.

He snatched off the cap and kneaded it in his hands. "My Uncle Jambonneau?"

"Your uncle's name is Jambonneau? You call him Uncle Pigs-knuckles?"

Jerome scratched his cheek. He could not remember Uncle Jambonneau's real name. He had always been called Pigs-knuckles. "He has the same last name as me, Sister. It is Jardin. He is an old soldier from des Invalides who has pneumonia. He is here. I must get word to him."

The nun busily pored over her book. "Jardin. Jardin . . . *oui.* Jacob Alfred Jardin. He is here, but you may not see him. He is better but still a very sick man. Children are not allowed. But I shall see he gets a message that you have come by."

Jerome twisted his hat in his hands. How could he tell this woman who wore the black garb of the enemy that he and his sister had no place to go? that he needed help? Surely she would swoop down like a terrible black crow and lock him and Marie into a room until they could be deposited in an institution for homeless waifs. Papa would not like it. Marie would die from terror.

"Madame," he said quietly and respectfully, "please tell my Uncle Jambonneau Jardin that his niece and nephew, Marie and Jerome, have come by to wish him well. Tell him also that his dog, Papillon, is fat and happy. That everything is fine and that he must get well because we all miss him very much."

She copied Jerome's words. "I will take him the note myself," she promised.

"Uncle Jambonneau is blind," Jerome warned her. "You must also read the note to him aloud or he will not know what is on the paper, Madame."

She agreed, and he hurried out of the hospital with his head spinning. What could he tell Marie? What were they to do now?

෴

Horst placed the telephone call to the Associated Press office in Berlin at nine o'clock on the morning of December 27 as the priest had instructed him. The telephone was answered by a German receptionist. In English, Horst asked for Josephine Marlow.

"Marlow?" The receptionist was puzzled by the request. "She is not in the office."

"When do you expect her?"

"Expect Josie Marlow? Well, I can't say. She doesn't work in Berlin, you see. She might have gone home to America."

Horst glanced at the baby, who was happily investigating a small space that Katrina had hemmed in with furniture. The priest had not told him what to do if the American journalist was not there!

Attempting to remain businesslike, Horst asked for some member of the staff who might know how she could be reached. A few moments passed before a man came on the line.

"Bill Cooper here."

It was a friendly male American voice. Horst breathed a sigh of relief. "I am trying to speak with Fräulein Josephine Marlow, you see."

"Josie Marlow? Sorry. She's on Paris staff."

Paris. There was no hope of Horst speaking with her directly. It was still possible to send wires to Paris—they were routed through Holland or Belgium—but those were subject to strictest scrutiny by the Gestapo. Any German attempting to contact someone on the outside could be arrested at the whim of the secret police and charged with treason.

Horst was certain that even this call was being monitored by the Gestapo. To say more now could cast some suspicion on Bill Cooper, as well as make the reentry of Josephine Marlow into the Reich very difficult when and if the time came.

"Is there something I can do to help?" Cooper asked.

"No. Herr Cooper, is it?" Horst wrote down the name, thanked the man, and quickly hung up the telephone.

Katrina did not speak English, but she clearly understood the disappointment in her husband's expression. "The woman is not in Berlin?"

"Paris."

She shrugged and smiled down at the child, who was picking at the bows on her black pumps with tiny, persistent fingers. "I will keep him here." Katrina scooped Yacov up. "He is a fine baby. And I will just keep him."

"No, Kat. Not a boy. It is dangerous enough what you have here. How many little girls learning to act like good Catholics? If it is possible, for your safety and the child's, I must do as the priest instructed."

"But if the woman is not in Berlin, then she is not in Berlin."

"If I could speak privately to Herr Cooper. He knows her. He could get word to her."

"Horst! You cannot dare go to the office of the foreign press! Every door is watched by the Gestapo. You know that! Such an act could land you in Sachsenhausen tomorrow!"

"Yes. Maybe if the baby can stay with you awhile . . . I must go to the Führer's speech in Berlin on New Year's Eve. There is always good attendance by the foreign press. If I can find this Bill Cooper among them, perhaps there is some hope to contact Fräulein Marlow after all."

"And if you contact her, what will the message be? There is no passage from France into Germany. How can she come here?"

He sat down hard in the rocking chair and took the baby from Katrina. "How can we send you on your way to Jerusalem, little man?"

"I will keep—"

"No, Katrina! I forbid it! He has a grandfather who no doubt would not think kindly of a Wehrmacht major keeping his grandson. Now help me think!"

It was clear she resented the command, but Katrina did as he wished. "There is my Aunt Lottie's house in Treves," she said thoughtfully. "It is just across the border from Luxembourg. Luxembourg is a neutral, so . . ."

He snapped his fingers as if that was the solution. "She is a journalist. Treves is full of neutral journalists. The Porta Nigra Hotel is crawling with journalists."

"And Gestapo?"

"Of course. The Gestapo is everywhere. Like fleas. Treves is no different. But it is right on the border. Fräulein Marlow can enter Germany over the Wasserbillig Bridge. That is it! I will contact this Bill Cooper, and he will carry the message to her. We must give her time to get the proper documents for him, of course. American documents."

"Can she do that?"

"If she cannot, then we will have a son."

✑

Jerome hoped that Marie would not ask him any questions for a while, because he needed time to think up answers.

They trudged silently back along the Quai Voltaire. The water of the Seine seemed very dark today. No longer like home.

Two large women, heads covered with scarves, walked past them. They nudged one another and made unkind comments about Papillon and the fact that Marie was skinny and her shoes were much too large for her feet.

Jerome turned and glared hotly at their retreating backs. He cocked a snook at them and muttered savagely that women who were fat as pigs should not say unkind things about such a little girl as Marie.

Marie's head went down. She looked at her shoes. "What will we do, Jerome?" she whispered.

The moment of truth. He did not yet have an answer.

"Uncle Jambonneau said—" he hesitated—"what do you think he said?"

Marie shrugged. "How should I know?"

"Guess." He was stalling for time.

"Tell me, Jerome. I am too tired to guess."

"Come on. I will surprise you. He has a very good solution. You know Uncle Jambonneau. He always has good ideas. He is a very smart man. He told me to take you . . . someplace . . . and surprise you." He held his head up as if he knew where he was going. "But do not ask me any more questions, Marie. And you must stop leaking all these tears."

She stopped crying. She did not ask any questions. Finally Jerome found himself back in Buci Market, leading her among the stalls of flowers and vegetables and pâtisseries and the open shop of the butcher. Only then did it come to him. Like a flash of lightning, his dim brain lit up.

"Stop here." They halted beside a basket of blue flowers. "This is what Uncle Jambonneau told me to do, *ma chèrie.*"

"He told you to bring me to Buci? But we have no money to buy food."

"Listen." Jerome took Papillon from her. "Uncle Jambonneau says that you must go to the window of Monsieur Turenne, the butcher. You must ask him where Madame Rose lives."

"Who is Madame Rose?"

"A friend of Uncle Jambonneau."

"Oh no!" she wailed. "Not another one like Madame Hilaire! What more can happen to us?"

"No! No, Marie, *ma chèrie.* Listen! Madame Rose is American. Nothing like Madame Hilaire. She does not drink."

"Not ever?"

"I do not think so. But anyway, go ask the butcher where she may be found. It is like a treasure hunt, Uncle Jambonneau says. When we find this Madame Rose, we shall find our treasure! Chicken to eat maybe, like in the old days. Like visiting day at des Invalides! A happy ending, Marie!" He nudged her forward as the great hulk of the butcher appeared, framed in his window by naked poultry and rabbits and loops of sausages.

Jerome ducked behind a handcart of flowers as Marie walked cautiously forward. He did not dare to look but strained his ears to hear.

"Pardon, Monsieur Butcher. My Uncle Jambonneau says I must find Madame Rose. The American."

"And how should I know where such a Madame Rose person is?"

"Uncle Jambonneau says you will know where she is. Like a treasure, Monsieur. And so I am sent to ask you."

"Why should you want to know?"

"Because he says I must."

Silence. "You look like something that would interest Madame Rose. Something the cat would leave on her threshold."

"What cat, Monsieur?"

"Never mind. If I give you her place of residence, you must say I sent you to her. She will like that, I think. She will think well of me."

"*Oui*, Monsieur Butcher."

"All right then. She lives with her sister and the urchins at No. 5 Rue de la Huchette. The house is a large one behind a heavy wood gate where the coaches used to go in and out of the courtyard. Ring the bell, little one. Wait beside the gate even if it seems like no one is home. By and by someone will come and let you in."

Jerome cheered behind the bunches of petunias. He kissed Papillon on the nose. He congratulated himself for the brilliance of his idea. Marie came back smiling. It was the first time she had smiled since they left the *Garlic*.

"No. 5 Rue de la Huchette. I heard. Well done, Marie!"

"Now what?"

"Now we go there. It is all so simple. Uncle Jambonneau says this is the kindest of all ladies in the Latin Quarter. She is nothing at all like Madame Hilaire. She is a large woman and has a mouth like a bullfrog, but you must not be frightened of her. She also has a sister who is scrawny. Her name is Betsy. There are many other children who are there. They eat chicken sometimes for dinner."

Marie caught Jerome's excitement. Madame Rose with a mouth like a bullfrog! Beautiful Rose! The treasure of Uncle Jambonneau! Chicken for dinner!

Located one block from the Seine, Rue de la Huchette was a short, narrow street bordered by Place St. Michel to the west and Rue St. Jacques on the east.

It was a close-packed street, lined with houses Uncle Jambonneau said were several hundred years old. A single gutter ran down the center of the cobbles. This had been used as a sewer in the old days when the contents of chamber pots were tossed out of the upper-story windows. But now Huchette was a much cleaner place, though still quite poor. Napoleon himself had lived in one of the houses when he was impoverished. This fact had always been used by Papa to remind Jerome that even poor boys could make good and end up with a nice tomb like the one Napoleon now occupied at des Invalides.

The neighborhood was ideally situated for student riots, rebellions, barricades, and bloody battles. Such events came around every few decades on the Left Bank, and the Huchette was a very popular street in those times. Beneath the buildings were deep cellars where the unfortunate prisoners of the Reign of Terror had been confined and tortured. Devices of torment were still to be found in some of those basements. Uncle Jambonneau had cheerfully informed Marie about this historical fact, which made her hesitant at first to walk down Rue de la Huchette.

But it was getting on toward dinnertime, and the scent of cooking food wafted through the air. Jerome wisely talked about Madame Rose and chicken dinner and how well liked the place was by all the children who lived there. And besides, No. 5 was only a few houses from the corner. Jerome told his sister that it was a newer house and that it had no skeletons in the basement.

"How can you know this, Jerome?"

"I know this because the house has no basement." He lied because it was easier than arguing. By the time Marie found out that this was one of the oldest houses and also that it had a cellar deeper than all the rest, it would be too late. "No. 5. And there it is."

An enormous arched wood gate sealed off the house from the street. The stone around the portal was rounded and chipped from the days when wagons and carriages had turned into the courtyard and clipped the edges with iron hubs. The heavy wood planks of the gate were black with age and scarred from ten thousand small encounters over four hundred years. It was a venerable gate that had experienced the knocking of Latin scholars, pilgrims, prostitutes, musketeers, and the angry fists of the Revolution's mob in search of priests or terrified aristocrats hiding within.

This evening, as twilight closed over the strip of sky, Jerome added the rapping of his knuckles to the history of the gate.

He waited patiently for some minutes. No one came. It was dark.

"Monsieur the butcher said to ring the bell," Marie insisted as the smells of garlic and fried potatoes made her stomach growl.

Jerome could not see a bell. A frayed red rope dangled from a hole in the wood. He pulled it violently, and a bell rang inside the courtyard.

More waiting. Another pull.

A woman's gruff voice called, "Patience! I am coming!"

The clank of a metal latch sounded, and the gate swung open a sliver. The aroma of food escaped like a strong current of water. Jerome could easily see Madame Rose framed in the light behind her. She was peering out into the street at an angle much above the heads of Jerome and Marie.

"A prank!" She spat and slammed the gate.

"No! No! Madame Rose!" Jerome grasped for the cord and pulled hard. He held tight to it as if it were a lifeline thrown out to someone drowning.

The hinges groaned back again, and the big face of Madame Rose peered out now at his level. The thin lips of the wide, bullfrog mouth curved up in a smile. "Who is there?"

"It is me, Madame Rose. Jerome Jardin . . . salami?" He attempted to jar her memory without giving away to Marie that Madame Rose did not know Uncle Jambonneau.

Silence. The crack widened. "Salami?"

"The butcher told us where to find you, Madame Rose," Marie interjected eagerly. "And Uncle Jambonneau says you will feed us if we come here."

The gate opened wide. The two stepped in. Madame Rose studied –

Jerome in the shadowed light. "But of course! Jerome Jardin! Did you bring your rat?" She closed the gate.

"And my sister, Marie, also."

Marie giggled. "You know Papillon, too!" Such relief. Such joy. "Papa is at the war. Uncle Jambonneau is in hospital. Madame Hilaire has sold our *Garlic,* and now we have no place to sleep. But you do not have devices of torture in your cellar because you do not have a cellar. So I am not frightened. And Uncle Jambonneau says you are a treasure, and Monsieur the butcher says you will think well of him since he told us how to find you! And you will also have chicken sometimes for dinner."

Jerome did not need to say a word. Marie was doing all the talking. Very little of it made sense to Madame Rose, but she put her big hand on Marie's scrawny shoulder and nodded and made contented noises as though she was interested in everything. Jerome was relieved. Marie babbled on gleefully.

The house was three stories high, with open terraces, built in a U shape around a cobbled courtyard. Young children gaped and twittered down at them from between the slats of the banisters. Laundry was strung out on lines like colorful flags above their heads. Blue shirts. White shirts. Red dresses. Calico dresses. Clean, white underthings. Knickers. Bloomers. Long and short socks of all sizes tiptoed in the air above the courtyard.

Even in the faint light, Jerome could see that the walls were clean white and like new. No doubt the building was very old beneath the façade, but it did not show its age. The two sisters had fixed it up beauti- fully! Jerome remembered that some French king had demanded all the wood-framed buildings be plastered over after a great and terrible fire had swept through the city some centuries before. No. 5 Rue de la Huchette would have been around in those days. But tonight the building seemed quite bright and cheerful even in its ancient coat of plaster of paris. It was not anything like what Jerome had pictured an orphanage would be. The courtyard smelled like whitewash and spring flowers. And also it smelled like cooking food, of course. A pleasant combination.

"We are not too late for supper?" Marie blinked up at Madame Rose.

Madame Rose laughed a big, boisterous, American laugh and called to her sister, "Do not put the leftovers away, Betsy dear! We have two more for dinner!"

23

Watchful Eyes

A record cold gripped Berlin this New Year's Eve. A coal shortage compounded the wartime gloominess of the holiday.

To add to the edgy mood of Berliners, Himmler had revoked permission for the bars to remain open all night for the celebration. The Gestapo chief had further warned against excessive drinking and requested that German citizens greet the new year with sober thought and consideration of the Führer's upcoming speech. In spite of that, the Kurfurstendamm was crowded with drunks who were drowning their troubles beneath the watchful eyes of thousands of Himmler's police.

Above the packed pavement of the Ku'damm, in ludicrous contrast, loudspeakers broadcasted the grim New Year's celebration of the Nazi Party as it unfolded in the great Sportpalast. It was a very sober affair.

The floodlights ringing the stadium produced streaks of brilliant white light that alternated with bands of deep black shadow. The view of the assembled crowd as seen from the high platform was like a thickly timbered forest. Thousands of brown-uniformed human trees were brightly lit, and thousands more were in darkness.

Ten men to a row across one streak of illumination . . . ten tens to an eagle standard . . . ten hundreds filling a strand of radiance to the far side of the stadium . . . a hundred bands of light and dark.

The crowd was mostly still. There was some jostling in place as necks were craned to see what privileged celebrities gathered on the stage. Any comments made were spoken in hasty, reverent whispers. The highest podium was empty, unoccupied except for a row of microphones that guarded a vacant lectern.

At an unseen cue, a barrage of drums crashed into cadence. The tempo was deliberate and measured, but the volume was so overpowering that the air itself seemed likely to split apart. A hundred thousand men found that they were breathing in time with the drums, their heartbeats mimicking the rhythm.

When the throbbing of the drums so reverberated through the bodies of the crowd that they no longer heard the sound but rather felt it, a legion of trumpets burst into a fanfare. An encircling ring of spotlight beams jumped upward into the sky from the rim of the stadium to tower over the scene like pillars of ice.

Between the sky and the assembly, a cloud of red-and-black banners unfurled, fluttering in time with the trumpet blasts. The expectation of the gathering had reached a fever pitch—exactly the right moment for the object of their worship to appear.

As if controlled by a single switch, all light and sound vanished. The arena was plunged into absolute blackness and total stillness with such suddenness that thousands believed they had been struck both deaf and blind in that instant.

And then . . . a single spotlight reached out from the back of the stadium, stabbing the highest podium. As if by magic, the lectern was now occupied by the stern, brooding figure of Adolf Hitler.

Hitler extended his arm and swept a salute across the crowd. *"Sieg Heil!"* burst from a hundred thousand throats, repeating and reechoing till equal in volume to the now-silent trumpets and drums.

At last the Führer motioned for silence, and the ecstatic adoration died away. Then he began to speak. Angry denunciations of the democracies flowed from the Führer in an unchecked stream. The hundred thousand Nazi Party members hearing him speak in person were ready to march against Western Europe at that very moment if Hitler so ordered.

"We are about to enter the most decisive year in German history. In 1940, the Jewish capitalistic world wants to destroy us. I have repeatedly asked France and England for peace. But Jewish reactionary warmongers and their puppets, like Winston Churchill, are unwilling to cancel their plans to destroy Germany."

Hitler stopped speaking and regarded the audience sternly, with folded arms. Like a father who is about to make an unpleasant demand of a child for its own good. "Sacrifices will be required—sacrifice of ease, sacrifice of comfort, sacrifice of personal choice for the greater good of the Reich—yes, even sacrifice of blood. But we will go on from victory to victory—unflinching and unstoppable—to secure the rightful place of the German people!"

Thunderous applause greeted these words, as if the speech were concluded. But Hitler had something to add. He waited patiently for the outpouring of patriotic spirit to subside before speaking again.

Now he addressed them in a more measured tone, the voice of a father who dotes on his children. He called upon their loyalty to him personally, not to their patriotism or their devotion to the Reich, but to himself as the living embodiment of the spirit of Germany.

"You see me before you tonight, uniformed as your Führer. Not in the simple garb of Citizen Hitler, not in the trappings of state, such as Chancellor Hitler would wear, but as your supreme commander . . . to lead you ever forward, until final victory is achieved! I pledge this to you: You shall not see me in any other form than this until our goal is reached—Germany everywhere triumphant and all its foes crushed!"

The *Sieg Heils* reverberated. The tide of emotion burst out of the stadium and echoed in the street over the loudspeakers. The revelers barely raised their heads to acknowledge the racket. Like people who lived near a train track, they had learned to ignore the predictable clamor and were even comfortable with it.

Unaware of the lethargy of the general populace toward his oration, Hitler acknowledged the accolades with humbly bowed head, as if in deep reflection. Then he turned and made his way down from the high platform.

And yet a closer look revealed that not every arm in the Sportpalast was raised in praise of the Führer. Among the rank of dignitaries gathered at the foot of the stage were the uniformed generals and officers of the Wehrmacht. They exchanged looks with one another. Their expressions spoke volumes without uttering a word. They had warned Hitler not to press his luck. Poland was one thing. France was quite another. Russia had attacked Finland with Hitler's blessings and now was taking a beating from the cold and the Finnish army. German resources could be stretched only so far. Why not quit while they were ahead?

This was the hope of the German High Command as the bells tolled the coming of 1940.

◌

Horst von Bockman stood as the Nazi Party dignitaries marched out. He marked the thinly veiled expressions of disgust as Himmler and Heydrich and Goebbels passed the officers of the High Command. Admiral Canaris, chief of Military Intelligence, was well-known for his disapproval of Gestapo and SS tactics. A man small of stature but of great heart, Canaris raised his hand for an instant as if in heil, then wiped his nose instead.

Located four rows behind the distinguished group of generals, Horst kept his gaze locked on them. Men of true valor, these few represented all of the Fatherland to Horst: von Bock, von Brauchitsch, Canaris. For these brave men, Horst would walk through the fire of hell itself. Each of them was under suspicion by the Gestapo. Each was monitored and scrutinized by the inner circle of Hitler's black-shirted elite. And yet they attended the speech tonight. They prepared their troops for battle. They listened silently to the rantings of the madman. They stood at attention when he and his minions passed. And if the order came to "sacrifice," they would do as commanded. But their faces spoke volumes about their contempt for the tyrant who now controlled Germany. Were they holding on, hoping for a chance to take the nation back?

This remote possibility seemed real to Horst tonight as he observed their subdued behavior. They filed out as a group, leaving junior officers like Horst to brave the massive crowd inching for the exits. Horst craned his neck, searching for the tribe of foreign press who always sat in a reserved section near the front.

He spotted them and fought his way against the current toward them. There were dozens wearing press badges issued by the Ministry of Propaganda, stamped with the approval of the Nazi Reich.

This thought halted Horst in his tracks for a second as he moved toward a cluster whose American accents penetrated the rumble of retreating voices. What if Bill Cooper, the American AP journalist, was a man who favored the Nazi policies? There were such political aberrations among the foreign press, Horst knew. Many actually approved of Hitler's conduct of racial oppression and conquest. As if in confirmation of his fear, Horst noticed the Englishman William Joyce, who broadcast German propaganda to England under the name Lord Haw-Haw. He was laughing and engaged in animated conversation with a young man wearing the badge of a Belgian journalist.

Horst pressed on. "I am looking for an American," he ventured to a thin, stoop-shouldered man with a balding head and thick glasses. "Bill Cooper."

The man squinted with amusement at Horst's uniform and pointed to where a short, round man in a dark suit chatted with an American photographer at the foot of the podium.

The aisles were clearing. The noise had quieted down.

Horst approached Bill Cooper, who resembled the round monk on a Munich beer stein. The men fell silent when Horst appeared, as though his uniform had taken the humor out of their private joke.

"Herr Cooper?" Horst ventured.

Cooper turned, unsmiling, to face him. There was curiosity in his eyes, but this was tempered by caution. *"Ja. Ich bin Cooper."*

Cooper's German was quite good, but Horst felt uncomfortable using his native tongue here. "Mr. Cooper," Horst began again, "we should speak English."

"Sure." Cooper shrugged, then shook hands in farewell to the photographer.

"Mr. Cooper." Horst lowered his voice and looked away. "I was trying to reach Josephine Marlow."

There was a flash of recognition on Cooper's face. "You're the guy who telephoned." He said this too loudly and then, catching the look of fear on Horst's face, also lowered his voice. "Sorry. How can I help?"

"I have something for Fräulein Marlow. She was in Warsaw."

"Right. Barely got out, thanks to the efficiency of your army." There was an edge of bitterness in the comment. This was a good sign.

Horst continued, "I have recently been in Warsaw. I have a message for her. From the priest at the Cathedral of St. John."

"From her priest?" Cooper seemed pleased. "She talked about him. I thought he would be dead by now."

Horst leveled his gaze on Cooper. "Not yet. But it cannot be long. Please, Mr. Cooper, can you take a message to Fräulein Marlow? I must trust you in this. . . ."

Cooper looked over his shoulder instinctively, as if he felt the probing eyes of the Gestapo on his back. "I'll see her in Paris next month."

"A month?"

"That's the best I can offer. You know the rules. I'll see her face-to-face, and that's the only way to carry a message out of Germany these days."

Horst nodded in agreement. What choice did he have? Katrina could manage for a while longer. There was no hope but this.

And so, in the shadow of the Führer's podium, Horst told what he had seen at the Cathedral of St. John—the doomed children and the one child who might be saved. Cooper listened intently as the stadium fell silent and the last of the crowd dissipated into the streets. Walking slowly out of the arena, Horst explained to Cooper about Josephine Marlow and the plan of the little priest in Warsaw.

◖◗

Madame Rose was a kind person. She noticed things. Like the fact that Marie squinted at everything and lost her shoes and socks regularly and could not read letters on the blackboard.

It was arranged for Marie to be examined by an oculist and get a free pair of glasses. Now she could see everything! Blades of grass and minutiae of every description became objects of wonder! She seemed almost intelligent at times. This surprised Jerome very much.

The gift of Marie's miraculous vision was paid for by the American rich man named Dupont who stayed at the Ritz Hotel. Mr. Dupont had met Madame Rose by accident when he was lost and looking for St. Chapelle. She had cheerfully guided him to the holy chapel of St. Louis and personally conducted him through the jewel-like building. "We have a child in our orphanage who simply cannot see anything but the colors of these exquisite stained-glass windows," she had told Mr. Dupont. "And we do not have the funds to get her glasses."

Her assistance, in the end, cost Mr. Dupont a pretty penny, Madame Rose later told her sister. By the time the tour was finished, he had agreed to donate Marie's eyeglasses as well as other items. New shoes were ordered for everyone, which had become very necessary since there were so many more children now at No. 5 Rue de la Huchette.

Jerome considered that if Madame Rose had not been working on the side of heaven she might have made an excellent *escroc*, a con man.

All the new shoes arrived in boxes brought on a delivery van. Children lined up and were allowed to try them on and choose whatever pair they liked. It was this great occasion that made Jerome believe that, if there was a God, Jerome would want God to be something like Madame Rose.

There were five boys at la Huchette who were in wheelchairs. Jerome was allowed to guide the chair of Henri whenever they went on outings. Because of this he had become good friends with Henri, who was ten years old and very bright.

On the day the shoe truck arrived, Henri was in an unhappy mood. He stayed in his room and told Jerome not to bother him because the present from Monsieur Dupont was not meant for boys who could not walk. Henri pointed to his brown leather shoes. They did not have even one scuff mark, and Henri said he had owned them for a long time.

"I used to wear out lots of shoes," he said. "My mother was always saying she never saw a boy wear the sole off the way I did. I could run faster than any boy in Kroulouse before I got sick."

It was difficult to know how to answer. Jerome had never imagined what it must be like to be able to run one day and then be stuck in a wicker chair with wheels.

Madame Rose came in. "Henri! We have been looking for you! Is your tire flat?"

"Not my tire." His chin went down.

"Are you out of gas?"

"No."

"Well, then! You are missing the party."

"It is not for someone like me." He pointed to the clean, unmarked leather.

She said the American word, "Fiddlesticks!" She stuck her lower lip out in a pout and grabbed the handles of the wicker chair. She made the sound of an engine revving up and tilted Henri back almost to the ground before she roared out of the building with him.

Among the boxes and boxes of wingtips and oxfords and patent leathers were seven boxes bigger than the rest. Five for the boys who were in chairs and two for the boys who walked with crutches.

"Riding boots." The old woman raised her chin and snapped her fingers, and the gates of Rue de la Huchette swung open.

A great long-legged bay horse stepped in beneath the arch. On his back was a tall, handsome Frenchman dressed in the old-fashioned uniform of a cavalry officer. His chest glittered with medals. The iron shoes of the horse flashed sparks on the cobbles. The rider pulled his animal up in front of the rank of wheelchairs.

On cue the animal bowed before them, executing the *courbette*.

The children gasped and applauded. The officer doffed his hat. It was then that Jerome recognized the man. Jerome had seen him only last Armistice Day as he led the parade on this very horse! He was the great hero Francois Monceau, who had lost both his legs fighting the Boche in the Great War! This was an amazing thing.

The officer saluted, then rapped his knuckles loudly on his wooden legs. The little girls shrank back in horror. "Gentlemen," Monceau said, "Madame Rose has asked that I come here today to teach you a few fundamentals of horsemanship. Rule one is that you must always wear proper footgear before riding. Ah! Yes. I see you have fine boots. Well then, you are almost ready. Rule two is that you must never be afraid. And rule three is that no matter what circumstance befalls you, you must never, never give up."

The rest of the afternoon was spent with the hero of France riding up and down la Huchette. The children held on behind him, sometimes two or three at once. Jerome was on the very tail and did not much like it. He broke rules two and three instantly. At the end of the lane he slid off and walked home.

But there was Henri and the other Special Ones, as Madame Rose called them. They wore their new riding boots and rode just in front of the brave French cavalry officer who had much less in the way of legs than they had.

The experience cheered Henri up considerably. He began to believe rules two and three were possible even for a boy in a wicker chair with wheels. Polishing his boots every day, he made plans to own his own horse after he invented something and became rich.

After that first day, the officer rode by at least once a week to retrieve a mysterious package from the two sisters. He often gave the residents of la Huchette rides and let them pet the nose of his horse, Alexander. He said it made him happy to do so.

The question was asked: Where did Madame Rose meet this famous fellow?

She had been washing his shirts for years.

24

A Diligent Defense

When Paul Chardon unrolled the map on the desk in his office, the three senior cadet captains found themselves looking at a detailed chart of the Lys River and the immediate area around the Ecole de Cavalerie.

"More war games, Captain?" Gaston inquired in a tired-sounding voice. "With respect, sir, my command is exhausted from just juggling their studies, the care of the horses, and the demands of Sister Mitchell."

Paul said with exasperation, "Gaston, the military education at a military school does not stop because you are tired, overworked, or underappreciated!"

Gaston exchanged questioning looks with Sepp and Raymond. The fictitious defense of the school and the banks of the stream had been enacted every year that the boys had attended.

It was said that the same simulation had occurred every year since the school's founding, except in 1918, when it became actual fact. In that last year of the Great War, the kaiser's forces had made a push toward the sea. A herculean effort by the Allies had stopped them near that very spot, but only after the cadets had been evacuated.

The same thought seemed to strike all three student officers. What if history repeated itself, and the Ecole was again in the path of the Germans?

Paul read their minds. "I am not saying that it will come to that, but it is possible. Certainly an invading army would want to seize the Channel ports, and Lys is right on one probable line of advance. My intent is to develop the plans for defending this sector, so that the Regular Army will have them to study, should the need arise."

Gaston looked crestfallen. "We practice the resistance for someone else to perform?"

Paul almost gave an angry retort but caught himself. He addressed the three boys in a kind tone. "We all have a role to play in defending France. What does it matter if you actually fire the shots, so long as the strategy we have worked out succeeds?" He studied their faces, getting a ready smile from Raymond, a quick understanding nod from Sepp, and a grudging squint from Gaston.

"Look now," he said, directing their attention back to the map. "I have already made unit assignments, and it will be your duties to work out the detailed plans. Gaston, to you is given the area of most immediate danger: the direct assault on the town from across the river. You must develop the defense of the bridges and their demolition . . . if opposition is no longer possible."

The fact that Gaston had no comment convinced Paul that he had gotten through to the young cadet about the seriousness of the responsibility. Besides, Paul remembered, in the history of the school, no war games had ever included demolishing the bridges. No one ever built a retreat into their plans.

⌬

The artillery barrage at the Maginot was called the Matins Salute, because every dawn about the time of morning prayers, the "heavies" began to murmur explosively on the wind.

The booming was distant and mellow. Mac commented that they were probably howitzers, judging from the dullness of the reverberating echo. Mac and Murphy felt no urge to flop out of the car and dive for cover.

There was no other sound or evidence of activity along the line. The highway passed between two green mushroom turrets on the hilltop that identified strongpoints of the fortifications. Mac and Murphy drove onto a narrow plateau in the highlands of the Moselle River. From there they could plainly see the muddy yellow military roads that branched off into the opening of Maginot tunnels. At each entrance gates were painted like barber poles, indicating that no unauthorized visitors were allowed. All around were piles of rusted metal and dumps of weathered concrete left over from the construction of this new Wall of China. Beyond the bastions was a thicket of tank traps. Known as asparagus patches because they sprouted up in stalks, these were painted a harmonious green to match the landscape. But there was no sign of life, no indication that anyone was really inside the turrets or beneath the mushroom buttons that topped the hills.

Murphy shuddered in the car. "It's too cold for them to be out. But it's a whole lot better than the last war, when our guys were left to shiver in the rain, isn't it?"

They left the restricted military area and drove along the Thionville Highway. Coming to a control point, Mac geared down and moved slowly through a barbed-wire chicane. A surly French lieutenant with a stubby, Hitler-like mustache examined their passes as if they were spies. Fortunately he was too wet and cold to argue. He waved them on to the muddy barrier of Evrange, their last stop before crossing into neutral Luxembourg.

It was pouring. The road leading to the frontier came to a stop at a lonely concrete barrier. A single guard manned the blockade that was enfolded by sandbags. Sloppy spirals of concertina wire ambled off down the hill.

It was Murphy who first commented on the carelessness of this outpost. The Maginot simply stopped somewhere back down the line. It was as if no one in the French government imagined that the Germans might possibly come through little Luxembourg to cross the border.

"Is this it?" Murphy said incredulously.

Mac nodded. "And it's pretty much the same all the way along the Belgian border, too. I asked Prime Minister Daladier's assistant why the Maginot only went partway along the frontier. He told me that the French didn't want to insult the Belgians, didn't want the Belgians to think that France didn't trust them. The nation of Belgium is the rest of France's line of defense. Get it?"

Murphy rolled his eyes and shook his head in frustration. It was as if the minds of French politicians were also made of concrete.

A man in a heavy oilskin coat stepped out of the door of the customs shack and crooked his finger at Mac and Murphy. Would they please enter the office? And would they bring their luggage?

It was at this outpost that France had stationed her toughest three officials. Perhaps it was believed that if the German army breached Belgium and Luxembourg, the French customs officials would stop them at the border. Perhaps it was true.

These three men were dressed in blue serge uniforms trimmed in silver braid. Before the war their kind had made the lives of tourists miserable at every entrance and exit of France. Now, with the war on, they exercised their duty with a double dose of diligence. They refined the harassment of tourists to a high art. Their lives were dedicated to increasing the mental anguish of every traveler to a level that matched the court officials of the Queen in *Alice's Adventures in Wonderland*.

Stained mustaches drooped over teeth yellowed by smoke from

years of confiscated tobacco. And this trio knew well how to strip a suit-case to the lining in search of smuggled chocolates.

As the shadows of afternoon lengthened, the officials provided Mac and Murphy with in-triplicate forms. Private life, military status, reasons for traveling to a neutral nation were all scrutinized. Authority for leav-ing France, the right to drive an automobile, and the permit to take petrol out of the country all received careful examination.

Sharp-eyed from years of searching for illegal cigars and contraband liquors, the eldest of the officials caught a flaw in the documents of Mac and Murphy. "You will notice that your papers state that you are to leave France by the route of Sierck. This is the gateway of Evrange. That is not in order."

"There is a slight battle in Sierck," Murphy offered.

The customs official looked stunned. "Is that so? And how do you know this, Monsieur?"

"We were turned back and unable to enter Sierck," Mac explained.

The officials conferred. "This is military information you ought not to have, Monsieurs. Yet you expect to be allowed to pass out of France and into a neutral nation where the enemy also has access?"

The Queen from *Alice* lurked in Mac's mind. At any moment he ex-pected them to begin shouting, *"Off with their heads!"* He drew himself up and addressed the clerk as "Chief," in hopes of using flattery to turn the tide. "If the French are fighting the Germans at Sierck, then surely the Ger-mans know it very well, and the information is no longer a military secret."

It made sense, did it not?

Mac and Murphy were taken to a small anteroom heated by a potbellied stove. The door was shut and the lock turned. There they baked slowly for three hours while the customs officials, bastions of the gates of France, checked their story.

Finally the officials returned. "I have telephoned Paris. Your papers are now in order," one of them declared.

At last they were set free with a slight apology. They had to repack their clothes and reinsert the insoles of their shoes. The cuffs and sleeves of their topcoats had been carefully slit. They were given the name of a tailor in Luxembourg.

It was after dark when they entered the Grand Duchy of Luxembourg. They were tired and almost convinced that at the French outpost of Evrange, perhaps the Germans would not pass after all. At least not easily.

⊘

War games at the Ecole de Cavalerie were like an elaborate contest of king of the mountain. For the exercise, two-thirds of the cadets were to play the part of the German army. One-third, under the command of Paul Chardon, were to defend the school and the north bank of the Lys River as part of an examination in military strategy.

But was it only a game?

The town of Lys, little more than a mile wide along the river of the same name, narrowed to a point as it climbed the hill north of the stream and ended against the military school.

From a knoll above the village and the river, Paul pored over a topographical map of the area that showed each point of defense in the battle that had taken place here during the last war. Officer Cadet Raymond was at his side.

"Our responsibility," Paul said, "extends from the bridge at Rozier downstream to a mile upstream, where the banks are too steep for armored vehicles to climb out."

The chart showed the island in the middle of the river over which the main road into Lys passed. Connected to both shores by bridges, the island was the first line of defense against attack. "Gaston is planning the protection of the island," Paul said, "and Sepp will figure the coverage for the banks of the stream in front of the town."

"And me?" Raymond asked.

Paul knew Raymond was aware that there had to be a reason his assignment had been saved to last. Paul reflected a moment. "This is just for practice. You understand that it will probably never be needed and certainly would never involve you actually in the defense."

Raymond nodded.

Paul stabbed his finger on the downstream crossing of the Lys, five miles away from the school. "This bridge must also be defended. But if a withdrawal had to be made, it is a long way back. For that reason, I want your plan to include the horses. We will need our vehicles elsewhere, but I do not want to leave you—the defender—without a means of escape."

Raymond looked Paul in the eye. The young man was the finest horseman at the school. The assignment was an honor. "Understood," the cadet replied as Paul struck out to inspect the positions of Sepp and Gaston.

Halfway down the hill toward the river, Paul and Raymond spotted Sepp with four younger cadets of his command. They were outside the Church of St. Sebastian and embroiled in an argument with Father Perrin and the mayor, Jacques Fontain.

"But Father," Sepp appealed, "we must climb the bell tower of the church in order to see across the river."

"You are spotting landmarks on the far bank to use for range finding," complained the priest. "I forbid it."

"I, too, forbid it," said the mayor, an elderly man who shook his cane in Sepp's face. "I will not have Lys turned into a battleground." Then, spotting Paul's approach, the frail, bent man said angrily, "You are the cause of this, Chardon!"

"I did not start the war," Paul defended.

"No, but you will bring it here," the mayor replied.

"It is only an exercise in strategy. Like every other year," Paul soothed. "A way of preparing the cadets for some future situation."

"Lys wishes no future situations with the Boche. Ever," spat the mayor.

"Of course. Certainly. Only for military theory, you see. What would you have our cadets do? Welcome the Boche with open arms? Invite them to take all the wounded in the hospital as prisoners?"

The mayor appeared to think that over. Was this really just the game of a few hundred students at the Ecole? "It is a British hospital," he said finally.

Even Father Perrin looked shocked at the mayor's statement.

Paul stepped between the mayor and the cadets. "We are simply making a study of how the town can be defended if need be. None of us wants—or expects—that to happen. But you remember the Great War, Jacques. Should we remain unprepared?"

The mayor fell silent. "No," he said at last. "I thought we taught the Boche a lesson when they called here twenty years ago, but perhaps they are stupid and will try again."

Sepp and his group gained entry to the church tower, and Paul and Raymond continued across the stone bridge to the island. Gaston, sounding like a drill sergeant, was barking orders to a dozen subordinates about the placement of the school's two antitank guns. "One here to cover the bridge. The other farther back to guard against the loss of the first."

"How is it progressing?" Paul inquired quietly.

Gaston jumped at the sound of his commander's voice. "I did not see you coming." He thumped his broad chest in a gesture of relief.

"It is a good thing we are not Germans, Gaston," Raymond teased and then ducked as Gaston cuffed him.

"All right then." Paul broke up the tussle. "Your situation, Gaston, if you please."

"Hardly enough heavy weapons. Any chance of adding tanks or artillery to this plan?"

"Nothing we can count on."

"What about the 75 mm piece up at the schoolyard?"

Raymond laughed. "You mean the one Colonel Larousse was afraid to fire even as a signal gun, for fear it would blow up?"

"You are doing fine work, Gaston," Paul encouraged. "Keep it up.

Take good notes. If the enemy were to advance this far, their defeat might depend on the information we could supply to our army."

"Captain," Gaston said as Paul turned to leave, "according to the *Principles of Modern Warfare*, how many defenders are required to guard this length of river?"

Paul thought a moment. "Fifteen thousand—provided they have adequate artillery support."

"And how many cadets remain at the school?"

"Nine hundred," Paul replied.

25

German "Tourists"

Perhaps the best view of the war was in the Luxembourg village of Remich on the terrace of the Hotel Bellevue. The Bellevue was owned by a former vaudeville performer named Lucien Klopp. After the last war, Klopp had retired from the London stage for peace and quiet. The quaint establishment he managed was in the area known as Luxembourg Corners, where a point of the Grand Duchy jutted out to touch the borders of France and Germany.

Klopp's terrace overlooked a valley so picturesque it might have been lifted from a fairy tale. An ancient castle with turrets, moat, and drawbridge topped a ridge on the left. Vineyards for creating sweet Moselle wine climbed the bluish hills. Along the river in both directions were clustered little white villages with perfect white church spires rising against the cloud-studded sky.

The river wound gently in the sunlight, a shining ribbon of light, before it left Luxembourg and flowed away. Beyond the border of the neutral country, the Moselle was the tangible dividing line between France and Germany. From Klopp's patio, tourists could see the beginning of the purple mass of the Maginot fortresses and the Siegfried Line across from it in Germany.

With the aid of binoculars the batteries of both sides were plainly visible: barbed wire, earthworks, and machine-gun-studded pillboxes. Right there, on display from the peaceful promenade, was The War.

Mac and Murphy came out onto the terrace. "They've taken an intermission," said Larry Beavers of the *Post*.

Four other newsmen were leaning on a stone wall, looking off to where the Schengen Bridge crossed the wide blue river.

Mac could hear birds chirping in the cleft of the hill. There was no artillery, no smoke. The peace of little Remich was tangible.

Bill Cooper, the stout, round-faced AP correspondent from Berlin, had turned his field glasses skyward. "You guys missed it. We had five airplanes up there a while ago. Two of Hitler's and three of Chamberlain's. Nothing happening now, though."

Murphy laughed and patted Bill on the shoulder. "So, Bill, things must be boring in Berlin, too, huh?"

"Deadly dull. The Führer's off in Bavaria with his band of Merry Men. If you ask me, I'd say everybody's about to forget about this war business and sign an armistice. Any takers?"

There were a few comments about the lack of news. Everyone standing in Klopp's garden had come here hoping to pick up at least a small story. Hotel Bellevue had ringside seats, but the bout appeared to be called on account of weather.

"It's too cold to fight." Murphy pulled up the collar of his coat. "It's too cold to stand here and wait." He retreated sullenly into the drafty breakfast room of the Bellevue.

Mac guessed that about now John Murphy was longing for foggy old London town and his wife sitting by the fire. The war, the separation, and the evacuation were turning out to be a lot of bunk. Not one bomb had fallen on London, yet Murphy had endured being apart from his family for months. The strain on this normally phlegmatic guy was definitely showing . . . now all the trouble of crossing from France into Luxembourg and probably nothing to show for it but days of groggy conversation with a bunch of rheumy-eyed journalists.

Bill Cooper cocked his head slightly and peered at Mac with interest. "Hey, Mac! Weren't you . . . are you still seeing Danny Marlow's widow?"

"Josie? Not really. I mean, I see her sometimes." Mac shifted uncomfortably at the question. He hoped Cooper would move on to other topics.

"Where is she?" Cooper looked around Mac's shoulders, as if expecting Josephine Marlow to stroll out onto the terrace.

"Paris." Mac did not add that she was most likely breakfasting with a French colonel.

"You're going back to Paris?"

"I might as well. There's no war here."

Cooper's ruddy face lit up. He lowered his voice. "Listen, I was supposed to pass along an important message to her from a German Wehrmacht officer I met in Berlin. He brought something out of Poland for her . . . from that priest she's so fond of. I thought I was going to be in Paris to give her the tale in person, but my kindhearted little Nazi press officer advises me that if I go to France I may not be allowed back into dear old Deutschland. And this isn't something you can put in a letter. The French authorities in the Anastasie would pounce on it like ducks on a bug. You know?"

Cooper was correct about the French postal service. The censors had been named after Saint Anastasie, the woman who had her tongue cut out on orders of Emperor Diocletian. The tongue of every letter that entered or left France these days was cut out, leaving the reader to wonder just what it was that the original document meant to say. Important matters like this could not be trusted to good fortune and the mails.

Cooper checked over his shoulder, as if Klopp's terrace might also be a hangout for Gestapo spies. He was right to be concerned. Luxembourg, Holland, and Belgium were packed with German "tourists" these days— many of whom had more sinister reasons for traveling in the neutral nations than sightseeing.

Cooper took Mac by the arm and led him to a path that wound down the face of the cliff toward the river. Out of range of prying ears he told Mac about the German major, the Catholic priest from Warsaw, and an old rabbi in Palestine. At last he opened his wallet and removed a photograph of a baby. A half smile flicked across his face. "This year in Jerusalem."

❧

The engine that would carry John Murphy to the coast of Belgium chuffed impatiently beneath the ornate train shed of the Luxembourg City terminal. Mac knew Murphy was just as impatient to be on his way back to London.

Mac extended his hand in farewell. "Kiss Elisa and the kids for me."

"Her wire says she'll be waiting at Victoria Station when I get there." Murphy's eyes were alive with anticipation. "I may take a few days off. It's been months." He glanced at his watch as if even the minutes were too long to wait now.

"I envy you," Mac said, and he meant it. "Someone to come home to."

"Well, then? Get busy. I told you what Trump said. He's ready to open a new section: TENS Newsreel in London. He needs a good man to head it up. Why not?"

"I'm not cut out for a desk job. Anyway, Eva'd still be off in Wales."

"That could change."

"Five months ago I never would've believed it . . . before Warsaw."

Murphy shrugged. "So hustle back and marry that girl. You know what they say about love and war."

Mac waved his hand in front of his face, as if the thought was a fly to be brushed away. "Never mind love. It'll kill me for sure. All I care about right now is the war. It's safer. Talk to Churchill for me when you get back to London, will you, Murphy? See if you can't get me and my camera on a ship of the Royal Navy."

Murphy just smiled as he boarded the train.

Mac eyed the two large men standing near the serpentine wrought iron of the train-station lightpost; they were in no way remarkable in either looks or actions. To anyone but a trained observer, the raincoat-clad figures, one in brown and the other in navy blue, would have been indistinguishable from hundreds of other middle-class businessmen.

But Mac was a trained observer. The watchful eye of the camera never captured interesting scenes unless Mac had noticed them first. And these two men, both wearing fedoras pulled low across their foreheads, were interesting. Mac was certain they had ridden the tram to the train depot with him and Murphy. But they had not boarded a train themselves, and now after Murphy's express had pulled out, they were still lounging in apparently idle conversation.

Mac's mind flashed back to the destruction of his hotel room. He still couldn't fathom the reason for the vandalism, but these two gave him a clue as to the identity of the criminals. This pair had Gestapo written all over them. Mac toyed with the idea of going straight up to them and demanding that they pay for his busted camera. Better to verify his suspicions first, though. Even if they were German agents, they might not be interested in him. And if they weren't, it was better to leave it that way.

One way to check. Mac turned sharply and boarded the tram that was waiting to return to the center of the city. Sure enough, when Mac had seated himself and glanced out the window, he saw that the conversation had come to a halt, and the two men were hurrying toward the tram.

Just as the first of the two—a dark-eyed man with a prominent nose—entered the car, Mac stood up and pushed past the other passengers, back onto the sidewalk. "Changed my mind," he said to the conductor. "Sorry."

Mac wanted to see how they would handle this. For both to get out again right behind him would be suspicious even to a blind man. Both figures took a seat. The one nearest the window had a heavily jowled face that he pointed everywhere in the tram—ceiling, walls, floor—except out the window at Mac. The tram pulled out.

Knowing he would now recognize both sets of features again wherever he saw them next, Mac's need now was for alternate transportation back to his hotel. No taxis presented themselves, so when the next tram pulled up, Mac boarded it.

There were no stops between the Gare Centrale and the ancient battlements that towered over the Petrusse River. The coach slowed as it crossed the viaduct that rose on spindly iron legs over the chasm. The heights of the rock wall were shrouded in mist, but eventually it crossed the ramparts of the medieval fortifications.

At his stop above the cliff face, Mac recognized his mistake. The man with the prominent beak had gotten off the earlier coach and was waiting in the fine rain. The last thing Mac wanted was to lead these thugs back to his hotel and risk another spree of destruction, so he tried to make the train-station trick work again. Mac waited until the big-nosed man seated himself and the tram door closed, then popped up and said apologetically that he had almost missed his stop and needed to be let off.

The raincoated figure stood and also demanded to get out.

At the now-deserted tram stop, Mac found himself face-to-face with his pursuer. "I don't know what you want," Mac said, "but you are one ugly customer."

"*Was ist?*" replied the figure, whose wide-mouthed grin revealed he was missing his front teeth. "Come now, Mr. McGrath. There is no need to be uncooperative. We just want to speak with you about a matter of great importance. You will come with me." The last sentence was punctuated by the sudden appearance of a small Mauser pistol from the raincoat pocket.

Mac's protest died unspoken, and he raised his hands. "There is no need for that."

A casual wave of the pistol accompanied the instruction. "Please walk on slowly, a pace ahead of me. And you will not try to run. Having your knee destroyed would be very unpleasant for you, and I could scarcely miss at this range."

"What do you want?"

"All in good time."

Turning aside from the tram line, they paced the damp stones of the walk that skirted the edge of the precipice. Sheer rock walls fell away into the depths of the narrow gorge. The slender path followed the line of the ancient fortifications, which were themselves carved out of the solid rock of the cliff.

It was a very lonely spot. There were no others out walking on the cold and damp day, and they had moved away from the tracks so that a screen of brush blocked the view.

"That is now far enough," the man said.

"Look, what's this all about? I know you're Gestapo, but I don't know why you want me. And why'd you tear up my room in Paris?"

The thickset agent smiled his gap-toothed grin but said nothing. He gestured for Mac to back up until his legs were against the rain-streaked boulders of the parapet.

"Is this just for fun? 'Cause I got news for you, pal. I'm an American journalist. My country won't like you strong-arming its citizens. Your boss won't be happy either."

"Enough chatter! Where is he?"

"Where is who?"

The German agent lunged with his pistol hand, striking Mac across the side of the face with the barrel. Mac's head snapped back, and the skin over his cheekbone split. Clenching his fists, Mac crouched into a fighting stance. But another motion of the pistol forced him to relax and drop his hands again. A trickle of blood ran along the line of Mac's jaw and dripped onto the paving stones.

The German leaned close. He put the muzzle of the Mauser under Mac's chin, lifting Mac up on his toes. With evil-smelling breath loaded with onions and herring he said, "Coy is not your style, Herr McGrath. We know you were with Lewinski getting out of Poland. Where is he now?"

"Wait, hold on. Let me think." Mac's mind was racing. Where had he heard that name? He really did not know what this thug was asking about. But he couldn't say that. The image of the flight from Warsaw scrolled itself in Mac's mind. He saw a replay of Ambassador Biddle and the staff people and a weird character in a gas mask. "Do you mean the strange duck who wears the gas mask and has the curly red hair?"

"Of course! That's Lewinski!" A backhand rake of the pistol barrel across Mac's mouth burst his lip open and knocked him to his knees. "Quit stalling! Where is he?"

Now what? Mac could not say that he didn't know this Lewinski character's whereabouts, even though he didn't. He'd never be believed. "Yeah, sure. I know where he is. He's in . . . Paris," he said, naming the first city that popped into his head.

The Gestapo agent hefted the pistol as if weighing it. "So, you are telling the truth? Lying to us can cause great pain."

"So what do we do now? Stay here till the other bully boy runs over to check my story? Can I get up?"

The dark eyes stared down the bulbous nose and into Mac's bloody face. He put the pistol back in his coat. "Of course," he said, extending his hand to help Mac get up. Mac knocked the offer away and unsteadily rose to his feet. "There's just one problem."

"Yeah? What's that?"

The burly man suddenly grabbed Mac by the neck and his belt. He hoisted the cameraman onto the wall and pushed his head downward over the drop-off. "The problem is, I don't believe you. You would never give away a secret as vital as Enigma so lightly. Where is he really?"

Mac was truly terrified. Blood from the cut on his cheek was now running down into his eye. And below Mac was a cloud that concealed a two-hundred-foot drop. "I really don't know. Don't you think I'd tell you if I did?" he gasped.

"Probably," the agent grunted, and he momentarily relaxed his grip.

It was the opening Mac needed. His hands, which had been down by his waist, burst apart the grasp. Mac kicked the man in the midsection, knocking him back a pace. But before Mac could get clear of the wall, the Gestapo thug charged in again, anxious to get his hands back on Mac's neck.

The agent's damp shoe slipped on a loose rock underfoot, turning his lunge into an unexpected sprawl. Mac slid off the wall. Grabbing the lapels of the agent's raincoat as he dropped, Mac stood up quickly, pulling upward as hard as he could.

With a startled cry that turned into a long, drawn-out scream, the Gestapo agent plunged over the edge of the precipice, hurtling into the canyon. The shriek made less noise than the sirens of the Stukas Mac had heard in Poland and stopped abruptly.

Mac wiped the blood from his cheek and lip. He resisted the urge to see where the man had hit. Instead he turned his thoughts to a more immediate problem: what to do now.

If he went to the authorities, what would he say? How could he explain that he had just murdered a Gestapo agent who had been trying to kill him over some secret that Mac didn't have? What was that all about, anyway? And what about the guy's partner? Where was he?

In the end Mac slipped into his hotel through a side door and checked out immediately to return to Paris.

A sympathetic clerk exclaimed over the condition of his face.

"Yeah, well, those slippery rocks are dangerous sometimes," was all Mac said.

26
Impossible Things

Josie had spent the night in the bomb shelter beneath the Foyer International after two German bombers had flown lazily over Paris just to have a look at the Eiffel Tower. No air-raid alarm sounded, no bombs were dropped, but the harsh crack of antiaircraft fire erupted from eager batteries across the city. It was a French shell that rained down near the Metro in the Montmartre District. Two men were killed, and one woman suffered an amputated leg. After the damage had been done, air-raid sirens sounded a few minutes before midnight, but there were no enemy planes overhead.

The morning paper offered no apologies to the families of the Montmartre dead and maimed, nor for the loss of a night's sleep. The headlines clearly blamed the victims for their own bad luck and offered this word of warning in the headlines of the front page:

"CITIZENS OF PARIS!
When You Hear the Sound of Antiaircraft Guns,
Go to the Nearest Air-raid Shelter!"

Josie spent the morning at the Ritz Hotel, covering a fashion show staged for the benefit of French soldiers. The lobby bustled with over-dressed ladies eyeing the latest fashions in the shopwindows. Nearly every one of the shoppers wore a tricolored ribbon with a paper rose pinned to the lapel. This was a sign that they supported the drive to beautify the Maginot Line for the soldiers of France by planting rose-bushes at the front. The explosion near the Metro did not concern them at all. After all, none of them were the sort who rode the Metro anyway. Limousines were their style, Josie thought, as she passed two women walking their beribboned Pekinese dogs. Something in their manner made Josie believe that these grand dames of society could not imagine a stray shell having the impudence to land anywhere near their domain.

"Did you hear it? It hit just outside the Metro station, my dear."

"But of course! It had the good sense to avoid the Ritz! Can you imagine what a scandal that would have been? What a racket last night. It woke me up, and I could not get back to sleep."

Josie tucked the newspaper under her arm and passed through the oblivious mob. She took the Metro to meet Mac McGrath at the Café Voltaire on Rue de l'Odeon and noticed that the faces of subway passengers were not smiling and carefree this morning. Who on this train had not recently climbed the steps of the Metro station at Monmartre? Nearly all on board had been there at one time or another. The incident had a sobering effect on the ordinary men and women who could easily imagine themselves in that place when the errant missile hit its mark.

Josie found herself examining the patch of blue sky and imagining planes and artillery as she ascended the stairs to the street. She comforted herself with the old adage about lightning never striking twice.

She walked quickly to the café, which was crowded with a mix of professors and political types who gathered each lunch hour to rehash theories about the war. A haze of cigarette smoke hovered over the noisy room. Josie spotted Mac at a small table in the far corner. He wore dark glasses and was miraculously dressed in the uniform of an American correspondent. He looked very handsome, Josie thought, in spite of a bandage on his cheek. It surprised her that she was actually impressed, like some schoolgirl swooning over a man in uniform. Mac sipped a glass of wine and stared sullenly out the window at the teeming crowd of pedestrians on the sidewalk.

She was at the table before he noticed her. His smile of greeting was almost guilty, as if he did not want her to suspect that he was brooding about something.

"You made it," he said, regaining his pleasant expression instantly. "I didn't think you would come."

"I told you I would." She smiled at her reflection in the dark lenses. "Clark Gable in sunglasses."

He raised them enough to reveal that his right eye was nearly swollen shut. "Gable would've fared better. Some drunk in a bistro didn't like Americans. I showed him what a friendly bunch we are." He let the frames slip back into place.

"All the same, you look . . . really wonderful, Mac."

He flipped his lapel absently as if his tidy appearance embarrassed him. "Oh, this. I had to give in."

"What have you done with your tweed coat and your lucky red tie?"

"I've still got them. The war won't last forever, you know."

Same old Mac. The uniform was only a temporary aberration.

"You look swell all the same, even if it won't last."

"I've hitched a ride with the British navy. John Murphy put in a good word with Churchill for me. They're old friends, you know. Murphy and First Lord of the Admiralty. But I had to get myself a regular uniform, he said. The Brits wouldn't have me on board otherwise. Maybe going to get some real action on film."

So he was leaving France, Josie thought.

"The sea. That's where the real war is," Mac continued. "This whole Maginot thing . . . well, you know how it is. The Phony War."

"I'm glad you called, Mac."

He put down his wineglass and took her hand. "Are you, Jo?"

"Yes, really." And she was, too, even though she thought about him less and less since Andre had become a regular part of her life.

"Why do I always feel this way when I see you? Like I'm fifteen or something?" Mac eyed her with the expression of a sorrowful puppy.

He needed a haircut. He needed someone to look after him like a mother. He was not the navy type. Hadn't he told her that he spent his first, second, and third transatlantic crossings with his head in a bucket?

"You'll do fine," she replied, as if he had already expressed his concern about unending weeks on one of Mr. Churchill's big boats.

"We're always saying good-bye, aren't we, Jo?"

"That's the problem all right. Hello and good-bye. I should be flattered, I guess. That you want to see me before you sail away."

He grinned sheepishly. "That's not why I called you."

"Leave me with my illusions, will you?"

"I can't. I saw Bill Cooper in Luxembourg. You remember Coop?"

"Of course. How are things in Berlin?"

"Dull as here unless you're on the Führer's bad list. But Coop has had some contact with a friend of a friend of yours. The priest in Warsaw?"

Suddenly charged with energy, Josie knocked Mac's wineglass over, splashing red Bordeaux on his tunic. "Oh no! Mac! Your new clothes!"

He gaped down at the mess and dabbed at it with his napkin. "That's all right. It needed something to break it in." He snapped his fingers at a passing waiter and ordered soda water for the stain and water for Josie. "As I was saying. Cooper. The priest sent a message through a German Wehrmacht officer. More than a message really." Tapping his temple, Mac said, "I carried it up here to avoid having it pinched by the Gestapo in Luxembourg or the French Anastasie. Then I wrote it all down for you."

He pulled an envelope out of his tunic and placed it between the salt and pepper shakers. "There's this kid. A little Jewish kid. A baby, actually. The Polish priest sent him out of Warsaw with this German major. Coop says he's not a Nazi. A really nice guy, Coop says. So this major has the kid. The priest says you're supposed to go get him."

"Get him? Where?"

"The Reich. Treves."

"In the middle of a war?"

"Not much of a war, Jo; you have to admit. Anyway, it's all there in the envelope. The date. The time. The place. All figured out. Neutral American newslady crosses the border in Luxembourg. Picks up kid and scrams back. Happens all the time, doesn't it?"

She picked up the envelope and stared thoughtfully at it. "If the priest says it can be done, I suppose it's that simple."

Mac's moody look returned. "Your Frenchman should be able to help you with the papers. Great for cutting through the red tape, these colonels."

"My Frenchman?"

"Don't play coy, Jo. I know, okay? The guys in the pressroom at the Continental are taking bets on whether you marry the guy."

"And how did you bet, Mac?"

"I didn't. See, Jo, there's this girl I met in Warsaw. . . ."

"Oh!" Josie said suddenly.

"And there's a possibility of a job in London. . . . Murphy told me about a position with TENS." He put his hand to the bruise on his cheek. "I've been thinking about living a life with a little less edge to it. I admit it." He paused. Then, "You love this Frenchman?"

"I . . . I'm not sure. Maybe."

They ordered and ate their meals in silence. The clatter of dishes and the murmur of other conversations went unnoticed.

∽

The dining room in the Adlon Hotel at No. 1 Unter den Linden in Berlin was full of eminent Wehrmacht officers and Nazi Party officials. Even though they outranked everyone else in the room, Heinrich Himmler and Reinhard Heydrich occupied an undistinguished table in a corner.

Himmler was fussing over a plate of noodles in a bland cream sauce, taking tiny bites and frowning at the plate. "This has too much garlic," he remarked to Heydrich.

Heydrich was halfway through a heaping mound of a fragrantly spicy stew. "How unfortunate, Herr Reichsführer," he consoled. "Why don't you try what I'm having? It's excellent."

The slimly handsome Heydrich was baiting his boss, and he knew it. Himmler had such a delicate stomach that the sight of blood from an underdone steak upset him. It was a dangerous game to play with the mousy little man who was the second most powerful figure in the Reich, but it helped Heydrich's ego. Working for a former fertilizer salesman was tough on Heydrich's opinion of himself.

Heydrich stopped eating to smile broadly at a pair of Fräuleins seated across the room who were openly studying him with interest. Heydrich's womanizing was another activity of which Himmler did not approve.

"What progress have you to report in the Lewinski matter?" Himmler asked. It was clear he knew exactly how to burst his aide's self-satisfaction.

"We're working on it, Herr Reichsführer," Heydrich pledged, turning his attention back to his meal. As head of the main office of Reich security, Heydrich was under pressure to get results, and he knew it. "We are pursuing contacts at all the universities where Lewinski is known to have connections: Oxford, Princeton, Stanford. Even the Sorbonne in Paris, although that is most unlikely."

"Does it seem that this investigation is rather slow to produce results?" Himmler said, squaring his sloping shoulders. The SS Reichsführer also knew how to needle an opponent.

"I assure you, Herr Reichsführer, that we are proceeding with the utmost *gründlichkeit*," Heydrich said. "Thorough in every detail."

"If the secret of Enigma should get out . . ."

"Let me reassure you. Since the code setting changes every day, and the method of establishing the new settings is quite secure, the most that is at risk is that a mind like Lewinski's might unravel one day's code . . . but certainly too slowly to be harmful." Heydrich gave a dismissive wave of his hand. "But let me say, Herr Reichsführer, so that you will not lose a moment of sleep over the matter, that we are closing in on the fugitive even as we speak."

Himmler paused to polish his already spotlessly clean spectacles, then put them back on his pinched, narrowly placed eyes before replying. "That is most comforting. For your sake, I hope you succeed quite soon."

⨍

It was an amazing thing when Madame Rose rolled her eyes toward the sky and said, *"With God all things are possible."*

Jerome soon discovered that Madame Rose did not mean that she should sit quietly at No. 5 Rue de la Huchette and wait for God to do some impossible thing. On the contrary, this meant that she went to work at impossible tasks and simply expected that because she was well acquainted with the Almighty, those things would become possible to accomplish.

This seemed to be true.

Was the orphanage low on potatoes? low on funds? low on beds as twenty new children arrived?

Madame Rose had a Scripture promise for every emergency. These promises were drawn upon and recited back to heaven regularly. "Lord, You have promised to care for the widows and the orphans . . . therefore, we need potatoes. A few plump chickens thrown in for good measure would be kindly appreciated. . . ." Then she would go out to Buci in search of potatoes and chickens. Always she would get what was needed and a little more besides.

She expected miracles each day. Jerome suspected that the miracles were the result of a very strong personality. When he said as much to Madame Rose, she laughed and said that if it was so, Jerome should thank God for giving her such a personality.

There was no way to argue with her without feeling confused.

Enough of this, Jerome thought. If Madame Rose believed that with God all things were possible, he decided that he must ask her to ask God if it would be possible for Jerome and Marie to get in to see Uncle Jambonneau at the hospital.

Madame Rose went alone the first time. Carrying Papillon in a paper sack, she walked to the hospital on a Sunday afternoon to visit Uncle Jambonneau.

She came back very cheerful and brought a note that the old man had dictated.

> *Dearest Nephew Jerome and Niece Marie,*
>
> *Madame Rose has told me what a terrible thing Madame Hilaire has done by throwing you off the Garlic and stealing it. However, I, your dear uncle Jambonneau, am certain that you are both better off with Madame Rose than with Madame Hilaire, who has a voice like a cannon and a personality like a crazed anteater. . . .*

Jerome knew that Uncle Jambonneau had mentioned the anteater because it was Jerome's least favorite creature at the zoo. Always sucking helpless ants out of their houses. Terrible. Jerome had experienced nightmares about anteaters sucking him out of the porthole of the *Garlic*, so it was appropriate to call Madame Hilaire an anteater.

The note continued:

Please take care of my little dog. I have missed his little whiskers at my ear. I miss you both also. Be good children and obey Madame Rose.

Your beloved uncle Jambonneau

The next week Jerome and Marie followed Madame Rose to the back door of the hospital. She waited until Rodrigo, the Spanish laundry deliveryman, arrived with a white canvas cart heaped with towels.

Madame Rose knew everyone on the Left Bank who did laundry because she had taken in washing for so long herself. She and her sister were very good friends with Rodrigo. She told him about Uncle Jambonneau and then about Marie and Jerome.

Rodrigo emptied the canvas cart, and Jerome and Marie got in. Towels were piled on their heads. Madame Rose gave Rodrigo the room number and said she would meet him there in five minutes.

In this way the impossible was accomplished. Jerome and Marie were trundled up the freight elevator to the floor where Uncle Jambonneau shared a ward with twelve old men. Madame Rose drew a curtain around the bed, and Marie and Jerome popped out of the towels like cabaret performers out of a cake.

Rodrigo stood guard. The other old men in the ward said they heard the voices of children. Madame Rose opened the window, peered out, and said, "You certainly do! Spring is in the air!"

Five minutes only. There were hugs and whispers, and Jerome told Uncle Jambonneau about Henri and the horse of the French hero with the wooden legs. Marie let him touch her glasses, and he said that it was a very fine thing to be able to see. He was very pleased for her.

Uncle Jambonneau stated that Madame Rose was a very well-connected woman. She knew some very important personages who were able to achieve impossible and wonderful things.

Jerome agreed that this was true.

27

Much about War

As a pleasure cruise, travel on the *Altmark* left much to be desired. Under any other circumstances, this observation would have been feeble humor at best, but to the prisoners in the hold of the German freighter, it was uproariously funny.

Trevor Galway spent the better part of each day dreaming up ways to keep up the men's morale. Over two months had passed since his capture. The steady northward progress since the brief glimpse of the battle involving the *Graf Spee* meant that the chances for rescue were decreasing. If the prison ship was not intercepted soon, she would be inside protected German waters and would have accomplished her purpose.

For the past two weeks the prisoners had lived with increasing cold. From the roasting tropical conditions of their capture, many of the men now suffered the opposite agony in the unheated hold. Perversely, the Germans had finally decided that the captives needed more fresh air, and they left the hatch ajar just enough to admit a frigid draft.

Now the crowded conditions were a blessing, without which some of the sailors would have frozen to death. As it was, the cramped space they had formerly complained about was now warmed solely by the packed bodies.

Trevor had worked out a shuffling spiral of motion. The activity kept the men moving and their blood circulating. It also made sure that everyone got a fair turn at being near the center and warmed on all sides.

But even this effort lasted only so long. Eventually they became too tired to do anything but sleep, though the men had nothing but their thin and ragged clothes with which to cover up. In their exhausted hours, the sailors kept up unconscious movement, like a herd of sheep in a snowstorm. One would worm his way into the center of the pile of sleeping bodies, only to find himself rooted aside again later and shivering against an icy steel bulkhead.

It was during one of these semiawake sleep periods that the forward motion of the freighter slowed and then stopped. "Do you think we're in Germany?" Dooley asked. "Even a nice warm prison camp would be better."

"Shhh," Trevor warned. "Listen!"

There were shouts from alongside the *Altmark*, answered by replies from her deck. Trevor could barely make out the exchange. "George," Trevor hissed, "wake up and translate this."

"One of them is speaking Norwegian," Daly replied. "Wait—now he switched to German. That one is demanding to come aboard and search . . . something about neutrality."

"Everybody up!" Trevor shouted. "Make all the noise you can! There are Norwegian officers alongside. It can only mean that we're inside their territorial waters. Bang on the walls! Yell your heads off! Do anything you can think of to make noise!"

Norway was officially one of the neutral nations. As such, she was entitled to see that the ships of the belligerents passing through her national zone carried no arms or other war material. The prohibition included prisoners of war. If the British could make their presence known, the Norwegian could demand their release.

The men stamped their feet, banged tin cans together, yelled obscenities, and even sang snatches of songs. "How can they not hear this?" Dooley wondered aloud.

From overhead came a shrill, whining sound, joined by the thump of an engine, then another engine noise and a long, drawn-out squeak. The air filled with what sounded like a thousand out-of-tune violins scraping and sawing.

Trevor groaned. "It's the cargo winches. They've started up all the engines to drown us out."

The *Altmark* shuddered into motion again, carrying its discordant noise away from the Norwegian patrol boats. A short time later the hatch was uncovered, and Captain Thun appeared with several armed guards. There was a clatter in the darkened hold as tin cans dropped to the decking. "I have been too lenient," he said. "Stricter measures are now required. You, Mr. Galway, and you and you." Thun pointed his flashlight at twenty of the prisoners who had been standing closest to Trevor or who were caught still holding things to make noise. "All of you, come out of there."

"What are you going to do with us?" Trevor demanded.

"New accommodations," Thun said without humor. "Hellhole."

☙

It was an American story: Two aging American ladies in Paris taking in a load of kids and a lot of laundry. Human interest. Just the sort of thing that could spice up the back page of American's·newspapers during the "Bore War."

It would make ordinary U.S. citizens feel better about themselves: "Read this here, Bertha. Us Amer'cans ain't isolated-whatevers after all! Amer'ca's still got heart, don' it? That's Amer'cans like us over there takin' care of them waifs! Just so long as they don' bring the filthy little things back here!"

It was the sort of story that would be quoted in Congress. Senator Borah and the rest of the anti-foreign-devil mob were dedicated to keeping immigration to a trickle: "It is noble American volunteers over there in that Paris slum! Proof of the grrr-eatness of the American spirit. But the average American citizen does not want more refugees coming to our great nation and bringing their slums to our grrr-eat shores. We've got trouble enough!"

Paris AP chief Frank Blake assigned the story to Josie. Who else? Nobody else on staff could stand to write bleeding-heart material. Too depressing. But Josephine Marlow? She actually felt this stuff—was moved by it! Every day she frowned at the blank sheet of paper in her Olivetti and grieved over what she was about to write, as if she was that Robert Frost guy or that Steinbeck troublemaker. She pondered internal questions and agonized over content: Would the story make a difference? Was she capturing the essence of it? the heart of the people?

Frank Blake always let the literary drama play out. He smiled and thanked her when she presented her piece, then told her to go take a break. In less than one minute, starting from the bottom up, he cut the article in half and wired it to the States. That was good clean journalism: heart surgery with a red pencil as a scalpel. Slice it up. Toss out the heart. She never knew the difference. No doubt it would be cut in half again and altered by every editor in the syndicate. Let the little woman have her illusions. She was really just a high school literature teacher, after all.

This was the cynically reasoned scenario that brought Josie to her next assignment.

☙

It was cold, but a few of the bookstalls were open on Quai des Grands Augustins. Josie was early for her appointment with Rose and Betsy

Smith, so she browsed from stall to stall in search of a copy of *Paradise Lost* for herself.

It was not easy these days to pick up English volumes on the quai. There were no more English-speaking tourists, and the average British soldier who came to Paris on leave was not interested in reading. But there were lots of tinted postcards of the Eiffel Tower and Notre Dame and etchings of the bridges across the Seine looking toward the cathedral from Pavilion de Flore. The troops of the British Expeditionary Force purchased such things and sent them home by the bagful: *Hullo, Mum. Wish you were here!*

Of course they were quite content that their mums were on the other side of the Channel so they could sow their wild oats. The German troops did not seem so youthful as the British, nor as old as the French. That fact was worrisome when Josie stopped to consider it.

Six young BEF soldiers browsed the open-air stalls this afternoon. They stopped at the booth of Monsieur Lemoine, who was a veteran of the last war and had the empty sleeve of his coat pinned neatly to the shoulder. The soldiers did not notice the bookseller. They could not look at such a withered old man and imagine that he had once been in an army himself.

Ignoring the bookseller's amused gaze, they winked at Josie and spoke to her in clumsy French. "*Parlez-vous l'anglais?*" The words were flat, without any pretense of correct pronunciation, as if they were being read from a guidebook. English-French. French-English. Barely recognizable.

She shook her head politely, shrugged, and smiled apologetically.

They nudged one another and made suggestive remarks about her in their native language, thinking that she really did not *parlez*.

She knew the old bookseller well and asked in distinct English, "*Bonjour*, Monsieur Lemoine. If you please, I am looking for a certain volume of the works of Milton."

"*Oui*, Madame Marlow!" He held up the index finger of his one hand in exclamation. He had just the thing.

"Blimey!" exclaimed the fairest boy. "She's a Yank!" He noticed the press badge on her topcoat. "A journalist!"

Josie raised an eyebrow regally. "What would your mother say if she knew you spoke this way to a lady?"

The boys blushed. British males were usually stolid when it came to women, unless they thought they could get away with something. And these were very young. Probably this was their first time out of their Yorkshire village. Tipping their service caps, they wandered quickly in the opposite direction.

"Well done, Madame," exclaimed the bookseller. "One hopes these English will learn something about women while they are in France, but they do not even know how to speak. I hope they know how to fight the Boche."

"Let's hope the whole thing will be finished before it matters, Monsieur."

"*Oui*, Madame." He accepted fifty centimes for the volume. Then, with his solitary hand, he deftly wrapped it in newsprint and tied it with twine. Josie held her finger on the center of the knot. "Are you working today, Madame?"

"An interview with the American sisters on Rue de la Huchette."

"Madame Rose and Madame Betsy?"

"You know them?"

"But of course! Everyone knows them."

"How long have they lived here?"

He shrugged. "Since before I came home from Verdun. For a time they cared for the son of my dear sister, who perished from the influenza in '18. The boy is at the front now. I hope he comes back in one piece." He pointed to the pinned-up sleeve in a gesture that indicated he knew much about war. "Take the ladies a gift from me, Madame." He counted the fifty centimes back into her hand, then added an additional twenty. "The church is rich enough. *Bonjour*, Madame! *Merci!* Good day!" He turned to a new trio of customers.

༄

The dark-eyed beauty with the long, black hair batted her lashes at Professor Alan Turner of Oxford University. Her passport indicated she was Portuguese by birth, and everyone knew Portugal was a neutral nation, so her presence at Oxford as a student of literature was no surprise.

What was amazing was her sudden interest in mathematics. She attended one of Turner's lectures on games theory and stayed around after class to inquire further. "Ees it true that the great Einstein lectured here and that his blackboard notes are still preserved?"

Turner was so delighted by her breathy accent and her way of leaning toward him when she asked her question that he promptly forgot what she had said. Noting the way she filled out the silk blouse she wore did not help his concentration either. Turner blushed into the roots of his thin brown hair. "I'm sorry. What was that again?"

"Einstein," she repeated simply.

"Oh, yes," Turner confirmed. "He was here . . . let me see . . . clear back in '31. His notes are still on the board in the basement lecture hall."

"Can we see them?" Miss Francesca Pereira asked.

Turner loved the way she said *we*. "It's a bit of an old, dusty room. But perhaps I can arrange it sometime."

"Why not now?" she asked, pushing out her lips in a pout to go with her disappointed frown.

"Now? It's after hours and there would be no one about," Turner said, inwardly groaning after his objection.

Miss Pereira fluttered her eyelashes again and inclined even closer to the mathematics professor. "But this way you could geeve me a private explanation of what eet means," she purred.

Turner found himself walking rapidly along the curve of the Sheldonian Theatre. He was vaguely uncomfortable to be under the disapproving gaze of the thirteen giant stone heads known as the Emperors.

Miss Pereira talked incessantly and actually pressed against Turner's arm. "And you know Professor Einstein personally?"

"Yes," Turner agreed and then, waxing brave, added, "and other important thinkers as well."

"Really?" Francesca said. "Who else? You don't know Lewinski, do you?"

"Richard Lewinski?" Turner repeated. "Certainly."

"Ooh," she said. "I just adore hees ideas on a universal calculating machine . . . fascinating, and so ultramodern."

"Richard and I have discussed his theory many times. In fact, we worked on it together while he was here at Oxford."

"You don't mean eet?" Francesca's voice rose in amazement. "But this ees fabulous . . . it will be the foundation of a whole new world. But tell me, where ees Lewinski now? Why has he not published his work?"

Turner wrinkled his forehead, worried that he might somehow fail an exam for which he had not properly prepared. "I don't know. I lost track of him after he went to Warsaw." Turner could tell that Miss Pereira was unhappy with the answer. "But I know where he isn't," he added. "He did not go to America, because a colleague of mine from Princeton wrote and asked me the same question. It seems someone from Poland was trying to locate him about some money he had coming."

"But you must be concerned for heem," Francesca urged. "Can't you think where a great mind like hees would go to continue hees work?"

Turner thought a moment. "Lewinski always said that he loved Paris better than anywhere on earth. I should think he is in seclusion there."

Francesca's eyes widened. "Does he have something to be frightened of?"

"No." Turner laughed, tired of so much talk about Lewinski. "He's just like that—solitary and reclusive. Anyway, I would bet on Paris if I were trying to find him. Shall we press on to the classroom now?"

Francesca consulted the watch on her slim wrist. "Oh, my goodness," she said with alarm. "I'm late already, but we can do it another time, yes?" She planted a quick kiss on Turner's cheek and hurried away.

"Yes," he called after her. "Another time, then!" Turner looked at his own watch. How could he have been so inattentive? He also was late to his work at Bletchly Park, where he oversaw the MI6 attempt to unravel the German code device known as Enigma.

28

Miracles Every Day

Josie Marlow pulled the bell rope, announcing her arrival at No. 5 Rue de la Huchette.

A thin young girl with straight, bobbed brown hair and thick glasses opened the gate and peered out curiously like a strange little bird. She wore a coarse, hand-knit red sweater and a high-collared yellow dress. Her shoes were scuffed. One blue sock was up and the other down, revealing a spindly leg.

Behind her in the confined space of the courtyard a group of boys played baseball. The noise of cheering was amplified against the high white walls of the building. Chalk squares drawn onto the cobbles served as bases. Beside each base was an umpire—a boy in a tall, old-fashioned wheelchair being pushed by a much smaller boy. An orb wrapped and bound by burlap and twine served as the ball. A tennis racket was the bat.

The girl at the entrance screwed up her face at Josie and shouted, "I am Marie Jardin. Do you like my new glasses? I can see everything very well now, thank you. I did not know I could not see before. But now I can. You see? Who are you? You have a nice face."

"I have come to see Madames Rose and Betsy."

"They are playing baseball." She stepped aside and swept an arm up to point to two old ladies in the thick of the fray. "You would like to watch? Madame Betsy launches the ball. Madame Rose is *a la batte*. My brother, Jerome, is the catcher of the baseball, which is a common potato all wrapped up. Henri, the boy who rides in the chair with wheels is the vampire, but he does not drink blood. Vampire. It is something you have in American baseball, no? You see him there? He holds Uncle Jambonneau's dog, who is a rat. Papillon is on his shoulder."

Josie spotted a rat riding on the shoulder of the grinning, wheelchair-bound child beside first base. "Very interesting, Marie." Josie determined that she would steer clear of the kid with the rat.

"The game, she is a tie. Last inning. Two outs. No one on base and two strikes on Madame Rose."

Josie stepped around her just as the scrawny Betsy wound up and tossed the wrapped potato over home plate. Rose swung hard and connected. The twine around the burlap broke, and the ball flew into pieces. Part of the potato struck Rose as she ran for first. The catcher, a thin-faced, male version of the little bird-girl, clawed at bits of the tuber in an attempt to find enough potato to throw her out. Madame Betsy called for time and shook her bony finger at her laughing sister. This required a judgment from the umpires. It wasn't fair, Betsy declared. Half of the potato had touched Rose, and Rose was out! She had busted the ball, and she was out!

The wheelchairs rolled together for the umps to discuss the situation. The boys mumbled and nodded as the rat looked on seriously. Finally they judged against the base hit. Madame Rose was definitely out. Remaining on first, Rose blustered her protest. She was promptly warned that if she argued further her team would be penalized one run. Josie concluded that in this French version of baseball, the rules must be very fluid and unpredictable—something like French politics.

Pursing her lips in obvious disagreement, Rose dusted herself off as if she were Babe Ruth and stalked from first back to home.

Thus ended the inning and the game with a tie: thirty-one to thirty-one. Both teams, the umpires, and the spectators lined up to congratulate one another beneath the banners of laundry drying above the courtyard. Jerome plucked the rat from the shoulder of the ump and placed it on top of his head. He danced around in joyous circles, then fed the rat a bit of potato left over from the ball. Josie was taken firmly by the hand and guided to the center of the mob by Marie, who blinked happily through the lenses of her glasses.

Madame Rose, who did indeed have a grip something like Babe Ruth's, pumped Josie's hand. "Hello, hello!" Her cheeks had bright spots of color. "You are Josephine Marlow. We have no room for a *terrain de football*—a soccer field—so we play baseball. My team usually wins."

Betsy pouted. "Rose cheats . . . makes up her own rules."

"When in Rome, as they say, Betsy dear!" Rose retorted cheerfully. "You have Papillon as mascot, don't you, Jerome? That draws all the best players. If I did not cheat a bit, how could I ever win?"

All good-natured, the hands of the children reached up to pat their

coaches in congratulations. It was a good game. The best kind of ending:
Nobody won.

"We do not want you to enjoy yourselves too much! Schoolwork!"
Rose clapped her hands, and Betsy spread her arms like a hen herding her
chicks into the coop. There was an audible groan. The crowd, with curious
looks at Josie, dispersed to trudge up the outside stairs that led to the upper stories. The four umpires in their wheelchairs were piloted toward the
wide door of a ground-floor room by Austrian boys in lederhosen who
growled like race-car engines and charged over the rough cobbles in competition. The catcher and his rat beat everyone up the stairs to the landing,
where he thumped his chest and yodeled like Tarzan.

"How many children?" Josie asked, looking after them as they disappeared from balconies into a half-dozen doorways.

"Seventy-two," Betsy replied. "From the tiny ones to age twelve.
More than twice as many as usual."

"And the rat?" Josie asked.

Betsy put a finger to her lips, letting her in on the secret. "They all
think he's a dog with a long, hairless tail. He belongs to Uncle
Jambonneau, and Jerome is taking care of him," she confided, as if this
was an answer.

"However do you manage?"

"We are never without help," Rose explained. "Students from the
Sorbonne come to tutor the children in exchange for meals. Grandmothers come to help us cook and help with the babies. The older children help with the younger. And with God's help, overall, it is not
difficult, Madame Marlow. He brings us little miracles every day."

"I'll bring tea." Betsy excused herself as six volunteer cooks banged
on the gate.

Josie remembered the seventy centimes. She fished in her pocket and
presented the coins to Rose. "From Monsieur Lemoine, the bookseller.
He says you cared for his nephew years ago."

"This is why it is not difficult. Every day God reminds our friends that
we are still here. Like Monsieur Lemoine . . . his nephew, Jacques, all
grown up now and old enough for it to happen all over again. France has
enough empty sleeves from the last one."

Rose shrugged, mopped the perspiration from her brow, and led
Josie to a cramped and cluttered office. Framed needlepoint Bible verses
hung on the wall. *Do unto Others* . . . She moved a stack of hymnbooks
from a battered wooden chair and gestured for Josie to sit. "And now,
my dear, how can we help you?"

Bells and whistles were going off in Josie's head. She remained serene and
hoped that Rose would not see the sparks flying out of her ears. Could it be

that this was not just one story, but an entire series? Tomorrow she would submit a newsy little human-interest article to the bloody knife of Frank Blake for AP. And then? Then she would write something new and wonderful each week and sell it freelance to *Harper's* or *Ladies' Home Journal*!

Josie calmly took out her notebook. "Would you mind starting at the very beginning?" The tea arrived and Betsy joined them. "How did you come to be here?"

The sisters exchanged looks, as if they had been waiting the longest time for someone to ask.

"You see, my dear. Josephine, is it?" Betsy began. "It started with a miracle that took place in 1870. We would never have been here at all, otherwise. . . ."

Rose got a faraway look in her eyes, as if she were hearing another voice speak to her. "Our father, Captain William Smith, was a sailor. . . ."

Somewhere in the telling of the miracle, the thought hit Josie that Madame Rose was just the woman who could help in the making of another miracle. She took out the envelope with the photograph of the baby from Warsaw and slid it across the desk of the old woman.

"I need help. I don't even know where to begin. This child is in the Reich. . . ."

The eyes of Rose brightened as she studied the photograph. "And you want to bring him out?"

"Yes. I have approached the American Embassy about the proper documents. They are intractable. The waiting period for immigration to the States is years. No Germans are being allowed out of the Reich. Especially not Jews."

"Of course. Unless he is your son. A handsome little fellow."

"Can that be done?"

"Certainly." Rose grinned and opened a cluttered file cabinet to remove the forms.

"Is it difficult?"

"Heavens no! I'll hand carry the letters myself. We'll have to pretend he started out here in Paris." She winked. "A little larceny for the sake of a child. God doesn't mind a bit. We're an orphanage, you see. A matter of two months, and you will be a mother. I know an excellent bookbinder who can conceal the documents for you to cross the German border. A simple matter. Done quite a lot these days."

◈

It was a fact that Trevor Galway doubted would be believed at home. There was a young navy chaplain named Gabriel Horne who shared the space of the men in hell.

Being a tiny, dark-eyed Protestant from County Tyrone, Chaplain Gabriel had more the look and sound of a leprechaun than an archangel. It was observed, however, that the little man did not possess the power of either being.

The area in the hellhole of *Altmark* was even more confined than the cargo hold had been. It was not possible for those imprisoned here to do anything other than stand up. Trevor thought it was amazing what humans could cope with and keep going. He and the others in the cramped cubical leaned against each other to sleep.

The hellhole was below the waterline. When the ship rolled in the waves of the North Sea, icy, foul, oily water from the bilges sloshed around the legs of the prisoners.

The darkness that clamped down when the hatch was shut was absolute. While it was true that Trevor could literally not see his hand in front of his face, that fact was far from being the worst of it. Left without any ray of light to register on the senses, the mind soon conjured up images to replace the lack. At first the figures were simple, like sunbursts and fireworks. But as time passed, Trevor imagined that he could see flowers and trees and recognize people in these pleasant outdoor scenes. It made him wonder if he was losing his mind, but everyone in the confinement experienced the same thing.

Chaplain Gabriel, being shorter than the others, suffered from saltwater ulcers on his legs. And yet he coped with his suffering without curse or complaint.

To deal with the physical pain and the gnawing possibility of going crazy, Chaplain Gabriel encouraged the others to tell stories. Every man in the bowels of the ship remembered more than he thought he did—sights from travel in distant lands or memories of home. It was decreed that they would not talk about real food or sex. Chaplain Gabriel declared that discussing mother's home cooking or the girls they left behind was the surest way to drive each other crazy. They should think of this enforced fasting—two crusts a day—as a sort of spiritual purification. This pronouncement was at first harshly booed by the boys in hell. But when Dooley began to conjure up fresh strawberries and cream and a pot of hot tea for breakfast with Greta Garbo sitting across the table, Chaplain Gabriel battled the phantoms using bits of song alternated with Bible verses.

"Seek ye first the kingdom of God, and His righteousness; and all these things shall be added unto you."

This sentiment caught the attention of every man in the hold.

Dooley was silenced. The discussion began: "Seek the kingdom of God and I'll be given Garbo?"

It was a beginning at least.

Chaplain Gabriel did not explain everything to his captive congregation, but from strawberries and Greta Garbo came great debate about the nature of heaven and the chaplain's belief that the power of heaven could be summoned and miracles could happen when people pray and speak the Word of God.

"Even here in hell?"

"Were there ever fellows more in need than we are?" Chaplain Gabriel asked.

And so even the doubters decided to give it a try. Nob—who had not spoken aloud to his Creator since childhood when he asked lightning to strike his Yorkshire schoolmaster—inquired exactly what a fellow said to God, anyway.

"Just have a nice chat," the chaplain urged. "That's all. And then listen for a while."

Halting, childish prayers began to be uttered by desperate men. It was a time when prayer became a reality—not the egocentric petitions of the well-to-do self-righteous or the frantic prayers of the drowning man, but something altogether different. The men in the hellhole prayed for each other.

"Lord, let Nob's cough be better tomorrow than it is today."

Then came the listening part: *"Seek ye the Lord while He may be found, call ye upon Him while He is near. . . . I will never leave you nor forsake you."*

"Jesus, take the ache out of Chaplain's legs."

"Father, protect our children from ever having to go through anything like this, ever."

And Chaplain Gabriel spoke the promises: *"Though I walk through the valley of the shadow of death, I will fear no evil . . ."*

There was resistance when Chaplain Gabriel suggested that they pray for their captors.

"Pray that they get caught out in the open and shot to ribbons you mean!" The normally soft-spoken Nob was not buying this "love your enemies" line.

"Nob," the chaplain asked, "where will you be in a hundred years?"

"What nonsense are you talking? I'll be dead, of course."

"And where will the guards be?"

"In a hundred years? They'll be dead, too."

"Can't happen soon enough to suit me," someone grumbled in the dark.

"But think," the chaplain replied. "Suppose you could change places with the guards right now, but doing so meant that you had to change with them again a hundred years from now."

There was a sober reflection in the hellhole.

"To stand before a righteous God and give account?" the chaplain continued. "I'd rather stay right here in this stinking hold for a while than stand in the shoes of Captain Thun on that day, thank you, sir!"

A point well made.

Later, as Chaplain Gabriel slept, it was quietly discussed by the boys in hell that one hundred years from now heaven was sure to be filled with women who looked like Garbo and all the steak and strawberries a man could eat. It was a great comfort to them all.

⬡

Norway's craggy coastline jumped up from the dark gray sea in front of Mac. The snow-covered outcroppings offered only tiny amounts of level shoreline. It seemed as if the Norwegian fjords wandered through a drowned country of which only the tops of the mountains remained above water.

A glistening coat of ice sheathed the forward rigging of His Majesty's Ship *Cossack*. The destroyer had been Mac's home for the past several weeks. It and the rest of the squadron patrolled the North Sea, pouncing on German merchant shipping and unwary U-boats.

At the moment the kind of action Mac had often witnessed was unfolding against the backdrop of the Norwegian coast. Minutes before, *Cossack* had intercepted a small freighter gliding along just outside Norway's territorial limits. When her skipper caught sight of the destroyer's knifelike prow cleaving the waves, he put his helm hard over and ran for the Norwegian coast.

It was a game of sorts. Intercepting German shipping was part of war. If the steamer was not armed and carried no military cargo, international law permitted her to seek refuge in neutral waters. The game turned more interesting due to the deceptions practiced by the German officers. It was made infinitely more complex by the ability of Adolf Hitler to intimidate the neutral nations.

The *Cossack* accelerated to more than twenty-five knots, rapidly overtaking the merchantman. "Put one across her bow, Mr. Longbow," Mac heard Captain Vian order.

The gunnery officer relayed the command, and seconds later the destroyer's forward five-inch gun barked a command to halt. The shell exploded a hundred yards in front of the steamer, now straining to turn out eight knots of speed. But rather than heaving to, the German ship steered even more sharply toward Norway and safety. Her shuddering frame and lone funnel streaming black smoke proclaimed her resistance to surrender. The name on the stern that waved defiantly in *Cossack*'s face announced her to be the *Schwartze Himmel,* the "Black Sky," out of Hamburg.

"I'll have another round closer in, Mr. Longbow," Vian ordered coolly. "Mind that your crew do not blow off her bow, like they did to that trawler last week."

"Practice makes perfect, sir," returned Longbow with a grin.

The next shot fired landed just under the freighter's nose. She abruptly pulled up and turned broadside to the warship. It was clear to the German vessel, as it was to Mac, that the next shell would not be a warning.

"Bravo, Mr. Longbow. Nearly clipped her anchor chains! Mr. Perry, hail the captain."

But the master of the *Black Sky* got his words in first. "Ve are loaded mit hospital und relief supplies only," he called over the loud-hailer. "Und ve are inside Norvegian vaters. Let us proceed, if you please."

"Tell him, right after we verify his cargo," Vian said.

When this was relayed to the *Himmel,* there was no further reply. The deck of the freighter was littered with cable spools and canvas-covered stacks of crates. It was difficult for Mac to see anything warlike in her appearance.

The destroyer put down a boat, and First Mate Perry led the inspection team. He and his men would become the prize crew to sail the freighter back to England if the German captain's story proved untrue.

There were groups of sailors clustered on the deck of the steamer, studying the progress of the launch. As Mac watched, they slowly resolved themselves from an aimless mass into two distinct formations. One set of men stood near a heap of crates forward, the other around a netting-shrouded pile amidships.

"Captain," Mac muttered.

"I see them, too, Mr. McGrath. Longbow, order those sailors to back away to the far rail. And tell them to step lively."

It was as if the command was the signal the Germans had been waiting for. Instead of retreating, the two teams of seamen pulled the tarps from the supposed cargo, exposing a pair of antiaircraft guns. At the same moment, the *Himmel* belched a sulphurous blast and shook herself into motion again.

"Sink her," Vian ordered. And to the helmsman he commanded, "Put us between the launch and the target."

One of the rapid-firing German guns opened up on the small boat. Whether this was planned as a way to force the *Cossack* to save her own or simply murderous intent, the result was the same. The quick chopping noise of the antiaircraft shells had not reached Mac's ears before the launch was splintered along with the men in it. Three figures were seen diving over the side into the icy water, and then Mac had to duck as the other antiaircraft gun fired into the bridge of the destroyer.

The five-inch gun of the warship boomed again, crashing into and silencing *Himmel's* midships weapon. The chatter of machine guns coming from both vessels added to the sudden cacophony. From hearing only the keening of the wind and the slap of the waves a few minutes earlier, the torrential blare of war now broke over Mac.

A shell exploded against the bridge, knocking the helmsman away from the wheel. Captain Vian took his place, aiming the destroyer's bow directly at the fleeing German craft. The marksmanship of the Germans proved no match for the Royal Navy. First the other antiaircraft position and then the machine guns fell silent.

"Put over another boat to pick up our survivors," Vian ordered. "Then we'll finish this business."

Into the carnage of the bridge rushed a young officer Mac vaguely recognized as the radio operator. He was waving a yellow cable form. "Urgent message, sir," he told Vian, who was silently urging the rescue operation to hurry as the *Himmel* limped slowly out of range of *Cossack's* guns.

"Not now!" Vian snorted. "*This* battle is not finished yet."

"But sir!" begged the communications officer. "It's the *Altmark*! They've located the *Altmark*!"

Against this piece of news, even the treacherous ploy of the *Schwartze Himmel* no longer mattered. As soon as a handful of remaining sailors were retrieved from the frigid sea, the *Cossack* shifted her course south. Soon all that remained of the deadly encounter were a few floating bits of debris and a smudge of the freighter's smoke on the horizon.

29

Political Wrangling

On the chart in *Cossack's* wardroom, Jossing Fjord resembled the head of a cobra. Less than a quarter mile across at its mouth, the inlet expanded just inside the rocky opening, then narrowed again till it pinched out one and a half miles back from the headland.

The skipper of the destroyer *Intrepid* conferred with British captain Vian of the *Cossack* about the situation as Mac listened in. "*Altmark* was spotted by a patrol plane as she made the passage between Iceland and the Faroes. I caught up with her a dozen or so miles offshore, but she made the run into the fjord before I could overtake. You see where our Norwegian friends have positioned their gunboats . . . that's when I contacted you."

Through the shrapnel-blasted shutters of the bridge, Mac could see the two Norwegian patrol craft. Their low profiles and ugly, blunt snouts reinforced the image of Jossing Fjord as a nest of vipers. Drifting floes of ice bobbed in the current, but an unobstructed swath in the center of the channel showed that something larger than a gunboat had recently entered the gulf.

Captain Vian explained the importance with which the *Altmark* was regarded. "The freighter accompanied the *Graf Spee* during the battleship's rampage in the South Atlantic. When the *Spee* was surrounded, the *Altmark* eluded capture, carrying away with her perhaps as many as two hundred British sailors."

"So she has remained at large ever since the *Spee* was scuttled? Nine weeks ago?" Mac asked.

Vian looked chagrined. "Not for want of trying on our part. She has been the subject of an intensive search. It was believed that she would try to return the prisoners to Germany for the propaganda value such a move would have. And from her position here, she almost made it."

"How do the Norwegians figure into this?"

"Commander Riks, the ranking officer of the gunboats, is arriving now to answer that question," Vian said, pointing at an approaching boat.

The Norwegian skipper was a stocky man with sandy blond hair and pale green eyes. He appeared uncomfortable from the minute he boarded the *Cossack*, saluting the British colors as he did so.

"Captain Vian," Riks began, "I must request you to take your warships out of Norwegian territorial waters at once."

"We have reason to believe that the German vessel sheltering in this bay carries British prisoners of war. As such, she is clearly a belligerent and has violated your neutrality."

Riks stared at the floor. When he spoke again, the words came slowly, as if dragged from him against his will. "We have already searched the craft in question. There are no British nationals on board, nor is the ship armed. She has requested and been granted asylum in our waters."

"Asylum!" Vian exploded. "You can't mean it! Do you think we will let her escape to take our people back to Germany? I'll board her and see for myself!"

"Regrettably," Riks said softly, "I cannot allow that. As you can see, the torpedo tubes of my gunboats cover the entrance to the fjord. I have been instructed to use them against any unauthorized attempt to enter the strait."

Vian appeared disgusted, as if he had bitten into an apple and found Riks inside. "You have delivered your message and may return to your ship, Commander," he said tersely, "while I confer with my superiors."

When the Norwegian had left, Mac stopped Vian on the way to the radio room. "Does this development discourage you, Captain?"

"Not in the least, Mr. McGrath," Vian said. "First Lord Churchill will be responding to the situation personally."

As always, the waiting was the hardest part. The torpedo tubes of the gunboats stared at *Cossack* like the muzzles of two-thousand-caliber guns. Mac supposed that the Norwegians did not want to fire on the British. He knew that they despised Hitler and all the Nazis stood for. But more importantly, they feared the Führer's intentions toward their skinny, poorly defended shoreline of a country. Fragile neutrality depended on not offending the master of the Third Reich, not giving him any excuse to invade.

Besides, U-boats and mines had already sunk over two hundred thousand tons of supposedly neutral Scandinavian shipping. "So sorry," the Kriegsmarine replied. "Better keep your ships out of the sea-lanes used by the Allies. Let them trade only with the Reich, and they'll be safe." As extortion, it was not very subtle.

Mac imagined the discussions taking place in the Admiralty offices back in London and the response from 10 Downing Street. It was like Czechoslovakia and Poland all over again, only on a scale where everything could be taken in at once. Mac was certain that Churchill's response would be belligerent: *"Show the Norwegians that we mean business and they will stand aside . . . show the Germans that the sea is still a British possession, and its freedom will be defended."*

But Mac was equally certain that Chamberlain's reaction would be one of dithering and fretting. *"What will the Norwegians do? What will the world say about us if we blast our way through neutral ships defending their own territory? What if the* Altmark *has already disposed of its captives?"*

And what about those captives? Mac knew that some of the prisoners taken by the *Graf Spee* had been in custody for as long as five months already. Had they given up hope of ever being rescued? Were they even still alive?

The hands of the clock silently registered the political wrangling going on in London. Its hands swept around the dial several times before reaching 1600 hours and a reply from the Admiralty was received. "Good old Winston!" beamed Captain Vian, waving the cable. "He says we are to ask the captain of the *Altmark* what he has done with the prisoners!"

Mac accompanied Vian to meet Commander Riks on the gunboat *Kjell*. "Are you prepared to withdraw from our territory, Captain?" Riks asked.

"Not exactly. My government has ordered me to place two proposals before you, either of which will be satisfactory. The first is that we jointly escort the *Altmark* to port in Bergen, where an international inquiry will be made."

Riks was already shaking his head before Vian had finished. "You know I cannot fall for that. It would mean effectively giving an unarmed ship into your control. What is the other proposal?"

"The second option is that you and I proceed to the vessel and inspect her together. Just in case your earlier visit . . . missed something."

Mac sensed the difficulty with which Vian was restraining his temper. But if the warning signs were present, Riks did not heed them.

"I'm sorry, Captain," Riks replied. "That is not in my power to agree to either."

"In that case, sir," Vian said coldly, "we are prepared to take action without your cooperation."

Riks pointed to the uncovered warhead of a torpedo ready for launch. "We will be forced to resist such an attempt."

"May God have mercy on you then," Vian spouted angrily.

With that the British captain and his followers returned to the destroyer.

⟨∽⟩

When the rolling motion of the *Altmark* stopped again at last, the men confined in the hellhole began to pound on the walls and shout. Trevor tapped Morse code messages on an overhead pipe. The feeling was that the effort to alert someone to their condition might not do any good, but they could scarcely be treated any worse for trying.

A strange grinding that came from outside the hull of the freighter replaced the vibration of the engines. It was the noise of metal being scoured with wire bristles, or the shriek of fingernails on a chalkboard.

"Sounds like the bottom is getting torn right out," Trevor said.

Dooley chuckled. "You never sailed the North Sea afore, did you, Commander? That's the sound of ice floes rubbin' alongside the hull. We must've turned into a fjord to hide out or somethin'."

The imaginations of the men went wild. Hiding in one of Norway's icebound waterways meant two things that spanned the gamut of emotion. The first was the despairing realization that their unwilling journey to Germany was almost over. If the *Altmark* passed the Skagerak Passage between Denmark and Norway, then hope of rescue was done.

On the other hand, stopping to lay over in a fjord this near to her destination must mean that *Altmark* was closely pursued.

No one answered the clamor made by the prisoners, nor did the engines start up again. The ice continued to creak and growl against the hull with sounds just like the English poet, Samuel Taylor Coleridge, described in the masterful *Rime of the Ancient Mariner*.

Presently a new fear crept into the hellhole.

"What if them Nazis have cut and run?"

"What if this tub is stuck in the ice and no one finds us afore we freeze to death?"

It was, in fact, getting noticeably colder. With only the thickness of the metal hull between the ragged men and the ice-covered sea, the temperature dropped, as did the spirits of the prisoners. It had been a long while since the last meal, though there was no way to judge the passage of the hours in the deep hold. The gnawing in Trevor's stomach alerted him that at least one issue of rations had been missed.

"That's it, then," Dooley said at last, voicing the despair the others all felt. "They've left us here to rot."

"Don't give up hope," Chaplain Gabriel urged. "Maybe all this means is that rescue is near."

"Sure, Padre," Dooley said. "I just don't want to get rescued after I'm already dead."

A tremor ran along the spine of the *Altmark*.

"What was that?" Trevor remarked.

"What was what? I didn't hear nothin'."

"Not hear, felt."

"I didn't feel nothin' either. 'Course, I haven't felt my toes in about three hours."

"There it is again," Trevor said as a shudder coursed through the freighter.

"I felt it, too," Nob agreed.

"You're both dreamin'," someone challenged. "It's just more ice buildin' up outside. Like as not, they'll find us froze inside a iceberg in a hundred years or so."

The bilgewater in the hold started sloshing from side to side. "They started up the engines!" Nob exulted. "We aren't abandoned after all."

The freighter rumbled with the returning life of her power plant, but she did not get under way immediately. "What are they playin' at?" Dooley wondered aloud.

The senses of the prisoners in the hellhole were so tuned in to feeling the rumble of the ship that they did not notice the hatch being opened until it was thrown back.

"*Achtung*, Tommies," Thun's guttural voice ordered. "We are about to be attacked by a British warship."

Loud cheering greeted these words, but Trevor was instantly suspicious. Why was the German captain telling them this?

The answer was not long in coming.

"Shout while you still have voices," the Nazi officer said. "Here is a little something to keep you company." He dropped into the hold an oilcloth-wrapped parcel, which was caught by the chaplain. "If we get away, I'll take that back from you. Otherwise it is yours to keep."

"What is it?" Chaplain Gabriel asked.

"I will scuttle the *Altmark* here in the fjord rather than let her be captured," Thun said. "That is the time bomb to do the job. It will go off if you unwrap it, or in thirty minutes if we do not escape." The hatch clanged down, shutting off the horrified protests of the men in the hellhole.

"Shouting will do no good, lads," Gabriel counseled, "but God can hear our prayers."

30

A Blossom of Radiance in the Darkness

Even after all the time he had spent aboard the *Cossack* in the high latitudes of the North Sea, Mac was still surprised at how abruptly and how early the sun went down. It was barely late afternoon, and already a curtain of blackness replaced the gray veil of the daytime sky.

The destroyer prepared for her entry into Jossing Fjord. Her gun crews stood by their weapons. The orders they had received were understood, but no less difficult to accept. They were not to fire unless fired upon.

"Blimey!" the loader on a heavy machine-gun team burst out. "Let them blokes what thought of that one come here and go eye-to-eye with them torpedoes!"

Cossack's sister ship *Intrepid* was to stand by and assist in defeating the gunboats when the shooting started. It was also understood that she would inherit *Cossack*'s mission if the lead destroyer was blown out of the water.

Captain Vian ordered the huge, incandescent searchlights lit. Beams that were millions of candlepower blazed across the dark water. "Like givin' them torpedos a track to run on," muttered the loader, earning himself a cuff on the ear from his crew chief. Vian wanted to leave the Norwegians no doubt as to his intentions. *Cossack* would proceed directly into the mouth of the fjord, daring the gunboats to fire. It was Churchill's precise instruction.

The blazing lights pinned the gunboats against the snow-crusted walls of the narrow entrance. Their lethal black forms were perfectly outlined in front of the icebound shore. They squatted like the lifeless stone guardians of an ancient temple, but Mac knew they could spring to life at any moment with the deadly animation of a coiled snake.

Cossack swept closer and closer to the entrance of the bay. At this distance, there would be no escape when the torpedos were launched, no room to turn with only unyielding cliffs on either hand. Mac saw that the helmsman's grip on the wheel was white-knuckled. So was his own on the iron ring of the bulkhead by which he steadied himself. Only Vian seemed undisturbed by the peril. He murmured instructions to the helmsman in a calm, quiet voice.

It was a staring contest at point-blank range. The stillness of the gunboats was so threatening, so full of menace, that Mac almost wished for gunfire to break the spell.

Then suddenly they were past the mouth of the fjord and into the widening reach of the bay behind. The Norwegian warships lay astern of *Cossack*; they still had not moved. A chorus of excited exclamations echoed off the towering walls of the ice canyon.

But if Captain Vian had been unmoved by danger he was no less implacable when it had passed. "Belay that noise," he ordered sternly. "This mission is far from over."

The gleaming cakes of drifting ice closed in around *Cossack* as her searchlights probed the recesses of the gulf. At slow speed she glided almost silently around the bends of the fjord, alert for her target.

"There she is," Vian observed at last.

Mac could not immediately make out the *Altmark* against the shore. He saw a pale, two-story building that stood on top of a cliff of black stone, then realized that he was looking at the superstructure of the freighter above the dark mass of its hull. The stabbing light beams swept from the deck of the German steamer, but no movement was seen from the cargo masts amidships to the heap of netting on her bow.

"She looks deserted," Gunnery Officer Longbow observed.

"All the more reason for us to look sharp," Vian countered. "Helmsman, lay us alongside." The British ship slipped through the water toward its objective as if being pulled along on the searchlight beams.

Cossack's bow, which had been pointed directly toward the center of the freighter, swung to port as the destroyer edged up next to the *Altmark*. When the warship's flank was opposite the merchantman's bow, a blasting siren from the German ship ripped the night apart. *Altmark* jolted awake, and her bow swung toward *Cossack*'s side.

"Ahead full," ordered Vian calmly. "She is trying to ram us. Mr. Longbow, give the order to fire."

The heavy bow of the German freighter swung after the destroyer with ponderous but inexorable motion. It was like being chased by an iceberg. There was no speed to speak of, but any collision with so massive an object would be shattering. Even the lines of tracers that reached out from *Cossack's* machine guns seemed a puny attempt to ward off such a crushing blow.

Altmark's starboard quarter swung across the fjord's width to swat the *Cossack* like a bug. At the last second before impact, the freighter's stern grounded on the shore of the inlet. Her movement suddenly stopped with a rasping noise and a shudder.

"Now, helmsman, hard to starboard," Vian commanded. "Mr. Longbow, rake her deck. Boarding party!" Vian's voice elevated to shout a command that had not changed in a thousand years: "Grappling irons away!"

In an instant the two ships were wedded together by barbs and cables of steel.

"Come on, lads." Second Mate Beard led the charge over the rail, waving his pistol.

In the superstructure of the steamer, shots were fired from ports looking down on the deck of the *Cossack*. A heavy machine gun pivoted upward to shatter an entire row of the openings, and the shooting fell silent as quickly as it had begun.

Mac saw a group of German sailors break out of a hatch amidships and make a dash for the netting-covered objects on the deck. But *Cossack's* earlier experience with camouflaged weapons had taught them well. Not a single figure even reached the gun emplacement before all had been cut down.

Racing from the bridge, Mac found himself across the rails and onto *Altmark's* deck before he was even aware of what he was doing. He was as caught up in the excitement of the rescue as all the others in *Cossack's* crew.

Mac sprinted toward the gangway that led below. The clatter of *Cossack's* machine guns kept the Germans pinned down as the British tars swarmed over the deck. Halfway to the ladder, Mack tripped over a coil of rope and sprawled. As he fell, a trio of shots splatted against the metal of the *Altmark's* superstructure, showering him with chips of rusty paint. The point of impact was just where his chest would have been.

Each gunshot was a blossom of radiance in the darkness. The blazing searchlights swayed across the surface of the steamer, pinpointing knots of armed Germans. The rapidly firing heavy weapons of the British destroyer swiveled to follow the path of the beams, making it seem as if the rays of light were doing the killing. The whole of the deck was a stage performance gone berserk: brilliant illumination, then pitch-darkness, popping sounds and screams, and rapid rushing movements followed by crouching stillness.

More German soldiers emerged from the cable tier at the far bow end of the freighter. Attempting to take the British from behind, they came out of hiding firing MG-34s from the hip and spraying the freighter with bullets. Two Englishmen went down, and the rest knelt to take aim at the new threat.

One of the Germans drew himself up to lob a grenade. At the peak of his motion, a searchlight pierced him and a single shot rang out from the bridge of the *Cossack*. The German clutched his side, bobbling the toss. The explosive clattered on the metal decking, bouncing amid shrieking men. Mac turned his head aside at the instant of the explosion. The *crump* of the grenade was followed by a renewed chorus of agonized groans.

Mac saw a handful of remaining Nazis throw themselves over the side of the ship, but whether into the water or onto the shore he could not tell. He had reached the stairway down and was rushed along with a knot of British sailors intent on freeing their countrymen.

The interior of the *Altmark* was absolute blackness, and though a few of the men carried electric torches, they were afraid to use them for fear of drawing a shot. The charge slowed abruptly as suspicion of an ambush took hold.

A muffled shouting and a riotous clanging noise reached the ears of the rescue party. "That's more shooting up on deck," someone called.

"It's water gurgling in the hold," yelped another. "The Germans are scuttling the ship."

"Shut up and listen!" ordered Second Mate Beard.

In the silence that followed his command, the din of metal on metal continued, but over it could be heard voices yelling "Help us! Get us out of here!"

"Come on, men!" Beard shouted. "It's this way!"

They met no more Germans on the descent into the *Altmark*. The hatch of the first hold they came to was dogged shut from the outside, but Beard still opened it cautiously, his Bren gun ready. The portal was a dimly seen silhouette that led from blackness to even deeper shadow. No sound came from the interior. "Are there any English in there?" Beard called out.

There was a momentary silenc. Mac held his breath, then heard, "Yes, mates, get us out of here!"

"Well," Beard offered by way of explanation, "the navy's here!"

Hatch after hatch was flung open to reveal scores of British prisoners crammed into unlit, poorly ventilated iron cages. Out of every cargo hold came sailors who had been imprisoned for months. By the improvised lighting of handheld flashlights and torches, Mac shot film of the emotional scene. Total strangers fell on the necks of their rescuers, shaking hands and hugging, offering their gratitude over and over. Painfully squinted eyes blinked against the unaccustomed glare, and trembling hands clutched bearded faces in an agony of fear that the deliverance was not real.

Mac backed up against a bulkhead to frame another shot when a small square hatch under his feet rang with the sound of repeated blows.

"That's the hellhole!" one of the rescued men shouted hoarsely. "Get 'em out of there!"

The hellhole was an unused fuel tank. It stank of bilge, diesel, and human waste. When the lid was raised, the muffled calls of "Hurry! Hurry!" increased rather than subsiding. Instead of men climbing out to freedom, a small parcel wrapped in oilcloth was passed up first. "Quick!" someone yelled as the object was handed to Mac. "It's a time bomb! Over the side with it!"

Like a child's game with disastrous consequences for the loser, the bomb was passed from hand to hand out of the hold of the ship and up to the rail. "It's a bomb! Get rid of it!" The device was launched over the rail of the *Altmark* to sink in the depths of the fjord. No one ever knew whether it would have exploded or not.

The fifteen-by-fifteen-foot steel cube disgorged twenty men. Their oil-streaked, pasty complexions and bony frames made Mac think of Jonah, half digested in the belly of the whale. He helped lift them free of the pit.

"When did you get captured?" he asked one young man, no more than age twenty-five, who nevertheless looked about seventy.

"I don't know what day this is."

"It's mid-February. The sixteenth, I think."

The emaciated form was racked with coughing. When the spasm subsided, he replied, "Almost three months?"

"Does your family even know you are still alive?" Mac asked.

The face narrowed in thought. "I don't know. . . . I doubt it. How could they?"

"What's your name?"

"Trevor," the figure replied. "Trevor Galway."

⸎

Adolf Hitler was in his office in the Chancellery when he got word of the fate of the *Altmark*. "And how many British destroyers were sunk in this action?" he demanded.

The Kriegsmarine officer swallowed hard. "None, Führer."

"*None?*" Hitler shouted, a speck of moisture flicking onto the naval officer's face. "No resistance? No courage?"

"Five sailors did die, Führer, and five more . . ."

But Hitler was not even listening. "All the way back from the South Atlantic. Two months of concealed movements. Nearly returned with all the prisoners, and then this! To give up without a fight! Shameful! Despicable!"

The officer knew better than to argue the point. "The Norwegians are to blame, Führer. They permitted the British destroyer to enter their waters and attack the ship after having granted *Altmark* their protection." He saluted crisply and exited the office.

Hitler barely acknowledged his departure. "Get me von Brauchitsch," he bellowed into the intercom, demanding the immediate presence of the Wehrmacht's commander in chief.

Heinrich von Brauchitsch was a quietly intelligent soldier, widely respected for his ability. But his will was no match for Hitler's, and he had long since given up trying to oppose the Führer's wishes.

"Have you heard of this outrage in Norway?" Hitler demanded without preamble when the general arrived. Von Brauchitsch barely had time to nod before Hitler launched into his orders. "We will not wait to attack Norway. The assault on the French will take place as planned, but I want the invasion of Norway moved up a month. A whole month, do you hear? Norwegian collusion will allow the British to use the North Sea ports against us. We will not permit it!"

∽∾

Horst von Bockman was home again. Really home.

He and Katrina lay together beneath the warmth of the down quilt, and it was as it should be. He was drowsy and contented beside her now. He felt somehow healed by her touch, whole again . . . as though they had never argued, never been apart. She kissed his neck and traced the line of his shoulder with her fingertips. Afraid to move, afraid she would stop, he pretended to sleep.

"Touch me," she murmured impatiently and took his hand, bringing it to her lips.

He wanted her again. Pulling her against him, she yielded with the gentle, urgent desire of familiar love.

"I knew you were awake." She laughed.

"I never really sleep when I am with you." He kissed her mouth and felt her heartbeat quicken to match his own.

"And when you are not with me?" Her voice was tremulous but still teasing.

"Then I sleep only to dream of you."

"Horst." Her breath was sweet. Whispered in his ear, her words made him dizzy. "I want us . . . to make a baby. Part of you to stay with me when you are away."

There was a kind of magic in her request. It charged him through with tenderness for her like he had never known. He could not speak to answer. He wanted to see her face, but it was too dark. He wanted her to look in his eyes . . . to know how much he loved her.

Her lips moved against his ear, but he could not hear her voice beneath the drumming of his own pulse.

It did not matter what she said. He would agree to anything—everything she asked him. He nodded as she ran her fingers through his hair, then strummed his back in rhythm as though she heard music playing.

EPILOGUE

That word above all earthly pow'rs,
No thanks to them, abideth;
The Spirit and the gifts are ours
Through Him who with us sideth.
Let goods and kindred go,
This mortal life also—
The body they may kill;
God's truth abideth still:
  His kingdom is forever.

News of the rescue of British sailors from the *Altmark* lifted the morale of all of England.

Eva Weitzman and John and Elisa Murphy traveled from Wales to London to meet Mac when he returned to England with Trevor Galway.

Mac's film footage of the rescue and then of Trevor's reunion with his sister, Annie, and his father, was viewed in a private afternoon screening for the royal family and members of the War Cabinet at Buckingham Palace.

Afterward, as Elisa and Murphy slipped away to be alone, Mac and Eva strolled along the Embankment overlooking the Thames. Barrage ballons, like giant silver kites, drifted above barges on the river. Ahead, Big Ben and Parliament were silhouetted against the twilight sky.

Mac held Eva's hand. It seemed natural to have her beside him. "Your letters . . ." He groped for the right words, faltered, and fell silent.

"Will you stay in London now? Or go back to Paris?" she asked.

"Paris. A few days here, then . . . Paris again."

"When will you come home again?"

He inhaled. "Home. You mean . . ."

"I mean here . . . back to me. Home."

Yes. Being with Eva was like a homecoming for Mac. "I don't know. I don't. This thing, the war . . . is . . . it's just beginning. When the weather warms up again, when it's spring again, we're going to see guys like Trevor Galway who have been through enough for a lifetime back in the navy, back on their battleships, and it will happen all over again. I knew that when I saw those British prisoners come out of the hold of the *Altmark*. Yes. The true horror is just beginning."

"I will wait for you, Mac."

He squeezed her fingers. "I know. I know, Eva. And I wish I could somehow . . . sorry. I wish . . . I mean . . . being here with you, Eva, well, it's all I want." He stopped and pulled her to him, cupping her face in his hands. "You're all I want. But how can I make any promises? I have the feeling this is going to last a long time and . . . how could I ask you to . . . you know?"

"Just ask."

"All right, then. Would you? Marry me? When I finish this assignment. When I come back from Paris. Would you?"

She sighed. "Mac. Mac . . . you know the answer." She lowered her eyes in acceptance as he kissed her.

"Then, Eva, I'll live and die a happy man." He held her close against him.

"Just live, Mac. Live . . . please."

Digging Deeper into *Paris Encore*

"Time levels all men. Good and evil alike. A century will pass in the blink of an eye, and who will sort the particles of dust? 'God will know you!' I look in the mirror each morning and say to myself, 'Andre, one day everything you think you believe about yourself will be put to the test! Then there will be no more empty talk over the dinner table. Honor? Love? Faith? Courage? They will become suddenly tangible truths that stand before you and require you to make a choice." —Andre Chardon (p. 158)

When you hear the word *hero* or *heroine*, what character quality first comes to mind?

Most would say, "Courage." Why? Because without courage, there can be no such thing as a hero or heroine.

In the fall of 1939, England and France have finally declared war against Germany, yet Hitler's evil continues to sweep across Europe, destroying everything and everyone in its wake. Will England and France be able to stop the great tide of evil that now threatens to wash over the sleeping neutral countries of Belgium and Holland? Who will awake in time to see the danger—and have the courage to make a difference?

In *Paris Encore*, there are many heroes and heroines who exhibit courage—both publicly and behind the scenes:

Winston Churchill continues to fight evil the only way he can—by resuming his position as First Lord of the Admiralty for England so he can counter the cowardly Neville Chamberlain's inaction.

Journalist John Murphy pens and publishes the truth . . . but longs to do even more to open the eyes of Americans to what's happening in Europe.

Photographer Mac McGrath risks his life on the front lines for rare footage. . . and then has to fight the censors who refuse to release his films.

Horst von Bockman agonizes over his conflicting loyalties to duty and the Fatherland, his love for and need to protect his family, and his compulsion to help Father Kopecky save "even one" of the Jews from Nazi-occupied Warsaw.

Horst's wife, Katrina, risks her reputation, property, and very life to save the Polish Jew Brezinski, his family, and the numerous Jewish children and nuns in her stable.

It is a time when few people can be trusted. As Old Brezinski says, "The only honest men left in Germany are in concentration camps. Holy places, those prisons. Full of saints and martyrs" (p. 131). And yet this humble Jewish man is himself a hero. Why? Because he has every reason to hate Nazis, yet he is able to act with courage and see with long-range perspective.

When Katrina becomes disillusioned with Horst, Brezinski offers this wisdom: "Not every man in the Wehrmacht is evil. . . .You know the Nazi law. If one family member commits a crime, all are punished. . . . Love sometimes calls for a peculiar kind of duty. . . . You are doing all you can. You have put yourself at risk for all of us. So be smart. But you must have mercy also on your husband. They hold a gun to your head, and he loves you. Believe that he will do what he can, but also what he must" (pp. 131, 132).

And that takes us to you, dear reader. Do you struggle with conflicting loyalties—doing what you can, but also what you must? Are you being put to the test, as Andre talked about? Are you in the midst of an agonizing decision?

We know how complicated life becomes, so we prayed for you as we wrote this book. And we continue to pray as we receive your letters and hear your soul cries. Following are some questions designed to take you deeper into the answers to these questions. You may wish to delve into them on your own or share them with a friend or a discussion group.

We hope *Paris Encore* will encourage you in your search for answers to your daily dilemmas and life situations. But most of all, we pray that you will "discover the Truth through fiction." For we are convinced that if you seek diligently, you will find the One who holds all the answers to the universe (1 Chronicles 28:9).

Bodie & Brock Thoene

SEEK . . .

PART I
Chapters 1–2

1. Winston Churchill was appointed to Chamberlain's War Cabinet so he could no longer criticize the British government (p. 3). Have you ever been put in a position because you've been critical of the way things have been done? If so, did anything change in you, the job, or the organization as a result?

_____

_____

2. Even in death, the Nazis wronged Pastor Karl Ibsen. They claimed he'd committed suicide, when he actually died as a martyr (p. 4). Have you (or someone you know) been wronged by slander against your reputation? What was the situation, and how have you handled it?

_____

_____

3. If someone you love died under "horrible circumstances" (p. 4), would you want to know? Why or why not?

_____

_____

4. Should we fight in wars that are "supposed to be none of [our] business" (p. 11)? Explain your view.

_____

_____

5. Have you ever been intrigued by a person you've seen or met in passing, as Josie was intrigued by Andre (pp. 17, 18) and Annie was "burned into" David's mind (p. 37)? What interested you most about that person? Have you seen that person since?

_____

_____

Chapters 3–5

6. Have you ever experienced any "miracle in the storm" (p. 21) that has helped pinpoint your "larger purpose"? If so, what was it? How has that experience impacted your life?

_____

_____

7. If you had to flee your home and could take only forty kilos (88 pounds) of personal effects with you, what would you take? Why?

_____

_____

8. When others tease you, how do you respond? Good-naturedly (like David Meyer did when called Tinman—p. 29)? In anger? Or in some other way? How has your response affected the other person's response?

_____

_____

Chapters 6–7

9. Jerome and Marie's papa has a realization that his life isn't what he has dreamed it would be when he visits his sick brother (see p. 47). Have you had a similar realization? When? Has it led you to change your life in any way? If so, how?

_____

_____

10. Have you ever felt lonely, as Annie, Josie, and Andre did (see pp. 59, 64, 75)? When? What do you do in those lonely times?

_____

_____

11. When Mac McGrath's front-line footage is confiscated by the French censors (p. 63), he is understandably angry. But who do you agree with—the censors or Mac? With all the media available today, do you think wartime footage should be censored in any way? What "rules" would you establish?

_____

_____

12. Frank Blake, the Paris Associated Press chief, claims, "The English fight for tea, crumpets, and mother. The French fight for sex, a good table in a restaurant, and the right to a pension" (p. 65). What would *you* fight for?

_____

_____

Chapters 8–9

13. Have you ever had to choose between loving two different people (see p. 71, where Mac is torn between Josie and Eva)? How did you make that choice? Would you change that choice now? Why or why not?

_____

_____

14. Do you tend to be "a rescuer" (p. 71) for those in distress? Give an example. How has this worked in your favor? against you?

_____

_____

15. Andre Chardon says that his greatest fault is that he has a daughter and he has never met her (see p. 75). If someone you really trusted asked you, "What is your greatest fault?" what would you say? (If you couldn't say it aloud, what would you write in your journal?)

_____

_____

16. "Only one thing mattered. The rucksack containing his film was gone. And his DeVry camera was smashed. It lay in pieces on the floor" (p. 78).

    What is the one thing you would hate losing the most? Why?

_____

_____

17. Trevor Galway risked punishment to give the dying Frankie
    Thomas fresh air and paid with painful consequences:

    > The German captain shouted the order to have Trevor dragged
    > out of the hold for public flogging to precede the burial at sea of
    > young Frankie Thomas (p. 81).

    What qualities make someone a hero or heroine in your eyes?
    What "real-life" person do you consider to be a hero or a heroine?
    Explain.

    _____

    _____

PART II
Chapters 10–11
18. There is panic in Belgium because of the "hearsay that the Ger-
    mans will soon attack through Belgium and Holland" (p. 88). All
    of a sudden, any "outsider" is looked upon as a potential spy. If
    you heard a rumor that another country was soon going to attack
    yours, how would you respond? What—if any—preparations
    would you make?

    _____

    _____

19. Have you ever fallen for someone "like a ton of bricks" (p. 98) as
    David fell for Annie Galway? What happened in your relationship?
    Did you see that person for who he/she really is, or were your eyes
    covered by "rose-colored glasses" at any point? Explain.

    _____

    _____

20. Has anyone stood up for you (whether you did right or wrong) as
    Madame Rose stood up for Jerome when he attempted to steal the
    sausage (p. 103)? Explain the situation. How did that person's
    kindness impact your view of yourself? your future?

    _____

    _____

Chapters 12–13

21. "When the occasion demands it, we will put aside our differences, to be resumed at a more convenient moment" (Irene, p. 109).

    When have you worked with someone who would normally be on the opposite side of an issue? How did you put aside your differences to work together? In the process, did you learn anything about the other person? about yourself?

---

22. How would you respond to someone who says, "As long as an individual is left alone to live day by day, one set of principles is as good as another, isn't it?" (see p. 109).

---

23. "'No!' Delfina shot back hotly. 'Politics and war are not the same. It is war that ultimately decides politics, religion, and what your life will be like day to day! Not the other way around. Right and wrong survive every battle. But only the victor has the privilege to choose between the two. The Nazis have known that from the beginning. Hitler . . . Stalin . . . they are all the same. They enslave their own people by giving them something that politics and religion can no longer provide. They give them meaning to their existence that is beyond narrow self-interest. Give them a sacred war to fight! A reason to sacrifice! Some unity in a bloody cause! The real degradation begins when people realize they are in league with the devil. But they feel the devil is preferable to the emptiness of life that lacks larger significance. The Cause becomes their god. Right or wrong? What is that? The Cause is everything'" (p. 110).

    Reflect on your life and priorities. Is any "Cause" (whether work, a political issue, a social issue, a past event that has left you bitter, etc.) becoming "everything" over your time and thoughts? Why is this "Cause" so important to you? Is your life missing a "larger significance," as Delfina mentions?

---

24. Have you ever taken a "detour" into your past, as Andre does when he goes to visit Luxembourg City (p. 113)? If so, what did you find there?

_____

_____

Chapter 14

25. Paul Chardon is feeling sorry for himself because he has gotten into trouble by speaking so frankly with his brother and with General Gamelin (see p. 125). There is so much more Paul wants out of life, and now he wonders if he'll ever have the chance.

    Have you ever felt sorry for yourself? Or wondered if life had more "out there" for you and you were missing it? Describe the events. What has changed since that time? (Or, if happening presently, what step can you take to begin turning the tide of events?)

_____

_____

26. Through an unusual source (Brezinski, a Polish Jew—one of the very people the Nazis, including Horst, are fighting to exterminate) Katrina gains a new and startling perspective on her husband:

> "Your husband is a Wehrmacht hero, Katrina. His loyalty is unquestioned. Though the Nazis do not have his heart, they have his oath as a soldier. And as long as he continues to fight for the Fatherland? Well then, we might remain relatively safe" (p. 130).

    Think back to a time when you've been in conflict with another person. What—if anything—changed your perspective regarding that person or your conflict?

_____

_____

27. "Here was the question I put to myself: A man comes up to me on the street and puts a gun to the head of my wife. He tells me he will blow her brains out if I do not break into the house of my neighbor and steal his gold. What will I do? . . . In Poland now the Nazis have made Jews to be policemen to arrest their fellow Jews. Good men are made to be traitors to their own friends. Their wives and children are hostages" (Brezinski to Katrina, re: Horst, pp. 131, 132).

If you had to betray your neighbor, whom you've known for years, in order to save your family, would you? Why or why not?

_____

_____

Chapter 15

28. Josie Marlow suffered through a lot of teasing during her growing-up years because she was poor, she had an accent, and she was ordinary and too tall. Andre notices that "her gaze held the knowledge of sorrow too great for her years" (see p. 135). But these same circumstances also gave her a heartfelt compassion for the evacuated children from Alsace.

Think back to your childhood. What two or three events made the most impact on you? How do they continue to affect your decisions and the way you live your life? Would people say that you have "a nobility of spirit and a strength untainted by bitterness" (p. 135)? Why or why not?

_____

_____

29. "I promised myself after I lost Danny that I would not get involved. . . . So common sense prevails over love, and he's gone" (Josie, p. 136).

When Josie wouldn't allow herself to love Mac McGrath and when Andre chose not to marry Elaine Snow, the mother of his child, common sense prevailed over love.

Has common sense ever prevailed over love in *your* life (whether in a romantic relationship, with a family member, or with a friend)? What happened as a result?

_____

_____

30. Horst von Bockman cannot shake the woman Sophia from his mind (see p. 136).

   When you lie awake at night, what images replay through your mind? Is there something you can do (for example, Andre phoned Abraham Snow and took his mother's doll to the daughter he'd never met) to take a step toward healing?

   _____

   _____

   If you are struggling with a heavy burden of guilt, as Horst is, let Father Kopecky's words encourage you:

   "The condition of your soul is between you and the Almighty. No one else. Not the church. Not a priest. The only hope for any of us is that God alone is good and merciful. It gives Him joy to forgive us freely. Even the angels rejoice at the turning of one sinner's heart toward heaven. So says the Scripture. But then we must be willing to live as if we are forgiven. Showing mercy to others" (p. 149).

Chapters 16–17

31. Have you ever *given* a gift to ease your guilt (see p. 150, when Abraham Snow accuses Andre of doing this)? When? Have you ever *received* a gift that eased someone else's guilt? How did it feel to be on the receiving end?

   _____

   _____

32. When Andre took Josie to see Louvemont, how did her perspective change on Andre? the war? (See pp. 156–159.)

   _____

   _____

33. "I look in the mirror each morning and say to myself, 'Andre, one day everything you think you believe about yourself will be put to the test! . . . You will live out your Truth even to the death, or Truth will die inside you even if you survive" (Andre Chardon, p. 158).

   Have you ever been "put to the test" to see who you really are inside? In what situation? What ultimate "Truth" do you believe in?

   _____

   _____

34. "There are no righteous wars. There is only, regrettably, sometimes the necessity to fight" (Andre Chardon, p. 158).
    Do you agree with Andre? Why or why not?

    _____

    _____

35. "I have already made so many wrong choices. Hurt so many. Thrown away so much. Everything important, wasted on my own selfishness. Now I may lose my life, when living is precious to me at last. But for the first time in a long time, I think I have found something—*someone*—to live for" (Andre, p. 159).
    Are any of Andre's words true for you? In what situation(s)? What small step can you take this week toward reconciling the situation(s)?

    _____

    _____

Chapters 18–19

36. How is "the Christmas story . . . itself the ultimate reproof of all tyranny" (p. 168)?

    _____

    _____

37. "'This is why Papa hates you'—he lifted his voice to the vaulted ceiling—'and now I will hate you forever also. We come all this way, my sister and me and Uncle Jambonneau's dog, and you are not really here. We will go away cold and with empty bellies from this place that looks like a church but is not a church'" (Jerome Jardin, p. 171).
    Have you ever been disappointed by, or hurt by, the church? How has that experience affected your view of God and the church?

    _____

    _____

Note the irony: After Jerome says he hates the church, it is indeed the church that fulfills the Bible's promise to feed the hungry and clothe the destitute. The Communion bread provides dinner for three hungry individuals, and the beautiful altar cloth provides a warm blanket for the shivering and wet Marie. Two of God's "small miracles"! What miracles are you overlooking in your life?

_____

_____

38. The German pilots were David's enemies, yet he decided to go see them. Although one was friendly and the other bitter, David felt compassion for both of them (see p. 176).

If someone was trying to kill you and was injured in the process, would you go to see him or her? And if so, what would you say?

_____

_____

Chapter 20

39. "'You are here tonight as one of God's footsteps,' the priest replied quietly. 'You came tonight because tomorrow may be too late'" (Father Kopecky to Horst von Bockman, p. 182).

Has someone been "one of God's footsteps" to you? Have you been "one of God's footsteps" to someone else? Tell or write about the experience.

_____

_____

40. "It is in your hands now to change the future of one," the priest tells Horst (p. 182). When you see the needs around you today, it's easy to grow overwhelmed—"*So many! Too many to count!*" Horst thinks (p. 193). But how could you help to change the future of just one?

_____

_____

41. "Jesus said, 'Whoever welcomes a little child like this in My name welcomes Me.' Don't you see, Horst? How God loves them! Their angels are constantly before His throne. To have compassion on a child . . . there is no act so holy. It is as if you carry the Christ child in your arms!" (p. 182).

What is your attitude toward children? In what ways does it resemble Jesus' attitude? In what areas do you need to grow in compassion?

PART III
Chapters 21–22

42. "I am so sorry . . . God? Hear me," Horst whispers (p. 192) on the train from Warsaw to Berlin.

Do you need to say these words to God today? Then why not do it now and feel the sweet relief of His forgiveness? For as the Bible promises:

> *The Lord is compassionate and gracious,*
> *slow to anger, abounding in love.*
> *He will not always accuse,*
> *nor will He harbor His anger forever;*
> *He does not treat us as our sins deserve*
> *or repay us according to our iniquities.*
> *For as high as the heavens are above the earth,*
> *so great is His love for those who fear Him;*
> *as far as the east is from the west,*
> *so far has He removed our transgressions from us.*
>   —Psalm 103:8-12

---

43. "I have done this because . . . because I must! That is all!" Horst tells Katrina (p. 195). When have you dared to do something just because you knew it was the right thing to do, regardless of the consequences?

---

44. When have you felt helpless around another person's emotions, as Jerome did around his sister, Marie (see p. 199)? What was the situation? What did you do?

_____

_____

45. Two women make "unkind comments about Papillon and the fact that Marie was skinny and her shoes were much too large for her feet" (p. 203).

   How do you respond when you see people who are not dressed well on the street? Has reading about Jerome and Marie's life in *Paris Encore* changed your attitude toward "people on the street"? If so, how?

_____

_____

Chapters 23–26

46. When Henri was feeling sorry for himself (see p. 215), how did Madame Rose respond?

   When a friend or family member feels that way, how do you decide what is needed—empathy, compassion, or action? What person you know needs to hear Monceau's rule three today: "No matter what circumstance befalls you, you must never, never give up" (p. 215)?

_____

_____

47. When have you, like Murphy, felt the strain of a long separation from those you love (p. 226)? How did you handle that time apart? Looking back now, would you have done things any differently? If so, how?

_____

_____

48. Step into Josie's shoes for a moment. You've just been told that you're supposed to travel through dangerous territory, in the middle of a war, to pick up someone who is considered a "criminal" by the reigning government (see p. 236). Would you take the risk of such a perilous journey? Give the reasons for your decision.

_____

_____

49. Do you believe, as Madame Rose does, *"With God all things are possible"* (p. 237)? What experiences in your life have led you to believe or not believe this statement?

_____

_____

Chapters 27–28

50. Should the United States have an immigration restriction (see p. 243)? List the pros and cons. If you had been in charge of immigration quotas in 1939–1940, would you have made any different decisions?

_____

_____

51. Madame Rose and Madame Betsy had a tremendous responsibility—providing for and caring for the numerous children at No. 5 Rue de la Huchette in Paris. And yet they also took time to play a good-natured game of baseball with the children.

When you look at your schedule and what it says about your priorities, what can you learn from Rose and Betsy? What change(s) do you need to make to your schedule in the coming week?

_____

_____

52. God is in the business of miracles, Josie realizes when she meets Madame Rose (see p. 250). Have you ever sensed that God "put you together" with someone else for a great purpose? What has happened since then?

Perhaps even now you must make a decision about an opportunity to do good . . . which is also risky. What will you choose to do about it?

_____

_____

Chapters 29–30

53. The men in the hellhole of the *Altmark* are in deep trouble . . .
    about as deep as they can get. But Chaplain Gabriel assures them,
    "God can hear our prayers" (p. 263). However, those who haven't
    talked to God before aren't quite sure what to say to Him. "Just
    have a nice chat," the chaplain replies. "That's all. And then listen
    for a while" (p. 254).

    Do you pray for "little things," such as a cough to get better? Or
    do you wait for the "big things" before you ask for God's help?
    Give a recent example.

    God says, "I will be with you; I will never leave you nor forsake
    you" (Joshua 1:5). Why not take Him up on His promise?

    _____

    _____

54. "As [Mac] fell, a trio of shots splatted against the metal of the
    Altmark's superstructure, showering him with chips of rusty paint.
    The point of impact was just where his chest would have been"
    (p. 267).

    Do you think Mac was saved by chance circumstances or by God
    for a reason? Explain your answer. Have you ever been in a similar
    position?

    _____

    _____

Epilogue

55. If you had fallen in love, like Mac and Eva, what would you do?
    Stay home and get married? Go back to finish your assignment
    since it's your duty and just hope you don't die? How would you
    make your decision, knowing it's possible you would never see the
    person you love again?

    _____

    _____

56. When times are uncertain, are you able to believe in God and trust
    him for the outcome? Why or why not?

    _____

    _____

   If you do not yet trust in Jesus—Yeshua, the promised Messiah
of the Old Testament, God's only Son—why not choose today as
the day to be courageous? to take a risk on God and see where that
commitment will take you?

In you, O Lord, I have taken refuge;
let me never be put to shame;
deliver me in Your righteousness.
Turn Your ear to me,
come quickly to my rescue;
be my rock of refuge,
a strong fortress to save me. . . .
Into Your hands I commit my spirit;
redeem me, O Lord, the God of truth.

I trust in You, O Lord;
I say, "You are my God."
My times are in Your hands;
deliver me from my enemies
and from those who pursue me.
Let Your face shine on Your servant;
save me in Your unfailing love.

How great is Your goodness,
which You have stored up for those who fear You,
which You bestow in the sight of men
on those who take refuge in You.
In the shelter of Your presence You hide them
from the intrigues of men;
in Your dwelling You keep them safe.
                    —Psalm 31:1-2, 5, 14-16, 19-20

About the Authors

Bodie and Brock Thoene (pronounced *Tay-nee*) have written over 45 works of historical fiction. That these best sellers have sold more than 10 million copies and won eight ECPA Gold Medallion Awards affirms what millions of readers have already discovered—the Thoenes are not only master stylists but experts at capturing readers' minds and hearts.

In their timeless classic series about Israel (The Zion Chronicles, The Zion Covenant, and The Zion Legacy), the Thoenes' love for both story and research shines.

With The Shiloh Legacy series and *Shiloh Autumn*—poignant portrayals of the American depression—and The Galway Chronicles, which dramatically tell of the 1840s famine in Ireland, as well as the twelve Legends of the West, the Thoenes have made their mark in modern history.

In the A.D. Chronicles, their most recent series, they step seamlessly into the world of Yerushalyim and Rome, in the days when Yeshua walked the earth and transformed lives with His touch.

Bodie began her writing career as a teen journalist for her local newspaper. Eventually her byline appeared in prestigious periodicals such as *U.S. News and World Report, The American West,* and *The Saturday Evening Post.* She also worked for John Wayne's Batjac Productions (she's best known as author of *The Fall Guy*) and ABC Circle Films as a writer and researcher. John Wayne described her as "a writer with talent that captures the people and the times!" She has degrees in journalism and communications.

Brock has often been described by Bodie as "an essential half of this writing team." With degrees in both history and education, Brock has, in his role as researcher and story-line consultant, added the vital dimension of historical accuracy. Due to such careful research, The Zion Covenant and The Zion Chronicles series are recognized by the American Library Association, as well as Zionist libraries around the world, as classic historical novels and are used to teach history in college classrooms.

Bodie and Brock have four grown children—Rachel, Jake, Luke, and Ellie—and five grandchildren. Their sons, Jake and Luke, are carrying on the Thoene family talent as the next generation of writers, and Luke produces the Thoene audiobooks. Bodie and Brock divide their time between London and Nevada.

For more information visit:
www.thoenebooks.com
www.TheOneAudio.com

suspense with a mission

TITLES BY

Jake Thoene

"The Christian Tom Clancy"
Dale Hurd, CBN Newswatch

Shaiton's Fire

In this first book in the techno-thriller series by Jake Thoene, the bombing of a subway train is only the beginning of a master plan that Steve Alstead and Chapter 16 have to stop . . . before it's too late.
ISBN 0-8423-5361-5 SOFTCOVER
US $12.99

Firefly Blue

In this action-packed sequel to Shaiton's Fire, Chapter 16 is called in when barrels of cyanide are stolen during a truckjacking. Experience heart-stopping action as you read this gripping story that could have been ripped from today's headlines.
ISBN 0-8423-5362-3 SOFTCOVER
US $12.99

Fuel the Fire

In this third book in the series, Special Agent Steve Alstead and Chapter 16, the FBI's counterterrorism unit, must stop the scheme of an al Qaeda splinter cell . . . while America's future hangs in the balance.
ISBN 0-8423-5363-1 SOFTCOVER
US $12.99

for more information on other great Tyndale fiction,
visit www.tyndalefiction.com

THOENE FAMILY CLASSICS™

✪ ✪ ✪

THOENE FAMILY CLASSIC HISTORICALS
by Bodie and Brock Thoene
Gold Medallion Winners *

THE ZION COVENANT
Vienna Prelude *
Prague Counterpoint
Munich Signature
Jerusalem Interlude
Danzig Passage
Warsaw Requiem *
London Refrain
Paris Encore
Dunkirk Crescendo

THE ZION CHRONICLES
The Gates of Zion *
A Daughter of Zion
The Return to Zion
A Light in Zion
The Key to Zion *

THE SHILOH LEGACY
In My Father's House *
A Thousand Shall Fall
Say to This Mountain

SHILOH AUTUMN

THE GALWAY CHRONICLES
Only the River Runs Free *
Of Men and of Angels
Ashes of Remembrance *
All Rivers to the Sea

THE ZION LEGACY
Jerusalem Vigil
Thunder from Jerusalem
Jerusalem's Heart
Jerusalem Scrolls
Stones of Jerusalem
Jerusalem's Hope

A.D. CHRONICLES
First Light
Second Touch
Third Watch
Fourth Dawn
and more to come!

THOENE FAMILY CLASSICS™

✪ ✪ ✪

THOENE FAMILY CLASSIC AMERICAN LEGENDS

LEGENDS OF THE WEST
by Bodie and Brock Thoene

The Man from Shadow Ridge
Riders of the Silver Rim
Gold Rush Prodigal
Sequoia Scout
Cannons of the Comstock
Year of the Grizzly
Shooting Star
Legend of Storey County
Hope Valley War
Delta Passage
Hangtown Lawman
Cumberland Crossing

LEGENDS OF VALOR
by Luke Thoene

Sons of Valor
Brothers of Valor
Fathers of Valor

✪ ✪ ✪

THOENE CLASSIC NONFICTION
by Bodie and Brock Thoene

Writer-to-Writer

THOENE FAMILY CLASSIC SUSPENSE
by Jake Thoene

CHAPTER 16 SERIES
Shaiton's Fire
Firefly Blue
Fuel the Fire

✪ ✪ ✪

THOENE FAMILY CLASSICS FOR KIDS
by Jake and Luke Thoene

BAKER STREET DETECTIVES
The Mystery of the Yellow Hands
The Giant Rat of Sumatra
The Jeweled Peacock of Persia
The Thundering Underground

LAST CHANCE DETECTIVES
Mystery Lights of Navajo Mesa
Legend of the Desert Bigfoot

✪ ✪ ✪

THOENE FAMILY CLASSIC AUDIOBOOKS

Available from
www.thoenebooks.com or
www.TheOneAudio.com